The drawer contained her most private files. There were only four of them. Four very special files. Those who thought they knew her would have said it was typical of Pepper that she should carry the key to that drawer with her at all times—wearing it as other women might wear a lover's gift.

There were no names on the files. She didn't need them. Each had been built painstakingly over the years, information garnered in minute amounts until she had found what she wanted.

And now the final piece of information was in her hands, and from it she would forge the tool from which she would orchestrate her revenge.

Revenge—not a word for the squeamish.

POWER PLAY

Penny Jordan

HARLEQUIN BOOKS

TORONTO·NEW YORK·LONDON
AMSTERDAM·PARIS·SYDNEY·HAMURG
STOCKHOLM·ATHENS·TOKYO·MILAN

Original hardcover edition published in
the United Kingdom 1988
by Worldwide Books

ISBN 0-373-97108-7

First Harlequin North American paperback edition 1990

CHAPTER ONE

IN LONDON perhaps more than any other city in the world there are certain streets whose names are immediately synonymous with money and power.

Beaufort Terrace is one of them; a graceful curve of stone-faced three-storey Regency buildings. Spiked black railings curve away from the flights of stone steps that lead up to each Adam door. These railings are tipped with gold, and rightly so—the rents for the suites of offices in these buildings are reputed to be the highest in the city.

Pepper Minesse was probably more familiar with this street than anyone else who rented office space on it. Her company had been one of the very first to move in when the renovators and interior designers moved out. She owned the three-storey building right at the heart of the Regency curve. As she paused briefly outside it she was conscious of the fact that a man walking down the opposite side of the street had stopped to look at her. She was wearing a black suit from Saint Laurent. It had a deep 'V' neck and looked as though she wasn't wearing anything underneath it. In actual fact she *was* wearing a black silk camisole, but Pepper had learned long ago the value of distracting people she was negotiating with, whether those negotiations were for business or personal reasons; she was one of those few women who exude both sexuality and power, and men felt challenged by her. When it suited her she let them think she was a challenge they could master.

5

Expensive cars were parked either side of the road, testifying to its exclusivity. Merchant bankers and money men fought like rabid dogs for premises here. Minesse Management did not pay any rent: it earned it. In addition to the building she owned in the centre of the terrace Pepper owned two others.

It had been a long hard fight for her to get where she was today. She knew she didn't look like a woman who headed a multi-million-pound empire; for a start, she looked too young. She was fast approaching her twenty-eighth birthday and there was nothing she didn't know about the complexities of human nature.

Minesse wasn't really her surname; she had adopted it by deed poll. It was an anagram of the word nemesis, and so, she thought, a fitting title for her business. She liked Greek mythology; its almost wholesale indictment of the emotions that ruled mankind appealed to the cynical side of her nature.

It struck her as ironic and very revealing that a society that could bury under the carpet child moles- tation and abuse could throw up its hands in righteous horror at the very sound of the word revenge. She liked it, but then she came from an old culture; from a race that knew the rightness of exacting a just penalty for a man's crimes.

As she walked into the building the sun caught the coiled chignon of her hair, throwing out prisms of dark red light. When she stood in the shadows it looked black, but it wasn't. It was a deep dense burgundy. An unusual colour; a rare colour even, nearly as rare as the dense violet blue of her eyes.

As she walked into the building the man across the road studied the slim length of her legs acquisitively. She was wearing sheer black stockings. They were pure silk and she ordered them by the gross.

As she caught sight of Pepper the receptionist smiled

nervously. All her staff held Pepper faintly in awe. She set very exacting standards, and she was known to be a tireless worker herself. She had had to be. She had built up the agency from nothing, and now it handled some of the world's top media and sports stars, negotiating for them advertising revenues that bolstered their incomes well into the millionaire bracket.

The girl behind the reception desk was twenty-one years old. She was a pretty blonde with the longest legs Pepper had ever seen. That was why she employed her. Looking at them kept the clients' minds occupied while they waited to see her.

Beyond the cool grey and black décor of the reception area, with its discreet touches of white and its Bauhaus chairs, was a luxurious interview room. Concealed behind its banks of pared-down designer wall units was the most up-to-date video and sound equipment on sale anywhere. Anyone who wanted to use one of her clients in any sort of televised promotion had to prove to her first that they knew what they were doing.

Pepper skirted the waiting room, knowing that she didn't have any appointments. Had anyone asked her she could probably have run through her diary for a whole month without missing out a thing; she had a brain that was needle-sharp and far more flexible than the most advanced computer.

Her secretary looked up at her as she walked into her office. Miranda Hayes had been with Minesse Management for five years, and she still knew very little more about her boss than she had done on the first day she started work there.

She caught the scent of the perfume that Pepper had specially blended for her in Paris, and envied the cut of the black suit. The body inside it was almost voluptuously curved, but Miranda suspected that her boss didn't carry an ounce of surplus flesh.

She wondered if she exercised and if so where. Somehow Pepper Minesse didn't look the type; Miranda couldn't in a thousand lifetimes imagine her cool, controlled boss hot and sweaty after a physically demanding workout.

"Any calls?" asked Pepper.

Miranda nodded.

"Jeff Stowell called to remind you about the cocktail reception for Carl Viner at the Grosvenor tonight."

A briefly upraised eyebrow suggested a certain degree of impatience that the young tennis star's agent should find it necessary to remind her.

"He said there's going to be someone there who wants to meet you," Miranda added.

"Did he say who?"

Miranda shook her head. "Do you want me to get him back?"

"No," Pepper told her decisively. "If Jeff wants to play cloak-and-dagger games he must play them alone. I'm too busy to join in."

She opened her office door and walked inside, closing it behind her, leaving only the lingering trace of her perfume.

There was nothing feminine about the room. When she had commissioned the interior designer, she had told him she wanted it to exude a subtle aura of power.

"Power?" He had stared at her, and she had smiled back sweetly. "Yes—you know, the kind of thing that goes with being the person who sits behind that desk."

"Men don't respond well to powerful women," he had told her nervously. Pepper reminded him of a large lazy cat just waiting to pounce, but then he was gay, and sexual women always made him feel nervously defensive.

Pepper hadn't argued with him. After all, he was right, but there wasn't a man born with whom she didn't know how to deal. It was her experience that the more powerful the man, the more vulnerable his ego; learning how to turn that fact to her own advantage had been the very first lesson she had mastered.

Through the closed door she could hear the muffled, staccato sound of her secretary's typewriter. The sun streaming through the window caught the delicate gold chain on her left wrist. She always wore it, and she looked at it for a moment with a strange smile on her lips before taking it off and using the gold key hanging on it to unlock one of the drawers of her desk.

This drawer contained her most private files. There were only four of them. Four very special files indeed, and they didn't belong to any of her clients. Those people who thought they knew her would have said it was typical of Pepper that she should carry the key to that drawer with her at all times, wearing it as other women might wear a lover's gift.

She paused for a moment before taking out the files. She had waited a long time for this moment; waited for it and worked for it, and now at last the final piece of information was in her hands, and from it she would forge the tool with which she would orchestrate her revenge.

Revenge—not a word for the squeamish.

In the writings of every religion known to man were warnings against the usurpation by man of that power belonging to the gods alone. And Pepper knew why. The pursuit of revenge unleashed into the human spirit a dangerous power. For the sake of revenge a human being would endure what would be inconceivable for any other emotion.

There were no names on the front of the files; she

didn't need them. Each one had been built up pains-takingly over the years; information garnered in minute amounts until she found what she wanted.

She paused again before she opened the first one, tapping a dark red fingernail on the folder.

She wasn't a woman who hesitated very often, and people who had heard about her were often surprised to discover how small she was, barely five foot two, with a delicate almost fragile bone structure. They soon learned that her fragility was like that of steel wire, but Pepper hadn't always been like that. Once she had been vulnerable, and like any vulnerable creature . . . She moved her head and stared out of the window. Her profile was pure as an Egyptian carving, her skin moulded firmly to the perfection of her bones. Her eyes slanted slightly, giving her face a mysterious allure.

She looked at the files for a long time before putting them back and locking the drawer. A smile curved her mouth. It had been so long, but now the game was about to begin.

Her phone rang and she picked it up.

"It's Lesley Evans," Miranda told her.

The young skating star had only recently become one of Pepper's clients. She was being tipped to win a gold medal at the next Olympics. Pepper had spotted her over twelve months ago, and had instructed her management team to keep her under observation.

It was said in the business that Pepper Minesse had a gift for putting her money on the right horse, and what was more she always backed outsiders, on good odds.

Pepper said nothing. It made good business sense to let the Press build her up into some sort of prophe-tess even if it wasn't true. It added to the mystique that surrounded her, and in actual fact her decisions

were based on carefully accumulated facts, leavened
by a flash or two of the intuition she had learned to
trust.

The skater had been approached with a contract to
advertise a range of clothes intended for the teenage
sports market. The company involved was well known
to Pepper. They liked cutting corners and they tied
their young stars up with punitive contracts. The mere
fact that they hadn't approached Lesley Evans through
her told its own story.

The afternoon brought a rash of further telephone
calls. Pepper's clients were big stars in the sports and
media world with even larger egos, and she was
prepared to massage them—up to a point.

At five o'clock Miranda knocked on the door and
asked if it was all right for her to go.

"Yes, do . . . I shan't be here much longer myself.
The reception at the Grosvenor starts at seven."

Pepper waited until a quarter past five before she
unlocked the drawer again. This time there was no
hesitation as she took out the files and walked into
her secretary's office, sitting down at the electronic
machine on her desk. Miranda would have been
chagrined to see the speed and accuracy with which
she typed. There was no hesitation; Pepper knew
exactly what she was doing.

Four files.

Four men.

Four letters that would bring them here, all too
anxious to see her.

In some ways it amused her that she retained
enough of her mother's racial heritage to feel this
deep, atavistic need for retribution—for justice . . .
Not justice as some people would see it, perhaps, but
justice none the less.

The years had developed within her an ability to

stand outside herself and observe and analyse.

Four men had taken from her something which she had deeply prized, and now it was only just that those four men should, each of them, lose what they prized most.

Each of the letters was perfectly typed on the thick headed notepaper of the company. Pepper folded them efficiently and put them in the envelopes, using the stamps she had bought especially for this purpose: part of the ritual.

The security guard smiled at her as she walked out into the early summer sunshine. She was his boss and he respected her, but he was still man enough to cast an admiring glance over her indolently curved figure and slim legs as he watched her stepping out into the street.

There was a post box on the corner where she deposited the letters. Her car was parked outside the building, a very dark red Aston Martin Volante with the number plate PSM 1. Pepper unlocked it and swung her body gracefully into the driver's seat. The upholstery was cream leather, the seat piped in the same dark red as the coachwork. The cream leather hood was electrically operated, and as she started the engine she pressed the button that would lower it.

She drove as she did everything else; with economy and skill. It took her less than half an hour to drive through the traffic to her home in Porchester Mews. A special card was needed to operate the wrought iron gates that guarded the enclosed development. Like her offices, the buildings were Regency. It was one of the most exclusive housing developments in London, a collection of mews houses and apartments constructed round a shared enclosed garden. All the owners and tenants had access to the special sports facilities within the complex. The Olympic-sized swimming pool was one of the most luxurious in London. The gym had all the latest Nautilus equipment, and the squash courts had been designed by the world champion. In addition to her own home Pepper owned an apartment, which she kept for the exclusive use of her clients.

Her house was three storeys high. Downstairs was the drawing room, a dining room and the kitchen. On the first floor were two guest bedrooms with their own bathrooms, and on the top floor were her own private quarters—a huge bedroom, her bathroom, a sitting room, and a dressing room lined on both sides from floor to ceiling with mirrored wardrobes.

Her daily maid had already left. In the fridge was a blender full of the fresh ingredients of her favourite health food drink. Pepper took it out and switched it on. Her figure was the sort that could all too easily take on weight, so she was scrupulous about what she ate and drank. And she did exercise—discreetly.

She thought about the letters while she sipped her drink. Four men about whom she knew more than they knew about themselves. Years of painstaking detail built up layer upon layer until she could almost crawl inside their skulls.

She glanced at her watch. It had a plain gold wafer-thin bracelet and came from the Royal jewellers. She always avoided the obvious. Let others wear their Cartier Santos or their Rolex Oysters; Pepper didn't need that sort of security. This watch had been specially designed for her and owed nothing to fashion's whims. She would still be wearing it in twenty years' time and it would still look good.

Her clothes for the evening were already laid out for her; she had left a note for her maid this morning, telling her what she would wear. She gave the same careful attention and thought to her clothes as she did to everything else, but once she had put them on she put them out of her mind.

Tonight she was wearing a Valentino outfit. Unlike many of the other top designers, Valentino acknowledged that not all women were six foot tall. The suit Pepper was wearing tonight was black—a black velvet skirt cut short and tight, and a black velvet long-sleeved top with a long knitted welt that reached from just under the full curve of her breasts to the top of her hips. The knitted welt was designed to hug her body like a second skin. On anyone with a less than perfect figure it would have been a disaster.

She showered first, luxuriating in the warm spray of the water, stretching under it like a jungle cat. This was the other side of her nature; the one that no one else saw—the sensual, sensitive side. The heat of the water brought out the evocative smell of her perfume. It was the only one she ever wore and it clung to her skin with subtle emphasis.

Pepper stepped out of the shower and patted her skin dry before carefully smoothing in body lotion. At twenty-eight her body must already be ageing, according to the laws of science, but she knew without having to look in the mirror that her flesh was luminously firm and that her body held an allure that few men could resist.

Her mouth tightened over the thought and she tensed abruptly. The male sex and its desire for her was not something about which she cared to think. She had been careful over the years to build up an image of herself as a highly sexual woman. It was an image that was so carefully constructed that as yet no one even thought to challenge it. And no one ever would.

A tiny silvery mark low down on her body caught her eye and she frowned, touching it uneasily with one fingertip. The Valentino clung far too tightly to her to allow for any underwear other than a pair of special stockings that hugged the tops of her legs. She had discovered them in New York long before they had been available in British shops.

While she waited for the body lotion to sink into her skin Pepper padded comfortably about her room. Here, alone in her own home with the doors locked and the windows closed, she felt secure enough to do so, but that security had been a long time in coming, and she was intelligent enough to know that no woman who professed to be as sexually experienced as she chose to appear could afford to seem ill at ease with her own body.

Men were like predators, and they had a predator's instinct for female weakness. Pepper controlled the shiver that threatened her, tensing until only the tiny hairs on her skin showed any reaction, standing up sharply as though subjected to an ice-cold blast of air. Ignoring her betraying reaction, she put on her make-up with the ease of long habit, re-coiling her hair into a fresh chignon. Round her neck she wore a fine gold chain suspending a single flawless diamond. It nestled in the hollow of her throat, flashing fire against her smooth golden skin. Pepper rarely exposed her body to the sun; holidays were not something that held any appeal for her and a sunbed was far less hazardous to her skin. Her face she never allowed to tan.

At a quarter to seven she let herself out of the house and stepped into her car. The hood was back up. She inserted a tape into the machine in the dashboard and switched it on. As she drove to her destination she listened to the sound of her own voice relating every piece of information they had on file about Carl Viner. It was part of her credo to know everything there was to know about her clients. By the time she handed over her car to the doorman at the Grosvenor, she had virtually memorised the tennis star's biography.

Over her suit she was wearing a short evening cape of black velvet lined with white mink, spotted in black like ermine. It was pure theatre—a necessary part of the façade she presented to the world, and although Pepper didn't show it she was humorously aware of the looks people gave her as she walked indolently through the foyer.

One of the staff behind the reception desk recognised her, and within seconds she was being escorted to the suite where the private party was being held.

The party was being hosted and paid for by the manufacturers of the tennis shoes that the young star Carl Viner had agreed to endorse. Pepper had negotiated a six-figure advance payment plus royalties for the deal. She took ten per cent.

Jeff Stowell, the star's agent, was hovering just inside the door. He grabbed hold of her arm.

"Where the hell have you been?" he demanded.

"Why? It's exactly seven o'clock, Jeff," she told him coolly, detaching herself from him and allowing the waiter standing behind her to take her cape. She could see that Jeff was sweating slightly, and she wondered why he was so nervous. He was an ebullient man with a tendency to bully those beneath him. He treated his clients like children, exhorting and coaxing the very best out of them.

"Look, there's someone here tonight who wants to meet you—Ted Steiner, the yachtsman. He's with Mark McCormack, but he's looking for a change." Jeff saw her frown. "What's the matter? I thought you'd be pleased . . ."

"I could well be," Pepper agreed coolly. 'Once I know why he's thinking of leaving McCormack. It's

only six months since he won the Whitbread Challenge
Trophy and signed with him. If he's into drugs and
he's looking to me to supply them he can forget it."

She saw the dull flush of colour crawl up under the
agent's skin and knew that her information had been
correct.

"Moral scruples," he bluffed.

Pepper shook her head. "No. Financial ones—apart
from the obvious potential hassle with the police and
the Press, a sports star who's hooked on drugs doesn't
stay the best in the world for very long, and when he
loses that status he loses his earning power, and
without that he's no use to me."

She stepped past him while Jeff was still pondering
on her words and looked round for Carl Viner.

He was fairly easy to find. He liked women and
they liked him. Half a dozen or more of them were
crowded round him now, tanned long-legged beauties,
all blonde, but the moment he saw Pepper walking
towards him they lost his attention. He had a well-
deserved playboy image and for that reason some of
the other agencies were wary of him, but he was
shrewd enough to know what would happen if he
played too hard, and it was Pepper's private conviction that he was a definite contender for next year's
Wimbledon title.

Unlike all the other men present, who were wearing
formal lounge or dinner suits, he was dressed in tennis
whites. His shorts were brief enough to be potentially
indecent. His hair was blond and sun-streaked, and
fell over his forehead in unruly curls. He was twenty-
one and had been playing tennis since he was twelve.
He looked like a mischievous six-foot child, all
appealing blue eyes and smooth muscles. But in reality
he had a mind like a steel trap.

"Pepper!"

He rolled her name round his mouth, caressing it as though he was caressing her skin. As a lover he would be the type of man who liked to kiss and suck. Pepper knew even before his eyes moved in that direction that his tastes ran to women whose breasts were high and full.

One of the blondes clinging to his side pouted, teetering between sulky acceptance of Pepper's presence and aggressive resentment. Pepper ignored her and looked down at his feet. He was tall and muscular and took a size eleven tennis shoe. The grin he gave her when she lifted her eyes to his face contained pure lust.

"If you want to see if the adage is true, I'm more than happy to oblige."

The gaggle of blondes erupted into sycophantic giggles. Pepper eyed him coolly.

"You already have," she told him drily, "but as it happens I was just checking to make sure you're wearing the sponsor's shoes."

Carl Viner's face reddened like a spoilt child's. She leaned forward and patted him on the cheek, digging her nails gently into his smooth flesh. "Real women always prefer the subtle to the obvious. Until you've learned that you'd better stick to playing with your pretty dolls."

The sponsors were a relatively new company in the sports footwear field and they had wanted a racy, sophisticated image for their product. Pepper had read about them in the financial press, and it had been she who had approached them. Their financial director had thought that that gave him an edge over her, but she had soon disabused him of that. She already had several tennis shoe manufacturers clamouring with offers of sponsorship. She had never had any intention of allowing her client to accept an offer from anyone but the company she had chosen—they had the soundest financial backing; and they had also designed a shoe whose efficiency and style would soon outstrip the others, but they had allowed Pepper's self-confidence and coolness to undermine their own faith in themselves, and Alan Hart, their Financial Director, had been forced to back down and accept her terms.

He was here tonight.

There had been a time when he had thought he could get Pepper into bed, and his ego still smarted from her rejection of him.

For a woman who wasn't very tall, she moved extremely well. Someone had once described the way she walked as a sensual combination of a leopardess's feline, muscled prowl and a snake's hypnotic sway. It wasn't a walk she deliberately cultivated; it was the result of generations of proudly independent women.

Alan Hart watched her as she moved gracefully from group to group, and he also watched the effect she had on people around her. Men were dazzled by her, and she used her sexuality like a surgeon with a sharp knife.

"I wonder what she's like in bed."

He turned his head and said without smiling to the man standing beside him,

"She's a tease."

The other man laughed.

"Are you speaking from personal experience?"

He ignored the question, his eyes following Pepper's indolent walk.

How had she done it? How had she built up her multi-million-pound empire from less than nothing? For a man to have achieved so much by the time he was thirty would be awe-inspiring enough. For a woman . . . and one who by her own admission had barely received the most basic sort of formal education, never mind gone to university . . .

Alan freely acknowledged his own sense of almost savage resentment. Women like Pepper Minesse challenged men too much. His own wife was quite content with her role as his mental and financial inferior. He had given her two children and all the material benefits any woman could possibly want. He was regularly unfaithful to her and thought no more about it than he did about changing his shirt. If he gave it any thought at all he assumed that even if his wife was aware of his infidelities she would never leave him. She would lose too much; she couldn't support herself, and he had been careful to make sure that she never had more than pin-money to spend. He didn't know it, but for the last three years his wife had been having an affair with one of his closest friends. *He* didn't know it, but Pepper did.

She left after she had got what she had come for— a tentative offer of sponsorship for one of her other clients; a boy from the back streets of Liverpool who was one day going to win a gold medal for his speed on the running track.

The preliminary skirmishes were over; now the hard bargaining would begin. It was a game in which Pepper was a skilled player.

In a London sorting office, electronic machinery relentlessly checked and despatched the unending sacks of mail, and four letters slid into their appropriate slots.

It had begun. On the chessboard of life the pieces were being moved into position.

CHAPTER TWO

THE FIRST member of the quartet received his letter at nine-fifteen exactly on Saturday.

Although Howell's bank did not open for business on Saturdays, it was Richard Howell's practice as its chairman and managing director, to spend a couple of hours there checking through the mail and attending to any small matters of business that might have been overlooked during the week.

It was only a half hour's drive from the Chelsea mews flat he shared with his second wife to the small private car park that belonged to the bank. A uniformed commissionaire was there to let him in. Harry Rogers had been with the bank since the end of the Second World War, in which he had lost his right arm. He was due for retirement at the end of the year—something he wasn't looking forward to, despite the generous pension he knew he would receive. He liked working at Howell's. For one thing, it gave him something to boast about when he joined his pals at the Dog and Duck on Friday nights. There were very few people who didn't recognise the Howell name; the merchant bank was famous for its meteoric expansion and profitability under the chairmanship of Richard Howell. It was regularly quoted in the financial press as an example to others of its kind; and those financial correspondents who in the early days had dubbed him as "reckless" and "lucky" now described him as "a man with diabolically keen financial insight; an innovator and a challenger." Howell's had been behind several of the more dazzling takeovers in the City in recent years, and the clients who came to them tended to stay.

At just turned thirty, Richard Howell still had the same relentless energy and drive he had when he first entered the bank, but now it was tempered by caution and a discreet amount of guile.

He was a man whose photograph regularly appeared both in the financial pages, and more latterly in those gossip columns that focused on media personalities, but very few people looking at those photographs would have recognised him in the street. No photograph could convey that restless, highly strung energy that became so evident when one met him face to face. He was not a particularly tall man; just a little over five foot ten, with a smooth cap of straight dark hair and the olive-tinged skin that was his Jewish heritage.

Several generations ago the Howells had anglicised their name and given up their Jewish faith; judiciously they had married into the lower and even sometimes upper echelons of the British aristocracy, but every now and again a Howell was born who looked remarkably like the Jacob Howell who had first founded their empire.

Richard Howell had the sculptured, pared-down face of an ascetic. His eyes were a very intense shade of blue, and they burned like the incessant fires of ambition that burned inside him. He knew quite well where it came from; this desire to build and go on building. His father and his grandfather had both been ambitious men in their different ways. It was unfortunate that in his father's case that ambition had not led on to success but to death! But that was behind him now.

His first wife had accused him of being a workaholic, and he had denied it. Workaholics were driven purely by the pedestrian need to work; Richard wanted more; he was and always had been driven by a particular purpose, and yet now that that purpose had been achieved he couldn't stop.

Inside his traditional striped shirt and Savile Row suit was a man who was basically a gambler. But unlike those men who must win and lose fortunes across the baize-covered tables of the world's casinos, he had had the good fortune to be granted an entrée into the most exclusive of all the world's gambling circles—the world of high finance.

Richard picked up the letter and studied the heading thoughtfully. Minesse Management. He knew of them, of course; there was talk in the City that it wouldn't be long before they went public, but privately he doubted it. Pepper Minesse would never give up her empire to others, no matter how many millions going public might earn her.

Richard had seen her once, briefly, at a cocktail party he had attended with his second wife. There had been something elusively familiar about her, but though he searched his memory all night, he hadn't been able to recognise what. It had annoyed him, because he prided himself on having a good memory for faces, and hers was so strikingly beautiful that he couldn't imagine how, having seen it before, he could possibly have forgotten where. In fact, he could have sworn that he hadn't, and yet . . . and yet that elusive, faint tug on his memory told him that somewhere he had. Linda, his second wife, worked for one of the independent television companies. Like him, she was career-orientated. Pepper Minesse had been at the party with one of her clients.

Richard Howell wasn't a man who had a bias against successful women, and Pepper Minesse had intrigued him. She had built up her business from nothing and no one seemed to know anything about where she had come from or what she had been doing before she signed on her first client, other than that she had once worked for the American entrepreneur Victor Orlando. She was a woman who was skilled at appearing to be completely open and yet at the same time remaining conversely secretive about her past and her private life.

Richard tapped the envelope thoughtfully on his desk. It wasn't all that unusual for him to receive correspondence from people he did not know; it happened all the time. Howell's bank was known to be extremely discreet about dealing with its clients' affairs.

He opened the letter and read it, then got out his diary. There was nothing booked in for Monday afternoon. He made a pencil note in it. The letter intrigued him. Pepper Minesse: he was looking forward to meeting her. It could be very . . . interesting.

He went through the rest of his mail and then his phone rang. He picked it up and heard the voice of his wife. They had arranged to spend the weekend with friends and she was just telephoning to remind him.

"I'll be home in half an hour." That would just give them time to make love before they set out. The adrenalin bounced round his veins, released by the intrigue and anticipation of Pepper's letter. It was always like this—the merest hint of a new deal, a new game, always gave him a sexual boost.

Linda was the perfect wife for him; when he wanted sex she was both receptive and inventive; when he didn't, she didn't pester him. As far as he was concerned they had an ideal relationship. His first wife . . . He frowned, not wanting to think about Jessica. Linda had accused him once of wanting to pretend that his first marriage had never happened. She put it down to his Jewish blood and his inherited need to preserve old-fashioned values, and he hadn't argued with her. How could he? His marriage to Jessica was something he couldn't discuss with anyone, even now. He felt the beginnings of anger build up inside him, draining his physical desire, and checked them automatically. Jessica was in the past, and she was better left there.

Alex Barnett received his letter when the postman dropped it off halfway through Saturday morning. His wife Julia picked it up from the hall carpet and carried it through to the sunny sitting room at the back of the house where they breakfasted in leisurely relaxation on weekend mornings.

Alex looked quickly at her as she came in, dreading seeing the now familiar signs of the depression which so often seized her. This morning there was no sign of it. She was still buoyed up by the visit from the adoption authorities. He and Julia had everything that an ambitious couple could want. Everything, but for one thing . . .

At thirty, Alex Barnett was known as one of the most forward-thinking and successful men in his field. The computer age had still been at the toddler stage when he took over his father's sewing machine factory. From sewing machines to computers had been quite a leap, but he had made it safely, and although the big boys tended to look askance at some of his innovations, he held a very generous share of the market.

In less than six weeks' time he would hear from the Government whether they intended to accept his tender and install his terminals in British embassies throughout the world. The contract was far more important to him than he had allowed anyone else to know. Their sales had slipped slightly recently—not enough to cause concern, yet enough for him to realise that they badly needed the profits from this Government contract to finance new development.

That was the key to success in the computer world, and it was a young man's business; at thirty, Alex already felt years older than most of his design staff.

"Anything interesting in the post?" he asked as Julia walked into the room.

They had bought the house four years ago when he first became successful. They had been spending a weekend in the Cotswolds, celebrating both their wedding anniversary and the success of his new computer. They had seen the house and the "For Sale" board, and both of them had known immediately that it was just what they were looking for.

They had always planned to have a family. Alex was an only one himself and so was Julia. Children were important to them both, and this was a house specifically designed for a family. It had large private gardens, surrounded by shrubbery, and a paddock large enough for a couple of ponies. The village was only ten minutes away by car, and there were enough good private schools locally for their children to attend as day pupils.

They had managed to buy the house at a good price, and Julia had given up her job to settle down to the business of renovating and furnishing it, and of course, getting pregnant.

Only she hadn't; and since the news last month that the second in-vitro fertilisation attempt had failed, Julia had developed a brittle gaiety that scraped on Alex's raw nerves like wire.

What made it worse, according to her, was that he could have children, but she could not be their mother. He had tried to reassure her that she was more important to him than any potential child they might or might not have, but she wasn't willing to be reassured, so they had come back to the possibility of adoption; something they had discussed and eventually discounted in the early days after they had first discovered Julia couldn't conceive.

But now they had tried every alternative avenue, and none of them had worked.

The strain of the last few years with their hopes and bitter disappointments had scarred them both, but Julia more so than Alex. She had pinned everything on the in-vitro fertilisation working, and when it had failed, nothing had been able to rouse her from her depression.

But now at last she seemed to be recovering slightly. She was smiling at him as she handed him the mail.

"There's a letter from the adoption people. A social worker will be coming to interview us soon to find out if we're suitable candidates to adopt."

She paused beside his chair to read through the letter again. The sunlight caught her blonde hair and Alex reached up to push it back off her face. He had fallen in love with her the moment he saw her, and he still loved her. Her unhappiness was his, and there was nothing he wouldn't do to give her the child she so desperately wanted.

"Mm . . . what's this?" she asked him, holding out a cream envelope. He took it from her, his eyebrows lifting slightly as he studied the insignia.

"Minesse Management—those are the people who sign up sports stars to endorse sports equipment and the like. It's very big business."

"Why are they writing to you?"

"I don't know . . . perhaps they're arranging some sort of pro-am tournament and they want us to participate." Alex opened the letter, read it and then handed it to her.

"Well, it doesn't tell you much at all, does it?" she commented.

"No, not really."

"Will you go and see them?"

"I don't see why not. Advertising is always useful, although of course it depends how much it's going to cost. I'll give them a ring on Monday morning and see what it's all about . . ." Alex stretched back in his chair, his muscles tautening, then laughed as he saw the expression in Julia's eyes. They had always had a good sex life, although neither of them had really enjoyed those years when they had had to make love to a timetable in the hope that Julia might conceive.

"I thought you were due to play a round of golf."

"Perhaps I'd rather just play around?" he teased her, ducking out of the way as she flapped the newspaper threateningly in his direction and then grabbing her in his arms. Even without children they had so much, but Alex sensed that Julia would never give up; they had come too far down the road to go back.

But if they weren't accepted by the adoption people? He shivered suddenly and looked into his wife's face. She was thinner and there were tiny lines drawn on her skin by tension. She had invested so much hope in this test-tube thing; they both had, and he had feared that she might have a complete breakdown when their last attempt failed.

She was so fragile, so vulnerable; he could feel her bones through her skin. A wave of love and compassion washed through him. He buried his face in the smooth warmth of her throat and said gruffly, "Come on, let's go to bed."

They went upstairs hand in hand, Julia praying that

he wouldn't sense her reluctance. Since it had been confirmed that their final attempt to conceive via the in-vitro fertilisation method had failed she had completely lost interest in sex. Sex, like marriage, was ordained for the procreation of children; knowing that there would be no children robbed the act of its pleasure; of that glowing excitement she had felt in those early days when every act of love had been enough to make her climax wildly, elated by the knowledge that this joyous climatic act was the start of human life.

That joy had faded over the years, but she had still enjoyed sex; still welcomed Alex's body within hers, but now suddenly there seemed no point any more. No matter how many times he made love to her she would not conceive his child.

Upstairs in their room as Alex took her in his arms she closed her eyes so that he couldn't look into them and see her rejection.

Simon Herries, Member of Parliament for the Conservative constituency of Selwick, on the northern borders between England and Scotland, received his letter just before eleven o'clock on Saturday morning.

A long meeting with a select and powerful group of Conservative lobbyists the previous evening had kept him out of bed until three a.m. and in consequence, it was well into Saturday morning before he walked into the breakfast room of his Belgravia home in Chester Square. As was his habit, the first thing he did when he sat down was to glance through his mail.

The butler had brought the mail in earlier on a silver tray, and the thick cream envelope with the Minesse Management crest caught his attention straight away.

As a politician it was his business to know those

companies and institutions who discreetly funded the Conservative Party machine, and he remembered at once that there had been an extremely respectable donation from Minesse at the end of the last financial year.

Conservative Members of Parliament, in the main a product of the English public school system, are trained almost from birth to adopt the "under" in preference to the "over" statement. It is a British tradition that some say started with Drake playing bowls while he watched the Spanish Armada advancing. The "respectable" donation had in fact been close to a million pounds.

Even so, Simon didn't open the letter straight away, but eyed it cautiously. Caution was a prime requisite of politicians, and in politics, as in every other power-based structure, favours have to be paid for.

The unanticipated cream envelope disturbed him. It was unexpected, and he wasn't a man who adjusted well to anything that did not fall within the strict controls he set around his life.

At thirty-two he was privately being tipped, in all the secret and powerful circles that really matter, as a future leader of the Tory party. He deliberately played down his chances, smiling ruefully, adopting the role of impressed but humble student, to the political barons who had taken him up.

He had known since coming down from Oxford that nothing but the ultimate seat of power would satisfy him, but he had learned while he was there to harness and control his ambitions. Overt ambition is still considered both suspicious and ungentlemanly by the British ruling classes. Simon Herries had every-thing in his favour; he came from a North Country family with aristocratic connections. It was well known in the corridors of Westminster that no one could be an MP without an additional source of income—left wing politicians were financed by their trade union; establishment right-wingers got theirs from private sources. It was from trusts set up by his wife's family that Simon Herries received the income that enabled him to live in a style which very few of his colleagues could match. As well as the Belgravia house he also owned over a thousand acres of rich farmland and an Elizabethan manor house near Berwick. The Belgrave Square house had been bought on his marriage by his new in-laws. It was conservatively valued at half a million.

He picked up *The Times* and turned to the first leader, but his eye was drawn back to that cream envelope.

At eleven o'clock exactly, the butler pushed open the baize-covered door that separated the kitchen from the rest of the house and brought in his breakfast. Fresh orange juice, squeezed from the Californian oranges that he preferred; two slices of wholemeal bread and a small pot of honey that came from one of his own farms; a pot of coffee made from the beans that were bought fresh every day, apart from Sunday, from Harrods Food Hall and which Simon drank black. He liked his life to be orderly, almost ritualistically so. When people commented on it, Simon said it was the result of his public school upbringing.

He was as careful about watching his weight as he was about everything else. Image was important; one didn't wish to project the glossy, too well packaged look of one's American colleagues, of course—the voters would find that insincere, but Simon would have been a fool not to take advantage of the fact that at six foot, with a well muscled athletic build which came from public school sports fields, and rowing for his college, he possessed an enviably commanding presence.

His hair was thick and dark blond. In the summer the sun added distinct highlights, and his skin tanned a healthy brown. He looked arrogantly aristocratic. Women liked him and voted for him and for his policies, men envied and admired his success. He was known in the popular press as the only MP with sex appeal. He pretended to find the description distasteful.

His wife was probably one of the few people who actually knew how much he relished it, and why!

She was away at the moment, visiting her family in Boston. She was a Calvert and could trace her family back to those first arrivals on the Mayflower. She had spent a post-graduate year at Oxford, after graduating from Radcliffe. Her cool Bostonian arrogance had amused Simon; just as it had amused him to take her back to his family's ancient stronghold in the Border hills, and show her the documents that traced his lineage back to Duke William's Normans.

Elizabeth in turn had invited him to Boston. Her parents had been impressed with him. Her father was a partner in the family bank, and it hadn't taken Henry Calvert very long to discover that Simon Herries came from a family that was almost as clever and conservative with money as his own.

The wedding had made headlines in all the Society papers—discreet ones, of course; after all, there was Royalty present. Simon's godmother was a Royal, and she had graciously consented to attend.

Of course the ceremony had had to take place at St Margaret's, Westminster. Mrs Calvert had been torn between elation and disappointment. It would have been very pleasant indeed to have hosted a dinner in Boston for her future son-in-law's godmother, but Simon had been adamant: the ceremony was to take place at St Margaret's.

There was a piece in *The Times* lauding the new legislation he was pressing for to tighten up the laws regarding child abuse. He was building up a reputation for being a fierce campaigner for law and order and a return to a more strict moral climate. He was known among his peers, sometimes acidly, as the "Housewives' Choice." He smiled as he re-read the piece. There were an awful lot of housewives, and all of them had the right to vote.

His assistant would no doubt cut the piece out for him and clip it to his PR file. She was a twenty-three-year-old Cambridge Honours graduate, and Simon had been sleeping with her for the past three months. She was intelligent, but a little too intense. His mind shifted gear. It was probably just as well that the long vacation was coming up; it would help cool things down a little. He had no intention of getting too heavily involved.

Simon opened the envelope, slitting it carefully with a silver-handled knife, which had been given to his grandfather by the monarch.

The letter was brief and uninformative. It simply invited him to present himself at the offices of Minesse at three on Monday afternoon, to discuss something of mutual benefit.

It wasn't such an unusual letter; and he checked in his diary to see if he had the afternoon free. He had, and he pencilled in the appointment and a note to ask his secretary to produce everything she could on Minesse and its founder Pepper Minesse. He had never met her, but she had the reputation of being a beautiful and very clever woman.

Miles French, barrister at law, and quite possibly soon to be Judge French, didn't receive his letter until

Monday morning.

He had spent his weekend with his latest lover. He was a man who liked to concentrate on one thing at a time, and when he was with a woman whose company he enjoyed, he didn't like anything else to distract him. He and Rosemary Bennett had been lovers for almost six months, which was quite a long time as far as he was concerned. He liked beautiful women, but he also liked intelligent conversation, and his mind frequently grew bored before his body.

Rosemary was an editor on *Vogue*, and occasionally if she felt he was stepping out of line, she liked to punish him by exhibiting him in front of her fashion trade cronies.

A barrister was a rara avis indeed in their enclosed world; the men derided his Savile Row suits and white-collared starched shirts, while the women eyed him sideways, stripped off the suit and shirt, and wondered how much of a chance they would have of stealing him away from Rosemary Bennett.

He was six foot two with a body that was solid with muscle. He had black hair that curled slightly. His eyes were the colour of iced water, and Rosemary claimed that it gave her the most delicious frisson of dread when he looked at her in his "courtroom" manner. They suited one another. Both of them knew the rules; both of them knew exactly what they could and could not have from their relationship. Miles didn't sleep with other women, but she knew that the moment she began to pall he would drop her and that there would be no court of appeal.

He picked up the letter along with several others as he opened the door of the flat he owned, conveniently close to his chambers. Along with the rest of his mail he dropped it on his desk before going upstairs to shower and change. He had no appointments for the day. He was a man who didn't like to rush anything he did; a man who was patient and thorough, and to those who didn't know him, surprisingly passionate. He had a dangerous temper, although it was slow to be aroused.

His phone rang as he stepped into the shower. He cursed and went into his bedroom to answer it, dripping water on to the carpet. His body was strongly made and taut with muscle from his bi-weekly games of squash at his club. His torso was shadowed with dark hair, silky fine and alluringly sensual to the female sex.

The phone call was from his clerk, and Miles answered the query, then rang off.

Once dressed, he went into the kitchen and made himself a cup of coffee. He had a daily woman who kept the apartment clean and sometimes shopped for him, but he preferred to be independent. He had never known either of his parents. As a very small baby he had been abandoned on the steps of a Glasgow children's hospital, and had eventually ended up in a children's home, where he had learned to value his privacy and independence.

He took his coffee with him into his study. It was a spacious room, the walls lined with bookshelves, and it was one of the reasons he had bought this particular apartment. He sat down at his desk and glanced through his mail, frowning slightly as he came to the Minesse envelope, his bottom lip jutting out slightly, a habitual gesture he wasn't particularly aware of but which women found sexy. The name of the company was familiar to him, but as far as he knew he had no legal dealings with them, and in any case most of his dealings with clients were via the medium of a solicitor.

Miles opened the envelope and read the letter with

a smile. Intriguing, and he would have known that it
was a letter from a woman even without his knowledge
of who headed Minesse Management. He couldn't
recall if he and Pepper Minesse had ever met, although
he had heard about her. He wondered what on earth
she could want, tossing several possibilities around in
his mind. There was only one way to find out, and he
had a free afternoon. Miles picked up the phone.

Pepper spent the weekend with friends who lived just
outside Oxford. Philip and Mary Simms were the
closest thing she had known to a family since the
death of her grandmother when she was fifteen. She
arrived just after eleven o'clock on Saturday morning,
having timed her journey to avoid the traffic.

The bright early summer sunshine had tempted her
to put the hood down on the Aston Martin, and her
hair, left loose from its chignon, had been tousled by
the wind. She was wearing a linen suit in a soft shade
of olive green, the skirt cut short and straight, and the
jacket fitting the contours of her breasts and waist.
Underneath it she was wearing a cream silk blouse.
As she stopped the car engine and swung her legs out
on to the gravel drive she saw Oliver Simms disap-
pearing round the side of the shabby Victorian semi.

She called to him, and he turned and waited for
her, a grave-eyed boy of ten. He blushed slightly as
she approached him, but the good manners instilled
by his parents made him wait until she reached him.

"Hi, Oliver."

Of all his parents' friends, Pepper was his favourite.
She didn't try to ruffle his hair, or worse still, to kiss
him, and she always remembered his birthdays and
Christmas with presents that were exactly what he
wanted, plus a small sum of money for his post office
savings account. At the moment he was saving up for

a new bike. His birthday fell in June and he was hoping that as a present his parents would make up the shortfall on his savings.

"Mum and dad are in the garden," he told Pepper.

He had arrived in his parents' lives when his mother was just over forty and his father was eight years older, and in all the ten years of his short existence he had never for one moment doubted how much they had wanted him. He wasn't spoiled in the sense of being indulged with material possessions—his father taught at the local comprehensive and the family were comfortably rather than well off, but there had never been a second in Oliver's life when he had not known the security of being deeply loved.

He was a good-natured boy who had learned quite young to analyse and judge logically, and already he knew that although there might be times when he envied those of his school friends who possessed the latest computer, or the latest BMX, in reality many of them came from families where their parents led such busy lives that their fathers and sometimes their mothers were almost strangers to them.

Oliver knew that it was a struggle for his parents to send him to the exclusive prep school he attended, but no matter what sacrifices had to be made there always seemed to be just enough money for things like new school uniform, and extras, like the skiing holiday he had had just after the New Year.

Once he had seen Pepper safely round into the back garden, he excused himself, telling her gravely, "I'm just off to cricket practice . . . I might make it on to the first junior team this year."

Pepper watched him until he had disappeared then headed into the garden.

"Pepper, my dear! You're early . . ."

"The traffic was in my favour for once." Pepper

kissed Mary's cheek and allowed the older woman to hold her close. Mary Simms was the only person she ever allowed to embrace her in that way. Instinctively Pepper always held herself aloof and remote from others, but Mary was different. Without Mary . . .

"You're looking very well, Mary—both of you are, in fact."

There was no emotion in Pepper's voice as she studied their faces. No one looking at her could guess how close were the bonds between them.

Mary Simms, who had grown up in a rambling old vicarage near Cambridge, populated by not only her parents but a collection of ancient aunts and uncles as well, had almost from birth been used to showing her affection freely and physically. It hurt her more than she could ever put into any words that Pepper had been denied the love she herself had known as a child, and with which she surrounded her husband and son.

Philip Simms greeted Pepper with his usual absent-minded bonhomie. Philip was a born teacher; he had the gift of communicating to his pupils the desire for knowledge. He had taught her so much . . . given her so much. Here in this shabby house she had . . .

"Did you see Oliver?" Mary's voice cut through her thoughts.

Pepper smiled at her.

"Yes. He was just leaving. He said something about cricket practice."

"Yes, he's hoping to be chosen for the school's junior team." Love for her son and pride for his achievements shone out of her eyes as Mary talked.

Philip was carefully transplanting some young plants, and Pepper watched him. He was always so gentle and careful about everything he did, so endlessly patient and understanding.

"Come on inside, I'll make us all a cup of coffee."

The kitchen had changed very little since the first time Pepper had seen it; true, there was a new washing machine and fridge freezer and a new cooker, but the large cupboards on either side of the fireplace and the heavy pine dresser were just as Pepper remembered them from long ago. The china on the dresser had belonged to one of Mary's aunts, as had much of their furniture. Money had never been of prime importance in the Simms' lives, and for Pepper coming back was like crawling back into the security of the womb.

As Mary made the coffee they talked. Neither of them ever ceased to marvel at Pepper's success; they were as proud of her as they were of Oliver, in some ways perhaps more so, but they didn't totally understand her—how could they?

As she sat on one of the battered formica-covered stools Pepper wondered what Mary would say if she knew what she had done. For a moment her eyes clouded, but it was pointless trying to apply Mary's code of ethics to her own actions. Her life, her emotions and reactions were so complex that neither Mary nor Philip could ever really understand what drove her.

They had been so upset when she first decided to leave Oxford, but neither of them had ever tried to dissuade her. She had spent nearly a year living in this house, cared for, cossetted and protected by its owners. They had sheltered her and given her something that she had never experienced before in her entire life. They were the only true good and Christian people that Pepper knew; and yet she knew many who would disparage and deride them for their simple lives and their lack of interest in wealth and success.

Coming here was something she needed almost as much as she needed revenge. She had to force herself to limit her visits. Once a month, Christmas, and birthdays . . .

She and Mary drank their coffee in the sort of silence that only exists between people who know one another well and are completely at ease with themselves and each other. Afterwards Pepper helped Mary to wash up and then prepare the lunch, simple domestic tasks that none of her executives or her staff would ever have imagined her doing, but no one else was ever allowed to see her like this, vulnerable and dependent.

After lunch they all went out into the garden, not to sit down and drowse in the early afternoon sun, but to attack the weeds that relentlessly threatened Philip's flower beds. As they worked, he talked. He was concerned about one of his pupils. Listening to him, Pepper was flooded with love and humility. But for this man she would still be exactly what she had been at sixteen, an uncivilised, uneducated, little savage, who knew only the laws of her gypsy tribe, governed by emotion rather than logic.

She left shortly after five o'clock on Sunday, after afternoon tea on the lawn, eating Mary's homemade scones and some of the jam she had made the previous summer. Oliver was there with a couple of friends, who studied her car with amused nonchalance. While she watched them Oliver had grinned at her, a conspiratorial, engaging grin that showed quite plainly the man he was going to be. Already in Oliver Pepper could see seeds of great personal charm; of intelligence and drive, and more.

All his life, wherever he went, whatever happened to him, he would have these years to look back on; the love of his parents, the security they had given him, and all his life he would benefit from those gifts, just as a seedling plant growing in good, enriched earth would grow stronger and hardier than one that had to struggle in poor soil.

Handicaps of any kind could be overcome, but they left scars like any other injury. Oliver would grow into adulthood without those scars.

Pepper got up and bent to hug and kiss Mary and then Philip. All of them walked over to her car.

"It's Oliver's school's Open Day in three weeks' time," Philip told her. "Will you be able to come down for it?"

Pepper looked at Oliver who grinned bashfully at her.

"Well, since he's my godson, I suppose I shall have to make the effort."

She and Oliver exchanged smiles. She knew that she had struck exactly the right sort of note in front of his friends. They had all reached the stage where any display of adult emotion was deeply frowned upon.

She got into the car and turned the key in the ignition. Ahead lay London, and Monday morning.

Would they respond to her letters? Somehow she felt they would. She had dangled a bait none of them would be able to refuse. All of them, for their varying reasons, would expect to benefit from a connection with Minesse Management. Pepper smiled grimly to herself as she headed for the motorway—a brief twist of her lips that held more bitterness than amusement.

CHAPTER THREE

ON MONDAY morning Pepper overslept and was late. She could feel the tension building inside her as a traffic jam in Knightsbridge delayed her still further.

Up ahead of her she could see people milling in and out of Harrods, Knightsbridge, the Brompton Road, Sloane Square; all of them had become a shopping paradise for those with money to spend.

Elegant women in Sloaneish Caroline Charles outfits, wearing Jourdan shoes, paused outside shop windows. It was here in Harvey Nichols that the Princess of Wales had shopped prior to her marriage to the heir to the throne, and in nearly every department in the exclusive store were girls whose sharply cut British upper-class accents mirrored hers. American and Japanese tourists gathered outside Harrods' main entrance. Pepper noticed absently that Arab women were much less in evidence now than they once had been.

She glanced impatiently at the clock on the car's dashboard. She had no morning appointments, but she hated being late for anything because it implied that she was not in full control of her life. Even so, she fought down her impatience; impatience made people careless and led to mistakes. Mistakes—unless they were other people's—had no place in her life.

It was so unusual for her to be late that the receptionist had already commented on it when Miranda went down to collect the post.

"Perhaps she's had a heavy weekend?" Helena

42

murmured suggestively as she handed over the envelopes.

Miranda was as curious as the other girl about Pepper's sex life, but she was too well trained to show it. Gossiping about one's boss had been the downfall of many a good personal secretary, and there wasn't much that slipped Pepper's attention.

"I wonder if she'll ever marry?" Helena mused, obviously reluctant to let the subject go.

"A lot of successful business women do combine careers and marriage," Miranda pointed out.

"Um . . . I saw a photograph of her in one of the papers with Carl Viner. He's terrifically sexy, isn't he?"

Miranda raised her eyebrows and said drily, "So's she."

Out of the corner of her eye she saw Pepper come into the building. There was no mistaking that distinctive, deceptively languid walk, a lazy flowing movement of hips and legs.

"Morning, Miranda—Helena."

Pepper acknowledged both young women and walked past them towards her office, leaving her secretary to follow her.

"Miranda, I'm expecting four gentlemen at three o'clock this afternoon. I'll see all of them together. Here are their names. She passed a piece of typed paper to her secretary.

"Right . . . Would you like coffee now?"

"Yes, please. Oh, and Miranda, you might alert the security guard to make sure he's on the premises while they're here, please."

Although she was far too well trained to betray any surprise, Miranda tried and failed to remember a single other occasion when Pepper had made such a request. Curiously she glanced at the names, recognising only two of them. An MP and an entrepreneur. Mmm. She shrugged her curiosity aside, knowing it would be satisfied when Pepper dictated to her her notes from the meeting. Pepper was meticulous about keeping records of all her conversations, both with her clients and with potential sponsors.

Putting the piece of paper down on her desk, Miranda walked into the small kitchen hidden away behind her office. A staff room opened off it—an airy, attractively decorated room with bookshelves and comfortable seating. Minesse Management did not provide their staff with canteen facilities; the small number of employees did not merit it, although there was a formal dining room adjacent to Pepper's office, where she sometimes lunched clients and sponsors. The food for these lunches was provided by a small firm that specialised in doing lunches and dinners for executive functions. It was often Miranda's task on these occasions to check out their guests' religions and preferences, and once Pepper had these facts to hand she would call in the caterers to discuss with them the type of meal she wanted them to serve.

In this as in everything else Pepper always displayed an insight and authority that was almost intuitive. If Miranda had ever expressed this view to Pepper, Pepper would have told her that she had long ago learned that attention to even the smallest detail was important when you were gambling for high stakes.

In the small kitchen Miranda made fresh coffee and poured it into a coffee pot. She set an elegant silver tray with the pot, a matching cup and saucer, and a tiny jug of cream. The china was part of the dinner service used in the clients' dining room, white with a dense blue band and edged in gold. It was both very rich and severely restrained—rather like Pepper herself in many ways.

When Miranda took in the coffee Pepper put down the papers she was working on to say,

"If any of the men on that list telephone, Miranda, I don't want to speak to them. If any of them cancel their appointments please let me know."

She didn't say anything more and Miranda didn't ask her any questions. Pepper didn't delegate. The success or failure of Minesse Management lay in her hands and hers alone.

She drank her coffee while she studied the newspaper clippings from the weekend's newspapers. It was part of Miranda's job to go through the papers and clip out any mention of their clients or sponsors.

At quarter to twelve she cleared her desk and rang through to her secretary.

"I have an appointment with John Fletcher at twelve, Miranda. I should be back around two, if anyone wants me."

John Fletcher was an up-and-coming designer. Pepper had seen some of his clothes in a *Vogue* feature on new designers, and she had commissioned him to make two outfits for her. As yet he was not very well known, but Pepper planned to change all that. She had on her books a young model who was being tipped to go far, and it was in her mind to link model and designer in a way that could promote and draw attention to them both.

Louise Faber had introduced herself to Pepper at a cocktail party. She was eighteen years old, and knew exactly what she wanted to do with her life. Her mother had been a model, and so through her Louise already had the looks and the contacts to get into the business. Several of her mother's contemporaries had grown from modelling into other more powerful areas of fashion, and Rena Faber had been able to call on old loyalties to give her daughter a good start. But

Louise was no ordinary dewy-eyed eighteen-year-old whose ambition was to get her face on the front cover of American *Vogue*.

Louise had her own ambitions. She wanted to own and run a Michelin-star restaurant, but for that she needed money, and training. Without money and influence she would have very little chance of being taken on at the kind of restaurant where she could get the training to fulfil her ambitions. Women were not chefs, they were cooks, but Louise aimed to prove that that was wrong.

Her parents had divorced while she was quite young, and from what she had told Pepper there was not enough money in the family anyway to finance either the training or the sort of restaurant she would eventually want to own. A chance remark by one of her mother's friends, that she would make a good model, had led to her deciding that modelling would be an excellent way of earning the money she needed. Once having made that decision she was determined that if she was to model, then she wanted to be the best.

She needed an image, she had confided to Pepper, something that made her stand out from the other pretty, ambitious girls, and remembering John Fletcher, it had occurred to Pepper that designer and model could well have something to offer one another. If in her off-duty hours Louise wore only John Fletcher models, both of them would benefit from the publicity. Pepper had the contacts to make sure the press picked up on the story. She had already discussed it with John, and today he was going to give her his decision.

Initially she would make very little from the deal; but this was her forte, to spot original and new talent, whether in sport or any other field, and to nurture it towards success, and then to reap financial benefit.

No sponsor would ever risk his money on an

unproven outsider, but only let one of her outsiders start winning and Pepper was then in a position to make her own terms. That was how she had started off—spotting a potential winner before anyone else.

John Fletcher had premises just off Beauchamp Place, an enclave of designer and upmarket shops off the Brompton Road. Because of the lunch-time traffic, Pepper hadn't used the Aston Martin, and her taxi dropped her off several doors away from her destination. Two model-thin girls emerging from Bruce Oldfield's premises turned to look at her. Neither of them was a day over nineteen.

"Wow!" one exclaimed to the other. "Now that was real class!"

There was no one in the foyer as Pepper walked up the stairs to John Fletcher's showrooms. She knocked briefly before walking in.

Two men were standing by the window, studying a bolt of scarlet fabric.

"Pepper!" John Fletcher handed the silk to his assistant and came to greet her. "I see you're wearing the black."

Pepper smiled at him. She had chosen to wear the black suit he had designed for her quite deliberately. Wasn't it a black skull cap that judges used to wear when pronouncing the death sentence? Miles French should appreciate the finesse of her gesture, even if the others didn't, but somehow she was sure that they would.

The skirt of her suit had been cut in the new short, curvy shape that clung to her hips and waist. She allowed John's assistant to help her off with the jacket. He was one of the most beautiful young men she had ever seen, sleekly-muscled, golden-skinned and golden-haired. A covert look passed between the boy and John which the latter acknowledged with a brief shake of his head.

Pepper intercepted it, but waited until she and the designer were alone before saying lightly,

"Very wise, John. I'd be extremely mortified if you were to offer me the services of your tame stud."

"He hasn't been with me very long, and I'm afraid he's still a bit gauche," John apologised.

"Do you get many clients asking for that sort of service?" Her voice was slightly muffled as she stepped into a cubicle and stripped down to her underwear.

"Enough. But how did you know? Most people walking in here take one look at him and assume . . ."

"That you're gay?" Pepper stepped out of the cubicle and flashed him a mocking smile. "I know when a man likes women and when he doesn't, John, but I should have thought you were making enough profit from your clients without that sort of sideline."

"Oh, I don't provide it. Any arrangement my clients come to with Lloyd is their affair entirely."

Pepper's mouth twitched. "But word gets round, doesn't it, and there are plenty of bored rich women who'll patronise a designer who can do more for their bodies than simply clothe them."

John shrugged. "I have to make a living."

"Mmm. Speaking of which . . ."

As he worked, Pepper discussed with him her plans that Louise Faber should exclusively model his clothes.

"I like it." He stood up and studied the dress he was pinning on her.

"Do you think you'll be able to get the tie-in with *Vogue*?" she asked.

"I should think so. I've got several contacts there. There should be a number of their fashion editors at the charity do you and I are going to tonight. We could talk with them and if it looks good, then Louise and I can get together to thrash out the details.

Pepper left half an hour afterwards, picking up a cruising taxi that deposited her outside her favourite restaurant. The head waiter recognised her instantly, and escorted her to a table that made her the focal point of all other diners.

The restaurant had originally been a decaying three-storey building in a row just off Sloane Square. Pepper had bought it when she first suspected that the rich were transferring their loyalty along with their cheque books and credit cards, from Bond Street to Knightsbridge. All three floors were let out at extremely good but not extortionate rents. She had provided the finance for the restaurant, and she had also been the one who had tipped off the chef manager that Nouvelle Cuisine was on the way out and something a little more substantial on the way in.

There wasn't a day of the week when every table in the place wasn't taken. A subtle PR campaign had made it the "in" place to go. Coveys of elegant well bred women sat round the tables, nibbling at food they had no intention of eating—their size ten figures were far too important. Anyway, they hadn't come here to eat; they'd come to see and be seen.

An artist who was another of Pepper's clients had transformed the drab interior of the building with outrageously erotic trompe l'oeil, and if one was sufficiently in the know it was possible to discern in the features of the frolicking nymphs and satyrs the facial characteristics of many prominent personalities. When a person faded from the limelight, their faces were painted out and someone else's, someone who was new and newsworthy, painted in. It wasn't entirely unknown for actresses and even politicians to discreetly suggest to Antoine that their faces would look good on his walls.

Pepper's involvement in the restaurant was a well

kept secret; her face did not appear on any of the
gambolling nymphs, but as she followed the head
waiter across the smooth dark grey carpet, every pair
of eyes in the place marked her indolent walk.

She sat down and gave her order, without reference
to the menu, her forehead creased in a slight frown.
Most of the women lunching together were in their
early twenties or late forties, young wives or bored
divorcees. The other women, those with careers, those
with money, spent their lunch hour dining clients or
extending their range of contacts; the sort of business
that their male equivalents carried out in their clubs.

Soon these women would need the cachet of the
same exclusivity. As yet there were very few clubs
catering for the new breed of career women; somewhere
they could entertain their clients, have lunch and even
stay overnight if necessary.

If Pepper's clients had provided the bulk of her cash
flow, then it was her own careful investment of those
funds that had given her the very secure capital base
underpinning her business. Pepper was always in the
market for a good investment. She smiled to herself,
her mind sliding easily into overdrive, exhilarated by
the challenge of her thoughts.

Although she knew people were watching her, she
ignored their covert looks, mentally weaving the
threads which could form the pattern of a new business
venture, at the same time thoroughly enjoying her
fresh salmon and its accompanying vegetables. Pepper
had gone short of food too often as a child not to
appreciate it now. She was fully aware of how many
of the women toying with their plates of salad were
secretly gnashing their teeth over both her appetite
and her apparent disregard for the effects of what she
was eating on her figure.

What they didn't know was that tonight she would

eat a very meagre meal indeed, and then before she
got ready to go out she would also have half an hour
of tennis coaching on the indoor courts belonging to
the private sports complex attached to her home.
Dieting in public drew attention to a possible weakness,
and Pepper had learned long ago never to let anyone
see that she could be vulnerable.

She arrived back at the office at five minutes past
two. Miranda followed her in to tell her that she had
received phone calls from all four of the gentlemen on
the list. Three of the four had asked to speak to
Pepper personally, but on being told that she wasn't
available had settled for confirming their appointments.

"And the fourth?"

Miranda consulted her list.

"Miles French? Oh, he simply confirmed that he
would be here."

She thought as she left Pepper standing beside her
desk that her boss was looking rather abstracted, but
she knew better than to ask questions.

At two-thirty, Miranda prepared a trolley ready for
the tea she would be asked to serve later in the
afternoon. The fine china was Royal Doulton and like
the coffee cups had been specially designed to Pepper's
specification.

All four of the men arrived within ten minutes of
one another. The receptionist showed them into the
waiting room, then rang through to Miranda to tell
her that they had arrived. She glanced at her watch.
Five to three.

Inside her office Pepper refused to give in to the
temptation to glance through her files one final time.
She had already checked her make-up and clothes,
and she fought against a nervous impulse to check
once more. At five to three her internal telephone

rang, and her stomach lurched. She picked up the receiver and acknowledged Miranda's advice that the four men had arrived.

Taking a deep breath, she said calmly, "Please show them in Miranda, then bring us some tea."

Across the hallway in the comfortably furnished waiting room the four men waited. They had recognised one another, of course, each a little surprised to see the others, but acknowledging the acquaintance-ship. Their lives touched only rarely these days. Only Miles French seemed totally relaxed. What was *he* doing here? Simon Herries wondered, frowning slightly as he studied him. Was he somehow connected with Minesse? Retained by them to handle their legal affairs, perhaps?

The door opened and an attractive brunette stepped inside. "Ms Minesse will see you now, if you would just come this way, please."

When they were shown in Pepper was standing with her back to the door, pretending to study the view outside her window. She waited until Miranda had brought in the tea things and closed the door behind her before turning round.

All four men reacted to her, but she could only see recognition in the eyes of one of them.

Miles French. Pepper deliberately let her expression go blank, hiding from him her fury and loathing.

Across the desk Miles studied her with curiosity and amusement. He had recognised her face immediately, but it had taken him a few seconds to place her. He looked at his companions and realised that none of them had; his senses, honed by his legal training, picked up on her tension. She had come a long way since Oxford, a long, long way.

Simon Herries was the first to speak. Pepper let him shake her hand and give her his practised smile, a judicious blend of male appreciation, sincerity and seriousness. He had filled out since she had last seen him, and it suited him. He looked what he was—a prosperous and successful man. The others followed suit. Miles French was the only one to look directly into her eyes, trying to put her at a disadvantage, she acknowledged, her heart thumping unpleasantly fast as she met the recognition in his smile.

That was something she hadn't anticipated. None of the others had recognised her, and that he should have done so threw her slightly off guard.

"I'm sure you're all wondering why I asked you to come here." Her smile was professional and tempting, promising that none of them would be disappointed in their anticipation. She had already unlocked the drawer that held their files, and now she reached down with one smooth practised movement and removed them.

"I suggest that it might facilitate things if you were all to read these." The files held only copies, of course. Duplicates of them were safely deposited with her bank. Pepper had no intention of seeing almost ten years of work torn up in front of her eyes.

While she poured the tea she waited to see how long it took for the secure, self-satisfied smiles to disappear.

Richard Howell's went first. She saw his eyes narrow and then leave the papers he was studying to stare at her.

"Milk, Mr Howell?" she asked him sweetly.

Each of those files held a secret that if made public could destroy their professional lives for ever. Each of them had thought that secret so deeply buried that it would never be uncovered. Each of them had been wrong!

Richard Howell was now a highly respected and respectable merchant banker; but once he had simply been a younger and much poorer relative in the banking empire run by his uncle David.

It had taken a lot of digging to discover how he had got the money that enabled him to secretly buy up enough shares to challenge and eventually overthrow his uncle's control of the family business. It had taken Pepper months of painstaking work to discover that he had first started buying up shares while he was working in the safe deposit department of the bank.

For many people their safety deposit boxes are simply a place where they leave their valuables to prevent them from being stolen. There are, however, those who find that safety deposit boxes are excellent places to conceal funds—or other items—gained by other and often illegal means: tax evasion, fraud and sometimes outright theft.

It had been Richard Howell's good fortune during the time he was in charge of the safe deposit department to come across a man who fell into this last category. In addition, since it was a rule of the bank that they should hold duplicate keys for their safety deposit boxes, he was able, by carefully choosing his moment, to unlock it and discover for himself exactly what was inside—but that had only come later, following the death from a heart attack of the man who called himself William Law.

"William Law" had had his heart attack in the street, half a mile away from the bank's premises. The evening papers had carried his photograph and a small paragraph on his death, only his name hadn't been William Law but Frank Prentiss, and he had at one time been a member of a gang who had been suspected of carrying out several wages snatches involving hundreds of thousands of pounds. The police had never been able to get enough evidence to convict Frank Prentiss and the other members of the gang, and when three months went by without either the police or the bank connecting Frank Prentiss with William Law, Richard Howell went painstakingly through the records, and then when he was sure that no one would ever know, he removed from William Law's safety deposit box everything but a couple of hundred pounds.

He had no fears about the money being traced back to him—a man as clever as Frank Prentiss must surely have had the stolen notes laundered, and if the police did make the connection between William Law and Frank Prentiss, and find the safety deposit box, then they would just assume that Frank had spent the money.

There was now two hundred and forty-five thousand pounds in Richard Howell's private account with Lloyds Bank, and by the time his uncle decided to query where on earth the money had come from it was already too late—Richard was the new majority shareholder of Howell's bank, having used that original £245,000 as the basis of a fund which through clever and informed dealing on the Stock Exchange he very quickly managed to turn into a very large sum indeed.

Pepper smiled gently at him as she handed him the cup of tea. It amused and exhilarated her to see the panic in his eyes. No doubt he had thought himself safe and invincible—now he knew better.

And what of Simon Herries, the up-and-coming politician; the upholder of decency and family life; the closet homosexual who got his real sex thrills with young boys—the younger the better! When he was at Oxford he had been the ringleader of a select group, all bound to secrecy, who had dabbled in black magic among other things.

Pepper smiled dulcetly into the furious blue eyes that glittered dangerously across the width of her desk.

Alex Barnett had also been a member of that select group—if only briefly. Still, it was long enough to prevent any adoption agency from ever allowing him on their books. Pepper knew all about Julia Barnett's desperate need to have a child, and she also knew how much Alex loved his wife.

And so, on to Miles French. He had disappointed her. It was true that he had a highly active sex life, but he was very selective when it came to choosing his partners and faithful to them while the relationship lasted. Pepper had waited a long time to get something sufficiently damning on Miles, but at last her patience had been satisfied.

Three months ago, the eighteen-year-old daughter of a friend had been smuggling cocaine into the country. She should have been caught. Pepper's information was that she had got on a plane in Rio de Janeiro, carrying the illicit drug disguised some way in her back pack. But somehow when she arrived at Heathrow the cocaine had gone.

Her flight had put down briefly in Paris. Miles French had also been in Paris at the time, and the pair of them had returned to London together. Somehow Miles had managed to persuade the girl to give him the cocaine, Pepper was convinced of it, even though as yet she had no conclusive proof. Even without proof, though, there was enough on her file to irrevocably destroy both his career and his reputation. A potential High Court judge involved in a drugs scandal—he would be de-barred at the very least.

She waited until they had all finished reading. Only Miles French was still smiling. He had far more control than the others, she acknowledged, but she wasn't deceived.

Simon Herries spoke first, flinging down the file and demanding savagely, "Just what the hell is all this about?"

Pepper didn't allow herself to be affected by his rage.

"All of you will now have read your files, so all of you will, I'm sure, realise the precarious position you're in. In those files is information which if it became public could adversely affect your reputation and careers."

"So that's it!" Simon Herries sneered. "Blackmail!"

Pepper froze him with an icy look.

"No, not blackmail," she told him softly, "retribution."

She had their attention now. All of them were staring at her, watching her without comprehension— all of them apart from Miles French, whose mouth was twisted in a very knowing smile indeed.

"Retribution—what the hell for?" demanded Alex Barnett acidly.

Pepper smiled and got up.

"For rape, gentlemen. Eleven years ago all of you, in one way or another, contributed to the fact that I was raped." She paused as she saw their faces change, and offered mockingly, "Ah, I see you do remember after all!"

"Why have you sent for us . . . what are you going to do?"

It was Alex Barnett who spoke, struggling against his growing feeling of disbelief. He remembered the incident, of course. He had never forgotten it, but he had thought he had successfully buried it along with his guilt, and all the other unpleasant aspects of his past that he preferred to forget.

He looked at Pepper and saw the expensive groomed

elegance of her, wondering at the transformation. The girl he remembered had been bone-thin, wearing shabby clothes, her accent thick and hard to understand. She had fought them like a wild animal, lashing out at their faces with her nails . . . He shuddered deeply, closing his eyes.

"What are you going to do?" he muttered.

Amazingly she was still smiling at them. "Nothing. Unless of course you force me to."

Behind her calm smile she was alert, with adrenalin-based energy, watching and assessing.

Rape. To her it was the most vile four-letter word in existence, especially when it applied to the sort of rape that had been inflicted on her. The terror of that night was something she would never forget. She wouldn't let herself; it had been her single motivating force for too long. It had brought her from poverty and deprivation to where she was today.

"You took from me something that was irreplaceable, and I've decided that it's only just that each of you in turn should lose something of similar value.

"You, Mr Herries," she told him, watching him with her mouth curved into a smile and her eyes as hard as metal, "will resign from the Conservative Party. I hear you're tipped as being a possible candidate for their future leader. However, I'm sure they wouldn't think you such a drastic loss if they knew the contents of that file, do you?"

Her smile assessed his rage and then dismissed him as she turned to Richard Howell.

"The bank means an awful lot to you, doesn't it, Mr Howell? But I'm afraid you're going to have to give it up."

"Resign?" He stared at her in disbelief.

Her smile was gentle but implacable. "I'm afraid so. I'm sure your uncle will be only too delighted to step into your shoes."

Alex Barnett waited, anticipating the blow falling, knowing what she was going to tell him. He had fought ever since leaving Oxford to establish his business; he had put everything he owned into it, all his energy, nearly all his time, and he felt a sudden savage desire to take that smooth white throat between his hands and squeeze until those full lips were silenced for ever.

One look at his face told Pepper he had already anticipated her ultimatum, so she passed on to Miles French.

"I know," he told her drily, "but you've forgotten something, Pepper . . ." She frowned at him, disliking his use of her christian name. Unlike the others, he seemed more amused than appalled.

"Vengeance is mine, saith the Lord," he mocked softly. "You're treading a very dangerous path, you know."

Pepper turned away from him.

"You all have one month to consider my . . . suggestions. If at the end of that time I have not heard from you, the contents of these files will be revealed to the press. Of course, I need hardly tell you that they're only copies."

"And that you've left a letter with your bank and your solicitor to be opened in the event of your disappearance or death," Miles mocked.

It irritated Pepper that he should continue to pretend that he was merely amused by her. He had as much to lose as the others. She met his eyes and shuddered, remembering. It had been his room she had woken up in that morning, his shirt had been wrapped around her bruised body; he had been standing looking down at her.

"You can't get away with this, you know . . ."

Richard Howell blustered.

Miles touched him on the arm and shook his head.

"A month, you say?" He looked thoughtfully at Pepper and then said to his companions, "A month isn't a long time, gentlemen, so I suggest we don't waste a moment of it."

Pepper didn't watch them go. She rang through to Miranda and asked her to come in and show them out.

"You may keep your files," she told them mockingly, then she turned her back on them and walked over to the window.

It was over, and somehow she felt curiously empty . . . drained, and yet unsatisfied in a way she hadn't expected.

She heard her office door open and knew they were leaving. Miranda came back five minutes later to remove the undrunk tea, but although her secretary waited for the rest of the afternoon Pepper did not call her in to dictate to her any notes on the meeting.

Outside in the street four men eyed one another.

"Something will have to be done."

"Yes," Miles agreed. "We need somewhere private where we can talk."

"Where that bitch can't overhear us," Simon Herries swore savagely. "She must have had us followed . . ."

"I suggest we go back to my place and talk the whole thing over." Miles flicked back a white cuff and glanced at his watch. "It's half past four now. I have an engagement this evening. Is there anyone who can't make it?"

They all shook their heads. They were each in their own individual ways very powerful and authoritative men, but now they were reacting almost like bewildered and dependent children. As he looked at them Miles suspected that none of them had really yet accepted what had happened to them. For him it was different; he had recognised her when they had not, and in recognising the tremendous leap she had made from what she had been to what she was, he had already been half way to acknowledging her power.

"I just can't believe it!" Alex Barnett shook his head like a man coming up for air, confirming Miles's private thoughts. "All these years she's been waiting . . ." His face changed, shock giving way to reality.

God, what on earth was he going to say to Julia? To withdraw their application for adoption now would destroy her.

"She's got to be stopped."

Numbly he heard Simon Herries speaking, without monitoring the words, until he heard Miles saying coolly,

"What do you have in mind, Herries? Not murder, I hope."

"Murder?"

"No way." That was Richard Howell.

"She *has* to be stopped." Simon Herries glared at the others. Inwardly his heart was thumping furiously. That bitch of a woman—she had enjoyed bringing them down, having them within her power. He could kill her for that alone, never mind the rest of it.

"If you are in agreement I suggest that we talk the whole thing over in private. Since I live alone my place would seem to be the best venue."

God, how could French remain so calm! He seemed almost amused by the whole thing. Staring at him, Simon remembered how little he had trusted him in the old days, and how much pleasure it had given him to . . .

He realised abruptly that Miles was watching him, and quickly veiled the hostility and resentment in his eyes. For now it suited him to play along with everyone else.

It was Miles who found a cruising taxi and flagged it down, giving his address in a crisp, contained voice. As a barrister he had trained himself long ago to step outside his own emotions and reactions and study things logically, and he did so now. Viewed from Pepper Minesse's—where on earth had she got that name from?—standpoint it was perhaps quite natural that she should want to punish them all for what they had done to her, but it took a remarkable strength of will to wait so patiently, and build so carefully.

He could feel the tension from his companions; Simon Herries was the worst, tense to the point of violence; he had always been a dangerous, volatile man. At Oxford he had been very much the gilded youth and very sought after, but beneath that gilding had lain something malevolent, cancerous even.

And the other two? Alex Barnett still looked blank and shocked. Richard Howell was sitting on the edge of his seat, hyped up with nervous tension.

None of them wasted any energy speaking until they were inside Miles's study. "Drink, anyone?" he invited. All of them nodded.

Although they had seen each other casually over the years, they had not kept up the relationship they had had at Oxford, and each of them registered the changes in the others, as they waited for someone to speak first.

"She isn't going to get away with this!" Simon Herries downed his whisky in one gulp and slammed down the glass. "I'm damned if I'm going to be told what to do by some upstart bitch of a gypsy brat!"

"I'm sure your female admirers would be very interested to hear that speech, Simon," Miles remarked coolly, "but you seem to be forgetting that we aren't dealing with an uneducated seventeen-year-old this time. Ms Minesse is an extremely successful and powerful woman."

"She wants to destroy us!" Alex Barnett's hand shook as he put his glass down. "We've got to stop her . . ."

"For God's sake, we all know that. How the devil are we going to do it?" Richard asked impatiently.

Miles pursed his lips and offered mildly, "I have a suggestion." They all looked at him. "As I see it, we need to be able to put Ms Minesse in a position where she will not only be willing to hand over those files to us, but where she will also refrain from attempting to gain . . . er . . . retribution again."

"Threaten her in some way, you mean?" Alex Barnett looked uncomfortable. Miles ignored him.

"It seems to me that the success of Minesse Management rests entirely in the hands of its founder. If Ms Minesse were to disappear for a while, it follows that without her Minesse Management would slowly start to collapse."

"If you're talking about kidnapping her, it won't work," Richard interrupted flatly. "You heard what she said about that."

"Yes, I did, and I agree. She can't disappear. However, she could go away with her lover—and then stay away long enough for her clients to start losing faith in the company. Superstars have super-egos which need constant attention. Without Ms Minesse to provide that attention . . ." Miles lifted one eyebrow and waited for their reaction.

"Great idea!" Simon Herries sneered. "How the hell do you propose to make sure that her lover keeps her out of sight, or that she'd even agree to go with him?"

"Why, by making sure that her lover is one of us," Miles told them silkily.

Stunned silence followed his words.

Richard Howell spoke first, turning restlessly in his seat. "For God's sake, Miles, this isn't the time to start making jokes! You know she'd never accept one of us as her lover . . ."

"She doesn't need to accept it."

They all stared at him.

"Of course she wouldn't agree to going away with one of us—or with anyone else, if it meant leaving her business unattended, I suspect. But if we can convince her staff, and everyone else close to her, that she has gone away willingly with her lover, then her absence would not be considered a disappearance and consequently the instructions she has left with her solicitor and her bank would not be activated. And of course, once having abducted her, we would both have ample time and opportunity to persuade her to withdraw today's ultimatums."

"There's only one problem," Richard Howell interrupted sardonically. "Which one of us is going to play the part of the supposed 'lover'?"

Miles raised his eyebrows.

"I thought I'd take on the role myself." He smiled at them. "I'm single; I can take as much leave from my chambers as I wish without causing anyone to question my absence." He smiled again and raised his eyebrows. "Of course, if one of you would prefer . . ." They were silent as he looked at each of them in turn, and then Simon Herries spoke,

"Very noble, but why should you do that for the rest of us?" he demanded suspiciously.

"I'm not," Miles told him calmly. "I'm doing it for myself, and to be honest, I'd prefer to rely on myself rather than anyone else. However, if one of you has a better idea . . ."

"Short of murder I can't think of a single thing,"

Richard admitted bitterly. "God, she's got us all by the short and curlies, and she knows it."

No one disputed his comment.

"So, then it's agreed." Miles stood up. "I would suggest that from now on until her disappearance has been accomplished we don't get in touch with one another. She's obviously had all of us watched, at one time or another, and could still be doing so, if she thinks we plan to move against her."

"Surely she can't expect that we'd just accept her ultimatums?" Alex Barnett still looked bewildered, but now he was getting angry. The reality of what was happening had brought a thin sheen of sweat to his skin. He thought he had put all that business with Herries behind him long ago—God, what a fool he had been, but he had been flattered by Herries' friendship—way, way out of his depth.

Richard Howell was engrossed in his own thoughts. How on earth had Pepper found out about that safe deposit box? He couldn't give up control of the bank. He had fought too hard for it, but would French's plans work? At the end of the day what they were talking about was abduction and kidnap, and if French couldn't keep the girl hidden, if his plan didn't work . . . He swallowed nervously. But what the hell alternative was there?

Simon Herries watched Miles. He didn't trust him—he never had; he didn't like him very much either. At Oxford French hadn't been one of his court. That cunning bitch! Could French pull it off? He hoped so, he had fought too long and hard to give everything up now. There had to be another way, but until he found it he had to play along with French.

"Well, gentlemen, what do you say—do we go ahead with my plan, or not?" He looked at them all in turn, waiting for their responses.

"I don't see that we have any alternative." Alex Barnett looked almost ill, haunted in fact.

"I hope to God it will work." Richard paced tensely. "Yes . . . Yes . . . All right, I agree."

"And you, Herries?" Miles looked across at him.

"I agree." But I don't trust you, French, I don't trust you one little bit, he thought silently, and I'm going to be watching you.

"Right. We have one month's grace, and I intend to use that time to our advantage." Miles shot back a white shirt cuff and glanced at his watch. "I'm sorry to be inhospitable, gentlemen, but I have an engagement for this evening."

His engagement was with Rosemary. He would have to tell her that their affair was over. He wondered a little wryly how she would react. It was a pity that Pepper had managed to learn about Sophie, he had thought he had covered both their tracks rather neatly.

Pepper Minesse . . . Where on earth had she got that name? he wondered ironically again after the others had left. In their Oxford days he had known her simply as "Gypsy." Everyone had called her that.

When and how had "Gypsy" become the founder of Minesse Management? Miles reached for the phone and then put it down. Tomorrow would be time enough to start uncovering the mystery of Pepper Minesse; tonight he would have to concentrate on disengaging himself from his affair with Rosemary. It saddened him that he was able to contemplate doing so with so very little regret. Hadn't he always chosen the women in his life with a view to his ability for distancing himself from them?

Pepper Minesse . . . He remembered how she had looked that morning, huddled in a corner of his locked room. She had been a virgin; he remembered having to destroy his sheets. He closed his eyes and swore suddenly.

Pepper lay supine in her bath, letting the warm water soothe away her tension. She didn't want to go to tonight's party, but she had promised Louise.

Half of her couldn't believe that it was over; that she had actually done it. Behind her closed eyelids images writhed and danced. She saw Alex Barnett's shocked face; Miles French's impassive one. Simon had been furious, and Richard disbelieving. What were they doing now? Probably trying to think of a way to stop her, but that was something they wouldn't be able to do. She had had ten years to plan; they only had a month, and she had protected herself. If anything happened to her . . . But nothing was going to happen. She had the upper hand now. She wasn't a semi-literate nobody now, of so little importance that she could be kicked about like a stray dog. Did they really think that she had forgotten; that they could get away with it?

She moved restlessly in the cooling water, wondering why she wasn't feeling more euphoric. Beside the bath was the bottle of champagne she had taken out of the fridge. She had put it there this morning to chill so that she could celebrate, but now she didn't want it. It irked her that she was able to take so little pleasure in her achievement. What was the matter with her? She had wanted to enjoy her triumph. Perhaps she would have enjoyed it had she had someone to share it with . . . The thought startled her and she examined it suspiciously, pushing it away from her as she got out of the bath.

The charity do was being held at the Grosvenor, in the ballroom. As her partner Pepper was taking one of her oldest friends. Geoffrey Pitt had been her financial adviser for several years.

She had met him just when Minesse Management was starting to grow from a small concern to a very much larger one, and it had been Geoffrey Pitt who had guided her first tentative steps when she started to expand. It had also been Geoffrey who had advised her to buy her premises rather than rent, who had helped her to invest her profits so that they too could make money for her.

These days she knew almost as much about the world of high finance as he did himself, but officially she still retained him as her financial adviser.

When Pepper first met him he had just been getting over a traumatic divorce. It had been inevitable that they should become very close, although Geoffrey, like those men who had come both before and after him in her life, had found that she had a trick of withholding from him the most essential part of herself. Most people thought she was frigid. But how could she give herself to any man after what had happened to her? It had left her with an acute and deeply rooted distrust of the entire male sex. Her fear of them she had managed to conquer, just—and only she knew what an effort of will it had been, but to allow one to be intimate with her; to even think about permitting for a second time the humiliation and degradation she had already suffered, made her flesh turn to ice.

She was not a fool; she knew that perhaps with counselling, with care, she could possibly overcome her fear, but Pepper didn't want to overcome it. As an observer she had seen what their relationships with the men in their lives did for other women, and she didn't want that kind of bondage for herself. All her life in so many ways she had been alone, and she had come to relish that aloneness—to see it in fact as the only way for her to live. And so cleverly, discreetly she had learned how to keep the whole sex at bay.

With Geoffrey it had been almost too easy, and now they had the sort of comfortable friendship that exists only between two people who both know and like each other and have no curiosity about one another sexually. There were still times when Geoffrey looked at her and ached to take her to bed, but he knew that Pepper did not feel a corresponding desire for him. And besides, since Nick Howarth had come into her life . . . He grimaced slightly to himself. If Howarth hadn't been abroad on business Geoffrey doubted that he would have been invited to accompany Pepper tonight.

He picked her up promptly at eight o'clock.

Geoffrey was the type of upper-class Englishman who looked his best in evening clothes, Pepper reflected as he helped her into his Rolls. He was tall, with mid-brown hair and kind hazel eyes, the sort of man mothers thought would make their daughters a good husband.

As they drove down Park Lane they joined the tail end of a convoy of cars, all disgorging their passengers outside the entrance to the Grosvenor's Ballroom. The charity ball was for mentally handicapped children. Its patroness was the Princess of Wales, and she and the Prince were expected to be present.

As Geoffrey followed Pepper into the ballroom he couldn't help speculating about her relationship with Nick Howarth. He knew that Howarth was one of her major clients. There was a discreet rumour among those in the know that they were also lovers, and it was certainly true that they partnered one another at a variety of social functions—functions often associated with the sport that Howarth sponsored.

Were they lovers? Geoffrey felt the old familiar jealousy at the thought of someone sharing Pepper's bed, and then valiantly dismissed it. At heart he was a kind, rather gentle man; the kind of man who, he told himself wryly, could never hope to hold the attention of a woman like Pepper—a woman who was so intensely and vibrantly female that no man, surely, could remain immune to her.

Pepper would not have been surprised if she could have read his thoughts. Geoffrey wasn't the only person who speculated about her relationship with Nick Howarth. They had known one another for several years now, and although both of them were regularly seen with other partners, it was generally accepted among their circle of friends that they were lovers.

Nick wasn't like Geoffrey. Not so very long ago he had given her an ultimatum. He wasn't the first man to do so; and he wouldn't be the last.

He was away at the moment, but soon he would be coming back, and when he did . . . When he did she would find some way of dealing with him, Pepper promised herself. At the moment she had more important things on her mind.

A tense spiral of excitement began to wind inside her. In four weeks, but no, she mustn't think about that now. There would be time enough when . . . She had long ago learned to control her thoughts and impulses, and so, dismissing everything else from her mind, she started to concentrate on her surroundings.

As she stepped inside the ballroom she saw that it was awash with Emanuel creations in tulle and chiffon. Her own ballgown had been designed by Bellville Sassoon. The rich blue raw silk skirt floated round her as she moved, the tightly fitting bodice just revealing the upper curves of her breasts. The off-the-shoulder sleeves and the hem of her skirt were trimmed with antique lace that had cost almost as much as the dress itself. She was wearing her hair drawn softly back off her face and caught back with a matching silk flower. Among the soft pinks and peaches of the other women her gown stood out dramatically.

The Duchess of York had made red hair fashionable, but that was not why so many of the other guests stopped to look discreetly at her as she walked into the room.

John Fletcher and Louise Faber were already seated at the table when Pepper reached it. She introduced Geoffrey to them and accepted the glass of champagne offered to her.

They all made small talk for several minutes while the tables around them filled up. A tiny frisson of excitement ran through the room when the Prince and Princess of Wales were announced. Chairs scraped back over the floor as everyone stood up.

"She's lovely, isn't she?" Louise whispered to Pepper as they listened to the chairwoman's welcoming speech.

John, who had been studying the Princess's dress, announced, "She's wearing a Bruce Oldfield. It must be a new one, I recognise his latest line."

Over supper they discussed business. John had had time to consider Pepper's suggestion and he liked it. He already had in mind the sort of wardrobe he would design for Louise.

"I spoke to *Vogue* after I left you today," Pepper told him. "One of their assistant editors is here tonight, apparently—Rosemary Bennett—do you know her?"

"Yes, I do. In fact I've seen her somewhere." John turned round and searched among the tables. "Over there—look, Pepper. The woman in the Giorgio Armani—the white satin. Do you want me to introduce you?"

"No . . . not here, I'll go and see her at *Vogue* later in the week." Pepper looked away from the table, and her body froze as she saw the man making his way through the tables. For one moment she thought he was heading for her, and her face lost all its colour, her body tense with shock.

"Pepper, what's wrong?"

Somehow she managed to drag her attention away.

"Are you feeling all right?"

John's forehead was creased in an anxious frown, his eyes dark with concern. God, what was the matter with her? She had everything under control, but just one unexpected glimpse of Miles French had thrown her so completely off guard that she was still fighting the shock.

This afternoon must have been more of a strain than she had realised. Miles French hadn't reacted like the others. He had been far more cool, far more in control of himself, and he had also recognised her. That was something she hadn't expected him to do. She had changed so much from the girl she had been that she had thought there was nothing of that girl left.

Miles French had shown her otherwise, and she had found the experience disquieting.

On the other side of the room Rosemary Bennett reached out and scored her long nails delicately over Miles's wrist.

"You're looking very pensive, darling, is something wrong?"

Miles gave her a perfunctory smile.

"Not specifically."

There was something different about him tonight, Rosemary recognised; something distancing. She was far too experienced and knowledgeable about men not to recognise the signs. Miles was bored.

It was time to end their affair. She didn't really want to lose him. As a lover, physically she doubted that she had ever met his equal, but emotionally there was always a part of him that he withheld, that remained aloof and unobtainable. Rosemary veiled her eyes and studied him. Miles was not the sort of man who could live without a woman for very long, which probably meant that he had already chosen her successor.

She wondered without rancour who the woman was. Whoever she was, she hoped she had the good sense not to fall in love with him. Miles turned his head and looked at her.

"I thought tonight we might leave early."

Trust Miles to deliver the coup de grace with style! she thought wryly, and wondered if he intended to tell her before or after he had taken her to bed. Knowing Miles, it would probably be beforehand, then he would make love to her as a way of saying goodbye.

Once she had seen Miles, Pepper couldn't relax. Sensing her tension but at a loss to understand the reason for it, Geoffrey asked her if she would like to leave once they had finished their supper.

She got up gratefully, making her excuses to John and Louise. "I'm afraid I have a rather bad headache," she lied, letting Geoffrey take her arm and lead her away.

"You stay here. I'll get your coat for you," he instructed once they were in the foyer.

Pepper sat down on one of the small gilt chairs and stared abstractedly into space. Another couple walked into the room, the woman's voice cool and faintly metallic, the man's deeper, almost laconic and somehow familiar.

She tensed and looked at them.

"Pepper, what an unexpected pleasure!"

She saw Miles coming towards her and was conscious of a tight aching tension constricting her throat. She struggled to stand up, catching the heel of her shoe in the hem of her skirt, overbalancing slightly. Miles reached out to steady her, and she flinched beneath the unexpected warm pressure of his hands on her bare arms.

Five feet away Rosemary saw the way Miles was looking at the other woman and knew that she had seen the lady who was going to take her place in his bed. She smiled bitterly to herself. At least he had taste. Pepper Minesse was no pretty fluffy doll.

They had gone by the time Geoffrey returned with her coat, but as he helped her into it Pepper was still struggling to obliterate the small scene from her senses.

CHAPTER FOUR

PEPPER didn't sleep well that night. The old nightmare haunted and pursued her. It always came at times like this when she was under stress. Long-suppressed memories surfaced and twisted through her mind, and she lay back against the tangle of satin sheets, her hand over her heart feeling it steady, as she forced herself to block out the too-intrusive memory of smothering darkness, of hands and voices, whispers pitched just too low for her to hear. In her nightmare she struggled to catch what they were saying, but in reality she had heard; had known what was happening to her.

Rape. The taste of the word on her tongue was sour and foetid. Her mouth twisted bitterly. It was a full mouth, wicked and sensual; men always looked at it, imagining its red moistness against their skin.

She was too hyped up to even try to go back to sleep. If she did she knew what would happen. She would be back in that shadowy room in Oxford with the door guarded by the men who had taken her there, while . . .

Her body shook, sweat glistening on her soft silken skin. Once more she felt the smothering sensation of fear engulfing her and fought against it, pushing away the terrifying memories of unseen hands touching her body, voices whispering softly just outside the stretch of her ears.

She reached out abruptly and switched on the lamp beside her bed, deliberately controlling her breathing as she willed herself to regain control. She was both hot and shivering, pursued by demons that owed nothing to any human life form. The May night was warm, but inside she felt deathly cold.

"You can have whatever you want from life," Philip had once told her, "but there's always a price to be paid for it."

Pepper had paid her price, and now it was time that others paid theirs.

She got up and padded downstairs, ferreting about in the kitchen cupboard until she found the tin of drinking chocolate. It had been there since Mary's last visit two years ago, for Christmas shopping. Mary and Philip had never felt totally at home in her London house. Its cool designer exclusivity overwhelmed them.

Happiness and contentment had always been the meter by which they had measured their own lives, and she knew that both of them in their different ways worried about her. Although they didn't know it, they had good reason to be worried. Pepper grimaced faintly to herself, as she made a milky drink and carried it back to her bedroom, curling up against her cream satin sheets and pillows, her dark red hair spilling out over the antique trimmings. Without make-up, with her hair curling extravagantly round her face, she looked about seventeen, like a little girl who had strayed into her elder sister's room. But she wasn't seventeen . . .

At seventeen . . .

She sighed and compressed her body against the intrusive memories, but it was too late, already they were flooding back, drowning her in pain and fear. She let herself relax and admit them.

Perhaps after all it was only right that tonight she *should* remember, she thought tiredly, with the acceptance of her mother's race, for the vagaries and implacability of fate.

Very well then, if she must remember, let her at least remember it all. She would go back to the beginning . . . to the very beginning.

In January of 1960 the gypsy tribe to which Pepper's mother belonged was camped in Scotland on a tract of land belonging to the laird of the clan MacGregor. It had been a bad winter, with thick snow and howling east winds straight off the Russian seas. Sir Ian MacGregor was a kindly man brought up in a tradition that made him, as chief of his clan, as responsible for their welfare as he was for that of his own immediate family.

The MacGregors had never been a particularly wealthy clan; they owned lands, yes, but the land was fit for nothing but running sheep and renting out as grouse moors to rich Americans. When his factor told him that the gypsies had arrived and were camping in their usual valley his first thought was relief that they had arrived safely. The gypsies had been camping in that valley for more than two hundred years, but this year the heavy snowfalls had delayed them. His second thought was concern for their survival in the bitter cold, so he sent his factor into the valley with bales of straw for the ponies and some meat from the deer that he and his ghillie had shot just before Christmas.

Duncan Randall was not just the MacGregor's factor, he was also his nephew and heir, a tall, rather withdrawn eighteen-year-old, with black hair and a narrow bony face. Duncan was a dreamer and an idealist. He loved his uncle and the land, and in his soul he carried the poetry of his Celtic heritage.

An overnight fall of snow had blocked the pass through the valley so that the gypsies were completely enclosed. Dark faces and wary eyes monitored his progress in the Land Rover as he drove towards their encampment. Smudges of smoke from their fires hung on the horizon, small groups of wiry, silent children huddled round their warmth.

It had been a bad year for the tribe. Their leader had died in the autumn, leaving the tribe like a rudderless ship. He had been sixty-eight years old and it was to Naomi, his widow, that the rest of the tribe now turned.

There had been only one child of the marriage—a girl. Layla was fifteen and according to the custom of their tribe she must now be married to the man they had chosen as their new leader.

Rafe, her husband-to-be, was thirty years old, the younger son of a leader of another Lee tribe. To Layla at fifteen he seemed both old and faintly alarming. Her father had spoiled her, because she was the child of his old age, even though her mother had warned him against it, and she was a wild, almost fey creature, as changeable as April skies. Naomi worried for her, knowing that hers would never be an easy way through life.

Naomi had pleaded with Rafe to wait until Layla was sixteen before marrying her. Her birthday fell in the spring, and Rafe had reluctantly agreed, but all the tribe could see how he watched the girl with jealous, brooding eyes.

Layla had always been contrary and awkward; Naomi despaired of her. Rafe was a man any other girl would have been proud to call husband, but when he looked at her, Layla tossed her hair and averted her eyes, giving her smiles instead to the boys she had grown up with.

Since this was his first year with the tribe, Rafe had

not visited the valley before, and he watched suspiciously as the Land Rover made its slow way in towards their camp.

"Who comes here?" he demanded of Naomi in their Romany dialect.

"It is the nephew of the MacGregor," Naomi told him, putting her hand on his arm to stop him as he moved forward. "He is a good friend to us, Rafe."

"He is a *gorgio*," Rafe protested bitterly.

"Yes, but we have been made welcome here for many generations. See, he has brought fodder for our animals," Naomi told him, watching as Duncan stopped the Land Rover and climbed into the back to unload the bales of hay.

The children ran to help him. Layla was with them, Naomi noticed, frowning as she watched the way her daughter's skirts lifted as she ran.

To a Romany it is a wanton act for a woman to reveal her legs to any man other than her husband, and although she knew this very well there were times when Layla almost seemed to deliberately flout their conventions.

Layla didn't want to marry Rafe, Naomi already knew that, but she had no choice, like must marry like, and Layla, like Rafe, was descended from one of their greatest leaders. Both of them carried his blood in their veins and it would be breaking an unwritten Romany law for Layla to marry outside her own blood. Even so, her heart was troubled for her wayward child.

The bales of hay were heavy and shifting them was hard work, but a year of outdoor activity had tautened and developed Duncan's body so that he was able to take the weight quite easily. He was aware of the gypsies' silent scrutiny, but he strove to ignore it even while it unnerved him.

Across the small clearing containing their fires he could see the old woman and the man watching them. He could feel the man's resentment and dislike and it made him uncomfortable. Poor devils, it was no wonder that they resented him. He would hate to live the way they did, almost on the verge of starvation, constantly moving from place to place. He shifted his glance away from the brooding intensity of the man's stare and saw the cluster of children staring up at him. Several of them had running sores on their faces, all of them looked thin and hungry. His uncle had sent down a sack of porridge as well as the meat, and as he reached into the Land Rover to get it out he saw the girl for the first time. She was standing slightly apart from the others, watching them as he did, but there was pride in her eyes and she had a way of holding her body that defied him to feel pity for her. Where the children were thin, she was slender and supple, reminding him of the reeds that bent beneath the wind at the edges of the lochs. Her hair was long and black, shining in the harsh sunlight, her skin smoothly golden. Her eyes flashed anger and arrogance at him as she met his stare; golden eyes like her skin. She was the most beautiful thing he had ever seen. The sack he was holding slipped in his slackened fingers and he caught it up, feeling the red tide creeping up under his skin and with it a fierce upsurge of desire.

Layla knew enough about men to recognise his desire. Although she hid it from him it excited her. There were very few young men of her own age in the tribe, and certainly none as handsome as this dark-haired, fair-skinned *gorgio* boy, who was so much taller and broader than the men of her tribe, and whose eyes betrayed his wanting for her.

She tossed her hair as she walked past him, filled

with a sudden surge of exhilaration. She didn't want to marry Rafe; he frightened her, although nothing would ever make her admit it. She sensed a cruelty within him that instinctively she feared.

Her mother called sharply to her and she scowled. She was not a child who needed to heed its parents' every sharp word. She was a woman; and she would choose her own way through life. Avoiding Rafe, she darted through the snow and into the caravan.

Duncan saw Naomi walking towards him and knew from his uncle's description that she was the wife of the leader of the tribe. Her English was thickly accented, but Duncan understood enough of what she said to realise that her husband was dead, and that Rafe was now their new leader.

Later, while he and Sir Ian ate the hot potato cakes smothered in melting butter and drank strong dark tea in front of the peat fire in his uncle's study, Duncan told his uncle how surly and uncommunicative he had found the gypsies.

"It is just their way. They are very slow to trust us, Duncan, and you can understand why. They are in many ways a persecuted and little understood race, whose habits and customs are not ours. They adhere to a much harsher code than our modern laws allow for, but then their life is much harsher than ours. Their women are still cruelly punished for adultery, and they consider their marriage to be a sacred rite that can be set aside by death alone. They are a fascinating people, though, and a very proud one."

It was on the tip of Duncan's tongue to tell his uncle about the gypsy girl, but before he could, the housekeeper came in with a plate of fresh scones.

Sir Ian lived well but simply, and already Duncan was ceasing to miss his more sophisticated life in Edinburgh at the University. His mother was Sir Ian's sister. She had married outside the clan, and her husband, Duncan's father, was a solicitor.

Ian MacGregor was much older than his sister. His only son had been killed at the end of the war. His wife had died shortly afterwards, of a broken heart, so some said, and Ian had refused to marry again, so that now Duncan was his only heir. Duncan had willingly given up his law studies to take over the job as his uncle's factor—a training for the inheritance which would one day be his.

Layla was bored and restless. She hated the confinement the snow enforced on them. She wanted to get away from Rafe's brooding presence. She wanted to escape . . . She wanted to see Duncan Randall again.

No one else was stirring when she slipped out of the camp in the early morning light. She moved quietly and silently across the snow, climbing as agilely and surefootedly as one of Sir Ian MacGregor's sheep as she headed up the narrow track that led out of the valley.

It took her half an hour to climb to the top. From there the moors stretched all round her in every direction, bordered by even higher hills. Here and there a dark crevasse in the snow indicated where other narrow valleys might lie, and against the skyline she could see a smudge of smoke. Layla was drawn to it even while caution urged her to retreat.

Duncan was also up early. He wanted to drop feed off with the shepherds before they had a fresh fall of snow.

Layla heard the sound of the Land Rover engine long before she saw it, the noise carrying well on the crisp cold air. She watched as the blue grey smudge came towards her, her body outlined against the sky, her hair flowing back like a dark banner.

At first when he saw her Duncan thought there must be something wrong with the tribe, but when he stopped alongside her and looked at her, there was no mistaking the look in her eyes. He felt the heat run through his body, and silently opened the Land Rover door for her.

She had dreamed about the *gorgio* last night, and now this morning she had found him. He was her fate, suddenly Layla was sure of it. Marriage to Rafe was not for her, she wanted more from life than that.

Uneducated, inarticulate, knowing only the feelings that flowed through her blood, she knew nevertheless that the feelings inside her were the same ones that flowed through the body of the *gorgio* boy beside her.

Layla was a virgin, but she was not ignorant of the ways of a man and a woman together. Her mother had told her when she protested that she did not want to marry Rafe that she would know when she was ready to be his wife. She knew now that her body was ready for a man's possession; she felt it in her responses to the way Duncan looked at her. She reached out and touched his arm and felt the muscles contract beneath his skin.

When he stopped the Land Rover they kissed as urgently and hungrily as though they had known and wanted each other for years. Despite their inexperience there was nothing fumbled or clumsy about the way they came together, both of them overwhelmed by a force stronger than their separate or combined wills.

Layla's sharp cries of delight, her firm thighs gripping his body, the soft feminine scent of her; these were the things Duncan remembered late at night, lying awake in his bed, aching for her, wanting yet again to expend his life force inside her.

Curled up in her narrow bunk, Layla too was thinking of him. She had enjoyed the pleasure they had shared, but more than that she was exhilarated by what they had done. Now Rafe could no longer claim her in the ancient gypsy rite; now she would not have to bow her head to him or acknowledge him as her lord and master.

She knew that many of the others thought her proud and stubborn and said that her father had spoiled her. Maybe it was true, but she was not a horse to be sold into a man's keeping. All the resentment she had experienced since Naomi had first told her that she was to marry Rafe surfaced and coalesced into fierce rebellion. She had taken the *gorgio* boy as her lover and in doing so she had broken the most sacred of all gypsy laws, but she didn't care. No laws could bind or chain her. She was Layla . . . she was free.

For over a week the young couple continued to meet and make love. Duncan became so obsessed with Layla that nothing else had any importance. He lived for the brief time they could snatch together, when she managed to escape from the tribe. The fact that she knew that Rafe was watching her only served to increase her exhilaration whenever she managed to sneak away to be with Duncan.

It was only when the snow started to thaw, and Rafe started saying that it was time they were on their way, that Layla began to fear the consequence of her actions. She confided her fears to Duncan one afternoon as they lay together in the hay loft of one of his uncle's barns.

"Then don't go with them," he begged fiercely. "Stay here with me . . . we'll get married."

Layla moved restlessly in his arms. Marriage to Duncan? Was that really what she wanted? She loved him; she loved the smooth young feel of his body; she loved the desire he could make her feel; but she also loved the excitement of stealing away to be with him, the dangerous elixir of doing the forbidden.

If she stayed with him the tribe would reject her . . . her name would never be spoken by them again. Her mother . . .

Her mother had problems of her own. This Scottish valley had always been one of her favourite stopping places. Normally they spent two months or so here, but Rafe was now their leader, and Rafe did not like the valley. Rafe was also growing impatient and bitter about Layla's foolishness, Naomi knew that, but Layla was so headstrong, such a child still, as wild and fey as the most spirited filly.

She was getting old, Naomi thought tiredly. Her bones ached in the cold wind, and life had lost its savour for her since she had lost her Leon.

Rafe's surliness seemed to have infected the rest of the tribe as well. Some of the men were saying that the valley was not a good place any more. What was needed was a celebration of some sort to lift the tribe's spirits . . . a wedding feast. But Layla was the only girl of marriageable age with the tribe, and she . . .

Sighing faintly, Naomi picked up the worn pack of Tarot cards she alway carried with her, absently setting them out. One card stared up at her and her body froze colder than the snow outside her caravan. Death. She put the cards down with trembling fingers.

The Tarot cards never lied, she knew that. She shuddered deeply, sensing danger, aware of it waiting, lurking, not visible to the human eye, but there all the same, an indefinable presence that cast its shadow over the whole tribe.

One morning Rafe announced that they were leaving. No one queried his decision, not even Layla— no one could query the decisions of the leader of the tribe, but just as soon as she could she slipped away from the valley, heading for her meeting place with Duncan.

Only this time she was followed.

Rafe tracked her with the cunning skill of their race, keeping her easily in sight without letting her know that he was there. Panic had made her grow careless. Once they had left the valley behind Layla knew that Rafe would insist on marrying her. Now that she and Duncan had been lovers the idea of marriage to Rafe was even more abhorrent to her.

Duncan would marry her, she knew that, but to cast herself off from her mother, from their way of life . . . Her thoughts tumbled through her mind like a mill race in full spate. She was deaf to the tiny, betraying sounds Rafe made as he followed her.

Outside the barn, Layla hesitated briefly, glancing over her shoulder. There was no one in sight. She ran inside, and Duncan, who had heard her come in, hurried to meet her, taking her in his arms and kissing her passionately.

When he released her Layla told him of Rafe's decree.

"Don't go," he urged. "Stay here with me."

"I want to."

Neither of them knew that their whispered confidences were being overheard. Rafe had crept into the barn while they were kissing, and was now standing in a shadowy corner, watching and listening.

A fierce rage possessed him. Layla was his . . . but she had shamed him by giving herself to this *gorgio*. She had broken the most important of the Romany rules. She was a wanton who would be cast out by the tribe if they knew what she had done. She wasn't fit to be his woman, but even so he would take her and show her just what she had scorned by giving herself instead to her pretty *gorgio* lover. But first . . .

Neither of them saw him move until he was close enough to reach out and push Layla away from Duncan. His knife, so sharp and so deadly, slid between Duncan's ribs with ease, and up towards the heart.

Duncan made a small sound, a choked protest, that brought a rush of blood to his lips as he dropped to the floor. Rafe had stabbed him through the heart, and as Layla watched with horrified, disbelieving eyes she saw him die in front of her, still reaching out towards her, his eyes so terrified and frightened that she knew she would carry their expression with her to the grave.

As Rafe bent to retrieve his knife, Layla whirled away from him, running as fleetly as a hare over the snow-packed ground, not daring to pause to look behind her.

Rafe let her go. After all, where could she run to? He wiped the blade of his knife clean of Duncan's blood and stared emotionlessly down at the inert body of his rival. The *gorgio* had stolen his woman from him and it was only right that he should forfeit his life as punishment. Layla he would punish in a different way. His mouth curved in a cruel smile as he contemplated just how he would punish her. He would not take her as his wife now, of course; she was unclean, tainted by her physical contact with the *gorgio*, but she would lie in his bed nonetheless.

Rafe had a rare taint in a Romany; he liked to inflict pain. As a small child he had enjoyed setting traps for rabbits and other small animals, not because he needed the food, but because he liked seeing the tormented look of agony in the small creatures eyes.

His father had tried to beat the trait out of him, but all that had done had been to suppress it. Normally Rafe was only able to indulge his taste for inflicting

pain on the women he bought whenever he had
enough money to do so, but now Layla had provided
him with a convenient opportunity to indulge himself
to the full without restraint. By her own actions she
had set herself apart from the rest of the tribe; by
Romany law now, no one would lift a hand to stop
him punishing her.

He was in no hurry to pursue her. Where could she
go? Her *gorgio* lover was dead, the tribe would not
allow her mother to shelter her from his wrath.

One look at her daughter's face was enough to tell
Naomi that something was wrong. She had a clear
mental vision of the Tarot cards, and saw death
grinning up at her.

Layla was too distraught to conceal the truth.
Naomi recoiled from her in pain and shock when the
girl revealed that she and Duncan Randall had been
lovers.

"And now Rafe has killed him," she told her
mother.

Naomi's mind worked furiously. Her first and most
important loyalty was to the tribe. Through Layla's
folly, and Rafe's reaction to it, they would all suffer.
The tribe needed a leader . . . they needed Rafe. They
would have to leave the valley, and quickly, and once
they were gone from here some story could be
concocted that would prevent the truth from coming
out. Once the *gorgio*'s death was discovered the police
would question them, of course, but somehow . . .
there must be a way out.

"Go into the van and stay there until I come to
you," Naomi told Layla abruptly.

There was so much to do . . . and Rafe was not
here. She went from van to van, urging everyone to
pack up ready to leave. The camp fires were stamped
out, the children and animals suddenly restless as they

scented the imminent departure.

When Rafe returned to the camp half an hour later he saw from her face that Naomi knew.

"She has told you, then?" was all he said.

Naomi nodded, unable to meet his eyes, so great was her sense of shame. Layla . . . her daughter had shamed her. How grieved Leon would have been had he lived to see this day!

"We must leave here. The police will come. They will ask questions . . ."

"To which our people will not know any answers," Rafe warned her. He looked at her. "Tonight you will send your daughter to me."

One look at his face was enough to silence Naomi's protests, and she returned to her own van with a heavy heart. Layla had offended against one of the strongest of their tribal taboos, and it was only right that she should be punished, but the look in Rafe's eyes had chilled her through to her bones, and Layla was after all her child.

She found Layla curled up on her bunk staring blankly into space. When Naomi told her of Rafe's edict, she shook her head vehemently.

"I will not go to him!"

Pain and grief shadowed Naomi's eyes as she looked at her daughter, so beautiful and so wild. Even now she held her head proudly . . . too proudly, perhaps. She was completely untouched by her own shame.

"I will not go to him!"

"My child, you will have no choice."

"No choice." The words hammered at Layla's brain. She hated Rafe . . . if she could she would have killed him herself for what he had done, but she had no skill with a knife, and her strength was puny when compared with his.

Even now she could not comprehend what she had

lost. It was impossible to believe that Duncan was dead, shock protected her from reality, and she had not yet accepted that she had lost him.

When the police came to the camp to question the gypsies, all of them responded stoically to their questions, each providing an alibi for the other. Rafe stood apart, silent, watching.

Sir Ian, who had come with the police, looked shrunken and old. Naomi pitied him sincerely. He had lost one who had been as a son to him, and she saw defeat written across the kindly face.

The police had already questioned Rafe. He had been hunting for game, he had told them, producing two other men as his witnesses.

No matter how many questions the police asked they could not break through the wall of silent suspicion emanating from the gypsies. They knew that one of them had killed Duncan; it had to be, and a knife, used so expertly and efficiently, had to have been wielded by a Romany hand.

"Clannish as the devil, if you'll excuse me from saying so, Sir Ian," the police sergeant said, as they walked back to the Land Rovers. "We'll get nothing out of them."

"But why . . .why? I don't understand it. Duncan was such a kind boy . . ."

"That's something we'll probably never know."

"One of them's done it, for sure," the sergeant told his superior later at the police station, "but I doubt if we'll ever find out which one. They've given each other alibis that we'll never break."

At dusk, the tribe ate in silence, a pall of mistrust and fear falling over the entire camp. Not a word had been spoken to Layla since her return. She had eaten alone in her mother's van, and now the time was fast approaching when Rafe would demand his vengeance.

She shivered as she contemplated what he might do to her. Duncan's lovemaking had opened her eyes to her own sensuality. She had responded to him as joyfully as a flower unfolding to the sun, but she felt no desire for Rafe, only fear and hatred. He had killed the man she loved, and she hated him for that and always would, but she feared him as a woman always fears a man who she senses wants to inflict pain upon her.

"You must go to him," Naomi told her quietly. "If you do not, you will be taken to him by the other men, and that will be worse. Better to endure what must be with your pride intact."

"Even though my body might be destroyed!" Layla cried hysterically. She was still young enough to want to cling to her mother and weep tears of fear, but Naomi was right. And her mother would not be able to protect her, no matter how much the tribe might revere her.

It was a night that would haunt Layla for the rest of her short life. She went to Rafe's van sick with fear. When she managed to crawl out of it hours later when he had finally fallen asleep her body was a mass of bruises and raised weals.

Naomi bathed them for her, her own eyes stinging with tears, but there was nothing she could say. Layla looked at her with the eyes of a wildcat caught in a snare. Her daughter's spirit was as broken as her body.

Layla did not have the stoicism to endure such physical abuse; hatred for Rafe was the only emotion she could feel now. Not even to her mother could she describe the things he had done to her; the manner in which he had abused her, taking her not as a man but as a perverted animal. Her body shook as she tried to blot out what had happened. Naomi gave her a soothing potion to drink, thinking to help her sleep, but while her mother's back was turned, Layla poured it away.

She could not endure another night like this one; she would *not* endure it.

While the rest of the camp slept she crept silently away. The constable on duty at the police station listened to her story in stunned shock, wondering whether or not to believe it. The sergeant, woken from his bed and brought grumbling to the station, took one look at Layla's white, bitter face, and knew that he had found the motive for Duncan's death.

They arrested Rafe at dawn; and he was sentenced to death two months later. He never reached the hangman's noose. Somehow, from somewhere, he obtained a secret poison. He was found dead in his cell one morning, his body already stiffening, his eyes glaring bitterly into emptiness.

The rest of the tribe shunned Layla. They elected a new leader, who decreed that Naomi must be allowed to stay among them, but that Layla must leave.

When Naomi discovered that her daughter was pregnant, she pleaded with the tribe for clemency, and it was granted; Layla would remain as an outcast from the tribe, but she would be allowed to travel with them.

Her daughter's frail, wraithlike condition appalled Naomi. The thought of the coming child was the only thing that kept her alive. Duncan's child. Layla said the words over and over again to herself like a mantra.

"It could be Rafe's child," Naomi told her.

Layla shook her head, and looked at her mother with eyes far too old for such a childish face.

"No, it could not. He did not take me as a man takes a woman; he did not spill his seed inside me."

Rachel Lee was born to her mother during her

eighth month of pregnancy. To see Layla's thin, almost sticklike body bloated almost obscenely with her pregnancy caused Naomi almost constant pain. Some fierce spirit seemed to burn in Layla, giving her a pride and a determination she had never thought to see in her fey, spoiled child.

The birth was a difficult one, and although they paused to listen to the cries coming from the caravan, none of the other women came to help. Naomi did not mind. She was an experienced midwife, and the child was well positioned, although perhaps a trifle large for Layla's emaciated frame.

It was only when she placed the child in her daughter's arms that she saw Layla smile properly for the first time since Duncan's death.

"She is beautiful," she told her mother. "You will call her Rachel, and you will love her for me, won't you, Mother?"

Already a swift-flowing river of red blood was carrying Layla away from them, and Naomi knew it could not be staunched; that her daughter was dying. She had known it from the moment Layla gave birth. In some ways she felt her daughter had willed herself to stay alive only as long as she carried her child. She had in any case been as one dead to the rest of the tribe from the moment she betrayed Rafe.

There was no burial pyre for Layla, no grieving or lamenting for the brief life so quickly extinguished, and although the tribe accepted Naomi, little Rachel grew up knowing that she was not truly part of it; that there was something mysterious about her own birth and the death of her mother, that set her apart from the others.

She soon learned that her mother's name was one that must never be spoken and that she and Naomi were allowed to stay with the tribe as a favour rather than as a right.

Her pain at the way she was excluded was something she learned to cloak with pride and indifference, and she was soon being described as far too much her mother's daughter. She was not popular with the other children, and she knew it. It made her only more aloof and withdrawn. Only Naomi loved her, only Naomi stood between her and the hostility of the others.

CHAPTER FIVE

YES, SHE HAD learned young what it meant to be an outcast, Pepper reflected wryly.

Almost from the moment she could toddle she had been shunned by the other Romany children, but through their cruelty she had learned two valuable lessons.

The first had been to conceal her hurts. As a child she had been sensitive to a degree that had meant the other children's contempt and dislike of her had constantly lacerated her. She had known as children always know that they neither accepted nor liked her, but she had not known why, and so she had learned to cover her feelings with a protective stoical acceptance. That had been the second lesson she had learned—not to let others see that they had the power to hurt her.

Not that the others had deliberately wanted to hurt her; it had simply been that she was not one of them; that her mother had offended so far and so deeply against their code that her child would never be one of their number.

Pepper's childhood had been spent moving with the tribe through the country in their nomadic annual journeyings; formal schooling for gypsy children in those years had been spasmodic at best—not even the most ardent of school inspectors could spare the time to check up on the constantly caravanning tribes and their children—but Naomi had been taught to read and write by her husband and she was immensely

95

proud of her skills.

She too had seen what was happening to her grand-child, and while she grieved over it, she knew that according to the rules of her people they were not being deliberately unkind.

Occasionally it crossed her mind that she should approach Sir Ian MacGregor, but she doubted that he would welcome Rachel any more than her own people did, and then the winter that Rachel was seven Ian MacGregor died and the land passed to a very distant member of the family.

Since Duncan's death, the gypsies had not revisited the Glen, knowing that they would not be welcome, and the loss of the privileged campsite was chalked up as another black mark against Rachel.

It was Naomi who insisted that she learn to read and write; who sent her to school whenever the tribe stopped long enough for her to do so.

Knowing how proud her grandmother was of her own ability to read and write, Rachel never told her of the purgatory her own schooldays were. Just as she was unacceptable to the tribe, so she was also an outcast to the non-Romany children. They laughed at her clothes, calling them rags, and they sneered at her heavily-accented voice and the gold rings she wore in her ears. The older boys tugged on them until her lobes bled, and called her a "dirty gypsy", while the girls huddled together in giggling gaggles to gaze at her darned jumpers and patched skirts.

With no man to protect them or hunt for them, Naomi and Rachel were forced to depend on whatever Naomi could make from telling fortunes and selling pegs. Occasionally in the depths of the night, one of the women of the tribe would knock on her door and ask Naomi for the special potions she made in the summer months from wild flowers and herbs.

Rachel watched these transactions wide-eyed and curious about what it could be that brought the women of the tribe to her grandmother's door late at night, but all Naomi would say when she asked her was that she was too young to understand. The herbal lore which she had learned from her own mother and which she had tried to teach her own feckless daughter was something Naomi was not going to pass on to her granddaughter. None of the women of the tribe would come to Rachel for advice and potions the way they did to her. She was, after all, one of them, and still respected, although now their respect was tainted with pity, but Rachel never would be; she was the daughter of a *gorgio*, and it had been for the love of this man that Layla had betrayed one of her own, breaking the sacred gypsy code. Now when she grew older Rachel's life would lie apart from that of the tribe, and this troubled Naomi.

She was getting old, and her bones ached in the cold and the damp. She hoped that by sending Rachel to school she could in some way prepare her grandchild to enter into the *gorgio* way of life, and because Rachel loved her grandmother she didn't tell her that she was derided and disliked as much by her father's people as she was by her mother's.

School, which had been a place of fascination and delight at first, when she had absorbed everything the teachers could tell her, had now become a hated prison from which she escaped as often as she could, often spending her days in complete isolation in the hills and the fields.

When she was eleven her body started to change, and with it the reactions of her peers. Boys at school who had pulled her hair and jeered at her now tormented her in different ways, trying to pinch the small swellings that tightened the fabric of her shabby clothes.

Her hair, always thick and lustrous, seemed to darken and curl with a vivid life of its own, her body alluringly changing shape. Rachel knew what the changes portended; her tribe lived close to nature, and its girls were taught to be proud of their womanhood.

Even one or two of the young men glanced at her sideways as she helped her grandmother to gather kindling or worked with her on her pegs and baskets, but they didn't forget who her mother was, or what she had done.

While the other girls of her age in the tribe tested their new-found femininity, laughing and flirting with their male peers, Rachel instinctively suppressed hers. She was a child of the shadows, her grandmother often thought sadly, watching her pensive face and too knowing eyes. As though she had been gifted with second sight Rachel knew instinctively that the rest of the tribe were looking for signs of her mother in her; as long as she was quiet and unobtrusive no one bothered about her.

But some things are impossible to hide, and the way her body was blossoming and developing was one of them.

The pinches and lewd remarks of her schoolmates was something she quickly learned to ignore, just as she had learned to ignore their jibes about her clothes and her speech. She wasn't the only girl who had to endure this rough male teasing, but the others all had friends, families, supporters and protectors whom they could call upon if the boys' tormenting became too familiar. Rachel had no one; she knew it and her tormentors knew it.

The gypsies' progress through the country was an annual one. At the time of the Whitsun fairs they were always in the north of England; among the mill towns of the north-west; grimy, enclosed ribbons of towns set in stark valleys, whose inhabitants were the inheritors of the Industrial Revolution; a grim and starkly realistic people who had often known the harsh bite of poverty.

The lives of the people were as enclosed as the hills surrounding their valleys; their minds as narrow as their habitat.

The mills were closing, being driven out of existence by imports from Pakistan, cheap cloth produced by cheap labour. The secondary school in the valley was overflowing with teenagers who would have no jobs to go to; the mills that had employed their parents and grandparents were closing, and the atmosphere within the valleys was one of resentment and bitterness.

This particular stopping place on their annual pilgrimage was one that Rachel had always detested. The poverty of the people in the valley was almost on a level with that of her own tribe, and because of it the valley people jealously guarded their rights and privileges. Outsiders weren't welcome whoever they were; and the gypsies were disliked and detested here much more than they were in the richer south of the country.

There were few pleasures to be had for the people inhabiting these valleys full of "dark Satanic mills". Whitsuntide was one of them.

The religious persuasion of many of the inhabitants sprang from Methodism, the cornerstone on which the Industrial Revolution had been built, but this did not prevent the people from throwing themselves into their Whitsuntide celebrations with enthusiastic vigour. The highlight of these celebrations was the Whit Walks. For weeks beforehand the females of the family would gather round to gaze consideringly at the "catalogues" to choose the all-important outfit for the Walk. The Whit Walks were an unashamed opportunity to show off. A new outfit was an absolute essential, if family pride were to be upheld. Everyone would line up to walk through the streets in their new clothes; afterwards families would gather for high tea, and then later still the teenagers would be let loose to attend the fairs that had set up in the market squares.

It was these fairs which brought the gypsies to the north-west. There were rich pickings to be had from them, what with fortune-telling, working on the fairs themselves and selling their wares.

Rachel hated the whole thing. She hated the taunting looks the other girls in her class gave her while they giggled behind their hands about their new outfits. She hated knowing that she was an outcast, that she was being made fun of, but now this particular spring, with her body burgeoning into that of a woman, she hated it even more. The girls resented her glowing prettiness, and the boys lusted after the growing development of her body. The fact that she wasn't one of them, that she was an outcast, made her an easy target for their malice and male vulgarity.

She had long ago perfected the art of ignoring all that was said about her, of pretending that she simply hadn't heard the insults. But this particular morning, knowing that the whole school would be seething with excitement over the coming Whitsuntide break, she knew she could not face them. Always sensitive to the opinions of others, she had found that with the onset of puberty her sensitivity had increased. Sometimes the effort of forcing herself not to cry in the face of the jeering taunts of her schoolfellows made her drive her nails deep enough into the palms of her hands to draw her own blood.

The northern valleys possessed three modes of transport; the road, the railway and the canal. Rachel was walking alongside the latter, pausing now and again to watch a moorhen with her chicks or to study the fleeting shadow of tiddlers as they changed direction at the sight of her shadow. The canal had been abandoned as a transport route long ago, and the rotting lockgates and weed-filled waters gave silent testimony to its decay. Mills long abandoned by owners who could no longer afford to compete with foreign imports reared up darkly alongside the towpath, casting dark shadows, their windows gaping emptily, the glass broken, their interiors long silent.

Occasionally a golden bar of sunlight slatted through the bleakness of the building. Rachel liked walking. It soothed her, gave free rein to her thoughts. She shivered as she walked beneath one of the narrow bridges, feeling the cold and damp seeping down through the stone. She passed few people as she walked. The occasional old man walking his dog; courting couples, giggling. Across on the other side of the valley she could see men working in their allotments alongside the railway lines, the narrow black lines of terraced houses blotting out the sunlight.

This particular valley was very long and narrow, the hillsides treeless. It was a grim and depressing place and Rachel hated it. Whenever they came here she suffered a sense of being shut in; she loathed the oppressive atmosphere that infiltrated the place.

Outside a row of terraced houses overlooking the canal she could see one woman donkeystoning her steps. She was wearing the all-enveloping pinafore that was the uniform of the married woman here. She looked up and saw Rachel and scowled at her.

"Be off with you!" she called out harshly. "We don't want no dirty gypos round here!"

Rachel was impervious to her insults, and walked on to where the river Calder ran alongside the canal. The towpath had crumbled away at the edges here. On one side it was level with the canal and on the other it dropped away to where the river ran sluggishly below, its progress choked with the detritus of human living—old rusty prams and bicycles, tin cans, and a variety of other rubbish that had been slung out of back yards and into the river.

She paused by a gap in the dismal line of terraced houses to enjoy a warm bar of sunlight. In front of her was the back door to a small pub. A man came out and staggered across to the gents', and then changing his mind, instead relieved himself into the river.

Rachel moved on, ignoring him. One day she would escape from all this, from people who disliked and taunted her. One day . . .

Daydreams were the only things that made her life bearable, and she escaped into them whenever she could. She enjoyed reading and from the books she read she knew that there was another way of life, very many other ways of life, and one day . . .

Her daydream was brutally crushed when she heard someone call out her name in a jeering voice. Her whole body tensed as she recognised the harsh male voices and came to an abrupt halt in front of a gang of boys she recognised from school. They were all older than her, due to leave school at the end of the summer term. They were all dressed in grubby jeans and cheap leather jackets. The rank smell of young male bodies closed offensively round her as they came closer. Resolutely Rachel stood her ground, deliberately avoiding any form of eye contact. Her heart was pumping like a terrified rabbit's, but her body was completely still.

"Lost yer tongue, gypo?" one of them taunted. His eyes shifted from her face to her breasts. "Got a fine pair of tits growing there, ain't yer? They say gypos make good lays . . ."

The coarseness of his comments and the laughter of his friends increased her terror, but Rachel knew it would be madness to even try to run. That was what they wanted her to do. They could hardly rape her here in broad daylight, she reassured herself stoically, as the lad reached out and pressed a filthy hand against the front of her dress. She had to fight against her instinctive desire to tear at him with her hands and nails, to rid her body of his unwanted presence, but long after they had jeeringly let her go past, calling out obscenities after her, she felt tainted by the encounter, her body still shaking with a mixture of outraged pride and feminine fear.

During the Whit week festivities her grandmother was busy telling fortunes, and Rachel escaped to the hills, ranging over the moorlands where thin half-wild sheep foraged and the land was barren and bare. Here and there the remnants of some long-ago drystone wall boundary darkened the landscape, but in the main it was untouched by man's hand apart from the odd reservoir mirroring the swift movement of the clouds across the hills.

At Whitsuntide the people of the valleys went on holiday, the more affluent of them sometimes for as much as three or four days, the poorer just on a day trip, but all of them to the same venue—the Lancashire coast and Blackpool. Rachel watched the coaches depart filled with them, and heard them come back at night. The gypsies were camping on a spare piece of land, close to the market square where the buses terminated, and late at night the coaches would disgorge their passengers, replete on beer, candy floss and fish and chips.

Here in the small town centre a viaduct spanned the canal and road, carrying the railway overhead, and at night these arches were the haunt of eager lovers. The tribe looked down on the *gorgio* teenagers and their lack of modesty, but Rachel knew that many of the young men, especially those who worked on the fairs, slipped away late at night to enjoy the favours of the girls who gathered in giggling masses beneath the viaduct.

One night as she walked beneath them on her way back to the camp, she recognised one of the intertwined couples. Ann Watts was in her class at school, although she was two years older than Rachel. Ann Watts was described as "slow", but there was nothing slow about the way she responded to and attracted the opposite sex. Jealous of her position as acknowledged sex queen of the school, Ann Watts was one of Rachel's most vindictive enemies.

It would be many years before Rachel would be able to recognise the other girl for what she was and to pity her for it, that night as she saw Ann voluptuously pressing her body against that Tyler Lee.

Tyler Lee was the oldest of the three brothers; tall for a gypsy, with a shock of wildly curling black hair. At seventeen his body was hardened and well muscled by the work he did on the fairs and labouring in the fields during the summer. His skin was brown, his eyes black as jet. He was proud of his Romany blood and destined to marry his second cousin. Rachel knew this, but Ann Watts did not. To her Tyler Lee epitomised the glamour she saw every week when she visited the local flea pit. He was the best-looking boy she had ever seen, far better-looking than the lumpy dull boys she was at school with; and better still, Tyler was dangerous. He rode a motorbike that he had put together from parts garnered here and there during his travels, and he knew exactly the effect he had on a girl when he looked at her from out of those night-dark eyes.

Although Ann Watts didn't know it Tyler despised her, just as he despised all the *gorgio* women who desired him, and Ann Watts was very far from being the first. Tyler had first realised the potential of his sexuality when he was fourteen years old. He had lost his virginity to a bored, thirty-odd-year-old housewife in Norfolk, exchanging it for his motorbike and enough money to buy himself the coveted teenage uniform of black leather jacket. Since then there had been more bored housewives and Ann Watts than he had cared to count.

Ann Watts was not destined to remain in his memory for very long. She wriggled against him provocatively, enjoying the rhythmic thrust of his hips. Tyler would be the third boy with whom Ann had "gone all the way", and already she was enjoying savouring what she was going to tell her friends afterwards. She liked the shocked, wide-eyed way they listened to her confidences. They were all younger than she was, and still virgins.

Out of the corner of her eye she watched Rachel go past, and glared at her. She disliked the proud way the younger girl moved, almost as though she thought that somehow she was better than anyone else. How could she be? Everyone knew that gypos were nothing better than thieves, and that they never washed.

Ann had a bath once a week, in the new bathroom that had just been installed in the terraced house. Theirs was the only house in the street to have an indoor lavvy as well. Ann's father was a foreman in one of the few mills still working and her mother served school dinners at the local Tech. And Ann was their only child. Already Mrs Watts was boasting proudly that her Ann would marry young, she was that pretty. All the boys were after her.

Sensing that he had lost her complete attention, Tyler pushed her firmly against the hard stone of the viaduct wall, thrusting himself against her open thighs, demanding, "Who you looking at?"

"That Rachel Lee."

Ann saw the expression on Tyler's face and realised that he liked Rachel no more than she did herself.

"What's up?" she asked him curiously. "What you got against her?"

"Her mother was a murderer," Tyler told her.

No one in the tribe had talked about Rachel's mother, but they all knew the story, and Ann's eyes widened in malicious glee. She had always known there was something odd about Rachel Lee. Just wait until she told the others at school about her! At that moment Tyler moved more determinedly against her, pushing up her skirt and pulling down her pants with one experienced movement, and Rachel was forgotten . . . but not for long.

Rachel knew the moment she walked into the schoolyard that something was wrong. Her senses, always attuned to danger, alerted her to the menacing quality of the silence engulfing her the moment she walked into the tarmacadam yard, but she looked neither to the right nor to the left as she walked past the silent huddles of watchers.

Ann Watts waited until Rachel drew level with her before launching her first salvo.

"Whose mother's a murderer, then?" she sang out, swiftly followed by her friends, as they picked up the taunting chorus and rang it across the schoolyard.

By now Rachel knew the story of her conception, but she still felt sensitive about it, and about the cloud hanging over her birth. She lashed out instinctively and her open palm caught the side of Ann Watts' nose, and almost instantly blood spurted from it.

Almost as though the scent of blood drew them like hounds to a fox, the schoolyard was in an uproar. It took four teachers to separate the seething mass of bodies, and when they dragged Rachel out from beneath her attackers, she had a broken collarbone and three cracked ribs.

Despite questioning from her teachers and from the police Rachel refused to say what had caused the fight. The police constable was only young—he had recently been moved into the area from Cumbria and he was finding the brooding violence of the valley difficult to take. There was poverty where he came from too, but it was a different sort of poverty from this, just as his people were a different sort of people. Privately he felt sorry for the little gypsy girl, but his expression betrayed nothing of this when he questioned her. She looked very forlorn and alone in the starched hospital bed, and he suspected that the nurses weren't any kinder to her than her peers had been.

It was after her stay in hospital that things began to change for Rachel. She saw the change in her grandmother almost from the moment she came out. Naomi had aged, but more than that, there were new lines on her face that could have only been put there by pain. For the first time in her life Rachel knew the terrible fear of being all alone. What would happen to her if her grandmother should die? The tribe didn't want her.

Would she have to go into a home? Rachel knew very little about these institutions other than the fact that they were held over the heads of hapless gypsy children as a threat of what could happen to them if they misbehaved. Somehow in Rachel's mind, children's homes had become confused with prison, and she thought of being sent away to one of them as a form of punishment.

Every day she saw her grandmother fade away a little more. Sometimes when she thought no one was watching her Naomi massaged the outside of her breast. She was in deep pain, Rachel knew that. She also knew that her grandmother had to drink some of the special poppy drug she made to help her sleep at night.

Rachel was frightened, but as with everything else she learned to lock the fear up inside her.

Naomi knew that her time was short. There was pain inside her that ate into her, a gnawing, bitter pain that was destroying her from within. The pain came from the lump she had discovered in her breast, she knew that. She was going to die, and when she did what would become of Rachel?

Winter came and the tribe was once again in the far north, not camping in the tranquil valley on the MacGregor lands this time, but on a barren piece of waste ground outside a small town.

Where once they had commanded a certain amount of respect and fear, gypsies were now almost consistently reviled. The townspeople called them "dirty thieves", and Rachel was more conscious than ever of the way others looked at them. She had never felt more alien and alone. There was no one she could turn to. Naomi was dying, but Rachel still doggedly hoped that somehow her beloved grandmother would grow well and strong again.

She spent hours searching for special herbs that were supposed to have magic properties to heal her. She saved the choicest pieces of meat for her, but none of it did any good; Naomi was dying.

The spring that Rachel was fifteen they stopped off

in the north for the Whitsuntide fairs again. Ann
Watts was still at school, but now she was in her last
year. Last year's plumpness had given way to unsightly
fat, and she eyed Rachel with spite and bitchiness
when she arrived at school.

"I see the gypos are back," she sneered, giving
Rachel a wide berth. "I thought I could smell
something bad!"

Blotting out the laughs and jeers, Rachel held her
head high and walked into the classroom. She loved
the deep tranquillity of its silence almost as much as
she hated her fellow pupils. Inside her something was
yearning desperately for knowledge, but her lessons
were so fragmented that in all her years of schooling
she had learned almost nothing.

To the teachers she was just another gypsy brat,
who would be gone before she could learn anything
worth knowing. She could read and write and add up
simple columns of figures, which in a school like the
one she was in now was as much as many of their
pupils would achieve by the time they were ready to
leave.

They had been back in the valley for almost a week
when one afternoon Rachel was struck by the
knowledge that Naomi needed her. When the class
stood up and the teacher left, Rachel darted out after
him, taking the short cut to the gypsy camp, along
the canal tow path. She ran all the way, and arrived
out of breath and scared out of her wits. This was the
first time she had felt for herself the power that ran
so strongly in the women of her family.

As she had known she would, she found her grandmother close to death. Naomi recognised her, and
forced away her pain for long enough to take her
hand. She had spent many hours worrying about this

child, this changeling who was neither Romany nor *gorgio*.

Pulling Rachel close to her so that she could whisper in her ear, she told her where she had hidden the small amount of money she had managed to scrape together since she had realised she was ill. She had saved the money with one purpose only in mind, and now she told Rachel what she was to do.

"You must leave here now, before . . . before I die. You must pretend that you are older than your years. You must get yourself a job and live as a *gorgio* would, Rachel. The Romany way of life is not for you, and I do not want you to become any man's whore. Remember always that my spirit goes with you."

Hot tears fell on her cold hands as she pushed Rachel away from her. Rachel was losing the only person on earth who cared about her, but if she stayed the tribe would reject her, and the school authorities would come and she would be put in a home. Naomi was right . . . she had to leave.

Alternately shivering and crying, Rachel found the small store of money. She bent down to kiss Naomi's cheek and murmured the secret Romany words of farewell. She would not be here to see her grandmother's funeral pyre; she would not be here to wish her spirit well.

Naomi opened her eyes and saw the indecision on her grandchild's face. Summoning the last of her strength, she took Rachel's hand in hers. "Go now . . . go with my blessing, my child . . . Go now."

From the moment she had learned to read Rachel had realised that it was education that was the only escape route from poverty, and now she was drawn as count-

less thousands of others had been drawn before her to
the gilded spires of Oxford.

She had passed through the town many times with
the tribe. She knew from her reading what it was . . .
but in her ignorance she knew nothing of the taboos
and rituals it represented; just as strong and damning
as those of her own people.

Rachel reached Oxford in the late summer of 1977,
when she was just short of her seventeenth birthday.
She travelled mainly on foot, using the ancient Romany
paths, carefully eking out the money her grandmother
had given her by taking casual work along the way—
mostly on farms, but always taking care to choose a
farm where she could be sure of being taken under
the wing of the farmer's wife. Rachel had learned
enough about the male sex in her short life to make
her wary of putting herself into any man's powers.
She still remembered the hated sensation of being
touched by male hands, and it was a man who had
led to her mother's rejection by her people. Men of
any age were to be avoided.

By the time she reached Oxford she had added to
her small hoard of money and had two hundred
pounds tucked away in the leather bag she had tied
to the inside of her skirt. Her clothes were in rags, too
short, too skimpy, augmented here and there by the
odd cast-off given to her by kind-hearted farmers'
wives who had taken pity on her.

Where once their pity would have offended her,
now she accepted it with a brief smile, because Rachel
was realising for the first time in her life the power of
freedom. Oh, she missed her grandmother, but she
didn't miss the oppressive disapproval of the tribe,
which she was only just beginning to recognise for
what it was; nor did she miss the contempt and dislike
of the people in whose towns they stayed. Here in the

country it was different—she was different, because she no longer wore the hated tag of "gypsy".

Only now was she coming to realise that she was free; that she had the power to choose what she would be. The farms where she stopped off to work thought she was just another of the itinerant band of teenagers who spent their summers working in the fields; gypsies didn't travel alone, and her skin was pale enough, her hair dark red enough for her not to be picked out immediately as a member of the Romany people.

She was willing to work hard and she was consequently awarded respect by the farmers' wives who employed her. Rachel didn't mind what kind of work she was asked to do, just so long as it didn't bring her into too much contact with any male members of the households where she stopped, and that too was a point in her favour. Several times she was asked to stay on, but she was slowly coming to realise that there might be more for her in life than the drudgery of such menial tasks.

At one farm where she stayed in prosperous Cheshire she was allowed to sleep in a room which had once belonged to the now adult daughter of the family, and this room came complete with its own television. Several members of the gypsy tribe had had television, of course, but her grandmother had not been among them, and Rachel spent her free time absorbing information via this new source like a desert soaking up rain. She watched all manner of programmes—educational, political, cartoons, American cops-and-robbers series, and everything she saw only confirmed to her that there was another form of life out there.

She remembered how her grandmother had always told her that education was the key that unlocked many doors, and how she had believed her. But how could she get the sort of education she needed? Because now Rachel had a goal. She wanted to be like the women she saw on television, polished, glamorous . . . loved. How did they get like that? They were like no women she had ever seen before, with their long blonde hair and their pretty faces—and their clothes.

Up until now as far as Rachel was concerned clothes had simply been something she had worn to protect her body from the weather, but now she was seeing girls wearing pretty clothes, and she ached to wear them herself.

When she wasn't working she spent more time than she had ever done before exploring the various towns she passed through on her way south. She stared in through shop windows and watched . . . and soon she had plucked up the courage to walk in through the plate glass doors of one of the stores. If the girl who served her was shocked by the state of the clothes she was wearing, or surprised that Rachel didn't even know her own size, she kept it to herself.

Rachel spent her money carefully. She knew exactly how she wanted to look. When she came out of the store she caught sight of herself by accident in a plate glass window, and froze, shocked by this new image of herself. She no longer looked different—poor. She looked just like everyone else.

She turned her head to make sure. All around her young girls dressed in the timeless uniform of the young strolled, flirted and laughed, and she was now one of them. She stared down at her jean-clad legs— her grandmother hadn't approved of girls wearing any form of trousers—then touched the soft fabric of her new T-shirt. The feel of clean new fabric beneath her fingertips was sensuously pleasing. It felt good to know that no one had ever worn these clothes before her, that they were hers and hers alone.

By the time she reached Oxford Rachel had lost all

but the faintest tinge of her Romany accent, and she had also removed her gypsy earrings. She was dressed just like any other teenager, and wore her new-found confidence like a patina of pleasure.

Oxford drew her like a magnet. She had seen a programme on television about it, and that had increased her yearning to be there.

She arrived just before the start of the Michaelmas term, and the town was almost empty of students; the bicycles that later would fill the narrow streets were few and far between, and the pubs and discos that later would be the haunt of the young were almost empty. During the long summer recess Oxford belonged to its inhabitants and its tourists—American in the main, come to stroll among the colleges, and examine the quaintness of this ancient seat of learning.

Rachel found a job easily enough in one of the hotels, but the pay wasn't as good as it had been on the farm, and the work was hard. The majority of the other chambermaids were foreign; an Irish girl with an accent so thick that Rachel could barely understand it made friendly overtures towards her, and by the end of the first week she was beginning to feel she was settling in.

When she complained to Bernadette about the poorness of her wage the Irish girl grinned at her.

"Well, why don't you do what I do? Get yourself a job in one of the pubs in the evening? They're looking for someone at the place where I work. I could take you along and introduce you if you like?"

Rachel agreed. Although the hotel provided its chambermaids with board and food, the meals they were served were very meagre indeed, and she was almost constantly hungry.

She got the job in Bernadette's pub. The manager was a plump cheerful man in his late forties, with two

girls of his own who were away at university, and his
wife kept a stern eye on the more flirtatious of the
barmaids.

Rachel felt happier than she had ever been in her
life, but when she shyly asked Bernadette if she knew
how she might go about joining a library, the Irish
girl filled the dormitory they shared with the other
chambermaids with her rollicking laugh.

"Joining a library, is it, you're wanting? Well, sure
there's a fine thing! Oi'm thinking that a pretty girl
like you can get all the learning she wants from the
men . . ."

Bernadette was a flirt, Rachel had quickly realised
that, but she hadn't realised until now how great a
gap yawned between them. For the first time since she
had left them she felt homesick for the tribe. They
were, after all, her people.

When Bernadette asked her if she wanted to go to
a disco she refused.

"Ah well, suit yourself, then . . . I'm sure I don't
mind having all the boys to meself." Bernadette tossed
her dark hair as she walked out, and Rachel knew she
had offended her.

Fortunately Bernadette had a mercurial temper and
a kind heart, and by morning she was her normal
friendly self, chatting animatedly to Rachel about the
boy she had met the previous evening, as they worked.

"Keep away from Number Ten," she warned
Rachel. "Helga . . . you know, the German girl, she
was telling me that when she went in this morning he
came out of his bathroom stark naked and asked her
if she'd mind giving him a rub down! Dirty old man,
he's fifty if he's a day . . . and married. I mind he's
stayed here before with his wife . . ."

All the chambermaids gossiped, although Rachel
tended to keep herself aloof. She wasn't used to such

friendliness, and she treated it with caution, half expecting them to change and turn on her, unable to forget what she had suffered during her schooldays, but now she was different, now she wasn't a despised gypo but simply another young woman like themselves.

The seventies were a good time to be young; the world was full of optimism, and youth was petted and fêted by all. To be young was to hold the world in the palm of your hand. Rachel was constantly meeting other young people who, like herself, cherished their freedom, but who, unlike her, had travelled the world. They came into the pub in their faded jeans, carrying their backpacks, the men thin and bearded, their girlfriends long-haired and kohl-eyed, drinking beer while they told their tales of Kathmandu, and worshipping at the feet of the great ashrams. Everyone who was anyone was into meditation; Rachel read the magazines left behind by the guests and learned that she was living in an almost magical era.

As the summer heat faded into autumn, and mists began to hang over the river in the early morning sunlight, Oxford gradually began to stir back to life. Students arrived in dribs and drabs, trickling back into the town; life began to stir beneath the somnolence of the summer, as the tourists left to make way for the undergraduates.

By the beginning of Michaelmas term life in the town had changed, its pulse hard and heady. Bernadette was delighted.

"Now we'll see some foine young men," she promised Rachel one morning as they finished their work. "You wait and see!"

It was impossible not to respond to the surge of excitement beating through the air. Rachel felt it in her own thudding pulse. The crisp tang of late summer with its nostalgic undertones of autumn hung on the air. Almost every night the pub was full of young men in shabby jeans or corduroy trousers, University scarves wrapped round their necks, their long hair brushing their shoulders. They talked with a multitude of accents, but almost always in the same studiedly throwaway fashion; they were the cream, the *jeunesse doré*, and they knew it.

In some of the staider colleges it was still necessary to have permission to run a motorcar, and so the traditional bicycles were very much in use. Rachel had to run across the road to avoid being knocked down by one of them one evening as she hurried to work. Behind her she heard a great shout and then a crash, and turning round she saw a tangle of jean-clad legs and bicycle wheels.

Instinctively she started to walk away, until a plaintive voice halted her.

"I say, don't go and leave me here! I might have broken my leg . . ."

His voice was cultivated and teasing; the voice of a male used to being courted and flattered. As she turned her head to look back at him Rachel caught the blond flash of his hair. She hesitated.

"Come on . . . it was your fault I fell off, you know. I haven't ridden one of these damn things for years, and when I saw you . . . pretty girls oughtn't to be allowed to cross the roads in front of learner bicycle riders!"

He had called her pretty, and immediately Rachel stiffened, but there had been none of the hated near-violence and dislike in his voice that she had heard from the other men.

Caution urged her to walk away, but something deeper, stronger, and much more potent, urged her to stay. Slowly she walked towards him and watched him disentangle himself from his bicycle. He was tall, over six foot, with shoulder-length fair hair, and the bluest eyes Rachel had ever seen. They were the sort of eyes that always seemed to be full of light and laughter. He was laughing now, grinning ruefully as he brushed himself down.

"Damn! I think I've twisted my front wheel. That'll teach me to look at pretty girls!" He moved and then winced, taking his weight off his left foot. "I seem to have twisted my ankle as well. My rooms aren't far from here . . . If you give me a hand I should be able to make it to them without too much difficulty."

At any other time Rachel would have found his assumption that she would automatically agree to help him off putting, but for some reason she found herself responding to his smile and walking towards him.

"If I could just put my arm round your shoulders . . ."

His arm was muscular but thin, and she could smell the scent of his body mingling with the oily odour of wool from his sweater. He smiled at her, his teeth white in the tanned darkness of his face. For some reason she almost wanted to reach out and touch him. Shocked by her own reaction, Rachel dragged her gaze away.

He was like no other boy or man she had ever known. There was an aura about him that she could feel herself responding to. She looked at his hand, cupped round the ball of her shoulder. His fingers were long, the nails well cared for.

"Cat got your tongue?" he demanded with another grin.

Rachel shook her head. He was going to make her late for work, but recklessly she didn't care.

He said it was only a little way to his rooms, but in actual fact it was half a mile. Rachel gazed up in reverence at the ancient buildings of his college. She had explored them all during the summer recess, combining her walks through their hallowed grounds with knowledge she had gained from the books she had borrowed from the library. It had been the publican's wife who had come to the rescue and shown her how to join the library, and now she touched the weathered stone as they rounded the corner of the building and entered the enclosed quadrangle.

"Tom Quad," her companion told her cheerfully, glancing sideways at her.

Rachel only smiled. She knew all about the history of Christ Church College; that it had first been commissioned by Cardinal Wolsey, four years before he fell from Henry VIII's grace. Christopher Wren had added the Tower over Wolsey's gate, in 1682, and Rachel glanced up towards it automatically, just as Great Tom, the bell, tolled its curfew.

"Bang on time as usual! Come on, my rooms are up here."

His weight was beginning to make her shoulder ache, but it never occurred to Rachel to refuse to go with him. During the summer recess she had learned to parry the flirtatious remarks of the pub's patrons, but both Bernadette and the landlord's wife had warned her that Oxford's students could be remarkably persistent.

"You'd think they'd have better things to do with their time than spending it trying to get you into bed with them," Bernadette sniffed disdainfully.

It was from Bernadette and the other girls at the hotel that Rachel had gradually learned to be a little more worldly. Now when she worked she often hummed the latest pop tune. She wore make-up— something her grandmother had always disapproved of, and she was gradually adopting the manners and fashions of her peers.

For the first time in her life she felt that she was actually accepted on equal terms with her peers, and she liked that feeling, but Rachel was by nature cautious. When the other girls disappeared for the evening with flurried giggles, and didn't appear until the following morning, Rachel listened to their whispered confidences about the boys they had been out with, but when anyone tried to date her she kept them firmly at bay. She wasn't interested in boyfriends and romance; there wasn't time in her life for them. She had so much to do; coming to Oxford had opened her eyes to all that was missing from her life.

These students who flocked through Oxford's streets would one day go out into the world and become people of eminence, secure and respected. The bitterness of her childhood haunted her and Rachel was determined to make herself inviolate. The only way she could do that was by achieving financial security.

She had a quick intelligence and had soon realised that she could never be content with the goals Bernadette and the other girls set themselves. They were happy to drift from day to day, spending their wages on new clothes, dating a different boy every night. They were like the poppies that bloomed in the cornfields in the summer, Rachel thought wryly— pretty and giddy, blowing this way and then that at the will of the wind, but once summer was gone they wilted and died; they could not survive without the sun, without warmth.

"Think you can get me up the stairs?"

Rachel frowned and looked consideringly at him. He wasn't the first student who had shown an interest in her, and caution warned her to tread carefully.

"I have to get back," she told him. "I should be at work."

"You work?"

He said it with such amused condescension that
Rachel could feel her skin flushing with resentment.

"Yes," she told him curtly, "at the King's Arms."

"Ah . . . Yes. I see."

He was looking at her differently now, consideringly; and Rachel knew what was going through his
mind. In her almost teenage uniform jeans and cotton
peasant blouse, her long hair down on her shoulders,
he had mistaken her for a fellow student. Now that
he knew she was not, he was looking at her in much
the same way the village children had regarded her
and her contemporaries when they camped near their
homes. Only the suspicion was absent from his eyes,
and in its place was an intense glitter of sexual speculation.

"So you're not a student."

Her head lifted, her eyes coolly meeting his and
dismissing the look of desire he gave her.

"No."

"What's your name? Mine's Tim . . . Tim
Wilding."

His abrupt change of tack caught her off guard,
and unwillingly Rachel found herself telling him,

"Rachel."

The blue eyes laughed down into hers. "I don't like
it . . . it's far too biblical for you! I shall call you
Gypsy . . . it suits you far more."

Her heart almost turned over with shock and fear,
but he seemed not to see it.

"Are you a gypsy at heart? I am."

Up above them a window opened and he stepped
back to look up. Rachel followed his glance and saw
a man leaning out to look at them. He was about the
same age as her companion, but physically very
different. He had a shock of dark hair, worn slightly
shorter than the prevailing fashion, and wildly curly.

His face was all planes and angles, his skin brown and his eyes a clear sharp grey.

"Miles, I've ricked my ankle, and this fair charmer came to my rescue. Come down and give me a hand, will you?"

The dark head was withdrawn, after the cool grey eyes had cast a sardonic look at them both, and the window closed.

"Miles French, my room-mate." Tim Wilding pulled a wry face. "He's a mite too Celtic for my taste, but I suppose that comes of studying law. Very phlegmatic, is our Miles, unshockable and unshakeable, although it's always fun to try."

Rachel pondered his comment as his fingers wrapped round her wrist, preventing her from leaving. She got the feeling that Tim didn't entirely like his room-mate, and she shivered a little as she remembered the cool amusement in the other's almost analytic scrutiny of her. Something about him had frightened her, in a way that someone with Tim's overt sexuality never could.

"Bit of an enigma, is our Miles," Tim continued in his light drawl. He reached into his jacket pocket and produced a packet of cigarettes. "Want one?"

Rachel shook her head, and watched him extract and light one, the smile curling round his mouth making her feel curious. He looked like a naughty cherub. As he drew on the cigarette and expelled the smoke, she knew why. The unmistakable scent of pot surrounded her. It had been one of the other chambermaids who had enlightened her about the curious sweetish, sickly smell coming from one of their guests' bedrooms. It was a scent that sometimes seemed to pervade certain parts of Oxford, and Rachel drew back from it instinctively. Her grandmother had imparted to her some of her knowledge of herbs and

plants and their uses, and she had learned from her of
the dangers of abusing their powers.

The outer door opened before she could say anything
to Tim, her attention drawn by the young man coming
towards them.

Like Tim, he was wearing jeans and a cotton shirt.
Rachel saw his mouth compress slightly as he too
caught the scent of the doctored cigarette.

"Judgemental Miles!" Tim taunted him, catching
his expression. "My dear, what sort of lawyer will you
make if you haven't tasted for yourself all life's delights
and dangers?"

"I don't need to smoke those to know that they
addle your wits." He had a much deeper voice than
Tim's, now it was crisped with mockery and a finite
edge of anger. "Come on, Tim, stop showing off for
the girlfriend, and let me get back to work."

He ignored Rachel and hoisted Tim towards the
steps.

Rachel paused, angered by his indifference. Tim
turned to look at her, and called over his shoulder,
"See you soon, Gypsy!"

Turning on her heel, Rachel walked through the
lengthening shadows back out of the quadrangle. She
wouldn't see him again, of course; because if she did
she would make it plain to him that she wasn't going
to bed with him. This was the seventies, and sex was
free and easy, a new toy to be explored and played
with, but Rachel's heritage was an older, darker one.
She had suffered too much from her own parents'
careless rapture to ever treat sex lightly. It had held
her mother in thrall, making her dismiss the dangers
of what she was doing, and Rachel intended to make
sure that nothing ever had such dominion over her.
Nothing.

She was late for work that evening. Bernadette

frowned at her when she arrived behind the bar.

"You're late!" she declared. "Old man Wells has been looking for you."

Jobs weren't difficult to come by in the seventies, and Rachel was a good worker, besides being attractive to the customers, so George Wells, the bar manager, soon forgave her for her small transgression, although he kept her behind after the others had gone, making her do the final check of the tables for empty glasses.

It was dark when she finally stepped outside, and the street was empty. She turned to leave—then gasped as a hand closed over her arm, fear storming through her.

"Hello, Gypsy. I thought you were never going to come!"

She recognised his voice instantly, her head turning to look into the smiling blue eyes.

"Let's go and find somewhere where we can talk and get to know one another," he suggested winningly. "I want to know all there is to know about you, Gypsy."

The scent of drugs still clung to his skin, and his fingers when they laced with hers felt hot. Rachel wanted to pull away, and yet part of her wanted to stay with him. He was so different from her . . . she thirsted for the insight that he could give into another way of life.

Without even having to ask herself how she knew Rachel knew that he came from a wealthy background and that he had been shielded and protected by that wealth all his life. He lived a life she could only learn about second-hand, through books, and she ached to know what it was that gave him his patina of self-assurance and made him so uncaring of all the hazards that daily tormented her.

She *wanted* to talk to him, and she remembered that

there was a small café which she passed on her way
home at night that always seemed to be open. They
could go there.

CHAPTER SIX

TIM WILDING had never known what it was to want
something and have that want go unsatisfied.

From the day of his birth he had been surrounded
by adoring females, and as he grew older he had
learned to take their adulation for granted, to manipulate and exploit them, and in so charming a manner
that they continued to love and praise him.

He was the grandson of the Earl of Marchington;
an earldom that went back to the time of Elizabeth
the First. His family owned rich acres in Pembroke-
shire and the North. His grandfather's main seat was
in Dorset—a huge rambling mish-mash of buildings
extended and improved upon by a succession of
wealthy men rich enough to amuse themselves by
enhancing their home to suit whatever fashion had
held sway.

It was from Dorset that the first Earl had come—a
seaman turned pirate, turned one of Queen Elizabeth's
favourite courtiers, who had been repaid for his loyalty
and, some said, for his prowess in bed, with the hand
of one of the Virgin Queen's richest wards. Kate
Sothey had brought to her husband a fortune amassed
by her parents and grandparents, plus land in the
north of England.

Will Wilding had been forty-eight at the time of his
marriage, and rumour had it that his bride had been
more than unwilling. She was in love with someone
else, but the Queen's will had prevailed, and in due
time Mistress Kate provided her spouse with one son

and three daughters.

Not even the title of Countess had been enough to compensate for all that she had lost, though, and in family portraits she was shown as an unsmiling, frail-looking woman, very much in the shadow of her big jovial husband.

Will Wilding had set a standard that his ancestors carefully upheld, and the Wilding men had always married well, conserving and adding to what was theirs, with the result that the current Earl was a millionaire several times over. He and his son and his family lived at Marchington Place, and although his son's marriage had produced several children, only one of them was male—the only male heir, in the absence of any other near male relative. Tim had grown up perfectly aware of his own importance; of the fact that one day he would be the Earl. The fact that physically he was very attractive was something he had also learned young and played ruthlessly upon.

At Eton he had fagged for one of the school's most notorious bullies—until he caught the eye of one of the other seniors, who had bought him away from his peer. Paul Somerton had been wildly in love with his newly acquired fag, and Tim had deliberately encouraged and fostered his feelings, liking the power it gave him. For Paul he had no feelings whatsoever, but he had already learned how to manipulate people with his charm and his looks, and it was a skill he would use throughout his life as clinically and determinedly as any prostitute.

Sex to Tim was simply a means of subjugating his victims, and he was equally adept at making love to a male or a female. Age, looks, personality—none of these entered into his calculations, or influenced his choice of lover, until he met Simon Herries. Simon was one year his senior and thus ahead of him at

Eton. Being in different Houses they only came into contact with one another by accident, but Tim knew the moment he met him that Simon was different. He had a power, a fascination that held Tim in thrall, and under Simon's expert tuition he had learned to choose his lovers with more care.

At Oxford, among others, he had his eye on one of the tutors, a man whose influence extended widely throughout the college. They weren't lovers yet, but Tim knew that they would be.

He and Simon laughed at the ease with which their victims succumbed. They were still lovers, as they always had been, but sex was only a small part of their relationship, and Simon knew Tim well enough to accept that his sexuality demanded a very free rein. Sometimes Tim simply enjoyed the pleasure of the subtle chase and the ultimate downfall of his victim, at others he chose his lovers because they had something he wanted or needed.

His and Simon's room-mate fell into the former category, but as yet he had refused to succumb. Tim wasn't worried. He could afford to wait; it would make his ultimate victory all the sweeter. He and Simon had already been sharing rooms with someone else when Miles arrived at Oxford, and Miles had been moved against his will to fill the gap when the third member of the original trio had been sent down. Miles suspected that Simon Herries was as displeased with the arrangement as he was himself, and they both tended to give one another a wide berth.

Tim operated in a different way, delighting in tormenting Miles with deliberately provocative remarks. How he would enjoy seeing that enigmatic exterior crumble beneath the drive of desire! Tim thought, smiling to himself and watching Miles—and it *would* crumble. He had never failed yet. Perhaps he ought to invite Miles home for the Christmas vacation.

He frowned slightly, anticipating Simon's reaction to such an invitation, a petulant, almost adolescent rebellion darkening his eyes, and then his attention switched back to Rachel. She was still a virgin—he was ready to stake his life on it. He could always tell. So much the better for what he had in mind. A pulse of excitement thudded through him, a mellow sensation of pleasure yet to come as he anticipated the delights the future held in store.

Through this girl he would surely succeed in raising the Devil. Simon . . . Simon didn't really believe it could be done, he suspected, frowning again. Simon had been the one to instigate the formation of the revived Hell Fire Club, but the power and fascination it held for him was lost on his friend, Tim suspected. Simon had not as yet felt that strong pull of darkness with which he was so familiar.

But he would do; somehow he would convince him . . . Somehow? He knew how. Excitement kicked through him again. Virgins were scarce on the ground these days, and this one was perfect . . . perfect. He sensed the pride in her and the battened-down wildness. She would fight. He would like that. He could feel his body hardening, and immediately he switched off his thoughts.

The girl might only be a barmaid working in a pub, but Tim had sensed that she was intelligent, and wary too. He didn't want to alarm her . . . not at this stage. Later she could be as terrified as she wished.

The café that Rachel had mentioned was busy, but there was one table for two empty. Rachel sat down while Tim went to get them something to drink. She had noticed when they walked in how all eyes turned in his direction. He was one of the most perfectly beautiful human beings she had ever seen, and yet something in her was chilled by his perfection even while she was drawn to it. Age-old instincts warned her to be careful, but she told herself that no harm could come of simply sitting down to talk with him. They were among the last to leave the café. Tim insisted on walking her back to the hotel, but once they got there, Rachel turned firmly and repulsed him when he tried to kiss her. He accepted her refusal with a lazy smile and an amused look in his eyes that told her that he would not find it hard to find someone who was willing.

She was glad Bernadette was already asleep. She didn't want to talk to anyone about Tim. Not yet.

It was gone two o'clock when Tim eventually returned to his rooms. After leaving Rachel, he had felt so excited and pleased with himself that he had gone on to one of the discos. He had found a girl there, cheap and tarty, and more than willing to take him back to her bedsit with her. He left her in a tangle of grubby bedding, fast asleep, revelling in the way her cheap scent mingled with the odour of sex and clung to his body.

Miles looked up but didn't betray any reaction when he walked in. "Still up? I thought you'd have been tucked up in your chaste little bed hours ago, or were you too frightened to go to bed in case I joined you there?" jeered Tim.

It was part of his technique to goad his victims, normally it drew some sort of response, but Miles merely smiled impassively and said nothing.

His lack of reaction brought Tim down from his earlier high. He reached for a cigarette, inhaling deeply, watching the controlled way Miles moved as he started to clear up his books. Damn the man, he was far too controlled and clever about the barriers he put up. Tim wanted to see that control shatter, to break through that reserve and trample his pride into the dust.

"Herries is looking for you."

Miles didn't look at him as he spoke, but Tim felt the slight tension in his body. So he wasn't completely impervious after all! He grinned to himself and stubbed out the cigarette.

"Jealous?" he purred softly, taking a step towards him. "My dear one . . ."

"Cut it out, Tim." The cool command was laconic enough to betray a certain degree of amusement. "You know, you really ought to try for OUDS. Who you choose to make friends with is your own concern, but I don't like Herries."

"Because he's homosexual?" One blond eyebrow lifted teasingly. "My dear, at least half of Academe . . ."

"Enjoys having sex with and then beating up ten-year-old boys? I don't think so."

So French knew about that. Simon must be slipping—he was normally more careful about keeping his vices hidden. Tim would have to warn him to be more cautious.

"Did he say what he wants?" he asked carelessly.

"Something about a meeting. Apparently the date's been changed to tomorrow night."

There were any number of secret and not so secret clubs and coteries at Oxford, so there was no real need for the exceedingly sharp glance that Miles gave him, but as always the scent of danger fired his own excitement. This was how he liked to live, always on the edge of that danger, always flirting with violence . . .

Miles watched him as he roamed round the room, still half high on drugs, and unless he was wrong about the smell clinging to him—sex. Odd, he hadn't thought that dark-haired girl he had seen him with earlier had been Tim's type. He normally preferred them far more overtly sexual.

Miles wanted to throw open the windows and let in some fresh air, but he knew from long experience that if he did so, he would be subjected to all manner of taunts and digs, designed to undermine his self-control. Sexually he had no interest in Tim, or indeed in any member of his own sex, but he did have a deeply buried vein of hot temper that he was always careful to keep well under control, and there were many times when Tim pushed him close to the edge of it. He suspected that like Simon Herries Tim enjoyed the frisson of sex with violence. Although unlike Herries Tim enjoyed receiving the violence rather than inflicting it.

His room-mate's sex life was no concern of his, he reminded himself. He was damn lucky to be up at Oxford, and he was here to work, not to get involved in precious cliques.

The undergrad who had shared with Tim before him had been sent down in disgrace, supposedly for supplying drugs. Smoking pot was endemic among the students, and it seemed an overly harsh punishment. Oddly, Tim never mentioned his former room-mate, although he had shared with him for twelve months.

Tim was one of a number of gilded youths up at Oxford because it was what the male members of their families had done for generations. Miles doubted very much that Tim would get a degree, or that he would care. For all his gilded beauty, Miles sensed something disquieting about him, and not just because of his sexual ambiguity. There was something essentially cold and dangerous about Tim; something that ran deeply contrary to his open face and lighthearted pose.

Had he been able to choose, Miles would have preferred to share with someone else; someone closer to his own background and ambitions.

His degree was important to him because it was the first step towards his ultimate goal. He had wanted to go into law for almost as long as he could remember, and to achieve even as much as he already had had been hard work for a boy brought up in a Doctor Barnado's Home.

He had been left on the steps of a hospital as a day-old baby in the classic fashion. His mother had never been traced, and because of medical complications following on from his exposure, he had been almost two years old before he had been given a completely clean bill of health—too old then to appeal to prospective parents who wanted to adopt only small babies.

He was philosophical rather than resentful of his fate. The orphanage had been well run, the staff kind, and he had developed early on in life a matter-of-fact resilience to protect himself from thinking too deeply about his mother's rejection.

If he had been lucky at all in his life, and he liked to think that he had, it had been having been placed in an orphanage situated on the outskirts of a small Cotswold village. One of the most generous patrons of the orphanage was a local JP and retired Army officer, Colonel Whitegate. The Colonel, a strict disciplinarian and a widower, was one of those men who although having no children of his own, had a genuine rapport with them. Small groups of children from the orphanage were regularly invited to the Manor House to help the Colonel with the small stud farm he ran, and afterwards to have tea with him in the informality of his comfortable study. The Colonel bred and trained polo ponies, having become an aficionado of the sport during his days in the Army. Although reasonably

well off he did not have the means to support a full
polo string, and to travel round the world attending
matches, so instead he had turned his skill to the
breeding rather than the riding of the ponies. He was
also a well-read man, simple in his tastes and in many
ways oddly innocent about life, one of the few people
who genuinely deserved the title 'gentleman'.

He was kind to all the children he came into contact
with—the orphanage was a relatively small one and
he made it his business to know most of them by
name, but it wasn't until Miles won a scholarship to
Rugby that he began to take any particular notice of
him.

It just so happened that Rugby was the Colonel's
own public school, and when the director of the
orphanage confided to him that he was concerned that
Miles might have to forgo the scholarship because of
the expense of equipping him to attend, he had
immediately said that he would pay all the incidental
expenses. These extended to far more than merely the
cost of the uniform and spending money and covered
the whole range of extra-curricular activities, all of
which the Colonel insisted that Miles participate in.

When Miles had tried, at the end of his first term,
to protest diffidently, the Colonel had told him that
part of the benefit to be reaped from a public school
education was to take full advantage of everything
that it had to offer.

"Do you think I'd ever have taken up polo if I
hadn't gone into the Army? Got any plans for the
future?" he added brusquely.

"The law, sir . . ." Miles told him hesitantly. He
couldn't explain where this fascination with the legal
profession had come from, it was just something that
was there deep inside him. The ramifications and
diversity of the law enthralled him and challenged

him; he also liked debating, and he had already discussed with his housemaster his desire to enter the legal profession.

If Colonel Whitegate was disappointed he hid it well. Miles already knew how expensive in both money and time acquiring legal qualifications could be. The law was also a very enclosed world, nepotistic and tightly gathered in upon itself. His ambition to become a barrister could only be fulfilled if other barristers opened their chambers to him and invited him to join them. There was no automatic right of entry, but the simpler, more workaday world of the solicitor was not the one he wanted to enter.

All this had been discussed with his housemaster, and he already knew how long and arduous the road ahead would be. He would need a degree, and if he could win a place at Oxford the worth of that degree would be increased tenfold. After that there would be more periods of study, more exams, a period of apprenticeship in counsels' chambers.

All this he already knew, and explained to the Colonel as he told him of his ambitions.

"He's a bright lad and intent on reaching high," the Colonel commented to the orphanage director later.

"Too high, perhaps."

"No . . . no man can ever do that."

The Colonel financed Miles through his last two years at school, and was enormously proud of what he had achieved. Miles had an open invitation to spend his holidays with him, but during the summer he had spent all but two weeks working as a rousta-bout off one of the North Sea oil rigs. The roustabouts were the lowest form of life on the rigs, the work was hard and dirty, but it paid well, and Miles now had enough in the bank to see him through to his finals if he was careful.

He had learned a lot in Aberdeen. Going ashore with his workmates, he had discovered that to say one worked on an oil rig was a magic incantation as far as a certain section of the female population was concerned. He hadn't been a virgin when he went up to Oxford; there had been a couple of fumbled, hasty episodes beforehand, but in an Aberdeen pub he had been picked up by the bored wife of one of the oil company executives, who had taken him back with her to her neo-Georgian home and taught him the difference between more immediate sexual gratification and intense sexual pleasure, and all the delicate nuances in between. Miles had been surprised to discover within himself a deep well of sexuality, and he had put the lessons the woman had taught him to good use since.

He didn't have a current girlfriend; he preferred to keep his relationships casual. The last thing he wanted was to be tied down into the sort of steady relationship some of the other students were burdened with.

His workload was heavy and he studied hard. His degree was important to him, but he still left himself with enough time to enjoy some of the peripheral pleasures. He was a member of several debating societies; he rowed and he played tennis. He enjoyed both folk and classical music, although he didn't play an instrument, and occasionally he submitted a witty piece to *Isis*, the university magazine.

What he didn't do was get involved in the heavy drinking and drugs scene favoured by the *jeunesse doré* he was too intelligent to get caught in that particular trap. He knew exactly why Tim Wilding was goading him. With another man he would have told him quite simply that he was wasting his time.

He had come across homosexuality quite early on

at Rugby. It wasn't his thing; he liked women, although he numbered several homosexuals among his group of friends and enjoyed both their wit and their intelligence, but in Tim Wilding he sensed something different; something destructive and dangerous.

Although they shared a set of rooms they didn't have the same friends. Tim wasn't the slightest bit interested in gaining his degree. He and his set tended to look down on the students who had made it to Oxford through the grammar school and direct grant system. Their petty snobbishness bored Miles; he suspected it sprang from unadmitted inferiority, rather than from the much vaunted superiority that they seemed to cherish and demonstrate at every opportunity.

The fact that Tim was the grandson of one of the country's premier earls had no effect on Miles whatsoever. If anything he felt rather more sorry for him. His grandfather had a formidable reputation; his father was an immensely successful businessman and Tim had a lot to live up to. Far better to be in his own shoes, Miles reflected, where he was not constantly being overshadowed by those who had gone before. No, he didn't envy Tim, and in fact he didn't particularly like either of his room-mates, although of the two of them, he recognised that Simon Herries was the more dangerous.

There was an aura about him, a power, that Miles instinctively mistrusted. He was a very charismatic man, there was no doubt about that, but sometimes . . . just sometimes when things were not going his way Miles had witnessed a darker, far more dangerous side to his personality, and he instinctively avoided both Simon and Tim, having no desire at all to be drawn into their circle.

Their sexual proclivities were no secret, but they

were far from being the only two bi-sexual men at
Oxford. Miles watched the two of them together, and
it sometimes seemed to him that Tim deliberately on
occasions tried to incite Simon to sexual violence—
incited it and enjoyed it, Miles suspected distastefully,
but they were both grown men and their private
relationship was no affair of his.

There was far more between them than just a
homosexual relationship, and even the reality of that
was suspect, given the fact that Tim made no secret
of the fact that he had many other lovers of both
sexes. And yet for all his sexual conquests there was
an air of almost asexuality about him, a bogus air of
innocence, like that of a child before the onset of
puberty. But where Tim could be both charming and
witty, Simon Herries had a brooding air about him
that repulsed all but his chosen band of friends.

Miles wasn't a member of that small clique, nor did
he want to be. He suspected that Tim and others had
formed some sort of secret club, although what its
purpose was he had no idea, nor did he really care.
Secret clubs abounded within the colleges; some lasted,
some died, some became hallowed institutions and
admission to them was highly prized. Miles doubted
that anyone would remember what Herries' club had
stood for once he had left Christ Church.

Tim had once told him that it was Herries' ambition
to enter the Church. It seemed very unlikely to Miles,
who thought he had never come across a more worldly
and less Christian human being, but he kept his
thoughts to himself, knowing Tim's propensity for
jokes.

He had overheard one of the tutors commenting
that Simon Herries would make a good politician.

"He's devious and dishonest enough for it," had
been the cynical comment.

Tim waited until he was sure that Miles was asleep before leaving their rooms. Curfews were no longer maintained at Oxford and there was no penalty to pay for being out of doors after a certain time, but to Tim secrecy was the very breath of life, and he enjoyed the challenge of slipping out silently, and hugging the shadows of the stairs as he made his way to their prearranged rendezvous outside the college.

Simon was waiting for him as he had known he would be. Unlike Miles, he didn't make any attempt to conceal his recognition of the scent that Tim brought with him, pushing him away abruptly when Tim reached out to embrace him.

Tim laughed softly, knowing he held the power to make Simon cry out with desire for him, should he want to do so.

"I got your message. Why has the meeting to be changed?"

"We've got to change the venue—apparently the vicar's getting suspicious. We'll have to find somewhere else."

"Oh dear, the original Francis Dashwood didn't have these problems, did he—but don't worry, my dear, I've found something that will cheer you up. A deliciously untouched virgin."

It was while he was at Eton that Simon Herries had first become attracted to Satanism. A history lesson mentioning the notorious Sir Francis Dashwood and his cronies had sparked off his interest in the occult, and over the years that interest had grown.

There were plenty of young men like Tim Wilding who were attracted to the idea of violence and sex, and when that was combined with secrecy and power, its lure was irresistible. The aim of their 'Society' was not so much to raise the Devil as to investigate whether or not such a thing was possible; thus by stating this as the society's aim, Simon was able to cloak it in an aura of respectability and spurious study.

Of course, in order to validate the claims of Dashwood and his coven, that they had been able to raise the Devil, Simon and his friends had to mirror their methods.

Up until now they had used a remote church in a small local village for their rites, but the vicar had obviously become suspicious. Now they would have to find somewhere else.

Simon himself had little belief in Dashwood's claim—he suspected that like himself he had enjoyed the sexual licence his role gave him, and the power. Because there always had been and always would be those who were chained in superstitious fear to the old pre-Christian beliefs. Simon had learned at Eton quite by accident that it was possible to control others through the threat of hidden power. Now he used this power in a different way.

Those he chose as his disciples were only people who were useful to him in some way. First he tantalised them with subtle promises of the pleasures in store, and then once they had partaken of those pleasures, he used them as a threat against them. Unlike Simon, however, Tim believed that Francis Dashwood had raised the Devil; the pull of Satanism for him meant far more than the means by which he could control others—after all, he could do that already.

The next important date in the Satanist calendar was All Hallows' Eve; the new Hell Fire Club would celebrate it with a Black Mass. And for a virgin to be sacrificed at that Black Mass would invoke the most powerful of all of black magic forces.

Tonight, quite casually, Rachel had revealed to him

that she was an orphan. He had felt the excitement beat up through his veins then, dancing like fire behind his eyelids, making his whole body come alive. Already he could picture the scene, feel the power that would be his, first at the moment when he penetrated her body and then later when he made the ritual sacrifice and offered her up to the power of the Dark Master.

No one, not even Simon, who had shaped and indeed initiated his exploration of black magic, knew how deeply Tim had been affected by his research into Satanism. He had followed its development through the centuries, traced it back over many lifetimes, and had felt the thrilled pulse of his blood. To raise the Devil would be the ultimate thrill, the pleasure to end all pleasures, a greater high than any drug, more sexually stimulating than any mere contact with alien flesh. He could feel himself grow hot and float away from his body at the thought of what was to come.

Simon watched him, and frowned. Tim had been smoking pot again; his eyes were glazed and vacant, a thin drool of spittle escaping from the corner of his mouth. Simon had warned him before about becoming too reliant on the drug. He used it himself, but only carefully.

A virgin sacrifice. He liked the idea, although personally he would have preferred the pale, sexless body of a young boy. He felt himself grow hard at the thought. There had been a boy last week . . . He shuddered and felt the sweat break out on his skin.

As a fag at Eton he had once walked into a senior's study when he was forcing Tim to perform the act of fellatio on him, and the thrill it had given him to see someone else being forced to another's sexual demands had remained with him for a long time. In fact that had been the first time he had realised that there could be pleasure in sex as well as pain.

He had been less than five years old the first time his father abused him sexually.

His mother died shortly after he was born, and he had been handed over into the care of his father's aunt. His father had been a remote, distant figure, spending most of his time in London on business and returning to the borders only at rare intervals.

Then when Simon was four his great-aunt had died, and his father had returned home for good. A sombre, brooding man, he frightened Simon, who kept out of his way, although he had had no reason then for his fear.

The first time his father had slid into his bed and started to touch him with rough urgent hands, he had cried out in terror. He had soon learned never to make that mistake again. The next day his father had birched him, leaving thin red weals across his buttocks that oozed blood. The memory of his parent going down on his knees to lap the bright beads of blood from his lacerated flesh was something that would stay with him always.

By the time he got to Eton he was stoically accustomed to his father's abuse of him, and he had learned to endure what he inflicted on him in silence. At the least possible excuse his father would beat him until his flesh bled and he was driven to an orgy of lust.

When Paul Somerton sold Tim to his friend, Simon took his place. The cruelty of his senior made little impression on a boy who had already endured all there was to endure at the hands of his parent.

For the rest of his life there would be no pleasure for Simon without his inflicting pain on the pleasure-giver, and just as he had learned as a child to blot out the anomalies in his relationship with his father, so he learned to blot out the sadistic impulses that governed his own life.

By the time he reached Oxford he was a past master at the art of throwing a cloak of camouflage over his true personality. People might not like him; they might sense deep, uncharted chasms within his personality, but none of them knew why. Not even Tim knew about Simon's childhood; it was something he had locked away inside himself and would never ever set free.

Already he loathed Rachel even without knowing her. He could feel the waves of sexual excitement emanating from Tim, and all because of some female bitch. Simon hated women; it was a woman who had died and left him at the mercy of his father; two women, in fact, first his mother and then his aunt. Sexually they left him cold, but he already knew that one day he would marry. His father was dead, and had left him his house and lands but very little else. Simon was ambitious, but ambitions had to be fuelled with wealth, and for that he would need to marry. He had already drawn up a short list of candidates.

Abruptly he turned his mind to more pressing matters. Since one member of the coven had been stupid enough to leave behind a small portion of their black candles at their last mass, they would have to find a new site for their next one.

"I have an idea!" Simon could hear the excitement in Tim's voice. He looked across at him. He was silhouetted against the window, his head thrown back challengingly, his eyes glittering. It was a pose Simon recognised. This was Tim at his most lethally charming and determined. "There's a chapel at Marchington. We could celebrate our next Mass there."

"Don't be a fool! It would be far too dangerous."

Simon forgot for a moment how much Tim loved danger, recklessly so. He had said completely the wrong thing, as he realised almost instantly, but it was already too late.

"The harder the achievement the more worthwhile," Tim told him softly. "Think about it, Simon. No one can interrupt or stop us at Marchington. We'll be able to do it there. We can raise the Devil. Think of the power that will be ours!"

Simon shifted uncomfortably from one foot to the other. Did Tim really believe..? He grimaced to himself. He already knew the answer to that one. Tim was almost obsessed by his belief that these ancient black magic rites held the secret of total power.

"We shall hold the Black Mass at Marchington, and we shall sacrifice our virgin there and I shall raise the Devil."

Simon checked abruptly. He started to speak warningly, then fell silent as he looked into Tim's face. He looked like someone in the thrall of some blinding revelation . . . or some blinding obsession. Tim meant every word he was saying. Simon could stop him . . . perhaps . . . but the girl by all accounts would never be missed, and he couldn't help thinking of the power that would be his if he let Tim go ahead with his plans. Not the power Tim dreamed of, but a far more earthly power. He would let Tim stage-manage the Mass. He would stay on the sidelines, in the background, making sure that everything was properly recorded for posterity. They would pick the acolytes for that night carefully . . .

His mind ran ahead, busily cataloguing those among their members who could potentially be most useful to him in the future. Those who would be weak enough to succumb to blackmail. Rachel was forgotten . . . whether she lived or died meant nothing to Simon. She was as dispensable as an empty cardboard carrier, as unimportant in his scheme of things as an insignificant ant. She was no more than a means to an end; if Tim wanted this Mass then let him have it. The knowledge of his own duplicity made Simon's eyes glitter with satisfaction. It always gave him a thrill to know how completely Tim was under his control.

"Very well," he said slowly. "But it must be carefully planned, and no one, no one at all must know what's happening until the very last moment. We don't want anyone getting cold feet and running out on us to tell tales, do we?"

"It will be perfect," Tim told him. He was breathing steadily, his lean body suddenly taut with desire. Simon, who had seen that look in his eyes many many times before, recognised it instantly and laughed softly.

"Here," he suggested knowingly. "You want me here . . ."

It was cold and dark, but neither of them cared. The sudden upsurge of lust carried them both far beyond any mundane awareness of their surroundings or the lack of heat.

Afterwards, as he lay surfeited on the ground, Tim opened his eyes and said softly,   "What a shame dear Miles isn't here to share this with us."

"Be careful," Simon warned him, not sharing his amusement. "He isn't like the others, Tim. He won't succumb."

Tim felt he was wrong, but he was too relaxed to argue. He closed his eyes and started mentally planning his Black Mass. The thought of it excited him so much that he reached towards Simon again, but Simon pushed him back. In their relationship, he was the one who made the rules—a fact which just occasionally Tim was inclined to forget.

CHAPTER SEVEN

SIMON and Tim had instigated their own version of the Hell Fire Club during Tim's first term at Oxford. Tim's original room-mate had been one of the founder members, but he had started to talk too much and so they had had to get rid of him. Simon had been the one to suggest they plant the drugs on him, and he had also arranged for him to be caught with them— Simon was very good at "arranging" things. Since then they had been very careful about who they recruited to their ranks.

For the coven to be fully operational and effective they needed thirteen members; in addition they also had several novice members; and among these were Richard Howell and Alex Barnett.

Both of them had been drawn into the Club almost by accident. Alex Barnett had come across Tim in the College library and had fallen into conversation with him. As a boy he had always been fascinated with the alchemists' search for the magic incantation to transform base metal into gold, and when he had seen that the book Tim was reading was on this subject he had found himself agreeing to join Tim and some of his friends at one of their meetings, not realising exactly what was involved.

Secretly he had been flattered by the invitation. He had arrived at Oxford via a State-run grammar school, and in his first term was very much in awe of Tim and his friends, and the air of aristocratic superiority that clung to them.

Richard Howell had joined the coven by a different route. His sex drive had always been phenomenal, and when he heard on the grapevine that a club existed to promote the sexual orgies indulged in by the eighteenth-century Hell Fire Club he had lost no time in making known that if such a club *did* exist he would very much like to join.

Both of them were now novices, and neither of them took at all seriously the Satanistic side of the club. To them it was simply a rather daring and exciting secret circle to which they were privileged to belong. Both of them would have laughed aloud if Tim had confided to them that he genuinely believed in Satanism; they thought that he, like they, considered it to be nothing more than a game. By the time they realised that they were wrong it was almost too late.

As novice members so far they had only been allowed to take part in the opening stages of one Black Mass. Simon was very careful about whom they recruited into the coven. By the time a new member was finally initiated Simon had secured enough material against him to ensure that if he ever did leave the coven, he would keep his mouth shut.

As far as Simon was concerned the club was simply another stepping stone on the path he had marked out for himself. He hadn't decided yet what form his career would take, but he had already determined that the more people within his control the better.

The new recruits to the club would have been surprised if they had known the mental files that Simon kept on all of them.

Richard Howell had connections in the banking world—small ones, maybe, but who knew where they would lead, who could tell how valuable such a connection might be in the future?

Alex Barnett belonged to a stratum of society that

frankly bored Simon. His background was middle class, and there was little money, but there was still something about him that Simon's well developed sixth sense told him was worthwhile cultivating.

As novices both Richard and Alex were to be initiated as full members at the next formal meeting of the club. They discussed it one afternoon in the library, where they had met by chance.

Of the two Alex was the more nervous, the less self-assured. He was perfectly well aware what his parents would say if they knew what he was contemplating doing, and he envied Richard Howell his amused sangfroid as the latter unashamedly discussed the sexual revels he was already anticipating.

If it wasn't for Richard's careless insouciance, Alex suspected that he himself might have backed out. He had felt acutely uncomfortable at his first Black Mass, conscious of an atavistic prickling of his scalp during the unhallowed service, coupled with a sensation of treading on very dangerous ground, but Oxford was a new environment for him, and he didn't have the self-confidence to say what he thought. Having come to the University via the grammar school system, he was consequently somewhat in awe of its traditions; of its students with their careless air of self-confidence; of their contemptuous mockery of those they considered beneath them, and so he trod very warily indeed.

He knew that both Simon Herries and Tim came from landed, wealthy families, and he couldn't help but be impressed by them, even while the still developing analytical side of his mind told him that the only worthy measure of any man came from within himself and not from his birth.

His parents had been thrilled and proud when he had won a place at Oxford. His father, remembering the rumours of the University and the life of its undergraduates during the thirties, had warned him to stay clear of politically biased groups, but the real life of the place was centred on its cliques and societies, and almost without being aware of what was happening to him Alex had found himself gravitating towards the group that surrounded Tim and Simon.

Both of them awed him; he longed to emulate their confidently arrogant manner, to be able to be as careless of wealth and position as they were, and without being aware of it he found himself adopting Tim's lazy drawl.

"I wonder what they've got in store for us with the initiation ceremony," Richard commented to him with a grin.

Immediately Alex felt his stomach muscles tighten. Oxford abounded with horror stories of the violent and sadistic "hazing" ceremonies popular in some of the country's top schools, and he couldn't stop himself from shivering slightly.

"Perhaps they'll give us a virgin apiece?" Richard suggested with another grin.

Unlike Alex, he had no dread of the coming ceremony. He had never suffered an excess of too much imagination. He had been brought up by a father whose bitterness at being ousted from the board of the family bank had hung over his entire life, permeating every corner of it. Almost before he could understand what his father was talking about Richard was aware of his bitterness. He had been brought up to feel that he had been deprived of something that was his right, and for a long time he had not been able to understand why his father was so bitter.

It was a simple enough story. Jacob Howell had been the younger son. His father had left a controlling interest in the bank to his elder son, and Jacob had never been able to forgive him for it, just as he had never been able to forgive his brother for being the elder.

On the morning of Richard's thirteenth birthday, Jacob Howell removed the gun he kept in the right-hand drawer of his desk and shot himself through the head.

His wife found him. Richard came home from school at the end of term to discover that his father was dead and his mother had gone to a "place where they would make her well again". From henceforth he was to consider his uncle David's house as his home.

But he never could. Unlike his father, though, he quickly learned to control and hide his feelings, screening them with a mask of cheerful insouciance, adopting a clowning pose which deceived everyone but his great-uncle Reuben.

"Mark my words, that one will be trouble," he told his nephew, but David Howell only laughed.

"The boy's a fool," he told his uncle. "He's more interested in making laughter than making money."

"No, nephew, *you* are the fool, if you can't see the way he looks at you when he thinks no one else is looking," Reuben Weiss told him, but David would only shake his head and tell his wife that her uncle was getting old and losing his once sharp wits.

Howell's bank, or at least the English branch of it, had first been opened in London in 1789, just in time to assist the fleeing French aristocrats as they came flooding to London, clutching their family jewels; delighted to discover that in London there was a bank presided over by someone who not only spoke French fluently but who also treated them with the deference they had once commanded by right. It was immensely soothing to sit in Monsieur Howell's office that was furnished so comfortably like one of their own *salons* at home, and to have their trials and just anger listened to with sympathy and understanding.

Monsieur Howell was understanding also about the need to convert their jewels into cash, and quickly— there were family members still in France and in the greatest danger. Monsieur Howell knew just how to help. He was in touch with a group of brave men dedicated to rescuing the French nobility from the rapacious jaws of the mob. It was a costly process, of course, and success could not always be guaranteed . . .

Jacob Howell was a cautious and a sensible man— too cautious for dangerous greed. It was enough if simply one in ten of those who came to him seeking succour for other members of their families should not succeed. And if that one was also very wealthy and prepared to pay very, very well, then how much more gratifying financially it was to Howell's bank when the rescue attempt failed.

Of course Monsieur Howell was always désolé to report a failure on the part of his friends—all the more so because some of his friends too had disappeared along with the person they had tried to rescue. Monsieur Howell could only wish that he could repay the sum that Monsieur or Madame had advanced, but unfortunately . . . Here the very gallicness of his shrug was sufficient to convey that when such a venture failed money was the very last consideration to be taken into account, and Monsieur or Madame found themselves leaving the bank with their views that Monsieur Howell was one of the kindest and bravest of men alive stalwartly reinforced.

Monsieur Howell's caution paid off. He had enough successful attempts to smuggle émigrés out of Paris to guarantee that he had a steady source of income for quite some time. When he was not successful—well, sometimes the fates were not kind, and because his failures were so few and so well planned, no one seemed to realise that it was always those who were prepared to pay most for the rescue of their relatives who had the least success.

Once Jacob had got a taste for this novel method of earning income, it was but a short step, given the complexity of the Howells' family connections throughout Europe—Jacob Howell was the fifth son of an Austrian pawnbroker, with brothers spread out throughout most of Europe—from rescuing émigrés to supplying both the French and the English secret services with information for which both sides paid well.

In France, Fouché knew Jacob Howell's brother as one of his most rewarding sources of information, and who would ever connect Raoul Lebrun, a staunch supporter of the Revolution, with either Felix Lewotiz in Austria, or Jacob Howell in London? The brothers had not grown up in the ghetto for nothing and knew well how to cover their tracks.

In London William Pitt treated Jacob Howell with respect and courtesy. Wars are expensive, and bankers who show their willingness to support their adoptive countries are always welcome, especially such wealthy bankers as Jacob Howell.

No one suspected that along with the letters he had smuggled into the country there also came smuggled goods of a more financially beneficial type—French silks and brandies, carried across the Channel by the route Jacob had established for his émigrés.

Thanks to his communication lines with his brothers, like the Rothschilds, Jacob Howell knew of the English victory at Waterloo before the Government and people of the country—and in plenty of time to buy heavily into "the funds", so recklessly and foolishly sold by those people who had dreaded and expected a French victory. Overnight his fortune more than quadrupled, and Howell's bank was now firmly established.

In 1818 Jacob Howell bought himself a peerage and married the only child of a wealthy London merchant. He had one son and three daughters. On his death his son inherited the bank, and his daughters nothing. The Howell tradition of primogeniture was thus established.

Richard's grandfather was not quite as hard-headed as his ancestor; but then *his* sons were twins, born only ten minutes apart, and of the two the one he loved was always Jacob, the most emotional, least rational.

Even so he could not entirely break with family tradition. On his death he split his shares in the bank between his two sons, but gave David the controlling interest, and the chairmanship, as was his right by birth.

All might have gone well, but young Jacob, always relentlessly jealous of his brother, was foolish in other ways as well. David followed family tradition and married the daughter of a wealthy, respected family— the only daughter, while Jacob fell recklessly in love with a girl whose family owned nothing more than a small suburban semi-detached and who moreover was not even pretty. Always stubborn in the face of opposition, he married his Phyllis against family counsel, and privately Richard suspected that he had lived to regret it. The heavy gambling and drinking that became part of the pattern of his father's life surely didn't come only from jealously of his older brother?

The crunch came when it was discovered that Jacob had given an IOU that he couldn't meet. David called him into the bank and told him that the IOU would not be paid unless he made over to him the major part of his shares, and agreed to resign from the board of the bank. Jacob had little choice other than to agree.

A month later he was dead, leaving his son with a legacy of bitterness and resentment that Richard was careful to hide from everyone else around him. He had been brought up in the knowledge that but for a minor circumstance of birth, a matter of ten minutes in time, *he* would have been the one to inherit the bank and not his cousin Morris.

Morris was three years younger than Richard, three years behind him. His uncle had already promised him that if he did well at Oxford there would be a position for him with the bank. Richard *wanted* that position, and he wanted more—much more.

His uncle had been impressed when he had casually mentioned Tim's name; he would be even more impressed when he heard that Richard had actually been invited to visit Marchington. Of course he would never know why.

It added an extra fillip of excitement to the situation that they were actually to be initiated in Marchington's chapel.

All of them were to go down for the weekend. Richard had read up on the place in the library. Unlike the original Francis Dashwood's estate, Marchington had no caves in which they could perform their secret rites, but Tim had informed them that his family would be away, and quite frankly Richard felt that he would prefer the comfort of one of Marchington's luxurious bedrooms to Medmenham's Gothic caves.

Every night for over a week Tim had met Rachel after she finished work in the evening. At first she had treated him warily, waiting for him to invite her into his bed. When he didn't she started to relax.

He was the first male of her own age she had talked to at any real length. When he wanted to be Tim could be an amusing raconteur; he had a string of stories about his family and their friends and a careless throwaway manner of telling them that had enchanted far more worldly and sophisticated people than Rachel.

Another girl of her age and looks in the seventies would have immediately questioned Tim's apparent lack of sexual interest in her, but Rachel wasn't like other girls. She had learned to fear sex, and Tim, like the skilled hunter he was, could sense that fear. It amused him to see how far he could go without frightening her. When he touched her apparently by accident she stiffened immediately and looked at him with wary, cautious eyes. What a rare find she was! She was as virginal mentally as she was physically, so perfect for his purpose that he thought he saw the Devil's hand in her almost magical appearance in his life now, at this point, when he needed her the most.

After that first evening he was careful only to take her to places where they could not be seen—long walks along the river; drives in the car kept outside the college.

When he told Simon that he intended to invite Rachel down to Marchington, the latter was furious.

"You can't do that, you fool!" he exclaimed.

"Why not? Marchington is my home, after all, my dear."

"She'll never fit in. Your sisters . . ."

"My sisters will tolerate her as they tolerate all my friends, including you. Besides, they won't be there."

Tim had a malicious streak when he cared to use it, and it amused him to see the dull red colour run up under Simon's fair skin.

"You were awfully obvious, you know," he taunted him. "Father would never have let you marry Deborah, even if you'd got as far as proposing to her. He's got other plans for her."

Simon glared at him. Sometimes, despite his physical desire for him, he almost wanted to kill Tim. Always sensitive where his pride was concerned, he had to grit his teeth against commenting that if Deborah hadn't been who she was he wouldn't have looked twice at her. She wasn't a beauty, none of Tim's sisters were— it was as though having poured out a cornucopia of gifts over him, the fates had turned their backs on the children that followed.

An invitation to visit his family home was the last thing Rachel had expected from Tim. She knew from his accent and his manner that he came from a wealthy family, but she had no idea of his true social position.

"Well?" he prompted, watching her with enjoyment, knowing he had completely bowled her over. Such a naïve little innocent! What did she think he had in mind—a proposal . . . marriage? He almost laughed out loud.

"You want me to come to your home for . . . for the weekend?"

"Isn't that what I just said?"

Watching him, Rachel was suddenly shaken by a frisson of sensation that wasn't pleasant, a shiver of something that chilled her to the bone but which she shook off, ignoring the warning of her mother's blood.

"I'll have to see if I can get the time off work."

Tim fought to control his impatience. He wanted to tell her to forget her stupid little job, but caution urged him to tread carefully. There was something pleasurably exciting about stalking this particular prey. He had a sudden mental image of her naked body laid out on the altar of the chapel at Marchington, of her bright blood dripping on to its pure white floor. A heat mist of wild excitement swirled through his brain. His head pounded with the force of it; he felt himself swell with power . . . the excitement of it all but choked him. It was going to be so good. He could almost feel the power growing in him at the very thought of what was to come. But he forced himself to the discipline of patience, skilfully coaxing away her doubts.

When she left Tim Rachel could scarcely believe what he had said. She was to go home with him. They would drive down in his car. She would meet his family. Judiciously he hadn't told her that they would be away—his grandfather in Scotland, his parents and sisters in the Algarve taking a late holiday, after the crowds had gone.

Bernadette noticed Rachel's silence as they prepared for bed. Always inquisitive, she asked archly.

"Seen the boyfriend again, have you? Where'd he take you tonight?"

"Oh, just for a walk," Rachel told her.

Bernadette sniffed.

"You want to be careful of that. Tell him to take you somewhere nice. You don't want to let him hide you away like he wasn't proud to be with you."

"He wants me to go home with him this weekend."

Until she said the words out loud Rachel hadn't really believed it herself, but as though Bernadette's shock was in some way an antidote to her own, she found herself facing the open-mouthed stare with a smile, amid a sudden lightness of spirit.

"You don't mean it!" gasped Bernadette.

"Of course I do. Why should I lie? Do you think they'll let me have time off?"

"Oh, sure, and if they don't we'll all cover for you

somehow," Bernadette told her, her generous nature overcoming her surprised envy. "Don't you be going saying anything to anyone. I'll speak to the others— you've done favours enough for us before. You'll have to tell them down at the pub, though, but they'll understand. It'll be the first weekend you've had off since you started. What will you be taking with you to wear? You'll want something besides your jeans."

Bernadette might have joined the rootless community of youth, but she hadn't left her Irish upbringing behind her entirely. Where she came from a girl always took special trouble when she was meeting her man's family, and in her eyes, an invitation to his home meant that that was exactly what Rachel would be doing.

What would she wear? Rachel hadn't even thought about it.

"Sure and you'll find something," Bernadette comforted her. "We could go shopping tomorrow if you like."

Rachel smiled and said nothing. Her keen eye had already noticed that there was a vast difference between the cheap clothes Bernadette and the other girls bought and wore like throwaway paper handkerchiefs and those worn by the female undergraduates.

Jeans were the anonymous uniform worn by them all, but the female students had other clothes as well, clothes the like of which Rachel had never seen before in her life, but which she instinctively recognised as a subtly different but equally give-away uniform—a uniform worn only by the privileged.

Bernadette pulled a face when she saw the groups of girls walk by in their skirts and sweaters worn over neat collared blouses. Tim had mentioned his sisters. Those were the kind of clothes they would wear, Rachel knew that by instinct. But even if she knew where to buy them she didn't have the money.

"You'll need something to wear in the evening if he's really posh," Bernadette warned her. "You know, something dressy."

Something dressy . . . Rachel worried about it nearly all night. Clothes were important to her. The taunts and slights she had suffered as a child had never been forgotten.

She was still worrying about it when she got up the next morning. At eleven o'clock, just as she was about to go for her break, the housekeeper told her she had to go and clean Room 112. Rachel knew better than to object.

Outside the door she knocked, then used her pass key, expecting the room to be empty. But a girl of her own age and build was standing in the middle of the room, surveying the tumble of clothes and carrier bags strewn across the bed and spilling out of an open suitcase.

"Hi," she greeted Rachel. "Look, could you give me a hand with this lot? I'm off to India with some friends. Running away, in fact!" She made a droll face and laughed. She spoke like Tim; her fair hair was artfully streaked and she had long beautifully manicured nails. "We're leaving this afternoon—five of us in an old bus, it should be terrific fun, but Gil says I can only take one case . . ."

Rachel was already automatically folding the clothes into neat piles.

"No, not that stuff," the blonde girl told her. "I'm leaving all that behind. I'm starting a whole new life." She made an expansive gesture with her arms and grinned at Rachel. "The parents will go mad when they find out! They sent me to Oxford to find a suitable husband." She made another face. "I'm going to send them a letter—once we're out of the country.

Gil and I will probably get married in Delhi . . ."

She kept on chattering while Rachel packed her clothes, breaking off from her confidences occasionally to say, "No, not that . . ." or "Yes, I'm taking those."

When the case was full there was still a large pile of clothes on the bed. Rachel looked at her.

"Is it full? Well, I'll just have to manage with what's in there. Help me close it, will you?"

When the case was locked she swung it down to the floor and picked up her handbag. She had reached the door before Rachel realised that she was actually leaving.

"But what about all these things?" Rachel protested.

The girl turned her head and looked at the clothes folded on the bed, then shrugged.

"Oh, get rid of them for me, would you? I'm already running late, and Gil said he wouldn't wait." And then she was gone, leaving Rachel staring at the closed door.

She must have sat there for a full five minutes, Rachel realised afterwards, and then she started to clean the room, all the time expecting the girl to come back to claim her clothes, but nothing happened.

She couldn't leave them there. She touched her tongue to her lips and walked over to the bed, carefully unfolding each item and holding it up. There were sweaters of the finest wool she had ever seen, cashmere in fact—although it would be some years before she had enough knowledge to realise that detail—neatly round-necked and long-sleeved, and blouses in fine sheer cotton and soft wool. There were skirts, pleated like kilts, such as she had seen some of the female students wearing, and two fine wool dresses with small lace collars and neat waists.

It would be years before she realised that what she

had inherited was the wardrobe of a girl who in the eighties would be described as a Sloane Ranger. All Rachel did know was that the clothes were different from anything she herself had ever seen or touched.

They weren't fashionable, Bernadette would have turned her pert retroussée nose up at them and so would the other maids, but they had something that Rachel instinctively recognised. Her mouth dry, she slipped off her uniform and tried them on.

She was a little taller and slimmer than the girl who had originally owned them, but they were still a good fit. She looked at herself in the mirror and her heart swelled with delight and relief. These were the sort of clothes she wanted to wear for the rest of her life, she thought, touching the soft wool of the skirt. In them no one would laugh at her, or taunt her. These were the sort of clothes that the girl Tim eventually married would wear.

Tim married! He would never marry a girl like her—Rachel knew that instinctively. Despite the way he treated her she had sensed within him his contempt for those whom he considered his social inferiors. She couldn't delude herself. She was just someone who had caught his interest, like a new toy that he would eventually grow bored with.

As she looked at herself in the mirror she was gripped with a burning ambition to be the sort of girl who would wear these clothes by right . . . to speak with the same careless insouciance as the girl who had just left here . . . to be one of the elite, privileged band who floated through life without responsibilities or cares. But how could *she* be like that?

She took off her clothes and put on her uniform. What was the point of going home with Tim? Their relationship could not lead anywhere. She looked at the clothes and remembered how she had looked in them, and her chin tilted proudly, her eyes flashing storm signals at her reflection. Was she not descended from one of the proudest races on earth? Had her father not been the nephew of the Laird of the MacGregor clan himself?

For the first time in her life Rachel felt pride surge through her body. She *would* go with Tim. Perhaps their relationship was only to be fleeting and transitory, but while it lasted she would learn from it.

She opened her mouth and made an attempt to mimic the speech of the girl who had just left. Somehow it didn't sound right, but one day it would. One day she would have that patina of wealth and security . . . one day she would be the one to offhandedly throw away half her wardrobe, without so much as a backward glance. For now, she decided, she might as well look on her good fortune as a sign that she was meant to join Tim this weekend.

She didn't say anything to the others about her new wardrobe. Bernadette wouldn't have understood. Instead she took everything to the cleaners, and then went out and bought herself a new suitcase. She spent a long time choosing it. Nothing she saw in the chain stores she visited appealed to her. Nothing they had on sale looked quite like the suitcase she had seen on the hotel bed, and that was the kind of case she wanted.

When she did find one it wasn't on sale in any of the stores, but pushed to one side of the window of a second-hand clothes shop down one of Oxford's narrow side-streets.

Rachel went inside rather uncertainly. The air smelled fusty and was faintly oppressive, and she had a panicky urge to turn tail and flee. Before she could move a woman emerged from the back of the shop, rattling the cane curtain. She was one of the weirdest sights Rachel had ever seen. Her hair was hennaed bright red, and despite the fact that she must have been well over fifty, she was dressed in an assortment of layered skirts and shawls more suitable to a girl of eighteen. In her ears she had large hoop earrings, larger than any Rachel had ever seen the women of her tribe wearing. Thick dark kohl surrounded her eyes, and the rest of her face was chalk-white.

"Can I help you?"

For a moment Rachel was too startled by the woman's appearance to speak. The shop was full of rails of clothes, hats, shoes, and an assortment of general clutter that made it impossible for anyone to move more than half a dozen steps in any direction from the small counter.

"I . . . I . . . wanted to look at the suitcase in the window," she managed to get out at last.

The eyes within their kohl surround were shrewd and dark.

"The Vuitton? You have excellent taste. Wait a moment and I'll get it out."

It took considerably more than a moment for the woman to remove the case from the window and drag it to the rear of the shop. It was covered in dust which she swished away with one corner of her shawl, before inspecting the locks.

"You're lucky, this one isn't initialled—most of them are. I had a whole set of them—they were specially designed to fit in the boot of a Rolls; this is the last one left. Do you want to see inside it? It's lined in silk. Look . . ."

Rachel couldn't resist touching the silk. It felt soft . . . and more than that, sensuous almost beneath her fingertips. Her fingers, rough from her work behind the bar, snagged on the fine fabric.

"How . . . how much is it?" Her mouth had gone

dry. She wanted this case more than anything in her life. Somehow it had become a symbol of all that she wanted from life . . . a goal that she could aim for.

The woman pursed her lips and said shrewdly, "To you, ten quid."

Ten pounds. It was more than twice the price of the cases in the other shops. Ten pounds . . . It would take a considerable sum out of her savings.

"When it was new it would have cost more than ten times that much . . . if I held on to it I could probably get twenty quid for it . . ."

It was only sales talk, Rachel knew that. She knew all about the different ways of tempting a buyer's appetite; she had spent her formative years among the greatest exponents in the world of that particular art.

"I'll . . . I'll take it," she said breathlessly.

The woman smiled, and it seemed to Rachel that there was a gleam of understanding in her eyes.

"You won't regret it," she promised. "This case will still be going strong in fifty years' time. You've got good taste." She looked at Rachel rather thoughtfully. "I've got something else here you might like. Hang on a tick."

She disappeared into the back of the shop before Rachel could tell her that she neither wanted or needed anything else. She was gone about ten minutes, and when she came back she was carrying something wrapped in what looked like a white cotton shroud.

"I got these in the other day—a house clearance. Just feel this fabric!"

She was unwrapping the shroud and revealing to Rachel's astonished eyes two dresses. The first was in a soft shade somewhere between amber and peach, the fabric so finely pleated that Rachel couldn't imagine how it had been done. When she held the dress up in front of her, it was nothing more than a long narrow tube.

"Fortuny," the shopkeeper told her admiringly. "Now there was a designer! Feel it." Rachel touched the rich fabric. No one wore dresses like this one, and yet . . . and yet there was something about it that appealed to her.

"And this one."

It was a twenties-style flapper dress in rich satin, heavily beaded and cut on the bias in pale cream. Never in a thousand lifetimes would she have any occasion to wear dresses like these, but even Rachel recognised their quality, and knew instinctively that they represented a way of life that was way, way out of her reach. For that reason if no other she yearned for them. She touched them lovingly, her eyes full of dreams.

"You can have them both for ten quid," the woman told her. "There's no market for stuff like this round here. I ought to keep them . . . one day . . . but when that day comes, I'll probably be dead and gone. Buy them!" she urged, and as she dug into her purse for the money, Rachel knew she was buying far more than two old-fashioned gowns—she was buying a way of life, a dream . . . her dream . . .

She walked out of the shop in a daze, quickly followed by a sick feeling of dismay. She had just spent twenty pounds—money it had taken her months to save. She turned round. She would take the things back, explain that she couldn't afford them—but even as she turned, she saw the woman putting up a closed sign. It was too late. She had bought them. She couldn't let the other girls see them; they would laugh their heads off at her stupidity.

Miserably she dragged the case back to the dormitory and hid it under her bed, the two dresses still wrapped inside.

Tonight Tim would ask her for her answer to his invitation. She might as well go, she decided recklessly. After all, what had she to lose?

The day Tim's father came home from honeymoon with his new bride, the church bells rang out to greet the newly married couple. Since then the church bells of Marchington village church had been rung on four separate occasions—each time to celebrate the birth of another child to the Viscount and his wife, but never so proudly or so joyously as the day they were rung to celebrate the birth of the heir.

The road to Marchington led through the village and swept past the church in a triumphant arc before curling languorously and then revealing Marchington Place itself through a veil of trees, like a magician performing an especially favourite trick.

Rachel saw it first in autumn, rising breathtakingly through the late afternoon mists, cloaked in the full splendour of its trees, glowing rose red like a jewel set in a crown of green and gold.

Tim had picked her up outside the hotel just after lunch. His car was long and low, its hood up against the fine autumn drizzle. Inside, the smell of the cream leather seats engulfed her. She was aware of his faint start of surprise when he saw her. She was wearing the pleated skirt, and a demure blouse, with its collar neatly out over the round neck of the jumper she had on. She had bought some toning fine wool tights, and a pair of plain brogue type shoes. Her hair fell in a shining curtain to her shoulders, her face free of all make-up apart from a gloss of lipstick. She knew that outwardly she looked no different from those female students she had envied so deeply, and her smile as Tim handed her into his car had a new confidence.

Once or twice during the drive to Dorset, Tim glanced at her. She looked different today. She was dressed more like his sister than was appropriate to her true status in life. For the first time he wondered if she had lied to him; had pretended to be an orphan. Doubts trickled coldly through his mind, upsetting his carefully laid plans. The closer they got to Marchington, the greater his doubts became. The others weren't due down until tomorrow: he had planned it that way deliberately. His body twitched suddenly, and he ached for a joint. He had kept off drugs all week, knowing that he would need a clear mind to plan. Now, suddenly, he felt depressed and edgy. He wanted Simon—Simon, who never seemed to experience doubts or to deviate from a chosen course.

Rachel sensed that something was wrong, but Tim's silence did not encourage her to ask what.

And then miraculously they were there, with the full splendour of Marchington spread out before them. Awe gripped her by the throat, tears suddenly filming her eyes. At her side she heard Tim saying conversationally,

"We have a ghost, you know, so don't be alarmed if you hear footsteps during the night!"

She looked at him with apprehension, suddenly longing for the familiar security of the hotel dormitory.

The gates stood open and he drove through them with a flourish, beneath the eagles with outstretched wings, whose beaks supported the ribbon of stone carrying the family motto, "Through our own endeavours shall we survive." A very apt motto indeed, and one that successive generations of Wildings had followed to the letter.

The deserted, empty air given off by the house

disconcerted Rachel. Where was the family Tim had brought her here to meet? The three sisters he had spoken of with brotherly contempt, the parents and the grandfather who also lived here.

She looked at Tim questioningly.

"Mmm, doesn't look as though there's anyone about—odd!" He stopped the car and got out. "Never mind, they'll all turn up sooner or later. Let's go inside."

Uncertainly Rachel followed him. The double doors opened into a cavernous and rather dark hallway. Rachel paused on the threshold, glancing back towards the car.

"My luggage . . ." she began.

"Don't worry about it, one of the maids will bring it in later."

One of the maids! A girl like her . . . Rachel quelled her feeling of panic.

"Come on, I'll give you a tour of the place while we're waiting for the family to turn up."

Tim caught hold of her hand, dragging her through a succession of rooms, all huge and sparsely furnished, all giving off a cold musty scent of age and decay. Rachel sensed the excitement in him, and the tension, and put it down to the fact that he was as apprehensive about introducing her to his family as she was about meeting them.

They were in a narrow corridor, icily cold, with a stone-flagged floor. There was a door at the end of it, and as they approached it Rachel had an intense reluctance to go any further. She stopped dead, and Tim, who was still holding her hand, turned to frown at her.

"What's the matter? I'm only going to show you the family chapel. It's famous, you know." He opened the door, ignoring her shudder of apprehension. "The family priest was murdered right here in front of the altar," he told her carelessly, dragging her inside. "There's a stain on the floor that's supposed to be his blood, and it won't come out . . ."

Rachel couldn't move. Her whole body was held fast in the grip of an intensely primitive fear. She couldn't have explained what she was feeling to anyone; she only knew that to walk into that small, essentially simple room with its altar and cross, and its stained glass window depicting Christ's suffering on the Cross, was to come in contact with something so evil and dangerous that her whole life would be contaminated by it.

Many, many times she had heard her grandmother talk about the "sight", and only once had she come anywhere near experiencing it, but now as she looked towards the altar it seemed to alter subtly, a grey mist darkening the room and obliterating the sunlight outside. Round the altar she could see dark formless shapes . . . men in robes. On the altar lay a body . . . a woman's body . . .

A deep shudder of panic and horror engulfed her, her body convulsing on a bitingly sharp pain. She felt the coldness of death, as she had felt it once before when her grandmother died. Instinctively she started to back away, not daring to take her eyes away from the altar, not daring to turn her back and run as she longed to do, in case to do so was to make that macabre and frightening mental vision she had had become real.

Tim, who had released her hand to walk further towards the altar, turned to look at her.

"What is it?" He was frowning . . . angrily almost, Rachel could see, but nothing, no power on earth, could make her go into that room. It was evil, the very air was rank and sour with it. She made the gypsy gesture to ward off evil spirits and stepped back into the narrow passageway.

"Rachel . . ."

"No . . . no! I can't go in there!"

Tim was fascinated, his original annoyance with her fading as he looked into her eyes. She had sensed something . . . seen something, maybe. God, she was going to be so perfect for his purpose . . . so very, very perfect. He could feel the power growing in him already. Almost dizzy with the strength of it, he laughed softly.

"Silly girl, there's nothing to be afraid of!"

There was a gloating, almost triumphant note in his voice, as though he found something intensely pleasurable in her fear.

She shouldn't have come here, Rachel acknowledged. She wanted to leave. There was something dangerous and alien here . . . something she didn't understand but knew instinctively threatened her. There was a smell of corruption and evil about this place . . . and about Tim, she realised. She looked at him, and it was as though she was seeing him properly for the first time.

He was weak, and dangerous, and he had brought her here for some purpose that she didn't understand but that she instinctively knew to be threatening. She had to leave . . . she had to get away. A fear like nothing else she had ever known in her life engulfed her; an awareness of evil and danger that obliterated everything else.

All the way back down the narrow passage she felt as though she would choke from lack of air, and when they finally emerged into an inner hallway with several doorways off it, she found that despite the intense feeling of cold inside her, her skin was bathed in perspiration.

From outside she heard the sound of a car. Tim frowned and went over to a window. The others were early. They weren't due until tomorrow. What were they doing here now?

As he looked out into the courtyard and realised that the car was his grandfather's Daimler, a feeling of helpless rage overcame him. What was the old man doing here? He was supposed to be in Scotland. Tim's hands clenched, his nails digging into the palms of his hands.

Lord Marchington had never been deceived by his grandson's good looks and facile charm. Long ago, as a little boy, he had once happened to come across an old woman wandering round the Elizabethan knot garden. She had been talking to herself as little Adam approached her to find out who she was and what she was doing in his mother's private garden. He had been aware of such a feeling of power and evil emanating from her that he had instinctively shrunk back. She had come towards him, so very fast and agile for such an old woman that she had taken him off guard, and even though he had been tall and strong for a boy of six it had taken the combined strength of her nurse and his governess to get the old woman's death-grip from round his neck.

Later his father had explained gently to him that the old lady was *his* elder sister and that until his birth she had expected that one day her son would inherit the title and lands. She was her father's only child and there were no other male relatives who would inherit the title. She had been twenty and a young wife and mother when, against all odds, her parents had at last produced a son and heir. When her husband realised that their son would not after all inherit the title, he had left her. The shock had turned her brain, so Adam's father told him, and it was several years before he realised that it was not so much the shock of losing her husband that had brought on her madness but her vicious hatred of the brother who had supplanted her.

Sometimes when he looked into his grandson's eyes Lord Marchington saw within them the same look of hatred and envy he had seen in the old woman's. A little insanity was not an uncommon thing among titled families where cousin had married cousin for generation after generation, but madness and the desire to kill . . . these were not charming eccentricities of the very rich, these were dangerous, inexcusable traits.

And not for the first time Lord Marchington worried about his grandson; his eventual heir.

This latest telephone call from an old friend at Oxford, warning him that Tim was known to be involved in drugs, was what had brought him back from Scotland. Until his chauffeur drove past Tim's stationary car he had no idea that his grandson would be home for the weekend, and he frowned a little, his concern increasing.

"What is it?" asked Rachel, watching the shadows close in on Tim's face.

"My grandfather's arrived."

He said it flatly, quietly, and yet Rachel was still intensely aware of the hatred running through him.

"Come on," he told her abruptly. "We're going back to Oxford."

And in that moment she knew that whatever it was he had brought her to Marchington for it was not to meet his family. Once again she felt that same chill that had invaded her in the chapel, saw in her mind's eye that white body on the altar, felt the presence of death.

Lord Marchington was surprised to see the girl with Tim. He never brought his lovers, of either sex, to

Marchington with him. The Earl was no fool . . . He was well aware of his grandson's sexual proclivities . . . but as long as one day he married and produced a son and heir, they did not concern him; but that Tim might bring the Marchington name into disrepute through his excesses did.

He listened grimly as Tim announced that they were just about to leave. He could not take him to task in front of this shy, almost fey little girl. He had not even expected to find his grandson at Marchington, but instead had anticipated having to go to Oxford to talk to him there.

What he had to say to his grandson could wait— another few hours at least. He bade Rachel a courteous goodbye and smiled at her, but Tim was not deceived.

Running side by side with his hatred of his grandfather, interwoven with it, was an even deeper vein of fear and resentment. A superb athlete in his time, a war hero, a man of great wit and charm, his grandfather was everything that Tim knew he could never be. But one day he would die . . . and one day he would be the Earl, and there was nothing his grandfather could do about it, and therein lay his own power, his own strength, and if it had not been for his grandfather appearing, interfering, this weekend, that power would have been intensified tenfold. They could not hold the Black Mass at Marchington now, and it was too late to make alternative arrangements.

All the way back to Oxford, Tim fed his growing sense of bitter hatred. Sitting silently at his side, Rachel knew that their relationship was over. Today she had sensed something in him that frightened her too much to allow her to see him again.

Tim dropped her off outside the hotel, unceremoniously. His greatest need now was to find Simon to tell him what had happened and to cancel their arrangements, to be buoyed up again by Simon's strength.

Rachel was forgotten, obliterated by the greater need. How he hated his grandfather! But he would not always be the one in a position of servitude. One day . . . one day . . . Inside him his hatred raged like a caged beast, demanding release.

CHAPTER EIGHT

TIM FOUND Simon just about to leave their rooms, and explained what had happened in a burst of angry, staccato speech. Simon had an appointment outside the town, so he suggested that Tim came along with him.

Simon knew all about Tim's hatred of his grandfather. He made it his business to be a sympathetic listener . . . for despite all that Tim had said Simon was determined that one day he and Tim would be brothers-in-law.

Tim could be very indiscreet when he was angry, the way he was now . . . very indiscreet. Tim's sister adored him and would do anything for him. If pressure could be brought to bear on Tim—and he would see that it was—all these thoughts and many more were in Simon's mind as he listened to Tim's rantings. Rachel's name spewed out alongside that of his grandfather, her ridiculous refusal to enter the chapel somehow becoming part of Tim's general vicious torrent of verbal hatred.

Simon was glad in a way; he had never liked Tim's suggestion that they held their Mass at Marchington, but he agreed with him that Rachel must be punished.

"She has to be sacrificed," Tim told him wildly, turning round and grabbing hold of his jacket lapels. By this time they were crossing a narrow bridge spanning the river, the current eddying forcefully round its stone supports. "It has to be, Simon . . . that's the only way I can get the power!" Rage was making

Tim's speech lunatic. Simon listened in growing shock and unease . . . he didn't like all this talk of sacrifice and spilling blood, but the moment he tried to remonstrate with Tim, Tim's speech became even more violent, his fingers white and rigid where they clutched hold of him.

"Come on, Tim . . ." Simon tried to release his grip on his jacket, dreading someone walking past and overhearing what was going on. He was physically stronger than Tim, and the only way he could release himself was to push Tim backwards against the low parapet of the bridge.

He heard the coping stone fall, and then as though it was happening in slow motion he saw Tim fall, striking his head against the stone support of the bridge as he hit the water.

He knew before he dived in that Tim was dead, the sickening sound of his head crushing against the stone had told him that, but still he dragged him out, torn between guilt and shock. He heard someone call out as he knelt over Tim's body.

Another student, someone he didn't recognise, came running up.

"He fell . . . he fell off the bridge," Simon told him.

They were the words he repeated until they were burned into his brain . . . to the police, to Tim's distraught family, to the Dean of the College . . . so many times that he actually believed them himself, and as his belief in his own innocence grew, so did his hatred against the person he thought of as the cause of Tim's death and the destroyer of all his plans for his own future. Rachel—she was the one to blame. It was as though at the moment of death Tim's madness had passed on to him and become his own.

Tim's death was recorded as "accidental", but Simon knew that it wasn't. Rachel had killed him, and she must be punished. But he couldn't punish her alone. He would need help. He remembered how Tim had raved about her being the perfect sacrifice . . . a virgin . . . and a plan grew in his mind.

But first he would need to choose his accomplices. His mind raced. The two new acolytes . . . Yes. Yes . . .

They both refused, and went on refusing until Simon pointed out to them how easy it would be for him to arrange for them to be sent down. And after all, what was he really asking for? Nothing really . . . only that they kidnap the girl and bring her to his room, that was all.

They had no other options . . . they had to agree. Richard Howell thought about the position his uncle had promised him and knew he had no choice. Alex Barnett remembered the sacrifices his parents had made for him, the hopes they had for him, and gave his reluctant agreement.

Simon arranged it for the evening of Tim's funeral— his own private farewell to him.

Rachel had heard about Tim's death, and following her initial shock had come a certain inescapable knowledge that it had been inevitable. She didn't know why she should feel like that . . . it was the same sort of inner knowledge she had had in the chapel at Marchington, something beyond logic and reason.

The shock of the evil she had sensed in the chapel, and which she had known instinctively emanated from Tim himself, had killed her burgeoning feelings for him, but it hadn't killed the desire, born at the same time as her knowledge that she could never be the sort of girl Tim would take home to his parents as his future wife, that somehow she would have to find a

way to have all the things that life had so far denied
her. Respect, wealth, status, education; she would
have all of them . . . all of them and more.

Tim's death, not surprisingly, made the headlines in
some of the national newspapers; there was talk around
the colleges of a severe clamp-down on the smoking
of pot and what the authorities considered to be the
general licentiousness of the undergraduate body.

The funeral was well attended. Simon stood at the
back of Marchington's village church, a sombre figure
clad in black. Once or twice Deborah Wilding turned
her head to look at him. She knew that he had been
Tim's best friend, but there was something about him
that frightened her. She had the inescapable feeling
that somehow he was responsible for her brother's
death. It was an instinctive, alarming feeling, and one
that she had not dared to communicate to anyone
else.

She knew that her mother liked him and that her
younger sisters, still at the giggly, adolescent stage,
thought him sexy, but she always felt uncomfortable
in his presence. He was like the light to which heedless
moths were drawn to die in its fierce heat. Tim had
followed him blindly in all that he said and did. He
had almost worshipped him, and sometimes Deborah
had worried that their relationship held such blatantly
sexual undertones. She had longed to be able to
discuss her fears with someone, but she had no close
friends of her own age; her father was too remote,
and her mother too naïve. She looked back over her
shoulder again and was chilled by more than the cold
of the chapel. Was she really the only person to see
the evil in that bland good-looking face?

She had loved her brother, but she had not been
blind to his faults. Tim had been heedless and hedon-
istic. He had been spoiled by them all, and now his

golden precious youth was gone and he was dead, and
she was sure . . . so sure, that the man standing at
the back of the church, claiming to be his best friend
and wearing his grief like a sombre cloak, was
somehow responsible for his death.

Rachel didn't go to the funeral. How could she have
done? She remembered the stern and proud face of
the old man getting out of his car, though, and
mourned for Lord Marchington even though she could
not mourn for Tim himself.

That sudden awareness of evil that had struck her
in the chapel had brought home to her the reality of
her roots. She felt as though she had walked unknowingly deep into the shadows of intense danger, and
she knew that it was her gypsy heritage that had
recognised that evil.

Tim, so beautiful and perfect externally, had been
rotten and corrupt inside. Rachel didn't know how
she knew this; it was just a knowledge that was as
much a part of her as her knowledge of her own name
and background.

For a while he had bewitched her in a way that evil
does bewitch, but now she was free of his spell.

She was not free of danger, though. She sensed it
all around her, pressing in on her almost suffocatingly.
And that worried her. It shouldn't be there. Tim was
gone. But her own sense of danger hadn't. For some
reason it was still there, hovering, waiting for her, all
the more frightening because she did not know from
where it came.

Simon had laid his plans carefully. The desire for
revenge burned deeply in him, supplanting his guilt in
a crazy inversion of reality, transmuting what had

really happened into what he wanted to believe had happened.

This facility to deceive himself so completely had begun long ago in his childhood, its roots so darkly enmeshed with his own deep-rooted fears that they were lost to him. He couldn't see that what he was doing was a frantic attempt to escape from the truth, from his own guilt, from a need to make someone other than himself responsible for Tim's death.

He had lost his closest friend, his most prized acolyte, the one person he could rely on to do his bidding no matter what. He had enjoyed his power over Tim. It had sustained and nourished him, and now it had gone. And that gypsy whore was to blame.

Simon had never shared Tim's belief that it was possible to raise the Devil, but now somehow it was as though, in dying, Tim had communicated part of that belief to him. Simon couldn't know that these bouts of megalomania were a psychological illness brought on by the horrors of his childhood, and if anyone had tried to tell him so he would have laughed at them. His belief in his own power, in his destiny of greatness, was all-consuming.

Rachel had got in his way. She had destroyed one of the tools he had intended to use to achieve his destiny, and for that she must be punished. It wasn't he who was responsible for Tim's fall and subsequent death, it was her . . . the gypsy whore . . . and she must be punished for it.

He hadn't eaten since Tim's death, having discovered during puberty that fasting in some magical way clarified and intensified the workings of his mind. Sometimes he didn't eat for days at a time, occasionally hallucinating and enduring horrible nightmares when his father manifested himself and came to him. He started to shake, and then controlled himself, concentrating instead on a mental image of Tim. Almost he believed that he could hear Tim crying out to him for vengeance. In his own mind his plans had taken on the cloak of a holy war of righteousness; it was as though some higher power had appointed him as Tim's avenger. Muddled images swirled in and out of his mind. If he closed his eyes he could see Tim crying out to him for vengeance, his dead eyes suddenly magically alive; he could hear him reminding him of the power that would one day be theirs; a power they would have shared in secret. And now Tim was gone, and Simon feared that his death might in some way diminish that power.

It was as though in exercising his ability to punish Rachel he was re-establishing that power, laying claim to it in the same way that King Arthur had laid claim to Excalibur. Reality blurred and became indistinct, and as always when he entered and elevated the state brought on by fasting, Simon tasted and succumbed to the heady wine of his own ego.

He had planned it all carefully. It hadn't been difficult to find out what time the girl finished work in the evenings. Simon had learned how to collate and use information during his days at Eton, and the simpering receptionist behind the hotel desk had been only too easy to persuade. He had made the excuse that he wanted the information for a friend.

As luck would have it, the evening of Tim's funeral was the night that Miles French went to a monthly meeting of one of his societies so that he would be safely out of the way; another sign that fate blessed his plans. Simon hadn't any real fears that Rachel would do anything like report him. Girls of her class didn't.

As always when he thought about Rachel hatred spewed up hotly inside him. If he had ever felt any

emotion for another human being that human being
had been Tim. And now Tim was gone, destroyed by
that milk-faced bitch. The anger that had always been
there within Simon against her sex boiled up fero-
ciously, pushing at his self-control. He had always
hated the female sex . . . it was weak and destructive
and deserved to be punished. His fingertips tingled
and he felt an enormous surge of power and euphoria.
It blanked out reality completely; a sickness that
would manifest itself over and over again throughout
his life, turning him from a logical, charismatic man
into something approaching a dangerous psychopath.

"I don't think we should be doing this," Alex confided
unhappily to Richard, as they waited for Rachel to
emerge from the pub.

"We don't have any choice," Richard reminded him
harshly, and Alex fell silent, acknowledging the truth
of his words. He was uncomfortable with what they
had been told to do; it went against everything he had
been brought up to believe in. Man cherished and
protected woman; that was the way his own parents
behaved, and it was the way he firmly believed to be
right, and now here he was waiting to abduct a young
woman and turn her over to . . .

"Stop worrying," Richard told him abruptly. "It'll
be easy. We'll just walk up behind her. I'll gag her,
and you tie her hands. We'll take her to the car and
then drive her over to Herries' rooms and leave her
there."

"What do you suppose he means to do with her?"

Alex couldn't help asking the naïve question. It was
beginning to haunt him. Simon had told them that
the girl in question had been leading both himself and
Tim on for weeks. He said he wanted to teach her a
lesson, not just for himself but for Tim as well, but

whichever way he looked at it Alex came up with the same unacceptable word—rape.

He said as much to Simon only last night and had then shivered, watching the other man's face harden dangerously. "It isn't rape when she's been asking for it the way she has . . ."

Alex hadn't wanted to be dragged into the affair, but he hadn't been able to back out.

The Hell Fire Club had disbanded amidst panic and fear following upon Tim's death; its members might think they could destroy his memory along with their robes, but they would find out that they were wrong, Simon reflected. Both Alex and Richard knew how much they were in his power.

Richard, less squeamish than Alex, hadn't liked what he was being told to do either, but he was worldly enough to know that Simon was quite capable of carrying out his threats, so he had given in. He had too much to lose now, and especially over a girl he didn't even know. One sighting of that damning photograph of himself, naked, dancing round a grave-yard illuminated by black wax candles, would be enough to destroy any chance he had of getting into the bank; he wasn't going to risk everything he had planned for the sake of some stupid little bitch who had the idiocy to get on Simon's wrong side.

Rachel was slightly late leaving the pub. She had refused to allow the landlady to send the nephew who was staying with them with her as an escort back to the hotel and stepped out confidently into the dark alley behind the back door.

She had no awareness of anyone behind her, no sixth sense to warn her before she felt the hand clamp across her mouth, and then the rough arms grabbing her like a vice. She tried to scream, but her throat muscles were paralysed, as a strip of sticking plaster was stuck across her mouth, her flaying hands held and tied behind her back.

Instinctively she knew that what was happening to her had something to do with Tim, but Tim was dead . . . She shuddered deeply, the superstitions of her Celtic and gypsy forebears stirring strongly within her. She tried to kick out, but she was lifted and imprisoned between two hard bodies. The car that Richard had hired was parked at the end of the alleyway and they bundled her into it, Alex sitting in the back with her, to prevent her from trying to escape.

Richard drove back to Simon's rooms, taking a long and circuitous route as Simon had instructed.

Beneath the terror that had engulfed her from the moment of her attack Rachel's natural strength reasserted itself. She was being taken somewhere and for some purpose; and she knew that purpose had something to do with Tim. Tim was dead . . . but the dead could reach out from beyond the grave. She thought of her own grandmother and clung hard to the memory of her goodness and power, trying to remember the incantations she had taught her as a child to ward off evil.

There was no evil in this car, rather a sense of fear that did not come from her alone, but evil waited for her.

The car stopped and she was bundled out, carried up some stairs, strong hands resisting her attempts to break free.

Simon had seen them arrive. He opened the door to his rooms in silence, indicating the bed which had been stripped down to its white undersheet. It was Miles's bed, not his own. He watched as Richard and Alex put Rachel down on the bed, then motioned for them to go, quickly locking the door behind them.

Beneath his robe he was naked, his body throbbing with a savage need to punish and denigrate this woman who had been responsible for the destruction of the one human being he loved. Tim dead was no use to him. No, he had wanted—had needed Tim to stay alive. He stared down at her, the coldness of his eyes boring into the fear of hers, his lips curled back from his teeth in a feral snarl.

Rachel knew immediately that he did not mean to kill her, even though she couldn't have said how she had come by the knowledge. She also knew that what he intended to do to her would be far, far worse. After all, execution could be carried out only once. She thought of her mother and wondered despairingly what it was about the women of her family that attracted all that was most vile in mankind.

"You're frightened, aren't you, you little bitch? So you should be, you . . . Do you know why you're here?"

Instinctively Rachel shook her head, sensing his need to talk, praying that a miracle would occur and she would be rescued.

"You're here to atone for a man's death, that's why. It was you, you little bitch, who killed him. You . . . casting your spell on him . . ."

Tim! He was talking about Tim! He had to be.

"He planned to sacrifice you to the Devil, did you know that?"

Shock turned Rachel's blood to ice. She heard Simon laugh.

"He thought he could raise Lucifer. All he needed was a virgin sacrifice. He had it all planned."

The chapel at Marchington . . . the sense of evil . . . Tim's fury when his grandfather arrived. Yes, she could understand it all now, and more. This man had been Tim's lover. She didn't know how she knew, she just did. She also knew that he had killed him. A vision flashed in front of her—two men struggling on a bridge, one of them falling . . .

"You did it . . . you killed Tim!"

"No!" Simon hit her hard, on the side of her head, almost stunning her. He reached out and she saw the knife blade flash in his hand. He grabbed hold of the top of the plain dress top she was wearing and slashed through it. The knife point touched her skin, raising a bright red weal.

A red mist danced in front of Simon's eyes. He was doing this for Tim, not for himself, but there was something about this pale, white girl . . . something about her fear, that was a thousand times more satisfactory than any other sexual encounter he had had with her sex.

He slashed through the waistband of her jeans in a frenzy of excitement, tearing her clothes from her body like a hyena stripping the flesh from one of its victims. Reality faded, the words of his own father thundering in his ears until he was repeating them in a thick hoarse chant.

"You've got to be punished . . . I have to do it . . . I've got to punish you."

He entered her awkwardly and roughly, and Rachel thought she would never survive the pain. Her body was tense with fear and rejection, the mere sight of his erection alone enough to fill her with fear. He thrust into her, breaking the delicate membrane of her virginity, his body powered by a lust to inflict pain that had its roots deep in the traumas of his own childhood. She felt his semen spurt hotly inside her, and the pain of his rough withdrawal from her was almost as great as the entry had been.

He was still erect, his body still charged with the pulsing force of his hatred. Her arms, still tied behind her, ached appallingly, her head was swimming, her body bruised and defiled in a way she would remember for the rest of her life, but deep inside her anger grew alongside her fear. She would remember this man, this night, and one day he would pay a thousandfold for what he had done to her . . . They would all pay, she thought hazily, remembering the two who had brought her here.

Simon got up and for a moment she thought it was over, and then with a cold rush of fear she realised it wasn't. He rolled her over, panting slightly.

"That was for Tim . . . for what you did to him, and just so that you'll never forget him . . ."

The scream flooded deep inside her as she felt the knife against the flesh of her right buttock, a vertical slash into her tender skin and then a horizontal one. T . . . T . . . for Tim. T . . . for terror.

"And that was for me . . . in memory of the man you destroyed!"

Rachel felt the sickness and pain rush from her stomach to her throat, and while she endured his degradation of her body and knew that it would live within her for the rest of her life, she promised herself that there would be retribution, and a retribution so terrible that he would long, as she now longed, to die rather than face another sunrise.

Before he left Simon ripped the plaster from across her mouth, making her eyes sting with tears, and proffered her a glass of some colourless unscented liquid. When she refused it he slapped her and said savagely, "Drink it, you little fool. It's only a couple of sleeping tablets."

Rachel didn't want to drink, but he held her nose and poured the vile mixture down her throat so that she was forced to swallow.

He watched her until she started to fall asleep, then

quickly went to work, picking up his clothes. They
would have to be burned. He looked at his watch. At
least half an hour before Miles was due back. Good,
he would be long gone by then. Simon tried to picture
his room-mate's face when he discovered what was
lying in his bed.

French might even be stupid enough to think the
bitch was lying there waiting for him . . . Well, he
would soon find out his mistake if he tried to make
love to her! Simon looked down at the pale colourless
face with its halo of dark red hair. He had done it—
he had avenged Tim's death. The madness of his lust
was gone, leaving him feeling calm and refreshed.

He would need an alibi for tonight, just in case the
girl was foolish enough to talk, but he doubted she
would. Girls of that class . . . little nobodies, with no
money or family behind them . . . if she told anyone
her tale, who would believe her?

He was smiling the calm peaceful smile of an angel
when he let himself out of the room and locked the
door behind him. The last thing he had done was to
cut through the rope binding Rachel's hands. It had
rubbed her skin raw.

Miles was later leaving the meeting than he had
planned. He had got involved in a heated debate,
which he had won, but underlying his satisfaction at
having made his point was an irritating sense of
unease.

Simon Herries was up to something. He sensed it,
smelled it in the air almost, if that wasn't too fanciful
a thought.

Tim's death hadn't surprised him; somehow he had
always been half expecting it, although in a rather
more spectacular manner than a simple fall from a
bridge—if Tim had fallen. He·had seen the way Tim

had taunted and manipulated people, and had often wondered how long it would be before one of his victims retaliated. What did surprise him was that Simon Herries had been the one to be with Tim when he died. As far as he could see, and his perception was very good indeed, Tim was far more valuable to Simon Herries alive than dead. Tim was Simon's tool . . . without him Herries would be dangerously vulnerable. And Herries would not like being vulnerable.

As any budding lawyer must be, Miles was something of a student of human nature. In observing the interplay between Simon and Tim he saw much that neither of them would have wanted him to see. He knew, of course, that in part their relationship was sexual, but he also knew that it was far more complex than that. He recognised and acknowledged the aura of power and danger that both of them gave off, Simon more strongly than Tim. Simon was a man who was driven by a relentless ambition to dominate everyone around him, while Tim preferred to toy with others like a cat with a mouse. Now Tim was dead, not killed by one of his enraged lovers as Miles might have expected, but dead from a drug-induced fall, his death witnessed by the one person Miles was convinced would have sold his soul to keep him alive. And yet something told him that there was far more to Tim's death than a simple accident, far, far more. There was something . . . something dark and dangerous, something almost evil . . . but he couldn't put his finger on it, and the logic that had been his training for so many years dismissed his thoughts as fanciful.

Taking the stairs to his rooms two at a time, he dug into his pocket for his key.

The study the three of them had shared was in darkness and he was tired enough to make his way straight to his own bedroom. An odd, unfamiliar scent hung on the air. It wasn't drugs. It wasn't even sex, but it was something that made the skin on his scalp tighten with tension.

It was fear, he recognised in surprise, fear and . . . and blood? He reached for the light and flicked it on, staying in the doorway, his eyes searching the room, noting its heavy stillness, and then fastening on the untidy disorder of his bed, and the naked girl sprawled across the white sheet.

Miles walked over to her, light-footed as a cat, recognising her instantly. Tim's girl . . . the little redhead. Little fool, what was she doing here? Surely she hadn't been stupid enough to get herself involved with Simon; to go from Tim's bed to his?

Nothing that happened at Oxford could shock Miles any more. It was a time of complete sexual freedom and uninhibitedness, when the only thing that caused any raised eyebrows was a refusal to throw oneself into the hectic sexual climate of the times.

He reached down and shook the inert body gently. Whatever her reason for being in his bed, he wanted her out of it. He noted in detached amusement that her body was particularly good . . . good enough in fact to make him suddenly achingly aware of how long it had been since he had had a woman—but he wasn't going to get involved with this particular woman.

"Very delectable," he said out loud in a bored voice. "But I'm afraid I'd like my bed to myself tonight, if you don't mind." He had no idea what she was doing in his bed rather than Simon's but presumed it was one of the latter's malicious jokes.

When she didn't wake he took hold of the edge of the sheet and yanked it tight, ready to tip her uncere-moniously on to the floor, only as she started to roll to the end of the bed he saw the blood on the sheet and the initial carved deep into the flesh of her small bottom, and he knew that whatever had happened in this room in his absence, it hadn't been anything as innocent as a practical joke—at least not as far as this small delicate-looking girl was concerned.

With fresh eyes he studied her naked body, and saw the rope burns on her wrists. He saw the glass, picked it up, and dipped his finger into the residue of fluid in the bottom. Had she been drugged before or after Herries had abused her? he wondered. Knowing his room-mate as he did, he was pretty sure it had been after. Now he understood the reason for the smell of fear infesting the room, and he also thought he understood why Simon had left her for him to find.

By the looks of it she had been a virgin. He touched the cuts on her buttock that were still seeping blood and gave a faint sigh.

Even if he knew where she lived he could hardly wake her up and turf her out in this state, but he was tired and wanted to go to bed. There was a bolt on the inside of the door. He looked at it steadily for a moment and then made up his mind.

Somehow he doubted that Herries would come back to their rooms tonight. In the meantime . . .

Miles had done enough work on farms not to feel offended by bruised and broken flesh, but a woman wasn't an animal, even if she had been abused like one. His mouth tightened perceptibly as he realised just how much Simon had abused the girl, and he wondered detachedly if she would ever recover enough to have a normal sex life after what she had endured . . . All the time he was cleaning her up she didn't move. He put her into one of his own shirts, fastening all the buttons and rolling back the cuffs, then he lifted her out of his bed and stripped off the soiled linen.

Despite his tiredness he didn't sleep much. He knew exactly the moment she woke up just before dawn, and got out of the chair he had slept in immediately to go over to her.

For Rachel to open her eyes and find another man standing over her staring at her was almost as terrifying as what had gone before.

She screamed as she scrambled off the bed and made for the door. It was bolted, and she heard Miles coming after her as she tugged the bolt free. Sheer panic lent her speed; panic and fear and the certain knowledge that she would die rather than endure another pair of male hands on her body.

Miles let her go. To go after her would only add to her fear. He recollected the terror he had seen in her eyes and involuntarily his hands curled into fists. He was not a violent man, but no one could have cleansed that fragile, delicate body without being sickened and disgusted by what had been done to it. He wasn't a naïve man, he knew that there were both men and women who found violence and pain sexually stimulating—and that was their affair, unless and until they began to inflict that pain and degradation on others who did not share their tastes. When *he* made love with a woman he liked her to share his pleasure, he liked to make her cry out with joy and fulfilment.

Only Bernadette knew that Rachel had been missing for most of the night, and like the good friend she was she had covered for her.

Rachel spent two full days in bed, shivering under the bedclothes, suffering from what the housekeeper thought was a bad attack of the "monthly curse". Because Rachel was such a good and willing worker she didn't reprimand her.

For two days Rachel thought of nothing other than how she might exact revenge for the crime committed against her. There was no point in going to the authorities, her gypsy upbringing had taught her that. How could a girl without connections or family, poor and ill educated, ever inflict vengeance for what had been done to her? She would find a way . . . She would *make* a way.

Simon returned to Oxford three days later. The shock of Tim's death had been too much for him and he had to get away, he told those who enquired. He had also taken the precaution of putting all his files in a bank safety box . . . In them were his records on all the other members of the coven. But safety deposit boxes have keys, and keys can be lost and found, stolen and forged.

Miles was waiting for him. He had known that eventually Simon must come back, if only to get his degree. He had never been a man of violence, had never thought he had it in him; but he beat Simon up so hard that afterwards he couldn't even crawl to his bed, but simply lay whimpering on the floor with tears pouring down his face.

"Now you know what it feels like to be hurt and vulnerable," Miles told him emotionlessly.

He had already made arrangements to move into other rooms. Perhaps he should have made an effort to seek out the girl and make sure she was all right, but he had been so sickened by the whole incident that all he wanted to do was forget it.

Rachel wanted to forget it as well, but she couldn't . . . The memory burned in her, causing her to be constantly sick and nauseous. It was over a month before she realised the truth. She was pregnant . . . she was carrying her attacker's child.

If she could have torn it from her body with her own hands she would have done so.

It was Bernadette who guessed first, approaching her quietly and worriedly to put her suspicions to the test.

"There's a woman that the girls go to who can get rid of it for you if that's what you want," she told her, "but you'll have to pay her."

An abortion! Rachel's grandmother had performed them occasionally. They could be dangerous, even with the most skilled of herbalists. Ergot, the fungus on the rye used to bring on the child early, could cause madness and death. But she didn't want the child. How could she?

She went to see the woman Bernadette had told her about. She was taken upstairs to a cold clinical-looking bedroom with a narrow bed, a sink and not much else.

"Umm . . . well, I'd say you were about six weeks on," the woman told her when she had finished her examination. Rachel had been tense throughout it, hating the intrusion into her body and its reminders of how this unwanted child had been conceived. "Twelve weeks exactly you'll have to be before I can do anything . . . That's the best time. A hundred pounds it'll cost . . . you'll have to bring your own soap—and a bucket. That way it means there's no chance of any infection, and no suspicion on me."

She saw Rachel's face and grimaced irritably.

"Gawd, you don't even begin to know what it's about, do you, lovey? What happened? Some young spark sweep you off your feet? And in these days! Why wasn't you on the pill? Well, it's done now, and if I was you I'd ask your young man for the money. A pretty girl like you . . . he'll be able to afford it. If he proves bothersome, tell him you'll go to the authorities. I'll bet he's a student, isn't he? Think they can get away with it, they do . . ."

"The soap," Rachel said, intervening huskily.

"A pound bar—good strong household stuff. We boil it up with plenty of hot water and then— well . . ." The woman looked at Rachel's pale set face and said wryly, "There's nothing to worry about. I don't go around ruining my ladies' insides, not like some I could name. After you've been here, you go home . . . twelve hours later it'll all be over. Just like having an especially heavy period, that's all it'll be."

Rachel stumbled from the room sick with cramping fear. Where was she to get a hundred pounds? Get it from your young man, the woman had told her. If only she knew!

No, she would never get a hundred pounds. That left only one way . . . Rachel felt her skin grow clammy with fright and nerves as she tried to remember what her grandmother had told her about the diseased seeds of the rye grasses which used properly could cause a woman's womb to contract and expel its foetus and which used incorrectly could cause the most agonising stomach cramps, and then gangrene, followed by death.

She knew what was needed, but how much . . . how often and when?

She walked far beyond the town and into the countryside, and kept on walking until the road shimmered dully in front of her and walking was simply a reflex action that kept her from thinking.

The woman saw her first, as her husband drew round the corner. She called out to him, and he braked immediately, but too late to stop the car bumper from catching Rachel. She fell awkwardly, tumbling on to the grass verge. The man cut the car's engine and they both got out, racing over to the unconscious figure.

"She's alive! We'd better get her to a hospital, though."

CHAPTER NINE

RACHEL woke up in a small sunny bedroom that was totally unfamiliar to her, and with no memory of how she had got there.

The door opened, and she stared at the woman standing there. She was small, plain and pin-neat, and her eyes were warm and very compassionate, Rachel noticed.

"Hello. How are you feeling?"

"I . . . What am I doing here . . .?" Rachel frowned as she tried to remember the woman's face, and then began to panic when she couldn't.

"It's all right." A gentle hand covered the restless movement of her own. "I'm Mary Simms. There was an accident—our car knocked you over. We took you to hospital and you've been heavily sedated ever since. Your friend at the hotel told us that you had no family of your own, so we brought you back here." For a moment the woman looked uncertain. "If you don't want to stay . . ."

Not want to stay! Rachel looked at her surroundings, felt the warmth and caring that came not just from the room but from the woman herself, and for the first time since her grandmother's death experienced an emotion she could only describe to herself as a feeling of no longer being totally alone.

And then she remembered why she had been walking down that empty lane and her hand went instinctively to her flat stomach. She saw pain flash in the older woman's eyes and wondered at it.

"No, you haven't lost your baby."

Rachel turned her head away.

"I wish I had!" She said it fiercely, bitterly, consumed with hatred for the life still growing inside her.

"Bernadette told us that your . . . your boyfriend had died in an accident. Have you . . . have you told his family you're carrying his child?"

It took Rachel several seconds to understand what she was being told, and when she did she looked at the woman and said bitterly,

"It isn't Tim's child. I was . . ." She swallowed back the venom threatening to choke her and spat out viciously, "It isn't anyone's child. I hate it!"

She felt Mary Simms flinch and looked curiously at her.

"You'll feel differently once he or she is born."

Rachel shook her head.

She wouldn't. She couldn't ever love the life that had been left within her in such violence and degradation. To her horror she felt tears gathering in her eyes and rolling down her face.

Mrs Simms made a sound of distress and remorse.

"There now, I've upset you! Let me go and get you something to eat and then you can rest. The doctor says you mustn't get up for another couple of days."

"Why . . . because I might lose the baby?"

Already, instinctively Rachel knew that in some way her child was important to this woman, more important than her, and she was jealous of that fact.

"No—because of the concussion you suffered when you fell."

Mary Simms went out, leaving Rachel alone, coming back almost immediately with a bowl full of homemade broth and some freshly made rolls. Rachel ate hungrily, appreciating the wholesomeness of the food.

"Rachel, you aren't fit enough to go back to work

yet. My husband and I would like you to stay here
with us until you are. Would you like that?"

Would she? The sensation of pleasure and relief
that rushed over her as she heard the suggestion was
its own answer, but even so she was suspicious, unused
to such kindness and concern.

"Why would you want me?" she asked baldly. "Is
it because of the baby?"

She wasn't sure what made her ask that, but she
saw from the shadow crossing the woman's face that
she had hit on a vulnerable nerve.

"Not entirely. Philip and I are concerned for
you . . . we feel responsible in a sense, because we
were the cause of your accident. You're all alone in
the world . . . a girl of only seventeen. Philip and I
have been married for fifteen years, and we have no
family of our own. Oh, several times we hoped,
but . . . We'd like you to stay with us, Rachel, for as
long as you care to do so."

"And the baby?"

"And your child too, when he or she arrives." The
woman got up and picked up the tray. "You try and
rest now. The doctor will be coming to see you later
on this afternoon."

The doctor when he arrived proved to be a jovial
man in his late fifties, and rather more forthcoming
about her rescuers than Mary herself had been.

Yes, he had known the Simms a long time, he told
Rachel in answer to her questions, looking shrewdly
at her as he surveyed her pale face and set mouth. She
didn't want this child she was carrying, and his guess
was that left to her own devices she would try to abort
it. He felt sorry for her; she reminded him of a small
wild creature caught in a trap and desperate for
escape.

Mary had told him of the child's vehement denial

of the suggestion that Tim Wilding was the father of her child, and yet according to her friend, he had been her one and only boyfriend, a fact which had been confirmed by the couple who ran the pub where the girl worked.

Something more than merely an unwanted pregnancy lay behind her almost savage resentment of her child, and the recently inflicted cuts on her bottom must have had something to do with her distraught state of mind, but whatever it was she wasn't ready to talk to them about it yet, so he talked to her instead, telling her about the couple who had taken her in.

"Philip is a schoolteacher . . . you'll like him, everyone does. Basically he's a very kind man."

And Philip himself would appreciate the agility and potential of her untrained young mind, the doctor reflected, as he got up to leave.

Rachel discovered that the doctor was right. Hard though she tried to hold the Simms at a distance, she found herself responding to their caring warmth. Days slipped by into weeks and weeks into months. The child inside her grew as she herself flourished in the tranquil backwater of the Simms home.

The old house they lived in was several miles outside Oxford and surrounded by a huge garden which Mary tended by herself. When she discovered Rachel's knowledge of herbs she was overjoyed, and gradually Rachel found herself disclosing more and more about herself to her unofficial guardians.

"What will you do, after the baby . . .?" Philip asked her one night over supper. He saw the suppressed look of need and intensity that crossed her face and wondered at its cause.

"I want to be rich," she told him simply. "So rich that . . ." Suddenly aware of the silence she had caused, Rachel broke off. Money wasn't important in

this household. There wasn't a lot of it, anyone could
see that, but it wasn't missed.

Had she grown up here, cherished by this secure
background, how different her life could have been.
How unfair it was that this couple who had so much
to give a child, that Mary, who yearned so desperately
for a family of her own, should be denied it, while
others . . .

"I . . . I want you to have my baby," she said
abruptly.

Colour fluctuated wildly in Mary's face as she stared
at Rachel unbelievingly. Both she and Philip had
learned to avoid the subject of the coming baby.
Rachel hated any mention of it, bitterly resenting their
attempts to get her to take an interest in her child.
She had said nothing to them other than that she
didn't want it, and Mary assumed that when the time
came she would opt to have the child adopted. Never
once had she allowed her thoughts to dwell on the
possibility of Philip and herself adopting the baby.

Once, yes . . . but now they were both considered
too old by the adoption societies. They had not
married until Mary was in her mid-twenties, and then
there had been the years of those hopeful pregnancies,
all of which had ended in tragedy, and then the years
when she couldn't even bear to hear the word "baby"
whispered, and now when she and Philip would have
gladly considered adoption she was forty and Philip
almost fifty, and it was too late.

Too late, or so she had thought—and now here was
this child abruptly offering them her unwanted baby.
It seemed like a dream, a mirage, and she desperately
wanted to reach out and grasp it before the offer was
withdrawn, but sanity prevailed, and she remembered
that Rachel was little more than a child herself, and
that her emotions were in such a turmoil that she

couldn't be allowed to make such a decision.

She reached out and covered Rachel's clenched fingers with her hand. "Oh, my dear, you can't know how much I want to say 'Yes', but when your baby comes you'll feel very differently, you'll see."

"And if I don't?" Rachel protested stubbornly.

"If you don't," Philip told her calmly, "then both you and your child will always have a home here with us, Rachel. You've become a part of our lives . . . an important part, and Mary and I love you for yourself and not for the child you're carrying. When I asked you what you planned to do with your life after the baby's birth, it wasn't because we want to get rid of you, but I can't bear to see you wasting the brain and the intelligence God gave you. You say you want to be rich. Be very careful, my dear, not to wish for the wrong thing from life, because you may very well get it."

Rachel felt as though he had twisted a knife deep inside her, and she wanted to cry out to him that he couldn't know what it was like to be her . . . that his soft words were all very well for others, for people with families and homes behind them, that until he had known as she had known what it was like to have nothing, he had no right to preach to her about not wanting to be rich.

Her labour pains started one Saturday evening in June. Mary stayed with her, soothing and reassuring her, but when her son was finally born, Rachel refused to look at him, saying tiredly,

"I don't want to see him. You take him, Mary."

She maintained her determination not to see her son all the time she was in hospital, and it was Mary who hung over his perspex cot and watched his every tiny movement, anxiously following his progress.

It was Mary who went out and bought the frilly Moses basket and the tiny sets of clothes, and it was Mary who held him when Philip came to take them home.

"Rachel, please . . . just hold him!"

Resolutely Rachel looked away. She had been back with the Simms for three weeks, and not once during that time had she touched or looked at her son. Inside her where her hatred and loathing of him had once been, there was now a tight knot of pain, and she knew instinctively that if she touched him, if she held him, there would be a bond between them that nothing would ever break.

Mary had been right, it was impossible for her to hate her own child, but Rachel had had plenty of time to think during the dragging months of her pregnancy, and with a clear-sighted determination she had deliberately plotted out a life for herself that excluded her child.

Here with Mary and Philip he would have the sort of love and security she could never give him. It was right that he should be here with them, and from the first moment she had thought of it, she had taught herself to think of him as their child. Here he would grow up free of the taint of his conception; here he would absorb from these kind, gentle people the sort of virtues and caring she could never teach him alone; here he would be safe, because when she took revenge for what Simon Herries had done to her, Simon would surely seek to hurt her in turn, even if that meant destroying his own child.

With her baby's birth, her determination to seek revenge had grown and intensified, and so too had her maturity, so she looked directly at Mary and said honestly and quietly,

"I can't. If I hold him now I may never be able to let him go. He isn't *my* baby, Mary, he's yours." She took a deep breath and told Mary what she had never told her before. "I was . . . raped by his father. I can't forget that. I don't want him to grow up in the shadow of that. *You* can give him so much . . . all the things I can't . . . love, security. I want him to have those things. I want him to have you and for you to have him. Don't you understand, Mary? I *want* him to be your child, because then he'll be safe, secure, loved."

It was all arranged very quietly and privately. The Simms had no close family, no one who knew their circumstances. Philip was a man who kept himself very much to himself. A change of house, a change of job, the quiet information dropped in one or two ears that they had had a child and that they had kept the pregnancy quiet because of Mary's age and previous medical history, and it was accepted that Oliver was their baby.

"And you, Rachel?" Philip asked her, as she helped him to pack away his books prior to the move. "What will you do?"

She had it all planned out.

"Go to college. I want to study languages, and secretarial skills."

She saw the disappointment in his face and knew why. He was convinced she could make it through university, but that took time—more time than she had.

"Then one of those cookery-cum-grooming courses . . . a short one. I'll work in the evenings to pay for it."

Rachel had learned a lot during recent months both from Philip and Mary's conversations and from what

she had read. She knew that for what she wanted
from life it wasn't enough just to have the ability; she
would need connections as well . . . the sort of
connections that were made at the very exclusive, very
expensive girls' courses that abounded in select private
colleges around Oxford.

"You must let us help you. At least stay with us,"
urged Philip.

Rachel shook her head.

"No, I can't, Philip. For one thing, there's . . .
Oliver."

He didn't argue with her, but when she left to start
her first month's tuition at the private secretarial
course she had chosen, he gave her a cheque for a
hundred pounds, which he told her she was not to
give him back.

Because she worked hard, Rachel was soon well
ahead of anyone else in the class. At night she worked
behind the bar in a pub—a new one where she was
not known—and she already had plans to get herself
a full-time typing job the moment she finished the
course. That would leave her evenings free for her to
take in night school language classes.

Philip found her her first job. He knew of a colleague
who was looking for someone to help him work on a
treatise he was preparing during the summer recess.
In addition to the straightforward typing there was
also a certain amount of research work to be done.
Although she was nervous, when she went for her
interview with Professor Crompton, Rachel hid it well.
She was still wearing the clothes she had been given
by the unknown hotel guest. They never went out of
fashion, and Professor Crompton's first impression of
her was of a neatly dressed, demure child.

He rapidly revised it when he discovered how well
she could work, and when he discovered by accident

that in addition to working full-time for him during the days she was also taking evening classes in French and German he was astounded.

"Why?" he asked her curiously. It was so patently obvious that she would be married by the time she was twenty-one that he couldn't for the life of him see why she was bothering.

Rachel simply shrugged her shoulders and evaded the question. Already she knew the sort of job she would go after when she had the qualifications she felt she needed, the gloss to go with them. Something in the media . . . something where she would be in contact with rich and influential people . . . something that would put her on the road to achieving her ambition.

At the end of the summer vacation, his treatise typed on time and to perfection, his files in immaculate order, and his books immaculately catalogued, the Professor gave Rachel a bonus and the offer of a full-time job as his secretary-cum-assistant. She turned it down. She wasn't going to make her fortune in Oxford.

Philip and Mary were disappointed. Oliver was a plump, contented baby now, who laughed and waved podgy limbs at everyone who came near him. Sometimes when she saw him Rachel's compulsion to touch him was almost uncontrollable, but she resisted it. She couldn't allow herself regrets, she couldn't allow herself to love him as her own child. He wasn't hers. He belonged with Mary and Philip. They loved him in a way that she could never have done. They loved him selflessly, and they would bring him up cocooned in care, protected from all the harsher realities of life.

She had almost saved enough now to pay for what she privately called "the gloss". Another couple of months' work and she would be ready to start it at the beginning of the Christmas term.

She bought herself a second-hand typewriter, and in addition to her night school courses, and her daytime job working for an agency that provided temporary secretarial staff—because that way she could get plenty of variety—she also took on the task of typing students' theses. These were hard work and didn't pay all that well, but it was work she could do in her own time, and extra income that she badly needed.

When she started her final course, she wanted to leave her present digs and move into something more upmarket. She knew the sort of place it would be . . . full of girls with languid accents and county backgrounds. These last months Rachel had started to erase the country burr from her own voice, mimicking the accents of those she sought to emulate. By Christmas she would have it just right.

Sometimes Philip and Mary were bewildered by her determination, her singlemindedness, her fanatical determination to achieve what seemed to them to be impossible dreams, but they loved her nonetheless, not for the gift of the child they loved so much, but for herself, and Rachel, sensing this, absorbing it, slowly let down her defences with them, allowing herself to love them in turn.

She found the new digs she wanted almost by accident, one windy Thursday afternoon in October. She was hurrying down the street, wanting to catch her bus, when she collided with a girl coming in the opposite direction. The package of papers the other girl was carrying burst open, depositing untidy typewritten sheets all over the muddy street.

"Oh gawd!" the girl exclaimed ruefully. "Neil's going to kill me!" As Rachel bent to help her pick up her papers, she went on, "He's my brother, and I promised I'd type his thesis for him. It's already almost a week late!"

She was a small brunette with a cap of shiny curls and dancing hazel eyes, and instinctively Rachel felt drawn to her. She was wearing a raincoat, woolly tights and brogues, and she exuded happy confidence in much the same way as a cossetted little puppy.

"Let me help you with them," Rachel suggested.

"Oh, would you? Look, my place is just round the corner. Do come back with me and have a cup of coffee. It will fortify me to face Neil!" The girl made a face which told Rachel how little she actually feared facing her brother's potential wrath.

Her "place" turned out to be an immaculate terrace house, with pretty shutters and a heavy front door.

"Ghastly, isn't it?" she said as she ushered Rachel inside. "But the parents insisted on buying it!" She rolled her eyes and grimaced. "Neil has the flat upstairs, and I live down here. Actually until recently I was sharing with someone, but she's left to go to Switzerland. The parents are now agitating for me to find a new flatmate. Heaven knows what they think I can get up to with Big Brother upstairs!"

The furnishings, the area, everything about the house told Rachel exactly what sort of background the other girl came from . . . discreetly moneyed and protected.

"By the way, I'm Isabelle Kent," the girl told her.

"I'm Pepper—Pepper Minesse."

Rachel had had the name there ready at the back of her mind for some time, but this was the first time she had actually used it, and she waited a little breathlessly to see what Isabelle's response was. There was none, apart from a total calm acceptance that let her release her pent-up breath in a faintly leaky sigh.

For her new life, Pepper had constructed a

completely new background. Her parents were dead, she had no guardian, and she had been living with family friends (the Simms) but was now branching out on her own. There was no money. (She had even perfected the face she would pull when she made the admission.) She had learned a lot during these last few months, and she had learned that money didn't necessarily matter if one had the right background and the right accent. Well, she had no background, but the accent . . .

"What are you doing here in Oxford? You're not at one of the colleges, are you?" Isabelle asked her nervously.

Pepper laughed.

"No. I'm . . . I'm not doing anything much at the moment, but I'm starting at Benton's, the Cordon Bleu place after Christmas."

"Oh, heavens, what a coincidence! I've just started there." Isabelle pulled a face. "It's awful! Well, not as bad as St Godric's—I was there for a while doing secretarial work, but I was hopeless. Mummy was furious with me when she found out I was still typing with two fingers! Daddy's a partner in a merchant bank and she wanted me to go and work there . . . well, you know the sort of thing, not so much work as find myself a suitable young man." She made another face and they both laughed. "Where are you living?" Isabelle added.

"Nowhere at the moment, actually. I'm between digs, and staying with friends of my parents."

"Oh, that's marvellous! Look, would you consider moving in here?"

Rachel's heart started thumping. It had never even occurred to her that Isabelle would make such an offer, she had simply seen her as an excellent person on whom to practise her new person, but now that the offer had been made . . .

"I don't know," she began cautiously. "I'm afraid I'm not frightfully well off. I . . ."

"Oh, that! Heavens, don't worry about it. Daddy pays for all this. All you'll have to pay for is your share of the food. Look, do consider it, because if you don't, I'll probably have one of Mummy's chums' awful daughters inflicted on me. You know what it's like . . ."

Rachel smiled. Her conscience pricked her for deceiving Isabelle like this, but if she told her the truth . . . that she was an illegitimate half gypsy . . . if she spoke to her in the Lancashire accent of her youth, if she told her she had worked as a chambermaid, had been raped and left with an unwanted child . . . if she told her all those things would Isabelle accept her so readily and welcomingly? No, she would not.

Her new life started here . . . today, she told herself firmly. The past had to be forgotten. From now on she had two aims, two goals . . . financial success, and revenge against the four men who had contributed to her rape.

From now on, Rachel Lee no longer existed. She was Pepper Minesse.

She changed her name by deed poll and moved in with Isabelle. Neil, Isabelle's brother, at first inclined to be a little suspicious of his slightly feather-headed sister's new "friend", soon relaxed his initial stiff distance.

At Christmas, just before she started her first term on the cookery course, Isabelle invited Pepper to go home with her.

Pepper refused. She wasn't ready yet to risk her new persona in front of too many others, it still needed practice and gloss. She thanked Isabelle for the invita-

tion, wrote her parents a charming letter, and explained
that she was spending the holiday with friends of her
parents in Oxford.

Mary and Philip were delighted to have her back.
The baby was now six months old, a happy, sunny-
natured child whom both Mary and Philip adored.

Pepper resolutely refused to think of him as anything
other than the Simms' child. She played with him,
bought him a Christmas present, but was careful to
remain in the background of his life.

Mary didn't know whether to be appalled by or
envious of the strength of her willpower. Neither was
she quite sure how to take the self-contained young
woman with her neat bell of dark red hair and her
laid-back upper-class drawl. Impossible to believe, if
she hadn't seen and heard it for herself, that less than
eighteen months ago this selfsame self-possessed girl
had been little more than a terrified child.

And it wasn't just outwardly that she had changed
but inwardly as well. Philip had never doubted Pepper's
intelligence, but now when he listened to the cool
positiveness of her conversation he marvelled at the
way she had developed it.

When she had first asked him how she might best
extend her general knowledge, he had suggested she
start reading the *Financial Times*, he had always found
it one of the only true unbiased reporters of world
news, but she seemed to have an ability to soak up
information like a sponge, and to retain what she
learned.

Privately Philip was beginning to suspect that she
had first-class honours degree material, but the
academic life wasn't for Rachel—or Pepper, as he
must now get used to calling her. She wanted material
success.

He sighed a little, then reminded himself that every

human being has different wants and needs. He looked at the downbent head of her small son as he played with his first set of building bricks and felt a familiar twinge of conscience. Perhaps they should have been firmer . . . Perhaps they should have tried harder to persuade Pepper to keep her child. Much as both he and Mary loved him, they were not Oliver's real parents. They . . .

"I'll never change my mind."

He looked up, stunned by Pepper's accurate reading of his thoughts.

"Look at him," she said softly. "Look at his eyes. He's loved and content. He's secure here with you, and I never want anyone to be able to take that away from him. Promise me you'll never, ever tell him the truth."

Did she know how much that had been exercising Philip's thoughts? All his life he had believed in total honesty, and yet at what stage did one tell a dearly loved and wanted child that he was not truly yours, that he was a gift? There would be bound to come a time when Oliver would want to know more, when he would need to discover himself the people who had given him life.

"It's for his sake that I'm asking you this," Pepper told him seriously. "Knowing the truth will do him no good, and could harm him. The man who fathered him . . ." She shuddered, then blanked her mind off from the tormenting images that still terrorised some of her nights. "I want for him what I never had . . . a safe, secure home. That will be something he'll carry with him all his life, my gift to him—the only thing I can give him. Promise me you'll never tell him."

And so Philip promised.

It was all for the best, Mary assured him when Pepper had gone, and he only wished he could accept that that was so as easily as his wife and Pepper.

Pepper's first few weeks at Oxford's premier cookery school might have been difficult if she hadn't had Isabelle to ease the way for her.

Isabelle, or rather Isabelle's parents, it seemed, knew everyone, as well they might. Isabelle's mother had been the most popular debutante of her year, and no one had been surprised when she carried off the cream of that year's eligible crop of young men, the heir to one of London's most exclusive private banking houses, Kent's. In fact, although no one but Pepper knew it, she had actually been accepted on the course in the first place following an introductory letter purporting to have been written by a close friend of her late mother's.

She had taken a chance on the fact that Tim's mother's handwriting would not be known to the principal of the college, since she remembered Tim saying that his sisters would all follow their mother to finishing schools in Switzerland, and that notepaper she had picked up on impulse from the desk in the hallway at Marchington had proved to be far more useful than she had ever imagined. She had taken it for no other reason than the fact that she had loved the thick expensive feel of it, so different from the notepaper provided in the hotel's bedrooms. Later she had burned with guilt over what she had done and had hidden the paper away, remembering it only when she had overheard two girls talking about a third, who would not be joining them at their exclusive secretarial school because her family was "not the right sort."

What she had done was wrong, of course, but justified, surely, since it would harm no one apart from those who deserved to be harmed . . . those who had harmed her. If she was ever to have the revenge she craved soul-deep she would need every advantage she could command, every advantage that her circumstances had so far denied her.

But even a letter of introduction from Tim Wilding's mother meant little when every other girl there knew or had heard of every other, through the social connections of their parents. She would have been very much the odd girl out, without Isabelle, Pepper recognised.

During their lunch breaks—the school had its own dining room and all the girls were expected to eat there—the talk was all of various parties and events that had taken place during the winter holidays. Some of the girls had been skiing with their parents, others had stayed at home in the country, but it seemed to Pepper, silently sitting at Isabelle's side and taking it all in, that all of them knew immediately to what the others referred.

Gstaad had gone dreadfully, frightfully vulgar, she learned, and the most awful types had started riding to hounds, and yet in almost the same breath the same girl would talk breathlessly about the absolutely super job one of Mummy's friends was giving her working in a shop. But Pepper learned that the "little shops" were always in Knightsbridge, and the holiday villas always in the South of France or the more exclusive parts of the Caribbean.

If anyone's parents owned a yacht, it was always a "tiny little thing really . . ." Large was vulgar, Pepper learned, and vulgarity in any shape or form was the biggest give-away in the world as to one's lack of social standing.

"What about you, Pepper, what will you do when you leave here?" one of the other girls asked her one lunchtime.

Pepper had no idea, but something Isabelle had once said to her popped into her mind and without even having to think about it she said airily,

"Oh, I'm not really sure, but I'm thinking of doing business lunches."

Business lunches, as a means of getting to know new young men and additionally proving that one had more between the ears than empty space, was a relatively new thing in the seventies. The rest of the class looked amazed.

"One of my cousins went in for that," a rather bored young woman remarked spitefully, "but she found it was horribly boring, and it meant she couldn't go skiing, so she gave it up in the end."

"Well, I think it's a marvellous idea," Isabelle leapt in defensively. "And what's more, Pepper and I are going to be partners."

Now it was Pepper's turn to be surprised. That was not what she had had in mind at all. She knew quite well from all that Isabelle had said to her that her friend had no thoughts of independence or making her own way in the world. For all her airy insouciance, she would marry young and well and settle down to much the same sort of life as her mother. And yet . . . and yet she owed Isabelle a lot, and she liked her. And then there were the connections she could make through Isabelle, Pepper reminded herself, telling herself that she was behaving logically and not emotionally, even while she knew the latter to be the case.

It was a very true adage that "he travels fastest who travels alone."

Perhaps Isabelle would forget all about the idea, she comforted herself as the bell rang and they all hurried back to their classes. But Isabelle didn't, and her excitement and enthusiasm for the idea was such that Pepper didn't have the heart to put her off.

"I was telling Mummy about our plans," Isabelle announced one weekend, after she had been home. "She thinks it's marvellous. She's dying to meet you, Pepper. I do wish you'd come home with me."

"Next time," Pepper promised, correctly interpreting Isabelle's mother's words. Dorothea Kent wished to inspect her, and in her shoes she would feel exactly the same. "Daddy thinks it's a good idea too. He said he'd give us a start by letting us do some for them . . . just for the Board at first," she added on a giggle. "He says he isn't prepared to let us loose on his clients until he knows we won't poison them!"

"And your brother?"

Incredibly, although they had passed occasionally on the stairs, Pepper didn't see much of Isabelle's brother. She sensed that there was a certain amount of disharmony between the two siblings.

"Oh, Neil! He's such a bore, and so dull. He doesn't think we'll be able to do it. He said we'd get bored within a fortnight. We've *got* to do it, Pepper, just to prove to him that we can! Oh, and I forgot . . . Daddy's told him to make sure he gets us tickets for the Commem. Ball at Magdalen—it's always one of the best bashes there is. Mummy's promised me a new frock for it. What will you wear?"

Pepper hadn't the faintest idea. Now that she was living with Isabelle it was impossible for her to work as well, and as it was she was having problems eking out her small savings. The only thing she had that remotely resembled a ballgown was that dress she had bought from the second-hand shop, she acknowledged grimly. She would just have to find some excuse not to go.

Only it didn't prove to be as easy as that.

Isabelle's great-aunt in Scotland fell ill, and her

mother had to go up and stay with her, and so Pepper's proposed visit to London to stay with the Kents had to be delayed. She had received a letter from Isabelle's mother apologising for this, and stating that she hoped they would meet at the time of the Ball, when they would be staying close to Oxford with some friends.

In other words, Pepper would have to attend the Magdalen Ball.

In the privacy of her room she took the fluted Fortuny dress from its protective wrapper and studied it. Beautiful though it was, it just wouldn't do.

Isabelle's mother subscribed to the *Tatler*, and Isabelle always brought the magazine back with her from her weekends home. By studying the photographs of Society's do's in its pages, Pepper had developed a fair idea of what she would be expected to wear.

She took the problem with her when she went to visit Mary and Philip. Oliver was walking now and trying to talk. He gave Pepper the impartial beam he gave everyone and hurled himself into her arms. She picked him up automatically, wondering a little at her own lack of mother love for him. Deep down inside she knew she had denied herself the right to such feelings from the moment of his birth when she had refused to hold him. Although she studied his features carefully she could see nothing of herself in him, nor anything either of the man who had fathered him.

He was just another chubby, smiling toddler.

The moment Mary walked into the room his head swivelled round and he wriggled in Pepper's arms. She put him down and watched the eager way he ran across the room. Yes, she had made the right decision . . . the right decision for herself and the right decision for him.

"Something wrong?" Philip asked her over supper. She had been quiet all day, and there was obviously something on her mind.

Pepper told them, pulling a wry face.

She had become more and more the girl she had created by her own hard endeavours and less and less the gypsy child she had been, Mary reflected, watching the naturalness of her gestures and speech. No one meeting her now would ever doubt that she had come from anything other than a comfortably wealthy upper-class home, the sort where the virtues and traditions of generations of established and orderly forms of life came as easily as breathing.

"Oh yes, you'll need something special for that," Mary agreed, when Pepper had finished telling them.

"I hadn't intended to go, but Mrs Kent is more or less insisting. She wants to inspect me and approve of me as a suitable friend and business partner for Isabelle."

"Probably more than that," Mary told her with an unusual touch of shrewdness. "You *are* sharing the same house as their only son!"

"Oh, heavens, we barely see Neil . . . he and Isabelle don't get on. I don't think he even realises I exist."

Privately Mary doubted that. Pepper was a startlingly beautiful young woman, and the new gloss of self-confidence she sported only made one all the more aware of that fact.

"I think I might be able to help out with a dress," Mary told her unexpectedly, "if you don't mind something second-hand."

"Anything," Pepper told her cheerfully.

"Well, I've been helping the Vicar's wife to sort out clothes for our 'good as new' sale for the annual fair, and I came across a bag of the most marvellous things.

Apparently they belonged to the niece of a friend of the Vicar's wife who had run off with an Arab prince . . ."

"Good heavens, what on earth possessed her to do that?" interrupted her husband.

"She's a woman, my dear," she told him wryly. "I believe the young man in question was extraordinarily handsome, and as rich as Croesus with it."

A short discussion followed on the folly of romantic indulgence and the reality of life that followed such folly, often with unpleasant consequences, which kept them all occupied for another half an hour, then Mary got up and said firmly,

"Yes, well, that's all very well. Left to it, I'm sure the pair of you could debate the issue for the rest of the afternoon, but if Pepper wants to see these things . . ."

Pepper did, she and Mary, with Oliver clinging to his mother's hand and refusing to get into his push-chair, set off for the Vicarage, which wasn't very far away. The Vicar's wife proved to be a sensible if somewhat harassed woman in her mid-thirties, who was quite agreeable to Pepper going through the bundle of things.

"They're far too good for our stall really, and because of that they probably wouldn't be bought . . . they're not the sort of thing the ladies round here would wear. Come and have a look."

There were three or four high-fashion outfits, that Pepper dismissed immediately despite their obvious quality—no one else at the college wore clothes like these, and standing out from the rest of the crowd was the last thing she wanted to do at the moment. As she looked at them she prayed that the dress wouldn't prove to be too outré.

It wasn't. It was white broderie anglaise, with an

off-the-shoulder top threaded through with blue ribbon
to match the sash round the waist. The skirt was cut
on the bias, and full, and there were several petticoats
to go with it. It looked like an upmarket version of
everyone's favourite Laura Ashley, and Pepper knew
immediately that it would be ideal—demure enough
to earn Dorothea Kent's approval and similar enough
to the dresses other girls would be wearing not to
merit any particular notice.

"It's ideal," she announced firmly.

The Vicar's wife was more than happy to accept ten
pounds for it, and the three of them left with the dress
bundled into a Marks & Spencer carrier bag.

"I'll wash and starch it for you," Mary promised,
"and I think we ought to get some new ribbon. What
do you think about a soft peach?"

For all that she herself was not particularly interested in clothes, Mary had an excellent eye for colour
and style, and Pepper was happy to agree with her.

It was the fashion to have one's hair put up for
formal balls, and Isabelle and Pepper spent a giggly
afternoon the Saturday before the Commem. Ball,
arranging and rearranging one another's hair.

"It's not fair! Yours is fantastic . . . thick and
obedient, while mine curls all over the place," Isabelle
wailed.

She had just spent half an hour meticulously ironing
the curls flat, beneath a thick wad of tissue paper, and
now she complained that her neck ached from the
effort and her hair was still insisting on curling.

Everything went according to plan.

Dorothea Kent took one look at the girl with whom
her only daughter was sharing and knew immediately
which of the pair was the stronger. Beneath the neat
blouse and pleated skirt, and later, the very pretty and

appropriate white dress, she sensed a determination
and power that Isabelle would never have. But five
minutes' conversation with Pepper was sufficient to
assure her that she was the last person likely to suggest
that the pair of them take off for a trek across
Australia, or indulge in any of the other equally
inappropriate ventures that so many of Isabelle's
previous friends had suggested.

It was a pity, of course, that she had no family to
speak of, but apart from that Mrs Kent could see
nothing to disapprove of.

Before they left to spend the night with their friends,
she graciously suggested that Pepper might like to
spend part of her summer holiday with them, and
Pepper equally graciously accepted.

Dorothea was also able to reassure herself that her
son, who was reading P.P.E., ready to follow in his
father's footsteps, was apparently in no danger of
succumbing to the girl's quite startling looks. That
was as well, as she and his father had other plans for
Neil . . . plans which in due time would include
marriage to a distant cousin whose father owned a
huge amount of Scotland, and a title.

Yes, it was all quite satisfactory really. Pepper was
rather an odd little thing, so earnest and determined
to make their little business venture work, but she
would be a good influence on Isabelle, and after all, it
wouldn't be for long . . . If Isabelle wasn't engaged
before her twenty-first birthday, Dorothea would be
very astonished indeed.

The Ball itself was an anticlimax as far as Pepper
was concerned. The all-important event of the day for
her had been meeting the Kents, especially Isabelle's
mother, who she sensed was the more determined of
the two adults. Isabelle's father had acknowledged her
and said he was looking forward to tasting the results

of the girls' time at college, but had said very little
more.

While Isabelle's mother had not previously been
loquacious, what she had said—or rather asked—had
been very much to the point. Pepper knew she had
created the correct impression, and that now she could
relax, but strangely, all she really wanted to do was
to go and spend the evening quietly with Mary and
Philip, talking over her plans for her future. In an odd
way they had become not only Oliver's family, but
her own as well. She loved them as much as she was
ever likely to be capable of loving anyone, she
acknowledged, as she listened to Isabelle's excited
prattle with half her attention.

Neil was escorting them to the Ball . . . Neil, who
tended to look down on his excitable, rather dim
sister. Neil was currently dating a fellow student. He
went for brains rather than beauty, Isabelle had laugh-
ingly confided to Pepper.

"I wonder what they do when they're alone together?
Make love, or add up columns of figures!"

Isabelle was at the moment extremely preoccupied
about the extent of other people's sexual experience . . . probably because she herself had none, she
had drolly confided to Pepper.

"I bet we're the only two virgins in the whole of
Oxford!" she had exclaimed ruefully one evening after
she had ditched her date and walked home, having
gone out with the express purpose in mind of ridding
herself of that unwanted stigma. "It was his hands,"
she told Pepper. "They were all clammy . . . I mean,
can you imagine . . .?" she appealed, giving a theat-
rical shudder. "No, I shall just have to find someone
else."

Pepper was now an accepted member of the small
circle of girls who attended the cookery college. Via

them she had made several contacts of her own and knew several young men, some of whom were present at the Ball. She wasn't left partnerless for very long, and while Isabelle was dancing with her latest conquest, Pepper was being swung round the floor by a succession of eager young men. None of them impressed her. A man . . . a lover . . . a husband. A man in any context was the very last thing she wanted, so she barely glanced at them.

Someone was looking at her, though.

Miles French had been persuaded to get tickets for the Ball by his latest girlfriend, an American on an exchange from Vassar. Tall and energetic with a waterfall of straight dark hair that she claimed came from some long-ago Red Indian blood, to Miles she seemed exotic and different from the other women he had dated. She wasn't a virgin and had no intention of settling down for a long, long time yet, she had told him frankly after their second date, when she had suggested they go back to his rooms to make love. They had been lovers ever since. Miles liked and admired her, but he was glad that he wasn't her chosen mate. She would be hard work to live up to, he thought in amusement, watching her as she danced with someone else.

It was then that he caught sight of Pepper. It was her hair that did it. That so unusual and vivid dark red banner of hair—that and the haunting beauty of her face. His eyes narrowed as he searched the milling crowds, seeking another look at her.

He had never forgotten the events of that night . . . nor quite forgiven himself for the violence he had felt afterwards. He had often wondered what had happened to the girl, and now, as he suddenly caught a glimpse of her cool shuttered face, he thought grimly that he knew.

She had changed, almost drastically so, but he still recognised her. That expression in her eyes, that cool wariness that warned against anyone trespassing too closely. Herries had put that there—Miles was ready to swear to it.

She was beautiful, almost flawlessly so, most men would say, but they would be wrong. She was flawed, inside, emotionally, he knew it as instinctively as though she had told him so himself, sensing the icy coldness within her even across the distance that separated them.

He thought about his energetic, ebullient American girl with her huge appetite for life in all it forms, her enthusiasm for sex and for living, and he looked for corresponding signs of such an enjoyment for life in Pepper's cool face, and knew he wouldn't find them.

Rape was an ugly word . . . a word he didn't even want to think about. He heard Beth call his name and turned towards her in relief, the decision whether or not to go across to the redhead and talk to her taken from him. She probably wouldn't have wanted to talk to him anyway . . . wouldn't have wanted to be reminded of what had happened to her. No, it was for the best—and yet Miles was left with a curious sensation of somehow having just made a very wrong and important decision.

CHAPTER TEN

ALEX BARNETT stood in Tom Quad waiting for his father. It seemed strange to think he would not be returning here in the autumn. He would miss Oxford, even though he had had divided feelings about coming here.

When he looked back from the vantage point of the sophistication he had gained over the last three years he felt rather amused by his younger self. He had been so anxious to do the "right thing" . . . to be seen to be au fait with the moods and manners of his new surroundings. With the benefit of what he knew now he realised that he should have chosen Cambridge and not Oxford. There he would have been right at the heart of the new computer industry.

Strange to remember that when he first came up to Oxford computers had meant nothing to him. Now . . .

He remembered quite clearly the first lecture he had attended on the subject, and those that had followed. He had known all along that when he finished university he would be going into his father's business, and that his degree and his years here at the famous college were simply icing on the cake . . . achievements that his proud parents could boast about to their friends, and to be fair, he had never imagined he might want anything else. And yet . . . and yet he envied those among his fellow graduates who would be making careers for themselves in what he privately considered to be the most exciting new development

in British industry that there had ever been. Alex
wanted desperately to be part of that industry. He
knew that beyond any shadow of a doubt, but he also
knew what his father was expecting. The company
had been owned and run by their family from his
great-grandfather's time, making sewing machines that
were a household name. His father was proud of the
business, proud of the reliability and sturdiness of the
machines they produced—machines that were still
exported to all four corners of what had once been
the British Empire. Lonely homesteaders in New
Zealand and Australia bought them; missionaries'
wives in Africa and China, the wives of captains who
sailed to South America and the Caribbean.

Nowadays their export sales were only minimal
compared with what they had been at the time of the
late Victorian and the Edwardian era, but the company
was still very soundly based. In the Nottinghamshire
town where the factory was situated they were known
as responsible and caring employers. His father was
the leader of the local Chamber of Commerce and his
mother was involved in all manner of local charity
work.

Had anyone asked Alex at the end of his first year
at Oxford how he saw his future he would have replied
confidently that he saw it falling into a similar pattern
to his father's. Now he was not so sure. He felt
disloyal in even admitting his restlessness. Others he
knew from Cambridge were travelling to Japan and
California to study the very latest technical developments; they were already talking about the future and
the changes their bright new technology would make,
like prophets granted a special vision.

He wanted desperately to be a part of that select
and small band, but he knew he didn't have it in him
to turn his back on his father and disappoint him.

And he would be disappointed. Alex had tried to talk
to him about how he felt, but his father had frowned
and dismissed computers as "a new-fangled idea that'll
be dead within a couple of years."

But he knew his father was wrong.

He frowned, brought out of his reverie by sounds
behind him, his frown deepening as he recognised the
man strolling towards him.

Richard Howell. It seemed a long time ago since
their first term together, and all that nonsense with
Herries' Hell Fire Club. God, how idiotic they had
been . . . dangerously so, he thought, remembering
how close both he and Howell had been to being
sucked into something that could have ruined their
lives if it had ever come out into the open.

With hindsight it was easy to perceive his own folly.
At the the time he had been too impressed by Simon
Herries and his crowd to realise what he was getting
himself into.

It had taken that incident with the girl Herries had
ordered them to kidnap to do that. Alex wondered
what had actually happened to her, then shivered,
even though not a breath of wind stirred in the quad.
It was pointless regretting that youthful weakness; he
couldn't go back and undo what had been done. He
had the future to think about now.

He saw his father's car approach and picked up his
bags, calling out a brief goodbye to Richard.

He and his father didn't talk on the drive home. In
addition to being a rather withdrawn and undemon-
strative man, Gilbert Barnett preferred silence to
speech, especially when he was driving.

It was early evening when they drove through the
small Nottinghamshire village and up to the large
Victorian house his great-grandfather had built. Still
as solid and plain today as it had been then, it

surveyed its surroundings from a slight hilltop, and
Alex registered the familiar change in the car's engine
note as they turned in through the gates and drove up
to the front door.

His father was not a mean man, but he didn't
believe in ostentation either. His Rover was four years
old and was still as immaculate now as it had been on
the day it had left the showroom. Alex already knew
that when his father got his new car he, Alex, would
inherit the Rover. Privately he would have preferred
a nippy MGB in traditional racing green. Several of
his Cambridge friends drove them—or if they could
afford them, bright red Morgans. However, he knew
that his father would not approve of his desire for a
sports car. The Rover was solid and reliable . . . to
match the company image.

Alex's mother was waiting for them in the drawing
room. She reached up and kissed him a little shyly.
His father did not approve of sons being too close to
their mothers, and consequently she tended to remain
rather in the background of his life.

"We're having dinner early tonight, because your
father has a business meeting tonight. It's your
favourite . . . roast duckling."

His room hadn't changed in ten years, and as he
looked round it, he felt almost uncomfortably alien in
it. It was only as he looked out of his window at the
surrounding countryside that he acknowledged how
little he had wanted to come home.

He knew it would be years before his father allowed
him any real say in the business, but how could he
simply turn his back on him and tell him that he
found it boring? That he wanted wider, more exciting
horizons? He knew he couldn't, so he showered and
changed, then went down to dinner, where he listened
to his mother's chatter about her social activities,

broken every now and again by a comment from his father. It was a scene that was as familiar to him as his own face, and yet now for the first time it felt alien. *He* felt alien.

He offered to join his father in his business meeting, but was told that he would only be bored.

"Which reminds me—better get you into the local golf club now, I think. You'll meet a good crowd there."

Golf! Alex grimaced to himself. He preferred something more active such as squash or tennis. A dull lethargic feeling settled round him like a grey cloud. Was this what he had gone to Oxford for? This . . . this stifling boredom?

At his father's suggestion he was taking a couple of months off before he started work officially, but he had expected to be going into the factory most days of the week, so that he could learn the business informally from the shop floor upwards.

However, his father surprised him by being rather evasive on the subject of when he should start work, and suggested instead that he take the Rover and give himself a well deserved holiday. Alex was too grateful for the opportunity to escape to question his father any more closely.

Although there hadn't seemed to be much point in keeping in touch with his fellow computer buffs, a letter from one of them had advised him of an informal group meeting to be held once a month, in Cambridge, just so that they could all keep abreast of new developments. Since he had been given a month or so's freedom, there was nothing to stop him from packing a suitcase and spending a leisurely fortnight driving through the Cotswolds and stopping wherever the fancy took him in a gentle peregrination which brought him to Cambridge just two days before the meeting was due to take place.

The acquaintance who had written to him lived on the outskirts of Cambridge itself, and on impulse, having found himself a hotel, Alex decided to drive out and visit him. He found the village easily enough and learned that his acquaintance was the local Vicar's son. The Vicarage was pointed out to him, a long rambling building set in a tangled, untidy garden.

Alex parked the Rover on the weed-infested drive and made his way to the front door. It was opened by a small, slim girl, with a cloud of soft blonde hair and large sherry-gold eyes. She was dressed in the shortest skirt Alex had ever seen, and her toe nails in her pretty sandals were painted a vivid fuchsia. She looked nothing like a Vicar's daughter, and his expression must have said so, because she gave him a rather aloof look before asking him to come in.

"I'm a friend of William's," he told her hesitantly. "He isn't expecting me, but . . ."

"We're in the garden. You'd better come on through."

She started walking away from him before he could object, and so, rather reluctantly, he had to follow her.

The back garden of the Vicarage proved to be almost as overgrown as the front, although someone had made an effort at mowing the lawn. William was sitting in a deck chair, immersed in some technical data, but his look of surprise quickly turned to one of pleasure when he recognised his visitor.

"I'm here for Wednesday's meeting," Alex explained a little awkwardly. "I just thought I'd call round on spec. Your sister . . ."

He looked round for the girl and discovered that she was sitting down in a deck chair applying another coat of varnish to her toe nails.

William frowned and then grinned at him.

"Julia isn't my sister."

To his chagrin Alex found himself flushing slightly. Trust him to put his foot in it!

"The folks are away at the moment," William explained, making him feel even worse. The very last thing he wanted to do was to play an unwanted third to a pair of lovers. "So Julia, being the kind little cousin she is, has come over to look after me."

So they weren't lovers but cousins . . . but that didn't mean . . . Alex looked from Julia to William and then back again, and still couldn't make up his mind as to whether or not there was a sexual relationship between them. In other circumstances he would simply have asked bluntly if he was in the way, but since leaving Oxford, some of his parents' genteel morality seemed to have rubbed off on him, and he found the words impossible to frame. He felt awkward and uncomfortable, and also very conscious of the fact that the girl Julia was watching him.

"Look, it was only a brief call. I'd . . ."

"Why don't you stay and have supper with us?"

Her invitation was the last thing he had expected. He turned round to look at her, but the golden eyes were veiled.

"Yes, do," William agreed easily.

It was gone midnight before Alex reluctantly stood up and said he must go. "Otherwise I'll be locked out of my hotel," he explained.

"Why bother going back at all?" Julia asked him, watching him with her quiet, unreadable eyes. "We've got plenty of empty rooms here."

"My things . . . I . . ."

What was it about this tiny slip of a girl that made him so tongue-tied and self-conscious? For a start, she was probably at least two years his junior.

She gave a delighted peal of laughter.

"Oh, William can lend you what you need. Have you got a spare pair of pyjamas, William?"

"Never wear 'em," William told her cheerfully, giving her a mock leer. "Look, forget about your hotel, Alex. We'll go over in the morning and collect your stuff. Like Julia says, there's tons of room here, and I'll be glad of your company."

And so Alex found himself agreeing to spend what was left of the holidays at the Vicarage. William, it seemed, was in touch with several other computer buffs who lived locally, and could introduce Alex to them.

"You see?" teased Julia. "What more could you ask for?"

Alex wasn't sure if he was imagining it or not, but he could have sworn at times that Julia was deliberately flirting with him. He had now established the fact that the only relationship between her and William was a strictly cousinly one, and he had also discovered that she was an excellent conversationalist, intelligent and witty. Her parents had brought her up to do "nothing more than become a wife and mother", she told him wryly, and it seemed that she divided her time between her home in Gloucester and the flat she shared with a couple of other girls in London. She had a job in an art gallery, and when she chose she could be quite amusing about the various personalities she met there.

They were late getting back from the meeting which had been the whole purpose of his visit to Cambridge in the first place, and Alex was buoyed up on a high from the conversation and stimulating company. He and William had gone there in the Rover and now they were driving back.

"What do you intend to do with your life, Alex?"

William asked him.

"I don't have much choice. I'm expected to go into the family business. And you . . .?"

"I'm working on my own personal design for a small computer . . . so small that it could become a household item, and so easy that a child could programme it. I've run into a few problems, though." William sighed. "A friend of mine's working on a similar thing, however, and I plan to fix up a meeting with him tomorrow. Would you like to come? How much longer can you stay?"

"Well, I've got another ten days of my holiday left, but . . ."

Alex had been going to say that he could hardly stay that long, but to his delight William said immediately,

"Great! How about staying on here? We could work on my project together."

"Your parents . . ." Alex began.

"Won't be back until the end of the month, and besides, they won't mind. We've got the room, so it's no problem. Unless of course you want to spend what's left of your free time roaming the fleshpots?"

William lifted a querying eyebrow, but Alex shook his head. He had had girlfriends through his time at Oxford—never anything serious, just the usual sort of experimentation. He enjoyed sex, but had never felt obsessive about it . . . and he had certainly never desired a girl to the point where his need for her obliterated everything else.

Until now.

It was the first time he had acknowledged how he felt about Julia. Every time she so much as looked at him, he could feel the surge of need dominate his body. He had hardly stopped thinking about her from the moment he met her. When he went to bed at night he had the most erotic fantasies about her. Sometimes he suspected that she knew exactly what effect she had on him. She had a certain way of looking at him, a certain knowing gleam in her eyes.

It was gone one when they got in, and Alex went straight to bed, showering in the bathroom adjacent to his room. Like William, he too no longer slept in pyjamas, and as he walked into his bedroom he simply wrapped a towel round his hips. His room was in darkness, a slight breeze moving the curtains. He reached for the light which he was sure he had left on—then froze as he heard Julia saying softly,

"No, don't switch it on."

He shut the bedroom door automatically, staring into the gloom.

She was lying on his bed; he could see the pale blur of her body. He walked uncertainly towards her, his breath catching in his throat as he realised that she was naked. Her skin gleamed like mother-of-pearl, tipped with rose over the fullness of her breasts. As he hesitated Julia lifted herself up off the bed.

"You do want me, don't you?"

Her voice was liquid with laughter, he could see it shaking the slender arc of her delicate frame.

A fierce mixture of anger and desire burst into life inside him. Beneath his towel he felt the fierce throb of his erection. She knew what she was doing to him, damn her! He wanted to punish her for that taunting laughter, to show that he was a man, and not to be made fun of. He reached the bed, and leaned over her, pinioning her there, his mouth smothering the taunting sound. He found her breast and caressed it urgently. She was making soft animal sounds in the back of her throat, her nails digging into the muscles of his shoulders, tracing the line of his spine.

He felt the heat explode inside him and reached

down between their bodies to find the moist feminine warmth of her. She trembled as he stroked the soft delicate petals of flesh, arching up against his hands.

"Now . . . I want you now . . ."

There was no laughter in her now, only a demanding urgency that found an answer in his own need. Alex parted her thighs and moved between them. There had been women before, but none like this, and his body seemed to echo the sentiments of his mind, swelling tautly as he filled her. She felt tight and hot, encasing him firmly, making him want to plunge himself into her until she was completely and entirely his.

He heard her cry out and smothered the sound with his mouth, caught up in the fierce tide of his own need. His flesh pulsed with it, driving him mindlessly on until he was spilling himself endlessly inside her. Only then did he realise that she had not reached her own climax. As he withdrew from her he was conscious of the tightness of her body, and of her small wince of pain.

Alex was not a particularly egotistical man; he knew that nature had endowed him neither more nor less than the majority of his fellows, and certainly not to the extent to cause that brief spasm of pain, unless . . .

"Was this your first time?"

He knew the moment he blurted out the question that it was the wrong thing to say, conjuring up all sorts of emotional taboos that no modern, free-thinking woman would ever acknowledge, and he cursed himself inwardly for his stupidity. Far better to have left it and discovered the truth discreetly for himself later. He felt Julia's body stiffen in rejection and tried to salvage what he could.

"I'm sorry you didn't . . . that I . . ." He swore under his breath as he felt her coldness grow and added helplessly, "I've wanted you so damn much. You've been driving me mad, and now see what you've made me do! I promise you it will be better next time."

He waited for some smart rejoinder that there wouldn't be a next time, and when all he got in response was a small sniffle, he jettisoned all his own carefully fabricated barricades and took her in his arms, comforting her with tender kisses, telling her how much he loved her.

They made arrangements to marry as soon as they could.

When Alex discovered that not only had Julia been a virgin, but that she was also not on the pill, and that nor did she intend to take it, he had hardly dared to allow himself to make love to her again. He wanted her as his wife, desperately so . . . but he didn't want to make her pregnant before their marriage.

Julia could be reckless, abandoned even in her attempts to get him to break his vow not to make love to her again until they were married
She had refused to take the pill. She wanted a family and she had heard that it could make some women sterile. She refused to allow Alex to use any form of protection, so what were they left with?

There were weekends, when he went up to London to stay with her in her flat, when she brought him so close to the edge of breaking his vow that he thought he would go mad from it. She seemed to enjoy driving him to that edge, touching him, caressing him with her hands and her mouth until he couldn't hold back any longer. There were no barriers between them now, she knew his body as intimately as she knew hers, but no matter how often he brought her to her climax she claimed that it wasn't enough until she felt the pulsating heat of him deep inside her.

Later Alex marvelled that he had held out as long as he had. The week before they were to marry, Julia greeted him at the door of the flat wearing nothing other than what looked little more than a brief silk G-string and a floating see-through robe. She had darkened her nipples with rouge and she was wearing a sensual, heavy perfume. As she drew him inside her hand went to his zip. She teased him until he was aching for satisfaction, withdrawing from him with a secret smile.

"You know what I want . . ." she whispered.

His child. Julia told him so over and over again, and with only a week to go to the wedding, her pleas were impossible to resist.

That weekend he seemed to have been granted the stamina of a stallion. They made love over and over again, as frantically as though they felt that life itself was about to tear them apart.

When he looked back Alex often wondered if for that brief space of time they had both shared a deep unacknowledged premonition.

Two days before the wedding his father had a fatal heart attack.

Alex had never even known that his father had a heart condition. He was stunned, but he had his mother to think of. She had gone completely to pieces.

The wedding had to be cancelled, of course, and instead Alex attended his father's funeral.

Julia stood at his side, a delicate, fragile figure in black. Her parents had agreed with Alex that the wedding would have to be delayed—"for at least six months, darling", her mother had told Julia in Alex's presence. Alex will be in mourning."

"Mourning? God, Mother, that's so old-fashioned!" protested Julia.

"Nevertheless," her mother continued with quiet calm, "the wedding will have to be delayed."

Alex had been tempted to suggest to Julia that they get married quickly and quietly in a register office, but he knew her parents would be horrified. She was their only child, this wedding was something they had planned for and anticipated for years.

"Six months will soon pass," Alex had promised her. He had a meeting the Monday after the funeral with his father's solicitor. By a rather outdated arrangement, the house would come direct to him, as it had done to his father on his father's death. He would buy his mother a cottage somewhere close by, he knew that it was what she would want. Julia pulled a face when he told her. She didn't care for his parents' house, and he couldn't blame her. It was gloomy and old-fashioned.

There was the business to sort out as well. So far he had done little more than mooch around the shop floor, his father showing a rather odd reluctance to involve him more deeply in what was going on. Alex had put it down to the old lion fearing the roar of the new, but on Monday morning he discovered just how naïve he had been.

Charles Willshaw had been his father's solicitor for as long as Alex could remember. He and his father were contemporaries, and Charles had attended the funeral. He looked gravely at Alex over the wide expanse of his desk.

"How much did your father take you into his confidence, Alex?"

"Not an awful lot—he wasn't that kind of man. It was understood that I would follow him into the business, but . . ."

"Yes Alex, I'm afraid I have some rather bad news for you."

It was worse . . . far worse than anything he could have imagined, and yet coupled with the shock was a tiny thread of relief that now . . . now he was free. Sales had dropped drastically over recent years; his father had borrowed heavily and at high set interest rates. He hadn't been able to pay back the loan, and now the threat of bankruptcy hung over the business.

"Just the assets are there?" Alex asked when he had digested his initial shock.

"Nothing in the business. Your father hated getting rid of anyone. He's been carrying far too much dead wood for years. There's the house, of course, that should fetch a reasonable sum, although it could take a while to sell. There isn't the call these days for such a large and expensive home."

A week of almost constant meetings followed—with the bank, with their creditors, with the foreman, with the accountants, and at the end of it all, Alex realised that he would be lucky to come out of the whole thing with anything more than ten thousand pounds. Perhaps not a small sum, but certainly not enough to provide his mother, Julia and himself with a home.

He thought back to his initial interview with Julia's father when he had asked his permission to marry her. Mr Henderson was the old-fashioned type, who sincerely believed that women were too fragile to worry themselves about financial matters, much less to work outside the home. Julia had been cherished and protected all her life, and Alex was honest enough to admit that her vulnerability was part of her attraction for him. He wouldn't change her in any way, but he was also very much aware of the fact that Julia was not the wife for a potentially poor man with his own way to make in the world. Always supposing that her parents would agree to such a marriage. Julia was still very young, and Alex very much suspected that once he knew the true situation her father would insist on them waiting until he was more financially secure.

The only decent, honourable thing to do was to go to Julia's parents and explain the position, and to temporarily cancel the wedding.

Julia took the news badly. In her parents' presence she clung to Alex and wept, begging him to change his mind. They could live with her parents, she pleaded, and in the end it had been her mother who had led her out of the room, leaving Alex alone to face his future father-in-law. It was just as he had expected. Politely but quite definitely he had told Alex that there was no way he would allow Julia to marry him until he was sure Alex could support her properly.

Later, as Alex tried to comfort Julia, he couldn't help reflecting a little bitterly that if his father had not died for another month he and Julia would be safely married. He was trying to see things from her parents' point of view, but it was hard, very hard.

Refusing to give in to Julia's pleading that they went ahead and married anyway was the hardest thing he had ever had to do. He pointed out to her that if they wanted to please her parents they had no choice. He hated leaving her with the tear-stains still damp on her face, but he would hate himself even more if he agreed to her suggestion that they marry secretly and then live with her parents. That was something his pride would not allow him to do. He wanted to marry Julia, desperately so; he would marry her tomorrow if he could, but not behind her family's back; not when he knew that such a marriage would virtually mean him being financially dependent on his father-in-law.

He was touched by Julia's earnest plea that they marry immediately, wondering what had happened to the girl who had so lately insisted that it was impos-

sible for her to marry without all the trimmings of the
large wedding her mother had organised. It strength-
ened his confidence in their love and made him all the
more determined to find some way of re-establishing
himself financially, even though he knew it would take
time. He and Julia were young, they could afford to
wait . . . at least for a little while, even though Julia
herself at the moment didn't seem to think so.

Her parents had fully understood and supported
Alex's decision; they had been the first people he had
told of his father's unexpected death, and now he had
to explain to them that his financial situation was
such that the wedding might have to be put off
indefinitely. He knew he might lose Julia, but he
couldn't tie her down to the type of poverty he might
have to endure if he couldn't find himself a job.

He had gone overnight from being a comfortably
off young man with his future securely laid out ahead
of him to someone with nothing . . . less than nothing
if he couldn't sell the house.

Julia's father heard him out in silence. He was a
remote, old-fashioned kind of man, rather like his own
father had been, and while he applauded his decision
to make finding a job his priority, Alex sensed a new
air of reserve about him, and guessed that Tom
Henderson was considering whether he was still worthy
of being considered a prospective husband for his
daughter.

Alex said as much to William when he met him less
than a week later in Cambridge. He had made the
journey at William's specific request.

"Have you found anything yet?" William asked
him.

Alex shook his head.

"No . . . and I'm not likely to be able to until I
sort out the unholy mess of the company's finances.

I've got the house up for sale."

He couldn't tell William about his mother's reaction to the news that she was to lose the home that had been hers all her married life. At the moment she was staying with a cousin in Norfolk. A sort of nervous breakdown, was how their doctor had described her condition. Alex grimaced faintly.

"How's Julia taking it?" William asked him.

"She's not too happy, and I can hardly blame her . . . having to postpone the wedding almost at the last minute." Alex shrugged. "And until I get myself some sort of decent financial status, no way do I see us getting married . . . do you?"

"I might," William surprised him by saying.

"What do you mean?"

"That small home-size computer we were talking about . . . I think I've found someone who's got the answer to one or two of our problems. He's got some money he can invest—not much, but I've been working out some figures, and . . ."

"Just a minute! Are you suggesting . . .?"

"That the three of us take a chance, set up our own company."

"But we're years away from producing anything!" protested Alex. "We don't have the facilities, the . . ."

"I don't think we're as far from a breakthrough as you think. Those last ideas you came up with could be made to work. We could have the equipment manufactured under licence. It would be less profitable, but it would give us a start . . . I reckon with, say, six to twelve months' real graft, we could have ourselves a product that no one else is anywhere near producing. "It's worth a chance," William finished.

Alex wasn't sure if it was fear or excitement that was coursing through his veins, he only knew that suddenly he felt more alive than he had felt in months.

Here was the opportunity to involve himself in the sort of project he had yearned to be part of. It would be hard work—the financial problems would be almost insurmountable, but . . .

He looked at William.

"When can I meet this other guy?"

Alex left Cambridge three days later buoyed up with plans and new confidence. When he got home and discovered the estate agents thought they had a buyer for the house, it seemed like a good omen.

He decided to go to London to see Julia. He didn't normally go during the week, but this was something special. She had been so disappointed about the wedding, so down . . . they might not be any nearer to getting married quickly, but at least now Alex had some prospects ahead of him.

Julia shared a flat with two ex-school friends, and one of them opened the door to him. Alex had never really taken to Frances Napier. There was something about her that he didn't like. A year older than Julia, she was far more worldly; her men friends were invariably a good twenty years her senior and rich.

She raised her eyebrows when she saw him, contempt darkening her cold blue eyes.

"Julia's in bed. She isn't feeling too good."

For a moment Alex thought she was going to refuse to let him come in, but then she stepped back, and he walked past her, heading for Julia's bedroom. She was sitting propped up by half a dozen pillows, her face almost waxen-pale. She looked at him when he walked in, her eyes lifeless and dull, and when he bent to kiss her, she turned her head away.

"Oh God, Julia darling, please don't be like this with me! I want us to be married just as much as you do . . ." he pleaded.

He tried to cheer her up by telling her about William's plans, but she seemed lethargic and uninterested. Her pupils seemed twice their normal size, almost as though she had been drugged, he thought worriedly. When he asked her what was wrong, tears filled her eyes, and then she said abruptly, "It's just the time of the month, that's all."

He stayed for a couple of hours, but she remained distant, wrapped up in her own thoughts, not the Julia he knew and loved at all really.

"He's gone, then?" asked Frances as she heard the front door of the flat close. "Did you tell him?"

Julia shook her head.

"No. What was there to say? I was having your baby, but I've had it aborted?"

"Come on, kid! Things aren't that bad. There'll be other babies . . . lots of them. Anyone can see that the guy's crazy about you!"

Julia didn't respond. She couldn't. Tears blurred her eyes. From the moment Alex had dropped his bombshell about their wedding being postponed, she had been living in a nightmare. She had known the evening they made love that she would conceive. She had deliberately planned it that way, knowing that Alex wouldn't be able to resist her . . . sensing that once they were married he might insist on them being sensible and waiting for a year or so, but she hadn't wanted to wait.

She hadn't been able to believe it when he told her that his father was dead, and when only days later her own belief that she was already pregnant was confirmed, she simply hadn't known what to do. Her parents were old-fashioned; an illegitimate grandchild was the very last thing they would want. Oh, if she had told Alex, he would have married her, she knew that, but how could she tell him . . . how could she burden him with not just her but a baby as well, when he had no money and no prospects? Julia had never had to budget in her life, and wouldn't have had the first idea how to do so. Her father was indulgent financially . . . but once she was married he would expect Alex to support her.

She had been panic-stricken then when she realised her position, and she had turned instinctively to Frances.

"So you're pregnant," Frances had shrugged. "So what, it's no big deal."

And Frances had proved right. A discreet visit to a small and very expensive private clinic where Julia had been treated with antiseptic indifference by the doctor and staff. An overnight stay, then back to the flat. She hadn't suffered any physical pain or discomfort, there had been none of the horrors one reads about.

No, the horror was locked away deep inside her, she acknowledged. She had destroyed her child . . . and it made no difference how many times she told herself there would be other babies, she knew that she would always grieve for this one. That would be her punishment, and she welcomed it. She ought to be punished . . . she needed to be punished, and Frances, who had had cause to visit the discreet private clinic on a couple of occasions herself, looked at her with cynical contempt.

If only she could tell Alex, but how could she? Had he known of her pregnancy he would have married her, no matter what, she knew that. But she hadn't been able to endure the thought of telling her parents, of people knowing, of . . . If only Alex's father hadn't died everything would have been all right. They would have been safely married.

Julia burst into tears and buried her head under her pillow, her hand automatically going to the empty flatness of her smooth young stomach.

Alex was lucky. A buyer was soon found for the factory, and when all the creditors were paid off he was left with almost twenty thousand pounds—double the amount he had hoped for. His mother had decided to stay with her cousin, and Alex divided the money between them, suggesting that his mother invest hers to bring her in a small income. It wasn't much, but it was better than nothing, and once their new venture took off he would be able to do more for her.

Within a year the new company was being praised for its innovative ideas, orders were pouring in, and Alex was able at last to tell Julia that they could set a fresh date for their wedding. They bought a small cottage not far from Cambridge, so that Alex could travel everyday. At night they made love, and Julia responded to him with a satisfying intensity, and then when they had been married for two years and she had still not conceived the child she so desperately wanted, he had bought her the house in Cotswolds, an old rectory, a graceful, mellow home—a family home.

The business had gone from strength to strength, but the home computer market was overloaded, and so three years ago they had started spending money on developing a new system. Because it hadn't been tried and tested, and because it was so revolutionary, orders were slow in coming in, but once they got the Government contract . . .

Alex arched his head back and stared out of his study window, not seeing the verdant spread of the lawn. Everything was going wrong. They should have heard by now . . . and this damned Pepper Minesse business hanging over them . . . If the Department ever got wind of the contents of that file of hers . . .

He broke out into a sweat at the thought, and found himself wishing to God he had never heard of Simon Herries, or the Hell Fire Club . . . never gone to Oxford. But no, that was stupid.

He saw Julia coming towards him. The tiny stress lines round her eyes seemed to have deepened recently. He knew how she felt about her inability to conceive their child. He wished there was something he could do to help her, but there wasn't. They were going ahead with the adoption process, but their social worker couldn't make any promises. There had been so many questions . . . endless enquiries into their private lives . . . Alex thought bitterly of what it might do to Julia if they were rejected. She looked so frail, her bouts of depression were surely more frequent . . . nights when she would lie beside him, silently weeping when she thought he was asleep.

Julia saw Alex turn away from her as he saw her and her stomach clenched in a familiar sense of panic. He seemed to be doing that so often at the moment, turning away from her . . . and why not? What man wouldn't turn away from a woman who couldn't give him a child, a woman who had destroyed the child he had given her. The black pit of despair that never seemed to leave her these days started to whirl round her, sucking her down into its dark depths.

Maybe Alex had found someone else, someone who could give him children. After all, he was an attractive man . . . a very attractive man, well off, kind. What would she do if she lost him?

Please God, haven't I suffered enough? she cried silently. Haven't I paid enough?

It was that abortion, of course, that antiseptic,

clean, painless operation that had taken away not only her child, but all her chances of ever conceiving again, because despite his air of calm assurance and competence, that doctor had made a mistake . . . a mistake that meant she would never be able to conceive. But only she and her specialist knew that. In the face of her near-hysteria when he had broken the news to her he had agreed that there was no need for him to tell Alex exactly why she could not conceive, and Alex, being the man that he was, simply accepted Julia's explanation without question.

He had been so patient with her. But what if he was running out of patience? What if . . .

Her footsteps slowed. She felt reluctant to confront him in case all her fears were justified.

Alex heard her come in and waited. He heard her go upstairs and sighed. He would have to go up and comfort her, but not now. He was too on edge, too tense. If only he could get word on that contract. If only Miles French would ring and say that everything was going according to plan . . .

CHAPTER ELEVEN

RICHARD HOWELL left Oxford the same summer as Alex. He too had a ready-made job waiting for him, but not as heir apparent. That role was reserved for his cousin Morris.

He spent his summer vacation working in the bank as holiday relief for members of the permanent staff, getting what his uncle David called a good grounding in banking principles. Richard hated it. At that level the pace of life within the bank was slow and pedantic. The daily routine of dealing with the bank's customers bored him. He wanted more . . . he deserved more, he told himself bitterly, especially when he learned that he had got a first-class honours degree.

David Howell was surprised, but not so his uncle-in-law Reuben Weiss.

"I told you to watch him! If you're not careful he'll snatch the bank from under young Morris's nose."

Morris was a plodder, a nice enough boy, but he lacked his elder cousin's cutting edge and both men knew it.

"What nonsense," David said uneasily. "Why, they're practically brothers . . . they've been brought up together."

"So were Cain and Abel," Reuben Weiss reminded him sardonically, and David remembered his own twin brother's bitter resentment of him and he looked rather thoughtfully at his nephew.

Morris wasn't going to Oxford—or to any other university. Only to himself was David prepared to admit his son lacked the brains of his cousin. There were times when Richard reminded him very much of his own father, that sharp-brained entrepreneur, whose shrewdness was responsible for the bank's present-day standing.

Perhaps a spell away, a reward to Richard for getting his degree . . . Morris was to start work in the bank within the next fortnight or so. He would be grooming him himself to take over his role as chairman. Morris was already a little inclined to take a lead from his older, far more sophisticated cousin, and it wouldn't do for the next chairman of the board to be seen to be in awe of someone who while they held the sacred Howell name was still destined to be little more than acting manager of the bank at the very most.

David Howell frowned thoughtfully. Yes, it would be a good idea to send Richard away for a while, but where?

In the event he had to push the problem of his nephew to one side. The morning brought a phone call from a fellow banker in New York who informed him that he and his wife and family were coming over to London for a brief holiday. David knew Dan Lieberman quite well. They had had business dealings over the years and David had stayed with the Liebermans on some of his visits to New York.

He and Dan had even tentatively talked about the possibility of Morris marrying Dan's daughter Jessica. It would be a good marriage . . . Lieberman's bank, while not of the status of Howell's, was well known, and its control rested solely in the Lieberman family's hands. Dan's son would follow him into the business, and Dan's father before his death had established trust funds for both his grandchildren, which would mean that Jessica Lieberman would one day be a very wealthy young woman.

David rang his wife and told her that he had invited the Liebermans to spend the weekend with them at Windsor.

The Windsor house with its surrounding acreage was a recent acquisition. David had been rather dubious at first when his wife suggested the move, but in the two years they had owned it, several prestigious new customers had found their way into Howell's books via the contacts David had made at Windsor. There was also the not inconsiderable cachet of owning a property in the Royal Borough, and he had sensed that Dan Lieberman had been impressed when he had casually mentioned the town.

Anna Howell was the ideal wife for a prominent banker. She was a superb hostess, and managed to combine the gift of making their home seem both elegant and welcoming. She had a placid nature and seldom allowed anything to ruffle her. She was also discreet and tactful and never made the mistake of interrupting her husband or any of his business colleagues, even when their conversation threatened to ruin her carefully planned meal.

As soon as she put the phone down she was busy planning.

Morris walked into her sitting room as she sat making lists. He had been playing tennis with the son of one of their neighbours, and Anna wrinkled her nose slightly at the smell of fresh sweat.

"What are you doing?" asked Morris.

"Your father has invited the Liebermans back for the weekend. They're coming to London later this week. You remember them, don't you? Their daughter . . ."

"The Jewish American princess," Morris interrupted with a grin. "Oh yes, I remember her."

His mother smiled indulgently. Morris might not have the intelligence and determination of his cousin, but he had something else . . . something that to her mind was far more important. Morris had a sweetness, a gentleness of manner and mind. Like his father, she regretted his subservience to his elder cousin, but for different reasons. She didn't like Richard. He reminded her too much of his grandfather, her father-in-law.

Anna knew quite well why David's father had been so anxious for them to marry . . . not because he liked or approved of her, but because she was Jewish and rich. And she didn't delude herself either. David would have married her no matter what she looked like, no matter what his private feelings had been, because it was what his father had wanted.

No matter how illogical it was, she feared that her son, her precious lovely Morris, might be held in thrall to his cousin in much the same way that her husband had been to his father. It didn't matter that David had never been the favourite son, the favoured and loved child, that he had time and time again been passed over for his brother . . . even when that brother had proved beyond any doubt that he wasn't worthy of his father's love or respect. Anna had known, just as they had all known, that her father-in-law, had he been able to change the order of things, would have preferred Jacob with all his faults to be his eldest son and heir.

"Don't call her that!" she chided Morris lovingly now. "She's a very nice girl."

Morris made a face. "She's spoilt to death and you know it."

"Well, never mind about that . . . you just make sure you're at home for the weekend."

"If I have to, but you won't be able to bring Richard to heel as easily."

It was another thorn in Anna's flesh that Richard continued to live with them, long after, in her opinion, he ought to have found a home for himself. It was the Jewish tradition for families to stay together, David reminded her, but they both knew that Richard stayed because there was no other way he could afford the life-style he had with them. And while he stayed he continued to overshadow Morris in everything they both did, whether it was swimming, playing tennis, or even dancing.

Unlike Morris, he received the news of the Liebermans' visit without comment when his uncle informed him of it. He and his uncle normally travelled down to Windsor together at weekends—the small salary Richard was receiving at the bank did not allow him to run a car . . . at least, not the sort of car he would have wished to be seen driving. He preferred to travel in the comfort of his uncle's Rolls to driving the sort of run-of-the-mill second-hand vehicle that would be all he could afford.

He also accepted without comment his uncle's statement that he should go to Heathrow and pick up the Lieberman family. As he inclined his dark head in agreement, David told himself that he had been imagining that flash of fury in those intense blue eyes that could only have come from his mother's blood. There were times when Richard made him feel acutely uncomfortable, times when he sensed within him that calculating, waiting intensity that Anna's uncle had warned him about.

Richard picked up the Liebermans as instructed. He had met them all before, and he greeted the older couple with the polite deference that he knew went down well.

Daniel Lieberman Junior wasn't with them. He was in his last year at Harvard and had elected to spend his vacation with friends at Bar Harbor, Mitzi Lieberman announced in response to Richard's polite enquiry.

Mitzi Lieberman liked Richard. She gave him a coquettish smile, something that Jessica observed with a sense of revulsion. Would her mother never realise that she was a middle-aged woman and that she was making herself ridiculous?

One only had to look at Richard Howell to know that he was the sort of man who would never go short of a woman. He must be laughing at her mother inside. Jessica writhed inwardly at the thought.

Jessica Lieberman was what is called a "Jewish American princess". She had known ever since she could remember of the trust fund set up by her grandfather and the millions she would inherit on her thirtieth birthday. It had given her an arrogance that had made her unpopular at her exclusive girls' school, with its antiquated WASP ideals and worship of lineage rather than wealth. She was not the sort of girl who could ever have been popular, no matter what her background, and her wealth emphasised her disdain for her fellow human beings, which was as much a part of her as the colour of her eyes.

One day of course she would marry. *That* was understood, but that was a distant event somewhere far off in the future. At the moment her mother was busy making plans for her fall debut into New York society, and Jessica went along with them.

Privately she couldn't think of anything more boring, but Jessica Lieberman was adept at hiding her real feelings and thoughts. The only thing that could move her to real emotion was art. Already she knew that the moment she could elude her mother her time in London would be spent in its famous galleries. There had been a time when she had dreamed of painting

herself, but the pedantry of her work, its sheer medio-
crity, had infuriated her to the point where she simply
refused to pick up a paintbrush. All through her life
she would never be able to bring herself to accept
anything less than excellence, in herself as well as in
others. If she couldn't be the best, then she wasn't
going to compete.

She sat in the back of the Rolls with her mother.
The boot was full of case after case of matched and
initialled Gucci luggage. Her mother firmly believed
that nowhere in the world could produce anything as
well as New York, and consequently when she
travelled, she did not travel light.

Although they had stayed with the Howells before,
they had never visited the Windsor house, and Richard
answered Dan Lieberman's questions about it, as he
drove them skilfully away from the airport.

Every now and again he looked at Jessica Lieberman
through his driving mirror. She had that gloss that all
rich American girls seem to develop. Her clothes were
expensive but unobtrusive—Mitzi Lieberman did not
approve of "fashion". Jessica's teeth, the product of
eighteen years of the most expensive dental care that
New York provided, gleamed white in the olive round
of her face as she talked. Her hair, dark and thick,
was naturally curly, her figure although petite was
curvy; she was almost the antithesis of the prevalent
fashion for tall, bone-thin girls with yards of water-
straight hair, and anyway he preferred blondes,
Richard thought, looking away from her.

The Liebermans were obligingly impressed with the
Windsor house. Anna Howell had taken a careful note
of the way her husband's non-Jewish acquaintances
furnished their homes and had firmly borne what she
had seen in mind when it came to re-vamping the
house. The result was a carefully subdued blend of

Colefax and Fowler, with just a modest dash of modernity in the Persian rugs and the plain walls.

David approved of what his wife had achieved, and the discreet diamond necklace he had bought her for their wedding anniversary proved it.

Mitzi Lieberman liked the house, but felt smugly pleased that for style it came nowhere near their New York apartment with its acres of off-white carpet and pastel leather couches. She had had the room copied from an article she had seen in *Lifestyle*—with one or two little touches of her own, like the pair of gold horses' head statues that supported the glass coffee table and the gold velvet floor-to-ceiling curtains.

She had had the entire apartment done out while Jessica was in her last year at Vassar. Jessica was such an odd girl, she thought fretfully. She had no interest in young men, or marriage. She hadn't even remarked on all the work that had been done to the apartment, Mitzi reflected indignantly. Sometimes she wondered how on earth Jessica came to be her child . . .

Jessica, who had been admiring a carefully grouped selection of small English watercolours that Anna had found in a local antique shop, looked at her mother and had a fair idea what she was thinking. Nothing on this earth would ever change her conviction that the New York apartment shrieked bad taste. She personally found it offensive even to look at it. This was much better . . . much more subtle, and somehow "right" for the house with its mellowness and large rambling garden.

Morris came in just as his mother was serving tea. Richard had been pressed into handing round the teacups, and the two cousins exchanged glances as David walked in.

Jessica had met Morris before; she found him dull and uninteresting, but she knew that her father was considering him as a prospective husband for her.

It was after dinner that David decided it was time to give Morris a delicate hint of what was in his mind.

"Jessica doesn't know any young people in England, Morris," he told his son when Anna was showing the Lieberman family round her garden. "I want you to make yourself available to show her round while she's here."

Richard knew instantly what was in his uncle's mind, and the jealousy he always kept meticulously under control raged inside him. Here was Morris, heir apparent to the wealth of Howell's bank, being handed the opportunity to marry a girl even wealthier than he would be himself!

Richard had no false conceptions about life. He felt sure that had his father married as had been planned his life would have taken a far different course. He resented his Englishness, the non-Jewish blood that came to him from his mother. Morris married to Jessica Lieberman, with that huge trust fund to come to her when she was thirty.

He saw the Liebermans walking towards the house and went forward to open the French windows.

Later, when his uncle accused him of deliberately setting out to seduce Jessica, he denied it.

He was telling the truth. He hadn't thought he would need to take things that far. But Jessica didn't want to get married . . . and that was really all he wanted from her.

Despite her years at Vassar Jessica had remained a virgin. She was too aloof, too self-contained to have much appeal on the casual dates she had had. Her remote manner put men off, and when there were so many other girls far more willing to give them what they wanted why should they bother with the Jessica Liebermans of this world?

And those young men who would have paid court
to her she avoided like the plague, knowing that what
they had in mind was the one thing she didn't
want . . . marriage. She wanted her independence,
the right to control her own life, and her own trust
fund. Jessica was no fool. She knew exactly why she
was being courted.

Even sensible young women can fall victims to their
hormones, though. To her horror Jessica found herself
responding to the physical presence of Richard Howell
in a way she had often dreamed of but never imagined
could ever happen to her.

He wanted to take her to bed, to make love to her
all night long, to kiss and explore every inch of her
body, he told her in the dark shadows of the garden,
and Jessica wanted it too. She wanted the brief indulgence of a passionate and intense summer-long affair
more than she wanted anything in her life. But Richard
wasn't after an affair, and when he realised that that
was exactly what Jessica did have in mind he knew he
would have to change his tactics.

He did it by keeping her in such a state of frustrated
anticipation that she made no demur at all when he
suggested coming to her hotel room. Her parents were
going to be out that evening . . . they were dining
with the Howells as a "thank you" for their hospi-
tality.

Richard knew that the evening would be over long
before Jessica or the Liebermans anticipated, because
he had purposely arranged, by bribing one of the
juniors, that the bank's alarm system would ring
halfway through the evening, necessitating his uncle
being called out by the police. The Liebermans returned
just in time to hear Jessica's guttural cries of fulfilment
pulsating round her bedroom as Richard made good
the promises he had been making her.

They had to get married, of course. Richard played his role to the hilt. He was contrite and guilty, but steadfast in his determined stance that he loved Jessica and wanted to marry her.

Jessica fought against her parents' edict like a caged fury, but it was no good. She would have to be married . . . *couldn't* she see that? her mother demanded.

The wedding took place in London, a lavish, full-scale affair, with the bride's face as white as her gown, and her mouth set in a bitter uncompromising line. She had no illusions. She knew now exactly why Richard had made love to her, and she could only marvel that she had been ever idiotic enough to want him to the point where she had been so blind to reality.

Dan Lieberman was irritated by his daughter's attitude, and by her stupidity. By rights she should have been marrying the Howell heir, not this cousin. David was furious with Richard, but said nothing, apart from pointing out to Morris that his cousin had snatched his prospective bride away from under his nose.

"But if Richard loves her, Dad," Morris protested, "I don't mind. I hardly knew the girl . . ."

Impossible to explain to Morris that he suspected that Richard didn't give two hoots about his bride and that his only interest in her was her trust fund.

Things wouldn't have been so bad if Dan Lieberman had suggested taking his new son-in-law back to New York with him, but he didn't. Richard's place was with Howell's, he announced firmly.

If Richard felt anything for Jessica it was mild contempt. She was far from being the first girl he had been to bed with, and it amused him that she should have wanted him so desperately. As yet she was too inexperienced to satisfy him, but he wasn't looking for sexual gratification in his marriage . . . he could find that elsewhere. His present girlfriend was a tall, leggy blonde, with a repertoire of sexual know-how that had even given him a few surprises.

In due course Jessica would produce a family—a son, he hoped. And if that boy should be Dan Lieberman's only grandson . . . but now, it didn't do to tempt fate too much.

The bridal pair honeymooned in the Caribbean—a wedding gift from the groom's uncle David.

Richard hadn't given any particular thought to how Jessica would react to their marriage. She was Jewish, therefore she must have been brought up to expect that she would one day be a wife and a mother. That she should be so furious about the way he had trapped her that she refused point blank to have sex with him was the last thing he expected. He tried cajoling, and when that didn't work he told her coldly that she was his wife and that he intended that their marriage would be consummated. It wasn't rape . . . but it wasn't anything like any of his previous sexual experiences. The cold rejection of her flesh irritated him, and by the time they returned to London they were barely speaking to one another, never mind making love.

Jessica's father provided them with a luxurious flat in one of London's exclusive Georgian squares. When Jessica taunted Richard with the fact that her father had had to pay for their home, he simply shrugged her taunt off. She could say what she liked to him. He didn't care. He had what he wanted, a wife who was going to make him rich.

Before they had been married six months they were sleeping apart in separate rooms. Richard wasn't dating the blonde any more . . . she had been supplanted by a redhead. He neither knew nor cared what his wife did in his absence. He spent as little time as possible at the flat, and made only duty visits to Windsor.

Morris was now working at the bank, and the bitterness and resentment which had subsided on his marriage to Jessica surfaced again. It wasn't just money he wanted, Richard acknowledged. He wanted the bank.

His first intimation that it was in financial trouble came when he walked into his uncle's office and overheard part of a telephone conversation. He gave no sign of what he had overheard, but started to delve discreetly into his uncle's financial dealings.

A speculative investment in the commodities market had wiped out a large part of his uncle's personal fortune; the bank had lost several important clients, and there were rumblings in the city that all was not well at Howell's.

And then, as though fate had finally decided to favour him, Richard was sent to work in the safety deposit section to cover for a member of staff who was off on extended sick leave.

By the time he and Jessica had been married four years Richard was well on the way to making his first million pounds, and Howell's bank was in grave danger of collapsing. There were rumbles from the board, open speculation in the financial press. Morris confided to him that he was worried about his father. Richard knew he had to act and act fast.

On the same day that he leaked the news of his uncle's financial misjudgements to the press, he also announced that he, as the son of David Howell's twin brother, had been approached by certain members of the board to take over as chairman.

The share price tumbled in the general panic, and Richard bought secretly and rapidly. When his uncle taxed him with the press announcements he said innocently that neither of them had anything to do with him. David Howell thought he knew better, but he had no proof . . . nothing. He was a man without power now, a man who had failed the great tradition of his family. The pains he had been having in his chest recently grew. He thought of his brother and his face . . .

Reuben Weiss found him, face down, at his study desk. He had died instantly, the coroner reported.

There was pandemonium at the bank. Someone had to take charge.

Richard had the authority. Richard had the shares . . . and now Richard also had the board's support. He had finally found his rightful place.

It struck him that he hadn't been home for almost seventy-two hours. He showered in what had once been his uncle's private bathroom, and which was now his, and got himself a taxi. He would sell the Rolls and get something else . . . He was pondering on what as he unlocked the door and walked into the hall.

He found Jessica in the drawing room reading a magazine. Despite his absence she evinced no surprise at his arrival.

"Guess what?" he told her flippantly. "I'm now chairman of Howell's bank!"

"Guess what?" she told him back acidly. "You're also about to be divorced."

She had all the evidence. She had been gathering it for months . . . or rather her private detective had been gathering it. It didn't matter how much Richard raged and argued; Jessica refused to back down. She wanted her freedom and she was going to have it.

Richard stormed out of the house an hour later, swearing under his breath. If she divorced him . . .

He thought of the settlement that would be hers on her thirtieth birthday and cursed again. Other men had affairs without their wives divorcing them. But other men weren't married to Jessica, he admitted bitterly. He hesitated for a moment on the pavement outside the house, then shrugged his shoulders. Since Jessica already knew that he was having an affair and that it wasn't his first, he might as well keep the date he had made with Rose.

He had been involved with Rose Marshall for just over three months. She was a model working for one of the new London fashion designers; a blonde English rose as different in temperament and looks from Jessica as it was possible to be.

She was waiting for him when he reached her flat. Richard was still so furious with Jessica that he forgot his own most important rule of never discussing either his wife or his marriage with his other women.

"Why not let her divorce you?" Rose asked him with a careless shrug.

At twenty-five she was beginning to be conscious of the fact that her looks and youth were not going to last for ever. And Richard Howell was a wealthy man.

Richard saw his mistake too late and cursed under his breath. Much as he enjoyed his sexual relationship with Rose there was no way he wanted to turn it into something more permanent.

"I can't," he told her baldly, adding, "Anyway she doesn't really mean it. She's found out about us and she's as jealous as hell."

"Oh, come on—I know all about your wife, Richard, I've heard about her from a friend of mine. How could she be jealous, darling?—unless of course you're trying to say that she fancies me?"

She saw from his face that he hadn't known, and she laughed shrilly, caught between triumph and a faint frisson of fear. Richard wasn't looking at her at all as though he was pleased by her disclosure.

"Don't tell me you don't know?" she asked him uncomfortably. "It seems to be pretty common knowledge."

Richard knew that Rose had a lot of friends and colleagues—people she had met through her work—who were members of the gay community, and suddenly he realised that she was speaking the truth. Little things that had meant nothing to him at the time . . . phone calls for Jessica from women he had assumed must be social contacts and friends, an oddly smug and defiant look in her eyes when she refused him sex . . . so many small pointers that he had either not noticed or had ignored. His wife . . . his wife would not allow him into her bed because she preferred to share it with a member of her own sex!

Rage and chagrin swelled up inside him. Rose saw it in his eyes and knew an increasing surge of fear. Even so, she had not expected him to head back to the door and leave.

"When . . . when will I see you again?" she asked him as he turned to leave.

Richard ignored the question. His wife . . . Jessica . . . God, how she must be laughing at him! No wonder she wanted to divorce him! Well, she could, but only at a price . . .

Jessica lay in bed staring numbly at the ceiling. She had been too confident, too careless somehow. She had never dreamed that Richard would find out, but he had, and now he was blackmailing her . . . threatening that if she didn't agree to stay with him until after her thirtieth birthday, until after she inherited under the trust fund, then he would tell her parents what she had become. And she knew he wasn't bluffing.

She wouldn't be thirty for another two years. It was unendurable. She couldn't stand it.

She got up and walked downstairs, pausing outside the door to Richard's study. If money was what it took to buy her freedom, then money he should have.

They were divorced two months later, but only after Jessica had signed a legal agreement to hand over to Richard two million dollars on the day of her thirtieth birthday.

As a woman she meant nothing to him at all . . . as a wife she had been important. He cared nothing for her feelings, and even less for her sexual preferences, Richard told himself, congratulating himself on having pulled off a good deal.

Under his guidance Howell's bank had gone from strength to strength. It seemed that the gods always smiled on him, and even more so, he had thought since he met Linda. She was his kind of woman. They had been married four years now, and life was good— at least it had been until that confrontation with Pepper Minesse.

He had to admire her. After all, she was doing no more than he himself had done, but she was a woman, and she wouldn't succeed. Miles French would see to that. Richard frowned, thinking back over the years. They had all of them changed. Nowadays he wouldn't do any man's bidding . . . And Simon Herries . . . There was something odd about him, something dangerous . . . something almost obsessive, but hadn't that always been there? That furious determination of his that Pepper was responsible for Tim Wilding's death and that she should be punished.

It was too late to go back and change things now. He only hoped that Miles French knew what he was doing. He hadn't struck him as a man who would make false claims about his abilities. What he had suggested had been so simple, and yet if he could pull it off it would be completely effective.

If he could pull it off.

Could he?

Richard mulled over what he knew about Miles, and then remembered that an eminent High Court judge had recently transferred his personal accounts to them, and made a mental note to get his secretary to make an appointment for him to have lunch. A little discreet foraging for information might be as well.

CHAPTER TWELVE

SIMON HERRIES left Oxford two years ahead of the other two. He had no money to speak of; the estate was bankrupt and he had to sell almost all of the remaining land to clear the debts. He knew that he needed money, and he also thought he knew how to get it.

He went first to Marchington, and Tim's mother, a gentle unworldly woman who thought she sensed loneliness behind the cold blue eyes and remembering that Simon had been her only son's best friend, invited him to stay.

He stayed for two months, and was quietly relentless in his pursuit of Deborah Wilding. The title would go to a distant cousin—the grandson of the Earl's mad aunt—eventually, but the Earl was an extremely wealthy man and so was his son, and all the Wilding girls had their own trust funds. If he could persuade Deborah to marry him . . .

Deborah guessed what was in Simon's mind and did everything she could to avoid him. She hadn't liked him when Tim had first brought him home, and she liked him even less now. In addition she blamed him for Tim's death. He was his friend, he had been with him . . . But she had kept her views to herself, knowing how much they would hurt her mother, who still grieved terribly for her only son. Deborah's two younger sisters couldn't understand her. They considered that Simon was both good-looking and sexy. Deborah couldn't explain her own feelings of revulsion to them; couldn't explain that she considered him to be evil and threatening; that she shuddered with fear every time Simon even touched her, and that the thought of marriage to him made her skin crawl. There was something about it . . . him . . . an aura which emanated from him that carried the smell of corruption so strong that she was amazed that only she was aware of it.

Her grandfather and her father had been away in Australia where they had joint business interests when Simon arrived, but when they returned the Earl was quick to notice the air of constraint about his favourite grandchild. She reminded him so much of his own wife, this quiet, withdrawn girl, who seemed to prefer to keep in the shadows rather than to live in the sunlight. Sometimes he thought there was almost something a little fey about her. She had an innocence, a modesty that was totally out of line with modern-day life, and often he worried about her future.

He had observed her Australian second cousins while he was away and had dismissed from his mind a half-formed idea that one of them might make her a good husband. She needed cherishing and spoiling, this granddaughter of his; and she would surely waste away and pine in the arid heat of the Australian outback.

He hadn't been pleased to discover Simon Herries in residence at Marchington. He had never liked nor trusted him, and when he saw how openly Simon was pursuing his granddaughter it added to his disquiet. When he tried to talk to Deborah, though, she refused to discuss what was troubling her. How could she, when she could see how much her mother enjoyed having Simon staying with them? It was as though having him there brought Tim back to her. After Tim's death, for a while they had thought that they might lose her too, she had grieved so intensely. The Earl wasn't deceived. Something was bothering Deborah and he intended to find out what it was.

He watched the way Simon followed Deborah and drew his own conclusions. Like her, he didn't like him, but with his much broader experience of life he knew why. Simon was a wrong 'un. The Earl could sense it . . . smell it almost. He had lived a long time and had come across other men who carried that same taint of inner corruption.

He didn't leave for Scotland at the beginning of August as was his normal habit but elected to remain at Marchington.

Deborah was glad. It didn't matter how often she told herself that there was no way Simon could make her change her mind, she still felt threatened and vulnerable. Having her grandfather there made her feel stronger, protected.

Simon was growing impatient. He needed a rich wife, and his own pride demanded that she be well connected, that she came from the same class as he did himself.

He knew Deborah didn't want him, and it infuriated him. What was she, after all? Nothing, if you took away her family and her wealth. She wasn't even particularly attractive, he thought sneeringly, watching her one afternoon as she and her sisters played croquet.

Simon's taste in women ran to narrow, athletic, boyish-looking girls with flat chests and long legs. He didn't question his preference, merely dismissing it in the same way that he had dismissed and turned his back on his homosexuality after Tim's death. He had the foresight to see then that what had been acceptable at school, that what was accepted in the cloistered confines of Oxford, would not be equally acceptable in the outside world. He had also recognised his own

need to marry well. Once he was married . . .
Deborah was annoying him with her stubborn resist-
ance. He knew that physically he was attractive . . .
far more attractive than a girl with Deborah's plain
plumpness could ever realistically merit. She ought to
have been falling into his arms in gratitude and adora-
tion, but she wasn't.

He was determined to have her . . . all the more
so because she insisted on resisting him. Somehow he
would find a way. He had already decided that they
would be married before Christmas, in the
Marchington chapel. His stomach gave a kick of
mingled remembered fury as he recalled the use to
which Tim had wanted to put the chapel . . . and the
tragic train of events that the decision had put into
action.

He had made her pay for it, though . . . that
common little tramp who had been the cause of his
friend's death. Simon remembered the sensation of
her body beneath his hands. She hadn't cried out a
great deal, but he had sensed her fear . . . felt it
almost, and that knowledge had charged his own
excitement. He had enjoyed possessing her, dominating
her. As he remembered, it came to him how he should
deal with Deborah . . . Nothing as crude as rape,
although he would have enjoyed punishing her defiance
with the dominance of his body . . . No, that would
have to wait.

Deborah was not a modern girl; quite the contrary.
No pill for her to give her the freedom to take as
many lovers as she chose. The Marchingtons were a
devoutly Catholic family. As Simon turned these facts
over and over in his mind, his excitement grew. Fate,
it seemed, was disposed to aid him.

The whole family were due to spend the weekend
with Deborah's uncle, but at the last minute Deborah

developed all the symptoms of a heavy summer cold, and it was decided that she shouldn't go. Simon tactfully announced that he would return home for the weekend, and Deborah heaved a small sigh of relief.

He left two hours before the family, but he didn't go very far . . . only far enough along the road to pull off it and wait until he had seen that they had actually left. He waited a further hour after that, and then when he felt comfortably sure that they would not be coming back, he turned round and drove back to Marchington.

It was still only early evening, but the sky was overcast; thunder had been threatening all day. The butler let him in, and accepted his plausible excuse that he had forgotten his house keys.

Instead of going straight to his room, though, Simon went into the library and poured out two glasses of the heavy, rich port that the Earl favoured. Into one he tipped the contents of a small sachet of paper which he had bought from a fellow student. It contained a powder nicknamed "stardust"—a powerful amphetamine-based drug that removed inhibitions and gave the user an intense sensation of power and freedom. It also had the benefit of being extremely fast acting.

Simon already knew which bedroom was Deborah's. He walked in without knocking. She had been half asleep, but the moment she saw him she sat upright, trembling with shock and dread.

"I forgot my keys," he told her, smiling at her, but neither of them was deceived. "Look, I've brought you a glass of port."

He sat down on the side of her bed and put her glass beside her, drinking slowly from his own.

There was no one in the house apart from the staff.

Deborah trembled, her brain numbed by his audacity. She had never imagined he would do anything like this. She felt sick as she reached blindly for the glass. Perhaps this would make it better . . . make her feel better. She knew what Simon meant to do . . . she could read it in his eyes, and there was nothing she could do to stop him. Even if she were to call out, no one would hear her. He had chosen his time well. She had just had her supper and the staff would be in their own sitting room watching television.

She wanted to plead with him, but the words stuck in her throat. He had no mercy for her . . . no feelings for her at all, she recognised as she looked into his eyes and saw her fate written there. He wanted only what she could give him.

He had finished his port and she drained hers quickly, wishing there was more . . . wishing she could drink enough to pass out.

"You know what's going to happen now, don't you?"

His voice lowered to a silken, whispering sound that shivered across her skin. It seemed to mesmerise her. She felt dizzy as she listened to it. Simon reached out and pulled the bedclothes away from her body, and she heard herself sigh in mingled resignation and dread.

As he looked at the lush curves of her breasts Simon quelled his own inner revulsion. He closed his eyes and pictured Tim's face. The remembered familiar heat surged through his body.

Beneath the crushing weight of him Deborah felt her mind and body spin out of control. Amazingly her sense of panic and revulsion was fading and in its place was a growing, dizzying excitement. She moved restlessly beneath him, catching her breath on a gasp as she felt the aroused hardness of his body against her own. Her mind disintegrated beneath the assault of the drug; she became a creature of pure physical need. She felt the fierce surge of him within her and went eagerly to meet it. How could this ever have been something she feared?

She wasn't Tim, but she held the key to so many things he wanted. Before he finally allowed her to fall asleep Simon had made use of the state of euphoria induced by the drug to introduce her to every sexual deviation he had ever learned—and had taught her to find sexual pleasure in them. It amused him intensely that this haughty, cold young woman could be reduced to such a demeaning, grovelling state, and he hoped that when the effects of the drug had finally worn off, she wouldn't have forgotten the events of the night.

Even if she had it didn't really matter. He had taken her and, he hoped, possibly he had impregnated her too. In the morning when the maid came to wake her she would find them both in bed. He would plead the folly of youth and love . . . he would say that he was the one to blame for agreeing with Deborah's plan that they take advantage of their elders' absence. There would be no arguments, no avoidance. They would be married.

He fell asleep on the thought.

Deborah woke up first. Her body ached unfamiliarly. She moved uncertainly, and stiffened as she encountered Simon's sleeping form. And then she knew . . . instantly and irrevocably she knew. She recoiled from the sleeping male body beside her, her mind playing back to her over and over again the events of the night. What had happened to her? Why had she allowed him to do such things to her? Why had her body craved his, like an alcoholic craving drink? She had broken every moral tenet that had formed her life. And she had destroyed for ever her own inner image of herself, creating instead a creature of such base grossness that she could not endure to live with what she had done. Her mind, never strong, and tormented by these horrifying images, disintegrated beneath the force of what had happened to her. She got up and stumbled into her bathroom, heaving sickly. She couldn't bear to look at herself, but scrubbed despairingly at her skin. The foul images still would not go away.

It was almost as though Simon had put some sort of evil spell on her. She remembered her own sharp cries of pleasure, her feverish, demanding response to even the worst of the atrocities he had inflicted on her, and she knew quite simply that the burden of her sin would be with her all her life. It could never be washed away. She let the sponge drop and got out of the old-fashioned shower. She didn't bother drying herself or wrapping herself in a towel.

No one saw her as she made her way down to the chapel. It was too early for the staff to be up. Deborah took down the ceremonial sword that had been her grandfather's, holding it carefully because it was heavy, and moving like someone in a trance.

She went towards the altar, images crowding one another for prominence in her mind. Her nausea had gone, but in its place was an implacable, cold determination to escape from what she perceived to be lying in wait for her. Her mind was suddenly crystal-clear, showing her the degradation that would be her future. She had sinned grievously, and in a way that had shown her how vulnerable she was to sin. She who had always held herself aloof, who had looked down upon those whom she considered to be weaker vessels. Now she was being punished. If her grandfather knew . . .

Tears shimmered in her eyes. Her last mental image

as she flung her body forward on to the sharp point
of the sword was of the Earl. She felt the pain searing
her flesh, cleansing her with fire, and her last conscious
thought was that she had finally and completely
escaped. Never again could she be dragged down into
the pit of degradation she had known last night.

She sighed, not knowing that her breath bubbled
from her throat on a wave of bright scarlet blood.

Simon found her. He woke up and found her gone,
and some instinct, some sense of awareness he hadn't
known he possessed, took him down to the chapel.
Fear and revulsion held him by the throat, his flesh
crawling with loathing as he stared at Deborah's
blood-spattered body.

He backed out of the chapel and looked round like
someone in a deep trance. He had to get away, to
escape, he thought feverishly . . . No one knew he
was still here. It was still early, only just gone six
o'clock. His car was outside, but the staff slept at the
back of the house. They wouldn't have known that he
hadn't left last night. He went upstairs, picked up
both the glasses and washed them, then he hurriedly
washed and dressed himself. He was just about to
straighten the bed when he remembered the stains on
the sheet.

He thought quickly, then stripped it off, going to
the cupboard just outside the bedroom to remove a
fresh sheet and make up the bed, deliberately untidying
it so that it looked as though it had been slept in. The
soiled sheet he bundled under his arm to dispose of
later.

He used the main staircase and let himself out
through one of the french windows. He drove twenty
miles before he stopped shaking.

It was Deborah's father who rang him to give him
the news. The shock of his granddaughter's suicide

had killed the old Earl, who had suffered a massive heart attack. There had always been a rumour in the family that they carried a streak of insanity, and now that he thought about his aunt he wondered uncomfortably if it had held any truth.

Simon went to the funeral, haggard and pale in dense black. He refused the invitation to go back to the house afterwards. One of the local papers had got hold of the story and there was some talk in the press about a family curse.

Simon escaped to America. He felt no guilt for what had happened, only a furious bitter anger. He was quite prepared to believe that Deborah had carried the taint of insanity—otherwise why on earth would she have chosen death in preference to marriage to him?

He pushed the entire incident to the back of his mind, locking it away with all those other things he preferred not to remember. His life had entered a new chapter.

The Americans loved him. They loved his accent, the way he looked, and most of all his air of breeding. He had armed himself with several introductions and talked nonchalantly about the family estate, shrugging dismissive shoulders when he added the fact that death duties had all but wiped out his inheritance. He fulfilled their image of what a member of the British aristocracy should be, and he in turn felt charged and challenged by their ambition, their drive.

He was introduced to Elizabeth Calvert by a mutual acquaintance. She was tall and slender enough to appeal to him physically, and when he discovered who she was he knew that he had found what he was looking for.

They were married just after Christmas. Simon's new father-in-law pressed him to remain in the States—

a place could be found for him somewhere within the family empire, which embraced both politics and the law—but he shook his head. He wanted to go home and restore his own family estate, he told him. In reality he had no intention of remaining under the watchful eye of Henry Calvert the Sixth, but he kept that bit of information to himself. His new wife's inheritance would make it more than possible for him to reclaim all that his father had lost, and besides, he had other reasons for wanting to return. Money, he was now discovering, wasn't enough. He wanted the power to go with it.

He thought of all that he had learned at Oxford; power came in many different guises. He would have to find the one that was right for him.

It was his new brother-in-law who first broached the subject of his entering the political arena, casually mentioning that he was due to go to Washington to address a small group of Senators.

Peter Calvert was a lawyer, and what he had to say made Simon think hard about his own future.

In their time both his grandfather and one of his uncles had represented their local constituency in Parliament. His father had had no taste for politics, and certainly it was not a career for a man without any financial backing behind him. But with his wife's family's wealth . . .

Before the newly married couple returned to England, Simon knew exactly what he intended to do.

Elizabeth Calvert wasn't sure exactly what she had expected from marriage. She had been at first astonished and then later triumphant when Simon Herries started paying court to her. At twenty-one, she had already and painfully realised that her narrow, almost curveless body did not appeal readily to the male sex. The brothers of her school friends, the young men who went to Harvard with her brothers, none of them actively ignored her, but they weren't attracted to her either. She had had only one love affair—born more out of sexual curiosity than anything else—with a totally unsuitable boy she had got to know while she was at Bryn Mawr. Neither of them had wanted anything permanent from the relationship, and when the time had come they had said their goodbyes without any regret.

Now at twenty-one Elizabeth was aware that she was becoming a social embarrassment to her family. Calvert women married young and produced families; they then went on to emulate their mothers and grandmothers by doing what generations of Calvert women had done. They worked for charity. If they didn't marry they either lived at home, or if they were very daring went abroad, and were henceforth known by other members of the family as "slightly eccentric."

Elizabeth fell into neither of those categories—yet! And the very last thing she wanted to do was to become the family spinster, aunt to her brothers' children, pitied by her female cousins and despised by her brothers' wives.

But one had to be seen to make the right kind of marriage. She knew that, just as she knew that her inheritance would find her a husband any time she wanted one, just as long as she set her sights on someone lower down the social scale than a Cabot or an Adams or a member of any of the other leading Bostonian families. And she had too much pride for that.

She had too much pride, full stop, she admitted. Far too much. Thus she had been at first wary and then reluctantly thrilled when Simon started paying subtle court to her. She wasn't a fool. She knew that financially she had a lot to attract him . . . several million dollars, in fact . . . but here was a man who could trace his family history back through countless generations more than any of Boston's first families. A man, moreover, who spoke with that upper-class English accent that no one could properly imitate . . . a man intelligent enough to hold his own with her father and brothers . . . a man who in short she could respect.

That she didn't love him didn't seem to matter. A Calvert woman did not have a career. It was a straight choice between marriage or remaining at home.

The thought of marriage had never particularly attracted Elizabeth; she knew that there was an odd coldness about her nature, a lack of responsiveness to men that she simply accepted as being part of her personality. Calvert women were not encouraged to discuss their sexuality. One married, one produced children—sons, for preference—and one worked for charity, and that was it.

Because she had never made any close women friends she had no one with whom to discuss her lack of feelings for Simon. He offered her an escape route from the label of "spinster sister" and she took it, telling herself that marriage at least offered a degree of freedom.

At first she thought she had made the right decision. After the first couple of nights of their honeymoon Simon seemed to be disinclined to make love to her—which suited her fine. He would want a son, of course . . . Elizabeth had heard all about his ancestral acres, and had quickly grasped that quite a considerable part of her inheritance would be used to buy back these lands and to pay off the mortgages on the Elizabethan house in the north. This did not worry her, her father had looked deeply into Simon's financial background, and since he had not been responsible for the debts that had overwhelmed his inheritance, Henry Calvert was quite content for his son-in-law to take charge of his daughter's financial affairs. He considered Simon to be an astute young man.

Simon had already confided to him his intention of securing the Conservative candidacy of his home town, and Henry Calvert approved of his plans.

He had never got on well with his only daughter. She was not like the other Calvert women, content to acknowledge the superiority of the male. There were even times when she made him feel uncomfortable. Privately he doubted that had he been Simon that he would have married her. There were plenty more wealthy young women in Boston far more compliant than Elizabeth. But Simon had his own reasons for choosing Elizabeth, and Henry Calvert would have been surprised to learn that her sexual coldness was one of them.

Simon did not want a highly sexed wife. He had no intention of being sexually faithful, and a wife who had little or no interest in sex herself was more likely to turn a blind eye to his own affairs—and less likely to exact retribution in the form of taking a lover of her own. As a potential MP, he would not be able to afford the scandal.

Already, though, he wanted more than merely to be a Member of Parliament. Already he was running through the contacts he had made at Oxford. Already his sights were set on a far higher goal . . . ultimately the very highest goal. He would make a good Prime Minister, he decided.

The newly married couple returned to England in the spring. Simon took Elizabeth first to the Borders, where he left her in the draughty, unheated, damp manor house while he went subtly into action. By the time he was ready to take his wife to London he had

fulfilled his own goals. The local Conservative party
would be adopting him as their new candidate at the
next election.

Left alone in the house, Elizabeth had discovered
she had more of the Calvert woman in her than she
had supposed. Workmen were called in, central heating
installed, damage repaired, decorators hired and
antiques bought to replace those sold. By the time
they left for London the house was already beginning
to glow with the burnish of money. One day it would
be featured in glossy upmarket magazines as an
example of all that was best about traditional English
country house taste, already it was beginning to show
all the hallmarks of what Simon privately considered
to be a "gentleman's residence".

He left a manager in charge of the home farm, and
told him that whenever land became available he
wished to be informed about it. So gradually he would
buy back all that his father had sold.

In London Elizabeth repeated the pattern she had
started in the Borders. The London house bought for
them by her parents as a wedding gift was an elegant
Regency building. Her parents came over on a visit
for the second Christmas of their marriage, and Simon
was delighted to be able to tell his father-in-law that
not only was he likely to secure the Conservative seat
for his own town at the spring by-election but also
that he had fathered his first child.

Elizabeth smiled wanly and accepted her family's
congratulations. She hadn't wanted a child quite so
soon. She seemed to spend the major part of her day
alone at home being sick.

Simon was out most of the time. She didn't ask
where . . . she didn't really care. Marriage, she was
discovering, was just as much a trap as spinsterhood.
She couldn't say that she disliked Simon, but there

were times when she almost ached to have her freedom. Now she could never be free. The birth of their first child would tie her to him even more firmly. And almost the entire Calvert family stood firm against divorce—not from any moralistic view point, rather from a financial one. Calvert marriages were always carefully arranged. When they broke up, so too did family fortunes . . . monies carefully garnered and cherished over many generations. Divorces were wickedly wasteful and totally unproductive. A Calvert man instead indulged his sexual proclivities with discreet and carefully picked mistresses who were content to remain in the background.

And as for the Calvert women . . . Elizabeth wondered idly if her mother had ever imagined making love with anyone apart from her father. She dismissed the question as irreverent, and tried to convince herself that she was fortunate to have so attractive and well liked a husband, and then wondered why it was that they had so few friends. Her husband dined out a lot with business and political acquaintances, but he seldom brought them home. They had very little social life.

That was something Simon too had been giving thought to. He had been using the connections he had made at Oxford to make sure of his future as an MP, but he needed spheres of influence . . . more power. He needed to please and flatter people into giving him their support, he recognised.

He looked at his wife. The right kind of wife was an undeniable asset to a politician, and Elizabeth was the right kind of wife.

She was surprised at the extravagance of his Christmas gift to her—a single strand of beautiful pearls. He added earrings when she gave birth to their first child—a son. And a delicate little pin with her initials on it when he secured the candidacy.

Only Elizabeth knew of the strain of months and months of dinner parties, of being pleasant to more local dignitaries than she could name . . . of constantly playing the part of the devoted wife of the ever charming and pleasant Simon Herries. Other women looked sideways at her, wondering what on earth Simon saw in her, she knew that. She also wondered how many of them discreetly found their way into his bed. She told herself that she didn't really care just as long as it kept him out of hers.

Once just after little Giles's birth he had lost his temper with her over some trifling incident. He had come to her room that night and made love to her, abused her, with such violence and menace that she could never forget it. She hadn't spoken of the incident to anyone, knowing instinctively that it sprang from far more than a mere male frustration at the long weeks of abstinence over her pregnancy and Giles's birth. There had been deliberate intent to hurt and humiliate her in the way Simon touched her, the things that he demanded that she do.

Elizabeth was no Deborah . . . no ignorant, shy teenager. She had immediately refused . . . and had carried the bruises on her body for weeks afterwards as a result of her defiance.

They never spoke of it, and it never happened again, but as she looked into the envious and sometimes amused faces of other women, she wondered if they would envy her if they really knew what her husband was like.

Simon was pleased with the way his life was going. At last he was getting somewhere. People treated him with respect and deference. He enjoyed all the small perks that went along with being an MP, just as he enjoyed the status which his wife's millions afforded him. For the first time he began to know the meaning of the word contentment. He no longer even thought about his relationship with Tim; that part of his life was over. An up-and-coming young politician could not afford to have any scandal attached to him.

When he wanted release from his sexual frustration he found it in a series of discreet alliances with sophisticated married women who shared his tastes. They weren't difficult to find, and although it wasn't anywhere near as satisfying as what he had once known, it was an adequate substitute.

When Giles was two and a half Elizabeth became pregnant again—much to her disgust. She hadn't wanted another child, and in fact had assumed that she and Simon would never sleep together again, but she was wrong. Simon wanted to have the perfect politician's family, and to that end he was even prepared to spend time in his wife's bed.

Luckily she became pregnant almost straight away. He sent her home to her family for a month's holiday as a reward, and thus established the future pattern of their lives.

Emma Catherine Herries was born just in time to celebrate her father's first appointment as a very junior junior minister.

Simon had changed outwardly over the years. No one looking at him now would ever imagine the young man he had been; the passions that had burned in him, his connection with the Hell Fire Club, and those who remembered it were too much in thrall to their own fear of their connection with its being revealed to betray him.

Simon sought every opportunity to prove his worth as a member of parliament. He was still too young to be considered for Cabinet membership, but he was making his presence felt. He was bound for success

and nothing and no one would stop him. Elizabeth
had broached the subject of a divorce and been told
that she couldn't have one. Her family supported him
in this decision and she had her children to consider,
so she resigned herself to her life, and tried to tell
herself it was no worse than many another woman's.

The friction between her son and his father worried
her. Giles was a quiet, gentle boy, who had avoided
coming into too much contact with Simon almost
from the first day of his life. Elizabeth had objected
when Simon wanted to send him away to school, and
for once she got her own way.

Giles contracted glandular fever just before he was
due to go, and Simon was forced to heed their doctor's
advice that he remain at home and attend a local
private school. Elizabeth knew that her son was aware
of the tensions in their marriage, just as she knew that
Emma was very much her father's daughter. She had
his arrogance, and sometimes Elizabeth suspected,
some of his cruelty.

They never shared a bed now, and she was glad.
She knew he had his affairs, but he was always
discreet. She longed to divorce him but knew that if
she did her family would disown her. They were proud
of Simon.

Her father thought, like Simon, that she was raising
Giles to be a weakling. Calvert men weren't allowed
to experience emotion. Like Simon, her family
preferred Emma.

It saddened Elizabeth to watch her daughter growing
up spoiled and arrogant. She wasn't popular with her
school friends, and although Simon made light of it,
Elizabeth had already had to deal with a couple of
complaints from Emma's exclusive girls' school about
her tendency to bully the young girls. Sometimes
Elizabeth felt herself shrink back from her and knew

that her own inner dislike sprang from Emma's resemblance to Simon. She wondered how much she was to blame for the way her daughter was growing up, but she couldn't bring herself to reach out to her.

As she did every summer, she dreaded her return to London. Simon had reached the point in his career where he was being seriously considered as a future candidate for the Party leadership. He had been tense and on edge before they left. He had embarked on a new affair—Elizabeth could always tell. She didn't want to go back . . . but she had no choice.

She arrived in London three days after Simon had received Pepper's ultimatum, to discover that her husband had gone up to the North, and that he wanted her and the children to join him. She had learned years before the folly of ignoring his commands, so she packed the clothes they would need for a week or so and told the chauffeur that they would leave immediately after supper.

The manor house, which had everything to make it a home full of warmth and serenity, was a place Elizabeth dreaded visiting. It had been here that Simon had launched his savage and never forgotten attack on her . . . and even before that there had been times when she had an awareness of an oppression of the spirit so strong and fearsome that it had almost made her cry out loud.

The house had been Simon's childhood home, and yet at times he seemed as reluctant to visit it as she was herself. Even the children seemed subdued when they were here, and yet it was the most beautiful place, built in cream stone, with views over one of the most unspoilt pieces of countryside Elizabeth had ever seen. The gardens had been designed at a later date, the grounds set out with rare specimen trees and an artificial lake. On an island in the lake stood a Greek-

style temple built by one of Simon's ancestors on his
return from Italy. The house and its grounds were
regularly described as architectural gems, and yet there
were times when Elizabeth felt she hated them.

The house was in darkness when they drove up,
and this made her frown. Where was Simon? It wasn't
that late . . . he would be expecting them. They only
kept a skeleton staff at the house normally, and their
estate manager normally took on extra help when he
knew they were coming up.

They spent a month here each summer, normally in
August, and then a week just after the New Year,
when Simon insisted on holding a lavish ball for the
local residents. He was a popular figure in the locality,
for all the short lengths of time he spent here . . .
but that was Simon all over, intent on maintaining
and polishing his image.

Elizabeth got the chauffeur to open the heavy door
and help them in with their luggage. She followed
him, snapping on lights, and shivering as she realised
the central heating wasn't even on! Where were the
staff?

She saw a thin light burning under the study door
and pushed it open. Simon was lying sprawled out in
a chair, and the smell of brandy hit her as soon as she
walked up to him. She saw the empty bottle and hid
her shock. Simon drunk! But he never drank . . . She
dismissed the chauffeur and quickly urged the children
upstairs, ignoring Emma's strident questions.

There was no one other than her to help them get
ready for bed. She saw to it that they had baths and
then went down to the kitchen to get them some
supper.

The cupboards and fridge seemed well stocked. Her
thoughts buzzed desperately inside her head as she
worked. What was going on? Had Simon gone mad

and dismissed all the staff? But no, he would never do anything like that.

Elizabeth took their supper upstairs and settled the children, and then went back into the study. Simon was snoring. She decided against waking him, and went down to the flat above the garage which the chauffeur occupied whenever he was with them.

She told him that the housekeeper must have gone out for the evening and suggested that it might be as well if he got his own supper. That would stop him from coming back to the house. Simon would never forgive her if someone other than her saw him in his present state.

She went back to the house and started brewing black coffee. She had just finished making it when she heard a car outside.

The housekeeper looked flustered when she saw Elizabeth. She and her husband took care of the house and its gardens on a full-time basis, and Elizabeth had always found her very reliable, even though she had had trouble in understanding her North Country accent at first.

It seemed that Simon had given them the evening off . . . because he had intended drinking himself to a stupor? The woman avoided looking directly at her, and Elizabeth's heart sank. What had been going on? Surely Simon hadn't been stupid enough to bring one of his women back here with him?

She took the coffee into the study and left it there on a hotplate she plugged in. She wasn't going to wake Simon and risk his temper. Giving him a bitter look, she closed the door on him.

Simon woke up abruptly, not sure where he was, only knowing that he was in danger . . . he couldn't breathe properly. He seemed to be tied up . . . a figure loomed over him . . .

His father . . . He screamed out wildly, his body already anticipating the pain, and then his mind cleared and he realised that the figure standing watching him belonged to his son. A surge of rage and hatred raced through him as he saw the rejection in the boy's eyes. All the frustrations and fears brought on by Pepper's disclosures coalesced into one fierce burning need. He reached for Giles, swinging him off his feet, holding him under his arm as he unlocked the French window. It had been a long time since he had been there, but he knew exactly what to do. He found the punt and dropped Giles on to its floor. When the boy started to cry he hit him, revelling in the sensation of the soft flesh beneath his fist.

There was no clear thought pattern in his mind, he was simply following an ancient inbuilt urge; exacting from his son the same payment that his father had exacted from him. He didn't question his motives or his feelings, ignoring Giles's strained, hoarse cries as he dropped him into the rocking punt and prepared to cast off.

The very act of getting into the punt had triggered off a wild excitement inside Simon. He felt his body stir with pleasure and a dangerous maniacal sense of power. It was only right that his son should suffer this . . . as he had had to suffer it.

He was unaware of Giles looking up at him, beyond words, beyond tears, beyond anything except a primaeval fear of his father. He shivered in the cold night air, and Elizabeth, who hadn't been able to sleep and who had come down to check on her sleeping husband, stood transfixed at the open doorway, staring at the small tableau in disbelief.

Where was Simon taking Giles? What was he doing with him? It was a cold damp night. Giles could get a chill . . . and then sickeningly she knew exactly what was happening, and she started to run, her heart pounding with fear and shock. She reached the punt just as Simon pushed it free of the bank. Desperately she reached forward, grabbing for the pole, and managed to wrench it away from him.

She had caught Simon off guard, appearing almost from nowhere, to shock him into a moment's carelessness, but now he was turning towards her, his lips drawn back against his teeth in a rictus snarl of rage as he tried to take hold of the pole.

At some time she must have waded out into the water, Elizabeth realised as she felt her feet becoming stuck in the mud. Her terror for her son lent her a fierce strength that enabled her to resist Simon's attempts to wrench the pole from her, and she prayed desperately that somehow someone would see them and come to her aid.

Giles sat huddled up in the bottom of the punt, his eyes dazed with shock and fear, his body shaking convulsively. He seemed to be looking past them at some unimaginable horror, Elizabeth realised, and her determination to protect him sent a strong surge of adrenalin racing through her blood. By some miracle she managed to grab the pole from Simon, and then without thinking about what she was doing she raised it and hit out wildly at him, smashing the slightly flattened end of it into his body. He stumbled and the punt rocked wildly. Elizabeth saw him fall and catch his head on the side of the punt as he collapsed into it. Throwing the pole, she waded out to the boat and grabbed her child, and then with him held tightly in her arms she stumbled back to the house.

It seemed to take a lifetime to wake Emma. She protested bitterly that she did not want to leave, but for once Elizabeth ignored her strong-willed daughter, the horror of what she had glimpsed in her husband's eyes too strong to allow her to hesitate.

There was a small Ford in the garage, used mainly
by the staff. The keys were kept in the kitchen.
Elizabeth was shaking as she inserted them into the
ignition, dreading with every heartbeat seeing Simon
suddenly appear around the corner of the garage
block.

It was only when they were on the southbound
motorway that she could finally accept that they were
safe. But for how long? Simon would hunt them
down—he could not afford to let her go free to tell
the world what he had tried to do to his own child . . .
what he might actually already have done, Elizabeth
realised on a shudder of sickness.

Knowing her own family's unshakable support of
Simon, she realised she couldn't turn to them for
help—at least not until she could prove her husband's
depravity. She mentally reviewed her London friends.
None of them were close enough for her to turn to in
a crisis like this. She had always held herself rather
aloof from the women she knew. And then she remembered reading about shelters that had been set up for
women like her . . . women whose husbands physically violated and abused both them and their children.
She had enough money with her to book into a hotel.
She wouldn't use her own name. And tomorrow she
would find out how she could approach one of these
refuges. There wouldn't be much time; Simon was
bound to come after them. Elizabeth dared not risk
going back to the London house. In the back seat
Emma whined and complained, while Giles slept. She
would have to take him to a doctor . . . not her own
doctor. Feverishly her thoughts ran round and round
in tormented circles, while she castigated herself for
not realising what her husband was doing to their son,

and while she did so, she prayed that it was not too late and that Giles might be safe from his father's corruption.

CHAPTER THIRTEEN

THROUGH the good offices of Colonel Whitegate, Miles was able to leave Oxford, complete his law studies, and go straight into chambers. At first the others were a little wary of him. He had no legal connections, no background, and it was well over twelve months before he was really accepted.

It was gruelling, demanding work, made more so by the additional studying he did at night. Unlike most of his contemporaries, Miles had no family to finance him, so in his free time he worked. He held a variety of jobs, but it was while he was working behind the bar in a sophisticated West End club that he heard about an escort agency that was looking for presentable young men to escort some of their female clients.

"It's all straight and above board," he was told. "The agency's quite genuine . . . of course, if you want to come to a private arrangement with the client then that's something else."

"What's the pay like?"

"Good—and you get a dinner suit thrown in."

"So why are you working here?" Miles asked laconically.

"I blotted my copybook—got too involved with one of the clients. It turned out that her husband found out what was going on and made a complaint, so I got the push."

Working as an escort—paid to accompany rich old women; it sounded the very last thing he wanted, but the money was good. He needed a new set of textbooks, and his flatmate was getting married and wanted the flat to himself.

Halfheartedly Miles gave the agency a ring and made an appointment.

Marilyn Vernon had started up her agency when she discovered that the permissive age was leaving many of her contemporaries marooned on the shores of divorce; these were women in their late thirties with sufficient energy and income to enjoy themselves, but still tied by conditioning and upbringing to the need for a male escort when they went out.

She was scrupulously determined that her *escort* agency would be exactly that. The young men she employed could make whatever private arrangements they wished with her clients, but private they must be.

Miles French immediately struck her as being out of the ordinary run of well-born but impecunious young men she normally employed. Despite his relative youth he already carried about him an air of masculine authority that piqued her interest. She asked him the questions she asked all her potential employees. Miles answered them honestly and openly. Marilyn's eyebrows lifted a little when he told her that he was studying for the bar, and her mouth twisted wryly when he countered her surprise by commenting smoothly that since her agency was exactly what it was supposed to be he need feel no scruples about taking a job with her.

"The pay's better than the money I earn working in a pub . . . and to be quite frank, I need the money."

To test him she hired him to accompany one of her clients to the opera. Lady Pamela Dulwich was one of her richest and most difficult clients. She was forty-five and had the brittle brilliance of a bitchy, brittle socialite, with a penchant for attractive young men.

Marilyn knew in advance the sort of offer Lady Pamela would make Miles. If he accepted it he wasn't for her. A discreet private arrangement was one thing . . . out-and-out prostitution was quite another. She wasn't sure whether to be pleased or disappointed when he rang her at her office the following morning and explained calmly that there seemed to have been a misunderstanding and that he was not prepared to provide the kind of service Lady Pamela wanted.

Marilyn hired him. She would have been a fool not to do so, and Miles, who had initially taken on the job purely through financial need, found as the months passed, that it was impossible not to feel sympathy and compassion for the loneliness of many of the women he was hired to partner.

Very few of them made sexual advances towards him. He had that type of maleness that made it next to impossible for all but the most determined of women to treat him as nothing more than an available body.

One of his favourites was Lady Ridley. She had in her prime been a well-known opera singer, but she had married and retired to become a wife and mother. Now in her seventies, she announced that she was far too old for anyone to look askance at her if she chose to be escorted by a handsome young man. Miles liked her. She had a salty, keen wit, and a deep appreciation of the human condition that he found endlessly entertaining. Their relationship was almost one of grandmother and grandson—her only daughter lived in Australia, and she was very much alone, apart from one goddaughter, who regularly visited her but whom Miles had never met.

He had heard a lot about her, though. Amanda Courant had married young—almost straight from school. She was the only child of an extremely rich and very eccentric Scottish peer, and she had been married at her father's insistence to her second cousin.

"Hamish believed that because they both had Stuart blood they could between them produce a second Bonnie Prince Charlie."

Miles already knew that Amanda's father was obsessed by the Stuart cause, but that because of his wealth his mild eccentricities were generally accepted. He also knew that the marriage hadn't been a happy one. The second cousin had been too poor to refuse the offer of such a rich wife, but he apparently loved someone else.

"They never produced a child—I suspect the marriage wasn't even consummated, and of course, Hamish blames poor Amanda. She's living in London now . . . her mother left her a small inheritance, luckily. She won't go out, though. Her father's instilled into her the fact that she's a failure to such an extent that she actually believes it. She should marry again . . . but how can she if she won't go out and meet people? I want you to take her out, Miles. I'll pay you."

"If you mean you don't want her to know . . ." he began.

Lady Ridley shook her head. "Oh no, nothing like that! My dear boy, I've just told you—Amanda suffers from a massive lack of self-worth, there's no way she'd ever believe that a handsome young man like yourself would actually want to take her out . . . but her inheritance isn't very large and I've only managed to persuade her to go out by insisting that it's my duty as godmother to make her do so. She needs to meet people, Miles, to put the past behind her."

Miles agreed to escort Amanda to a fashionable society cocktail party.

He didn't really know quite what he expected, but

it certainly wasn't the almost flamboyantly beautiful brunette who opened the door of the small Chelsea mews house to him, and then he saw the apprehension in the huge golden eyes and he realised that Lady Ridley had been right and that he was looking at a woman with absolutely no confidence in herself at all. Her voice was husky with nervous tension, and he sensed that it would only take the slightest thing to have her backing out of the evening.

His taxi was waiting, but as he turned to take her arm he felt her flinch away from him. She was so patently nervous that he was at a loss to know how to reassure her, and even close to in the taxi, she looked closer to twenty-five than thirty-five.

The evening wasn't a success. Amanda shook visibly every time anyone male came anywhere near them, and Miles saw in her eyes that she was painfully conscious of the fact that he had been paid to accompany her. Every attempt he made to talk to her was blocked by a deflective "Yes" or "No", and he sensed that she couldn't wait for the end of the evening to arrive.

In the taxi on the way back she kept rigidly to her own small corner of the seat, looking straight ahead, her whole body taut, and Miles knew that when he was called up to report to Lady Ridley on the success of the evening, he would have to concede that it had been a failure.

As Amanda stepped out of the taxi, her heel caught and she stumbled. His protective movement towards her was completely instinctive, something he would have done for anyone, but the way she shrank from even that casual contact was so palpably obvious that he released her immediately.

He felt a slow wave of anger burn through him as he got back in the taxi to go home. This was the

second time in his life that he had been made aware
of the irreparable damage the male sex could inflict
on its female counterpart. First that girl at Oxford . . .
and now this woman.

He wasn't surprised at not being asked to escort
her again. Lady Ridley suffered periodically from
bouts of arthritis which kept her housebound, and
Miles visited her when he could, tactfully saying
nothing when she continued to fret over her
goddaughter's single state.

"I've found the ideal man for her too. He's a
Cabinet Minister . . . a widower with two children.
Like Amanda he was brought up in Scotland. He's
just perfect for her, Miles, but how can I get her to
meet him?"

After that the very last thing Miles expected was to
see Amanda at a celebrity publicity party he was
attending as the escort of a well-known soap opera
star.

When he first caught a glimpse of her he stared in
astonishment, and as though the concentration of his
attention caught her awareness Amanda raised her
head and looked at him. Her face burned, but whether
with anger or embarrassment he couldn't say. She had
the clear pure skin colouring of a Celt, and the way
the colour ran up under its paleness gave him a sudden
urge to feel its heat beneath his fingers. He was
familiar with sexual desire, certainly sufficiently so not
to be caught off guard by it, but on this occasion he
was, and it was several seconds before he could drag
his attention away from her averted profile. Already
he could feel the familiar ache and pulse of his body,
the sensation of wanting to reach out and touch . . .
He shook his head, amazed at his own reaction. He
had only seen the woman once before, damn it, and
here he was aching for her with an intensity he hadn't

even experienced with his first girl.

For the rest of the evening he avoided coming into any sort of contact with her whatsoever, physical or visual. Commitment . . . marriage . . . they were not included in his plans at the moment. His career was all-important. It had to be if he was ever to make a success of it, and everything he already knew about her underlined the fact that Amanda Courant was not the sort of woman to participate in the physically pleasurable but emotionally unconstraining relationship he favoured. He made it a rule never to get involved with a woman who wanted more from him than he was prepared to give. So far that rule hadn't caused him any problems; there were plenty of young women about who wanted the same sort of casual no-strings-attached relationships.

Since leaving Oxford Miles had been involved in relationships with half a dozen or so different women, all of whom he remembered with affection. He never slept with a woman he didn't like and admire . . . he didn't need to; and sex was only part of what he wanted from his relationships.

He was an ideal lover, although he didn't know it, physically attractive and male enough to treat women with that very special brand of male tenderness. In bed he was a thoughtful and instinctively skilful lover, and out of it he was an intelligent and entertaining conversationalist, who never made the mistake of underestimating a woman's intelligence.

It almost made him hurt inside to see the way Amanda shied away from his sex; it was like looking at a delicate work of art that had been carelessly damaged by rough handling. He would have liked to have been able to show her all that a man-to-woman relationship could be, but he knew he would never get the chance.

He saw her once more before he left the party. The woman he was escorting had subtly indicated to him that she no longer required his company. She was flirting with a producer whom Miles knew only by sight, and he was discreetly about to slip away when he caught sight of Amanda Courant. She was hemmed into a corner by a large ex-rugby player type who appeared to be talking at her rather than to her, and Miles could sense her fear from all the way across the room. He told himself that the last thing she would want would be for him to interfere, and yet still he found himself going over to her.

He thought he saw the faintest flicker of relief lighten her eyes as he approached. The rugby player glared possessively at him, but he ignored him and to his own surprise he heard himself saying quietly,

"You did say you wanted to leave early!"

Was that relief in her eyes, or was it shock? Either way she was stepping past the hovering hulk and coming towards him. Neither of them spoke as they walked outside. Miles felt Amanda shiver beside him and he realised that she wasn't wearing a coat. He saw a taxi and flagged it down, ushering her into it.

To his astonishment when they reached her house, she invited him to come in. She was terribly tense, her body rigid with the intensity of it. She offered him a drink which he refused, wondering why she had invited him in when she so plainly wanted to get rid of him. She poured herself something and then put it down untouched, her movements jerky and uncertain.

The house was rented, Lady Ridley had told him, and its modern fashionable décor did not really suit Amanda. She belonged to another age, he told himself, then wondered at his own idiotic romanticism. He could see her dressed in rich velvets and satins . . . a tragic Stuart heiress . . . or was that simply because he knew her history?

She picked up her glass again, and Miles shifted uncomfortably in his chair. Her tension was obvious to him, and he suddenly wanted desperately to leave. She had her back to him and abruptly she turned round, hectic patches of colour burning in her face.

"Well, I suppose we might as well get it over with, mightn't we?" she said bitterly. "And then you can report back to my godmother that you've done what she's paid you for. How does it feel to be paid to go to bed with women no one else wants?" Her eyes glittered and he saw that they were filling with tears.

Beneath his own anger compassion rose up inside him. He got up quickly and went towards her.

"Is that what you think? That your godmother has paid me to take you to bed?"

"Why? Isn't that what you do?" Her head lifted arrogantly, but he could see behind the proud mask to the pain hidden inside her. "I hope she's paying you well, because . . ."

As Miles reached out to restrain her, she pushed his hand away, and suddenly he saw beyond the pain and the rage to what lay beneath those feelings.

His breath caught in his throat as he recognised her desire. She wanted him. He had seen desire too often not to recognise it now, and as he reached for her, despite the fact that she pushed him away, he refused to let her.

"Let's get one thing straight," he told her. "No one pays me to take anyone to bed."

"But you were paid to take me to that party . . ."

"As your escort, nothing else. Is that really how you see me? As a man who makes love for money?"

He felt the shudder run through her as he forced her to look into his eyes. He was already aroused and he knew that Amanda must be aware of it. He saw the knowledge flare in her eyes along with a frantic panicky disbelief.

"I want you." He mouthed the words against her lips and felt her muscles quiver.

"You can't . . ." He caught the shaky, breathless whisper of hope hidden beneath the flat statement.

"Why not? Because your husband didn't?"

Amanda shuddered again, and the feel of her, so light and fragile in his arms, intensified the pulsing ache of his flesh. He wanted her, and he wanted her now. He bent his head and silenced her protest with his hands. For a long time she didn't respond, then her body jerked spasmodically as the tension eased out of it and her mouth moved beneath his, uncertain, tentative, untutored little movements that made his heart ache with tenderness.

She had less experience than girls of seventeen. He felt emotion burn his throat at the waste of it. He wanted to give her all that she had never had . . . show her what she could be, what she deserved to be.

He eased her slightly away and looked down into the blind, white face, "I want to take you to bed . . . now."

For a moment he thought she would reject him; in fact he was more than half expecting it, and then with an effort he could almost see, she seemed to gather all her strength together. He saw her swallow nervously, the movement ridging her throat. She looked at him, wary and uncertain as an animal more used to kicks than caresses.

"I . . ." Her voice cracked and she swallowed again. Miles couldn't help her, much as he ached to do so. "I . . . I haven't had a lover before. My husband . . ."

She refused to look at him, but he knew what she must be thinking . . . waiting for.

She looked defiantly at him.

"Well, don't you think it's pathetic? A woman of my age still . . ." her mouth twisted bitterly, "untouched and virginal, still so undesired by the male sex that . . ."

Miles put his fingers to her lips to silence her and said savagely, "I don't give a damn whether you've had no men or a hundred. Right now I want you so much that I'm likely to take you here where we're standing. Can't you see what you're doing to me?" he demanded thickly, and he saw the hot colour run up under her skin as he deliberately took her hand and placed it against the pulsing heat of his body.

She swayed close to him on a small moan of acquiescence, and Miles picked her up, feeling the urgent hammer of her pulses.

Her bedroom was furnished with the same stark modernity as the rest of the house. By rights he should be making love to her in the depths of a huge fourposter, he thought absently as he stripped off her clothes and then his own.

He felt the tension invade her at the sight of his nudity, and he knew without her having to say so that she was terrified—not so much of him, he suspected, but of herself. It was cool in the bedroom, and he wrapped them both in the quilt, stroking Amanda's shivering flesh until it grew warm and pliant and began to quiver slightly.

He was possessed by a need to make up to her for all that she had missed . . . to give her such pleasure that the past would be completely wiped out. His own desire was pushed to one side as he used his skill to arouse her. He felt her tension as he fondled her breasts, small and dark-nippled. He kissed the narrow curve of her shoulder and the thudding pulse point in her throat, opening his mouth so that he could suck gently on it. Against his palms he felt her nipples peak and harden and he heard the tiny gasp of shock rattle in her throat. By the time he had kissed his way down to the swollen urgency of her breasts she was moaning softly deep in her throat, her nails digging into the muscles of his arms.

He sucked gently on the turgid peaks, taking care not to frighten or hurt her. He made love to her as though they had all the time in the world, gradually arousing her by such delicate degrees that she was barely aware of the transition from dread to aching wanting.

His hand opened her legs, gently stroking her. He felt the shock course through her and silenced her protest with his mouth, mimicking the delicate movement of his fingers with the soft stroke of his tongue as it rimmed and teased the outline of her mouth.

Even though Amanda was aroused she was tense; Miles could feel it in the underlying rigidity of her flesh, and he knew if he entered her now he would hurt her. His own flesh ached for release. Later he would show her how to caress and arouse him, but for now all his attention was concentrated on giving her pleasure. Her body was beginning to respond to the subtle rhythm of his stroking fingers. He kissed her deeply, thrust his tongue between her parted lips, not releasing her until he felt her response. He could feel her body starting to relax, to welcome him. Her nipples pressed eagerly against his hands as he caressed her. He took one gently into his mouth, sucking on it until he heard her moaning softly, and then he sucked harder.

Her skin was beginning to burn, her hips lifting as she pressed herself against the caressing intrusion of his hand. He released her breast and let his mouth drift lingeringly down her body until he reached the top of her thighs. As he had known it would, her body went rigid with shock when his mouth first touched her intimately. He felt her urgent movements to escape from him, her shock at the intimacy of what he was doing, but he had judged his moment well and the desire he had coaxed slowly into life flared hotly beneath the persuasive caress of his tongue.

The control which Miles had striven to maintain for so long splintered and shattered as he tasted the soft femininity of her body and felt its unmistakable response. His erection already pulsing and aching with need grew as he heard the soft, tormented cries of pleasure stifled in her throat and felt the tiny convulsive contractions of her flesh. He entered her quickly and determinedly, minimising the shock of pain and quickly reaching his own climax.

Later he made love to her again, this time bringing her to a brief but unmistakable climax with the controlled thrust of his body. She cried in his arms like a little girl, and he knew that nothing in his life had given him as much pleasure as restoring to this child-woman the power of her own sexuality.

They remained lovers for six months, and then one day Amanda told him that she was in love with someone else. She introduced them several weeks later at a party, and Miles was not surprised to discover that he was the Cabinet Minister Lady Ridley had mentioned to him.

He had always known that their relationship wouldn't last, but it hurt to lose Amanda, even though he had known she didn't love him.

His days with the escort agency were over as his bar examinations loomed, and then just after they had finished he got a telephone call from Colonel Whitegate's butler-batman to tell him that the Colonel had

had a bad fall. He went down to see him immediately, shocked to see how much his benefactor had aged in a matter of months.

"Not the leg," the Colonel told him gruffly from his hospital bed. "Nothing to do with that . . . Got some damned thing inside me eating away at me. Only a matter of time now. Never thought I'd go like this, stuck in some damned hospital."

Miles knew what he was trying to say. The Colonel's only living relative was the second cousin who would inherit from him, and so Miles made the arrangements for the Colonel to come home; he hired and paid for the round-the-clock nurses who were needed in the latter stages of the Colonel's illness, and he also arranged to take leave from his chambers so that he could be there with him.

Colonel Whitegate died peacefully in his sleep four weeks after Miles's twenty-sixth birthday. As it happened, he had had a bad night the evening before and Miles had elected to stay with him, so that he was there when the old man opened his eyes for the last time. He saw them cloud and darken and heard the creaky bluff voice soften as he called out a woman's name. Miles heard the death rattle in his throat and wasn't ashamed to realise that he was crying.

He had lost the first real friend he had ever had. Men like Colonel Whitegate were the unsung heroes of the world, and Miles knew that without him he might well have made nothing of his life.

Despite their closeness, he was astounded to discover that the Colonel had left everything but the house and its lands, which were entailed, to him, with the proviso that he fulfil the Colonel's wish that provision was made for his batman.

Miles bought him a small cottage in the same village where his sister lived, and provided him with a pension.

There was sufficient money left for him to invest in the purchase of his own house and his first car. The case of vintage port the Colonel had left him he kept, to be drunk on suitable occasions. All apart from one bottle, which he and the batman shared on the evening of the Colonel's funeral.

Miles felt it was a gesture that the old man would have appreciated.

It is a long slow climb up an archaic and slippery ladder for any young man aspiring to become a leading barrister, and Miles was hampered by his lack of connections, but he got there. The year he was first tipped to become one of the country's youngest Q.C.s—that select band of lawyers entitled to call themselves Queen's Counsel and thereby to take precedence over other barristers—he had an unexpected visitor at his Inner Temple chambers.

He recognised her immediately she was shown in by his clerk, even though she had given him a false name. The years hadn't really changed her and she was still a very beautiful woman.

"Amanda! What a lovely surprise!" Miles rose to greet her, kissing her affectionately.

She looked tense and he could see there were lines of strain around her mouth. He asked her gently, "What is it?"

"Miles, I need your help." Her hands twisted the platinum wedding ring and its matching diamond ring loose on the long fingers. "It's my stepdaughter—I've just found out she's heavily involved in drug smuggling. Gordon, my husband, has just been tipped off by a friend at Scotland Yard that Sophie is being used as a carrier. She's in Brazil at the moment and due to fly back to England, stopping over in Paris on the way. She's already booked on to the flight, but we can't get in touch with her to warn her. Once she gets on that plane . . ."

"Why have you come to me?" Miles asked her gently.

Amanda smiled nervously at him.

"I was reading in a magazine about the work you do with young drug addicts, and . . ."

There had been an article about Miles recently in one of the Sunday supplements following press interest in his elevation to the ranks of Queen's Counsel. He remembered that the young interviewer had accused him of being very establishment and out of touch with reality until she learned that he worked free of charge for several organisations which helped the under-privileged, one of which was an organisation that provided help for young drug offenders. Not pushers, though. Miles had seen too much of the destruction that drugs could wreak on innocent lives to have much sympathy with those who made their living from such misery.

Amanda must have seen the distaste in his face, because she said unhappily, "Yes. Yes, I know, she deserves to be punished, but Miles, she's only eighteen, and very much under the influence of a boy she's been going out with. She's always been rebellious. She's doing this to punish us . . . her father and me. I don't think she really realises exactly what risks she's running."

"Why come to me?"

Miles was frowning now, remembering the last drugs case he had handled. He had got the girl off, but uselessly, because she had died of an overdose several months later. He never handled cases unless he was absolutely convinced that the person he was defending was innocent. He held no brief for those who deliberately inflicted pain and degradation on their fellow human beings, no matter who they were.

"There wasn't anyone else." Amanda's hands twisted again. "Gordon can't do anything. His position in the Cabinet . . ."

Miles could see that. He looked down into her face and was half irritated by his own burgeoning feeling of responsibility . . . a need to protect and shield the weaker sex. That had always been one of his own weaknesses, and it hadn't lessened over the years. He wanted to help her, he acknowledged. He wanted to wipe away the pain and fear, just as he had wanted to all those years before. As he looked at Amanda, his mind was running over all the possibilities. If the girl was flying back from South America on a known flight the police were bound to be watching the airport. The only way he could stop her would either be to fly to South America, or to intercept her when the flight touched down in Paris.

"We can't even get in touch with her by telephone," Amanda told him, cutting off the former avenue. "We don't know where in Brazil she's staying, only that she's booked on to this particular flight home."

The timing would be difficult, almost impossible, and when Miles thought of the risk he was running, he knew what he was contemplating was pure idiocy, and yet when Amanda smiled her tremulous thanks he felt as though he was St George and had just been handed his sword. The irrationality of the male ego, he derided himself wryly as he rang the TV newsreader he was currently dating and cancelled their evening date.

Half an hour later he had made arrangements ostensibly to travel to Paris to consult with a legal colleague on a matter of international law.

He took the precaution of ringing the French lawyer he knew and arranging to have lunch with him. There was a case he was involved in concerning a French wine label . . . if questioned. His mind ran on, seeking out problems and trying to find answers for them, while all the time he acknowledged the sheer implausibility of what he was setting out to do.

The girl's flight was due to leave Rio two days later, by which time Miles had made all his arrangements. He flew out to Paris as arranged, and if Jacques Premier thought it odd to be asked out to lunch at eleven-thirty in the morning he did not say so. They discussed the problems of international law at some length, and then Miles called for the bill. If the French lawyer was somewhat confused about the purpose of their luncheon engagement he did not show it.

Miles arrived back at the airport just in time to meet Sophie's flight. Luckily his French was fairly good, and the girl at the check-in desk had been all sympathy when he explained that his niece was travelling on the Rio jet bound for Heathrow and that he had intercepted her flight while on business in Paris to give her some very grave news about her father's health.

The stewardess who brought Sophie from the plane was more interested in Miles than in the sulky, unkempt girl at her side. What wouldn't she give to have an uncle like that! she thought enviously as she handed Sophie over into his charge.

"You're not my uncle!" Sophie complained sulkily the moment they were alone.

Miles had taken the precaution of drawing her out of earshot of anyone else. She was dressed like one of a hundred thousand teenagers in jeans and a thin T-shirt, a backpack on the floor beside her. She looked both defiant and wary, and beneath both emotions Miles could sense her fear. If she was frightened so much the better, it made his task all the easier.

"We can't talk here," he told her calmly. "Come on."

He could feel her muscles bunching beneath his fingers as he led her towards the door. If he had to detain her physically she would be no match for him, but he hoped it wouldn't come to that.

"Here, I'll take that . . .".

As he made to take the backpack off her Sophie snatched it back, her face white. So it was true, Miles reflected tiredly. He had hoped . . .

"Who are you, and what do you want?" she demanded.

"I'm a friend of your parents," he told her quietly. "And what I want, or more properly, what I'm here for, is to stop you from being arrested."

Her mouth fell open, but she had herself under control again quickly.

"What for?" she sneered. "Being young?"

"No—smuggling drugs."

Miles watched the way her eyes slid away from his.

"You don't know that . . ."

"Oh yes, I do, and so do the police. Why else do you think I'm here?"

Sophie digested what he had to say in a sullen silence, and then objected bitterly,

"I don't believe you! If the police really do think I'm smuggling drugs, why did they let me board the plane in the first place?"

"Because they want to pick up your London contact as well," Miles told her curtly, forcing himself not to give in to his growing desire to give her a good shaking. Didn't she have any conception of what she was doing? No, she didn't. She was a spoilt, petted child, who was defying her family in the most satisfactory way she could imagine, with one blow destroying both her father's career and her stepmother's peace of mind.

"They've already got your boyfriend," he added brutally, watching her pale and flinch.

"Joachim? No—he's too clever . . ."

"You really think so? He doesn't love you, Sophie— he was using you, just as he in turn is being used. Smuggling drugs might be exciting and dangerous to you, but there are others in it purely and simply for money. Do you use the stuff yourself?"

She shook her head and grimaced.

"Do you think I'm a complete fool?"

"So, and yet knowing what they can do you still agreed to bring the stuff back with you?"

Sophie wasn't totally hardened, Miles acknowledged, watching her wince and seeing pain flare briefly in her eyes.

"Have you ever seen anyone *die* from drug abuse?" he asked her harshly. "It isn't an easy death, contrary to what you might imagine. And in my opinion anyone who contributes to that sort of death deserves whatever punishment they get. Don't think I'm doing this for your sake. I'm not."

The fight had gone out of the girl. She looked frightened and sick. Pity for her touched Miles briefly. She was young and vulnerable and had been dragged into the whole sordid situation by men old enough and cynical enough to know how to make best use of teenage rebellion.

"You can't stop me getting back on the plane," she told him.

"No, and I can't stop the French and English police taking you into custody either," he agreed. "No one likes drug pushers . . . you won't have an easy time in prison."

Prison . . . he saw that Sophie hadn't even thought

of that possibility and gave an inward sigh of relief. It was going to be easier than he had thought. She wasn't as hard as he had imagined.

In the end he managed to persuade her to leave the airport with him. He took her into Paris and booked them both into a quiet back-street hotel. When she gave him the incriminating package, he destroyed its contents, his face concentrated in grim disdain.

Afterwards he took her out and bought her an outfit more suitable for the teenage daughter of the Member of Parliament for Rochford West than the scruffy jeans and shirt she was wearing. Once she was reluctantly clad in the neat and unexceptional uniform of a Sloane Ranger teenager, Miles took charge of her passport and ordered a taxi to take them back to the airport.

Luckily they were able to get two empty seats on the next B.A. flight out. Sophie fidgeted impatiently beside him, and he could sense that she was still angry with him. He was aware of the quick silent scrutiny the airport officials gave them before they were allowed through to the departure lounge. Sophie looked like any other demure young schoolgirl in her cotton shirt and pleated skirt.

He could tell that she was stunned by the thoroughness with which their luggage was checked at Heathrow. The passport official stared and then frowned as he checked both their passports, and then they were asked to wait while their luggage was examined.

Sophie went white with shock when she saw the way the Customs officials took her backpack apart, and Miles hoped grimly that she was now aware of the risk she had run. There was no way she would have got through Customs, and he could tell from the grimly bitter expression on the faces of the men who had stopped them that they knew quite well what had happened. However, there was nothing they could do about it. Sophie was not carrying drugs. That did not help Miles to feel any better about the derisory look he was given by the senior Customs official as they were finally let through.

He found a taxi and escorted Sophie home. She sulked all the way, and Miles had seldom been more relieved to rid himself of a woman.

He found himself very uncomfortable with the thanks he received from the girl's father, mainly because had it been anyone else but Amanda who had asked for his help, Miles's own code of morals would have obliged him to have refused.

The whole incident had left an unpleasant taste in his mouth . . . a feeling of having done something Colonel Whitegate would not have considered honourable, but how could he have refused her? He pushed the incident to the back of his mind as one does with things that one feels do not reflect to one's credit.

CHAPTER FOURTEEN

To ISABELLE'S constant and ruefully expressed astonishment, the business she and Pepper started together after leaving college was an almost overnight success.

That this was due as much to Pepper's overwhelming appetite for hard work as to her father's influence and the patronage of his friends was something Isabelle was equally loquacious in mentioning.

Within four weeks of their starting up the business, it became obvious that Pepper was the one with the business brain; it was she who got up at four every morning to be at the markets to get the freshest and cheapest deliveries of foods; it was she who meticulously worked out budgets and profit margins; it was she who was scrupulous about keeping their books in order. Isabelle announced cheerfully that she found that side of their small business a boring chore.

Their first commission had been from Isabelle's father—a luncheon party for the bank's board of directors. Since every one of these gentlemen was related to Isabelle in one form or another, and since all of them had known her since she was a child, the description "sinecure" had slid almost instantly into Pepper's mind. But she was realistic enough to know that the old adage "It's not what you know but who you know that counts in life" was very true, and so she set to work, tactfully coercing Isabelle into the preparation of a menu that would make the board of Kent's bank sit up and take notice.

Alastair Kent was impressed enough to say privately

to his wife that it was one of the best, and most efficiently served lunches he had had in a long time. What he did not say was that the two extremely attractive girls who had served their meal had done nothing to detract from its appeal.

Pepper had learned during her chambermaiding days that male guests were always more ready to overlook a mistake in a pretty face than in a plain one, and she used this information ruthlessly when it came to hiring girls to serve their meals.

Isabelle had said breezily that there was no need for them to hire anyone for this task and that they could do it themselves, but Pepper had demurred, and Pepper had had her way. The sort of amateur, happy-go-lucky type of catering Isabelle was contemplating was not the image that Pepper wanted to project at all.

Within six months they had built up a reputation in City dining rooms that made Alastair Kent tell his wife that he was amazed by what the two girls had achieved.

Dorothea grimaced slightly. She had no illusions. Without Pepper, Isabelle would not have stuck it out for much more than six days, never mind six weeks! Even so, it was rather pleasant to hear that one's daughter was getting a reputation for having just a little more than feathers between her ears. Several of her contemporaries' daughters were doing similar things, and when she and Isabelle went to watch her husband playing polo at Smith's Lawn, it was rather nice to be able to take a maternal pride in her offspring's achievements.

Alastair Kent had been a polo fanatic ever since he was in the Guards. Lucky enough to have the wealth to indulge in such an expensive hobby, he was a member of a team headed by the Duke of Raincourt.

On several occasions during their first year of

business, Pepper was also invited to accompany the family down to the exclusive polo grounds at Hurlingham or Smith's Lawn at Windsor. She observed with a detached and often cynical appreciation the wealthy upper classes at play. This was a world that was as yet closed to the entrepreneurial and the mega-rich of the commercial world, but Pepper could see a day when this might no longer be the case. The polo-playing world was still small and enclosed, but wealth, the kind of wealth that was needed to be able to play this exclusive sport, no longer lay solely in the hands of the old-established families of rank and privilege.

Isabelle made no secret of the fact that she heartily resented these duty attendances. She even tried to persuade Pepper to fib to her mother that they were too busy at work to be able to go, but Pepper refused. Slowly, oh, so slowly, she was beginning to build up a network of contacts and acquaintances. Slowly, oh, so slowly, she was gradually being accepted and absorbed into Isabelle's social circle.

And then almost overnight things changed. Two events were responsible for this change.

The first was that Isabelle met and fell in love with a young ex-Guards officer.

The Honourable Jeremy Forster was everything that Dorothea wanted for her daughter as a husband. He was well connected, and wealthy; he was charming and not too intelligent, with a comfortable London home and a position with his father's stockbroking firm. In short, marriage to Jeremy would fit Isabelle as snugly and comfortably as a handmade glove.

Both families were pleased with the match. There was no need for a long engagement—Isabelle would be married at Christmas. And of course it went without saying that immediately upon the announcement of her engagement, she would cease working. For one thing, she simply wouldn't have enough time.

She explained all this gaily to Pepper the week before her engagement was due to be made public. Pepper accepted the information stoically. She had expected as much, and besides, she thought she had built up sufficient reputation to employ someone else to take her place. Someone from the same social set as Isabelle would be an ideal candidate, and she cast around, mentally wondering who, out of those young women she knew, would best fit into the gap left by Isabelle's departure.

Two days after Isabelle's announcement Pepper received a visit from Neil Kent. Mainly because she had shared so many of Isabelle's social activities she had come to know Neil a good deal better, and discovered that behind his reserved and rather formidable exterior there was a very sensitive and shy young man.

He did occasionally call round to see her when he was in the vicinity of the small Chelsea house she was renting, although normally it was by prearrangement.

It was gone eleven o'clock. She had spent the evening working on the business's accounts, and making out a list of possible substitutes for Isabelle. The previous weekend she had been to Oxford, and even while she knew that as far as both Oliver and herself were concerned, her decision to allow Mary and Philip to adopt him had been the right one, every time she saw him it left her faintly unsettled.

To counteract the feeling of tension that gripped her she had had a long hot soak in a bath full of scented hot water, and now she was wearing the tatty towelling robe she had put on afterwards.

To her Neil was simply Isabelle's brother. Pepper liked him as a person, but sexually she was completely indifferent to him—as indeed she was to all men, but with Neil she felt she did not need to hide behind her carefully cultivated role of a sexually experienced and available woman. She invited him in, conquering her surprise at seeing him.

For once he looked slightly dishevelled, and as he walked past her she smelled the sweetness of spirits on his breath.

Although the Chelsea cottage was rented, Pepper had added some decorating touches of her own. The mint green satinised cotton sofa was a perfect foil for her colouring, but when he sat down on it, it only served to emphasise Neil's sickly pallor.

"Neil, are you all right?"

She heard him groan and watched in dismay as he buried his head in his hands. She had seen too many men in the throes of drunkenness to mistake his condition, but what did shock her was that Neil of all men should arrive on her front door in such a state. He was normally very abstemious. Indeed, Isabelle often made fun of him because of his staid and slightly worthy image.

"I had to see you." The words were muffled by his hands. And as she looked at the vulnerability of his downbent head, for the first time in her life Pepper knew compassion for a man. She reached out to touch him comfortingly, an automatic reaction to his distress, shocked by the way his whole body went rigid under her touch.

Instantly a nebulous but thoroughly frightening alarm began to invade her.

"Neil, what is it? Is something wrong? Isabelle? Your parents?"

"No . . . no, nothing like that," he groaned, still refusing to look at her. "It's me . . . me, Pepper. Oh God, I'm so desperately in love with you! I don't

know what to do, where to turn . . . You fill my
heart and mind to the exclusion of everything else. I
never knew it was possible to feel this way about a
woman. I know you don't love me."

In an appalled silence Pepper watched his shoulders
heave as he struggled to master his feelings.

"I know I'll never be anything more to you than
Isabelle's brother, but wanting you is driving me
insane." He gave a high cracked laugh. "Me, of all
people! I've always thought sex was something I could
control rather than the other way round, but just the
thought of you is enough to send me crazy with
wanting you."

As she listened Pepper felt the chill inside her deepen
and spread, accompanied by a growing sense of panic.
She didn't want to hear any of this. She didn't want
to listen. She wanted Neil to go away. She wanted to
pretend he had never said any of this.

He raised his head and looked at her with tear-
blurred eyes, and she shuddered, knowing what he
was silently begging from her. He wanted her to invite
him into her bed. He wanted to stay here for the night
and make love with her.

She could feel the perspiration breaking out all over
her body, even though the room wasn't over-warm.
She wanted to scream and run, she wanted to blot out
the sight of him. She wanted . . . She shuddered
tensely, her voice hoarse and raw as she whispered
thickly,

"No . . . No! You mustn't want me like that.
I . . . I'm Isabelle's friend, I . . ."

She had no real idea of what she was saying, her
body and mind held in the fierce grip of the panic
clawing through her. It wasn't enough to tell herself
that this was Neil; gentle, kind Neil who wouldn't so
much as crush a spider, because somewhere deep down

inside her all she could think was that he was a man.
All she could remember was what another man had
done to her. All she wanted was to run away and hide
herself from him.

"Pepper, please . . . I want you so much. Please
let me!"

He was reaching for her. Her whole body froze in
shock and rejection as his fingers touched her wrist.
She wanted to turn and run, and she just couldn't
move. A scream bubbled up in her throat. She opened
her mouth and found that her throat muscles had
paralysed with fear.

"Pepper, what is it?"

The doorbell rang, the sharp sound cutting through
the thick tense silence. Instantly Neil released her, and
her fear evaporated, and she was once more her usual
self, in control, self-assured.

She went to the door and opened it.

"Hi, I've just dropped Jeremy off at his club and I
thought I'd drop round and see you on my way home.
Were you just on your way to bed?"

There was no way Pepper could stop Isabelle from
walking into the sitting room, and no way either she
could prevent her from leaping to the conclusions she
saw in her eyes as they went first to her brother and
then back to Pepper.

"Oh dear, I'm rather de trop, aren't I? I had no
idea . . ."

"Neil was just calling in for a chat," Pepper told
her firmly, knowing as she did so that there was no
way Isabelle would believe her.

As she had known she would, her friend grinned.

"Ok—it's ok. I'm broadminded," she assured them
both with a teasing smile. "How long has this been
going on? I never guessed a thing . . . Pepper, you
cheat! You might have told me. Is it serious?"

"Isabelle, it's nothing. Neil just called round by chance, just like you."

But it was no good. Isabelle wasn't going to believe her, Pepper recognised, not even when Neil elected to leave with her.

As all three of them stood in the small hallway, Isabelle turned her head and whispered in Pepper's ear,

"Sorry I spoiled your fun. Poor Neil, he's so staid and stuffy, the poor old dear. I suppose he thinks it might be setting me a bad example if he stays the night now." She gave a deep chuckle. "Much he knows!"

Of course it was too much to hope that Isabelle would keep her conclusions to herself. She was far too delighted at the thought of gaining her friend for a sister-in-law for that. Even so, Pepper was surprised when she received a telephone call at home one evening from Isabelle's father, asking if he could some round.

She had rather less contact with Alastair Kent than she had with the rest of the family, but she had always found him to be a fair, although somewhat aloof man, who still considered that women had a specific role in the scheme of things and that this role did not include the cut-and-thrust of business activities. Even so, he was an intelligent man and one who did not believe in wasting time in getting to the point.

He arrived punctually, on the dot of nine. Pepper led him to her small sitting room and offered him a drink. He refused.

"Isabelle tells me that you and Neil are rather involved," he began without preamble. "Is it true?"

Pepper, shrewder and more worldly by far than Isabelle, knew exactly why and what he was asking.

"Not as far as I'm concerned," she responded honestly, meeting his questioning look head on. She paused, choosing her words carefully. "Neil believes that he has feelings for me which he thinks are much stronger than they actually are." She paused delicately, and Alastair Kent relaxed a little.

Good, the girl was being sensible and open about the whole thing. He had half expected that she might be. It wasn't that he didn't like her. Pleasant enough girl and sharp as a needle, but not the wife they had in mind for Neil . . .

"And you . . . you don't share Neil's feelings?" he probed, watching her.

Pepper lifted her head.

"No, I don't. I want to make a career for myself, Mr Kent." She hesitated and then took a deep breath. "Marriage does not play any part in the way I visualise my life at the moment."

Subtly she had let him know both the depth of Neil's feelings for her, and her own reaction to them. She wanted it made perfectly plain that there was no question of there being any furtive sexual relationship between Neil and herself, or indeed of her ever even considering contemplating one.

Alastair Kent frowned. The affair was obviously more serious than he and Dorothea had realised. Although they had never spoken openly of their plans to Neil, they had been gently steering him in the direction of Alastair's cousin's girl; making sure that he accompanied them to Scotland in August, and then again in the New Year.

Fiona Campbell had the kind of lineage and background that made her eminently suitable to become Neil's wife, and in addition to that she was her father's sole heir. The crumbling castle and its grouse moors might not have a great deal of monetary value, but it had a heritage, a history that Alastair Kent valued far more. And now for this to happen!

Neil was a sensible enough lad—most of the time, but he was inclined sometimes to venture into a certain degree of sentimentality that his father suspected he must have inherited from his mother's family. It was no good appealing to his common sense, but Pepper was a different proposition.

He had not been quite sure how he would tackle the problem when he arrived. He had half expected tears and tantrums, pleas even. This cool, self-possessed rejection of his son's feelings had come as both a relief and a slight shock. It was the first time in his life he had ever heard of a woman decrying marriage in favour of a career, and he wasn't quite sure how to respond to it.

He and Dorothea had both discussed the matter. There had even been a mutual but soon dismissed suggestion that perhaps the offer of money . . .

"She won't take it," Dorothea had opined, slightly regretfully, conscience forcing her to add, "and she is one of Isabelle's friends . . ."

Left unsaid, but there nonetheless was the tacit understanding that friend of Isabelle's Pepper might be, but she was not really "one of us", not really totally socially acceptable. Even without the fact that they wanted Neil to marry Fiona, they would not have wanted him to marry Pepper.

Alastair Kent shifted uncomfortably.

"Well, you will understand, Pepper," he began with false heartiness, "that Dorothea and I have certain . . . plans for Neil." He avoided looking at her. There was something about that clear-eyed unwavering stare that increased his discomfort. Which was ridiculous when one took into account the fact that he was a partner in a reputable and highly professional merchant bank, while she was nothing more than one of his daughter's friends.

"You want me to tell him he's wasting his time. I've already done that," Pepper told him crisply.

"Well, yes . . . I'm sorry to say that I don't think that would be enough. Both his mother and I feel that it would be better if . . . well, if the pair of you didn't come into contact with one another for a time."

Pepper said nothing. She had already learned not to make it easy for any would-be adversary, and as though her silence somehow unsettled him, Alastair shifted awkwardly, his frown deepening.

Originally he and Dorothea had thought of sending Neil away for a time. They had cousins in America, although God knew what on earth Neil would find to do on a cattle ranch. It was already decided that he would follow his father into the bank, and really Alastair wanted him there now so that he could begin teaching him all that he himself knew.

He had come tonight to see Pepper chiefly to find out the lie of the land. Now that he knew she had no intention of encouraging Neil's infatuation with her, he needed to discuss the whole affair again with Dorothea. She was always much better than he at making this sort of decision.

Pepper's control and self-possession had thrown him. It wasn't what he had expected, and as he made his excuses and stood up he was visited by the uncomfortable realisation that had she actually wanted Neil, there would have been precious little he could have done to stop her from having him.

That realisation left him both disturbed and discomfited. It was not a good state of affairs for a senior partner of a merchant bank to feel that he was in a position where he could be bested by a little chit the same age as his daughter.

He said as much to Dorothea when he got home. She pursed her lips and shook her head. She was as alarmed as her husband. She contemplated making an appeal to Pepper to absent herself completely from their lives, but regretfully renounced it. It held too many pitfalls and problems.

"It's a pity that Pepper doesn't want to make her career in cattle raising," she said eventually with a rare touch of humour. "Then we could have sent *her* out of the way to your cousin's."

As though their conversation was an omen, the very next day, when Alastair was interviewing a potential client from America over a very formal lunch at his club, the latter told him that he was looking for a young woman to work for him as his P.A.

"You know the style of thing . . . one of your classy English girls, with a laid-back accent and the right connections. They're all the rage in New York at the moment."

Concealing his distaste, Alastair listened politely. His client was one of a new breed of amazingly wealthy entrepreneurs who almost made a virtue of bragging how they had amassed their new-found wealth. In the case of this particular man he had made his initial fortune by representing American sports stars and acting as their go-between-cum-agent in sponsorship deals.

He spent almost the entire luncheon describing to Alastair in detail how he had pulled off a succession of deals, but Alastair wasn't really listening. This could be the answer to his problem. Clever, ambitious Pepper could just be what this brash American was looking for.

He cleared his throat and interrupted his guest in mid-monologue.

"I think I know a girl who might suit you. A friend of my daughter's . . ."

"Classy, is she?" Victor Orlando asked, narrowing

his eyes. "The type of broad that's got plenty of SA?"

Hiding his distaste, Alastair said carefully,

"I think you'll find that Pepper will more than suit your requirements."

"Ok, give me her number. I'll call her."

Alastair frowned. Not even his desire to remove his son from the dangers of his infatuation for her would allow him to agree to place Pepper in such a potentially embarrassing situation.

"I think it would be better if I arranged a meeting," he said carefully. "Perhaps dinner one night . . . I won't say anything to Pepper beforehand."

"Sounds good to me. Gives me a chance to get a look at her without her putting on any special airs and graces, eh? Good thinking!"

Inwardly wondering which of their friends were least likely to be offended by the American's unfortunate manner, Alastair discreetly signalled for his bill.

The biggest hurdle would be Pepper herself. She had said herself that she was ambitious, and he suspected that working for Victor Orlando would be far more stimulating and demanding than running her own small catering business.

Alastair discussed the whole thing with Dorothea that evening.

"Well, she may agree to it," she said uncertainly, "but he sounds a dreadful man, Alastair."

"Pepper will cope with him."

Pepper did.

Dorothea Kent, who was not as sure as her husband that they should say nothing to Pepper about the purpose of the dinner party, called round at the Chelsea house when she knew Pepper would be there. Frankly and determinedly she told Pepper what the purpose of the dinner party really was.

"It could be an excellent opportunity for you," she explained.

And for you, Pepper thought cynically, saying nothing, instead reserving her judgement.

She disliked Victor Orlando on sight, recognising him as the very worst kind of male chauvinist bully, but the job as his P.A. was too tempting to pass up.

It took Victor less than six days to proposition her, and it took Pepper less than six minutes to convince him that not only was he wasting his time, but also that she could be of more value to him out of his bed than in it.

Thereafter an uneasy truce developed. Victor flew back to New York, leaving Pepper to follow him.

She arrived in the city in the first few days of the fall. It was quite a culture shock to discover women dressed in heavy tweeds in weather that would be considered hot at home, but New York was like that. On the first day of fall women wore fall clothes no matter what the weather, and Pepper quickly realised that she was going to have to follow suit.

As a gesture of goodwill, Isabelle's mother had arranged living accommodation for her, through her network of friends, and Pepper was sharing an apartment with the daughter of one of her friends, in a walk-up block in Greenwich Village.

Lucy Sanders was very like Isabelle, but she had a better defined sense of humour and a shrewdness that the other girl had lacked. She made Pepper welcome in a careless sort of fashion, once she had assured herself that Pepper hadn't been chosen by her mother to spy on her.

"Ma wants me to go home and get married, but that isn't what I want from life. New York is a crazy city and I love it—far more than I like the idea of marriage. A woman can be whatever she wants to be here." Lucy pulled a face and grimaced. "Provided she's prepared to be it without a man. They're a commodity that's in very short supply!"

Victor's offices were in an extremely expensive building on Madison Avenue, and Pepper soon accustomed herself to the advertising hype she heard all around her in the bars and restaurants.

Lucy introduced her to some of her friends, a gregarious crowd mainly involved in the theatre and design world, and Pepper soon became accustomed to listening to conversations that dealt almost exclusively with the latest off-Broadway shows. It was in New York that she put the final unmistakable gloss to her new persona.

Victor was a demanding employer and she had a lot to learn, but there was still time for dates with Lucy's friends, and business acquaintances she met through Victor. When she did date she employed the same tactics she had used at home, taking care only to date men whose own opinion of their sexuality would not allow them to admit to anyone that they had not taken her to bed. It was a wise ploy, establishing for her a very safe barrier behind which she could conceal the truth.

In the six months she was in New York she learned to call pavements "sidewalks", honed the perfection of the classy English accent; shopped at Bergdorf's and a variety of small food shops in SoHo; learned where to buy the cheapest designer clothes and where to get her hair cut, and beautiful though Central Park was in early spring, she was not sorry when the time came to leave.

Victor Orlando was astounded with her business flair—so astounded in fact that he very quickly sent her back to London to do the groundwork which would allow him to set up a similar sort of operation in London to the one he had in the States.

By the time Pepper got back Neil was safely married and living in Scotland. Isabelle welcomed her back affectionately, and she was very quickly drawn into the small élite upper-class circle she had inhabited before she left. She had an extra gloss now, a patina which once applied to her cool British upper-class accent and manner made her instantly stand out in a crowd. A good many men propositioned her, some even fell in love with her, but she had become skilled at holding them all at bay without causing offence. To one she would claim that she was involved with another, and to another that she was still heavily emotionally involved with a third. Only she knew the reason she kept them all well away from her bed. Only she knew the way she tensed up and froze when an unknown male so much as reached out and touched her.

Pepper was not stupid. She knew why she felt the way she did. She even knew how she might be able to overcome those feelings. An expensive and fashionable analyst would only add to the prestige she already had, but something told her that no amount of analysis, expensive and fashionable or otherwise, could undo the damage that Simon Herries had done. It would be with her all her life, and something atavistic and primitive deep down inside her hinted that perhaps she even deserved it, although she couldn't have said why.

Just as she couldn't have said why she still kept in touch with Mary and Philip. After all, she needed nothing from them now. She had her life and they had theirs, and they had nothing in common. Except Oliver.

Regular reports on Oliver still arrived from Mary, photographs, long newsy letters. Mary was not going to allow Pepper to simply vanish out of their lives, and even while part of her resented it, part of her rejoiced in it.

She had been back in London, working hard to establish the kind of network Victor would need, for six weeks when she had her first intimation of where the future of her life might lie.

Tennis and baseball were Victor's major sports, and Pepper had an appointment with a new up-and-coming tennis sportswear manufacturer in Berkshire who was keen to launch a new and expensive range of tennis wear, and who wanted an equally expensive and fashionable tennis star to sponsor it.

Pepper had heard about the company through one of her many contacts, and as she drove down to her late morning appointment with the sales director, she mentally reviewed all that she knew about them. The company was headed by a new and very dynamic boss who had acquired the sportswear company as part and parcel of a bigger deal. He was now completely revamping its image, and Pepper was hoping to persuade him that the as yet rather young but potentially very successful tennis player she had her eye on as one of Victor's first British sports stars would be an ideal candidate to become associated with the new label.

As she drove, Pepper mentally reviewed everything she knew about the company and its head. Nick Howarth was thirty years old. He had inherited a small scrap metal business from his father when he was eighteen, and in twelve short years he had built it up into a multi-million-pound business empire. She had heard about him through contacts in the business world. She still kept in contact with Alastair Kent, and Alastair was grateful enough to her for her co-operation over Neil's infatuation to give her the odd bit of information he thought might be useful to her.

A little to his own surprise he had found that he had come to like as well as admire Pepper. He sensed that she had lost nothing of that integrity which he had been so aware of being an intrinsic part of her, while she was in New York, and that he admired. It was so easy to be seduced by the lure of money and power, and Pepper had plainly not succumbed to it. She was still the same cool, self-assured young woman who had so disconcerted him.

In Nick Howarth, Pepper recognised a kindred spirit straight away. He was wickedly attractive, with almost wheat-blond hair and cool green eyes, tall and very lithe, sexually powerful in a way that very few men are. Even Pepper was aware of his sexuality, which was both heightened and muted at the same time by the rigidness of his immaculately pin-striped suit and white shirt.

Here was a man who liked using disguises, she recognised, a man who was well versed in the art of melting into his surroundings. What did he want from life that he didn't already have? she wondered thoughtfully. Pepper had learned in New York that it was the desire for new and more possessions that kept the commercial world turning, and where no such need existed—well then, it had to be manufactured.

What did *this* man want? she wondered, smiling dulcetly at him across the width of his desk.

The report she had prepared on her proposals lay on the blotter. Nick Howarth smiled at her, his smile as vulpine and controlled as her own.

"Well now, I must say your report packs a pretty powerful punch—very powerful indeed." He looked at her. "Are you sure that using such a very junior tennis player is a good idea, though? Wouldn't a more well known name be better?"

He was trying to throw her, to disconcert her and take the advantage, Pepper recognised.

"An *establishment* image?" she questioned thoughtfully, lifting an eyebrow.

He had made it plain enough that the image he wanted for the company was one of verve and style, and she hid her smile as she saw him check and frown. Round one to her, but round one wasn't the entire game.

He shrugged gracefully, as though humouring her.

"Perhaps you're right. But this young man . . ." he looked down at her file, "Tony Richmond, he looks promising now, but he's only, what? Sixteen. How do we know that he's not going to burn out in three months' time and never make it?"

Pepper showed him her teeth and said coolly,

"How did you know that you would make it, Mr Howarth? It's part of my job to be able to recognise and channel the kind of ambition that makes successes, not failures. That's why Victor Orlando chose me to set up the British side of his business."

"Umm . . . I was wondering about that. You do the work and Victor collects the prizes."

She smiled again, refusing to be drawn.

"I do have another appointment." She glanced at her watch. "I appreciate that what I'm suggesting is rather . . . radical, rather more . . . adventurous perhaps than you might want."

She was watching him and could see that he didn't like that. And well he might not. She had heard on the grapevine that he prided himself on his innovative style and flair.

"Perhaps you'd like a few more days to think it over?" she finished. She stood up, then tensed as he said abruptly,

"What are you doing this weekend?"

Normally they waited a little longer before propositioning her, but she had heard that Nick Howarth was a man in a hurry.

"I'm watching polo at Windsor," she told him truthfully. "A friend of mine's husband plays and she's invited me to spend the weekend."

It was true. Isabelle, newly pregnant and bored, had demanded her company, and Pepper hadn't been able to think of an excuse quickly enough to refuse.

"Polo?" queried Nick.

"You know, the game of kings," she told him flippantly, then realised that he was watching her closely. Her scalp prickled, all her senses alive and alert. Had she, albeit unknowingly, discovered his Achilles heel? Carelessly she added, "If you wished you could join us. I'm sure my friend wouldn't mind."

Childishly she crossed her fingers behind her back. She was taking a gamble based on instinct alone, something she very, very rarely did.

"You move in very exclusive circles for a PA. Polo is a very establishment sport. You might almost call it a closed shop." Nick Howarth laughed, but there was no amusement in his eyes. She had been right, Pepper thought, tiny goosebumps of excitement rising on her skin. Here was a very rich and a very successful man who wanted something he couldn't have. Adrenalin charged through her like electricity. Perhaps after all there might be a way she could persuade him to accept her plans. If so . . .

"Isabelle and I were at college together in Oxford. You may know her father—he's Alastair Kent.

"He plays in the Duke of Raincourt's team, doesn't he?" Nick Howarth responded, inadvertently telling her exactly what she wanted to know. No one who was not almost obsessed by the sport would have used that description of Isabelle's father, and especially not someone who might more reasonably be expected to say something along the lines of "Oh yes . . . the banker, I know him."

"I really must go now . . . but if you want to join us, please give me a ring. You have my number."

He was too careful and too experienced to commit himself there and then, Pepper recognised, and she would have thought less of him if he had. All the way back to London she wondered if he would take the bait. If she had judged him correctly. If . . . So many ifs . . . but then life was composed of them, wasn't it?

Nick rang her on Friday evening, quite late on Friday evening, just as she was about to leave the office, his voice carefully free of any hint of any enthusiasm.

"If the offer's still on for Saturday, it might be a good opportunity for us to discuss your plans in more detail. I'm off to Paris on Sunday morning and I shan't be back for some time."

Accepting his face-saving explanation, Pepper demurely agreed to his suggestion. Isabelle and Jeremy had recently bought a house several miles from Windsor. She gave him directions as to how to find it, and then phoned her friend.

Isabelle, scatterbrained as always, offered no objections when Pepper told her what she had arranged.

The afternoon went just as Pepper had hoped. Nick Howarth was totally involved and enthralled with the game. She had the lever she needed to make him agree to her sponsorship plans, and she had got that lever quite by chance.

Only days ago, Isabelle had happened to mention that one of Jeremy's friends, an ex-Guards player, was hoping to set up a new team, but that he couldn't find enough potential players wealthy enough to make up a full team.

Nick didn't join them for dinner, and when she got the opportunity to do so, Pepper discreetly sounded out her friend's husband on the subject of how his friend might feel about a new player who could well be in a position to underwrite the major proportion of their expenses.

"Well, it's the coming thing, isn't it?" Jeremy admitted. "The old guard don't care for it, but even HRH has said that if the game is to succeed, it needs new money to support it. Let's face it, there just isn't enough of the old stuff left to support it."

Pepper let that one pass and pressed on.

"So the team wouldn't be averse to—well, let's say at this stage, just talking to someone who might be interested in underwriting it?"

"Well, that depends on who it is." Jeremy could be shrewd enough when he wanted to be, and he looked at her consideringly. "Are we talking vaguely here or are we talking specifics?"

Pepper took a deep breath. "I was thinking of Nick Howarth."

There was a long pause and then Jeremy said thoughtfully,

"Well, he seems a decent enough sort of chappie . . . Not one of us, of course. It would have to go before the rest of the team. I could sound them out . . ."

A week later Pepper rang Nick Howarth and asked if she could see him. Over lunch she put to him her proposals that in addition to sponsoring an up-and-coming tennis star, he might also fancy getting his design team to come up discreetly with something new but subtle for a brand new polo team that was being formed.

"Several ex-members of the Guards team will be in

it. They're very keen to recruit, and . . ." she paused, delicately sensing his tension and deliberately drawing it out, "there could be a chance that they're also looking for some sponsorship money, discreetly given of course . . ."

Nick Howarth knew when he had met his match.

"How much, and what's in it for you?" he asked.

Pepper named a sum that he seemed to accept without so much as blinking an eyelid, then added coolly,

"And of course sponsorship of my up-and-coming tennis player."

He frowned and for one appalled moment she thought he meant to refuse. When he did speak he said in surprise,

"That's all? Nothing for you . . . no . . . special payment, no little sweetener?"

Pepper looked coldly at him.

"That isn't the way I do business."

"Well then, you're out of line with your boss," he told her frankly. "And Pepper, let me give you some advice. Orlando will drain you dry and then toss you on one side when he's finished with you. Don't look to him for concern or loyalty, because you won't get it." He frowned and then added, "Have you ever thought of going it alone?" He saw her expression and smiled.

"Ah, so now I've found something that *you* want," he said softly.

And so it began. Pepper owed Victor nothing. She gave him her notice and set up her own company.

Her very first deals were the ones she organised between her tennis player and Nick Howarth, and between Nick and Jeremy's new polo team. The commission she earned on those deals alone was more than she would have made in ten years of work for Victor.

Victor was furious with her. He gave interviews in the sports press verbally assaulting her, but they did her no harm. Rather they simply enhanced her reputation. A woman who could get the better of Victor Orlando was one tough cookie indeed, and within a surprisingly short period of time Pepper discovered that the sports stars were the ones coming to her, rather than the other way round.

Her foot was on the first rung of the ladder of success, and for the first time she was able to give her time and attention to something else. To Simon Herries, for instance, and to retribution.

She made discreet enquiries and found out the name and address of the best private investigator London could boast.

A man like Simon Herries, who enjoyed violence and degradation for its own sake, was not going to stop at one little rape. Oh no . . . sooner or later he would step out of line again, and when he did . . . She could afford to wait, Pepper reasoned. And she *would* wait . . . for however long it took.

CHAPTER FIFTEEN

MILES frowned as he surveyed the flimsy sheets of A4 paper on his desk. They might not be as detailed as Pepper's files, but each of them contained enough information to make him realise how very real and appropriate her threats of retribution were.

It was remarkable how much she had achieved in the years since Oxford, and along with the pity and anger he had felt all those years before was a growing admiration. And more, he admitted. There was a sense of comradeship . . . of pride almost, that he knew sprang from the fact that like himself Pepper had come through much adversity to achieve her present-day success.

This intense awareness he had of her as a person had a logical basis; both of them were after a fashion orphans; both of them had endured hardship and a sense of separateness as children; both of them had been lucky in having someone in their lives whose kindness and caring enabled them to rise above these setbacks and to go on and achieve their ambitions.

Miles, however, had not been savagely raped at the age of seventeen.

He had occasionally dealt with rape cases and he thought he had taught himself to adopt the correct distancing logic; to evaluate the facts without allowing his emotions to hold sway.

He remembered his first rape case as a junior barrister. The woman had been in her thirties, and nothing like Pepper, and yet all through the case it had been Pepper's body he had seen, Pepper's terrified condemning eyes.

She was, he acknowledged grimly, woven into the very fabric of his life in a way that he had not even previously recognised. He had never forgotten her, and perhaps even, who could tell, she had indirectly been responsible for his own attitude to the women in his life. He abhorred inflicting pain, either emotional or physical, and perhaps that was why he never allowed himself to get too involved with any of his lovers. There was always something of himself that he held back.

In the same way that Pepper held much of herself back.

Miles moved restlessly in his chair. He was here to evaluate the situation with a cold and critical eye, dammit, not to wallow in sentimentality. But he couldn't stop thinking about her; about the vulnerability so apparent to him and yet, it seemed, hidden from everyone else.

From the moment he had seen Pepper sitting behind that damned desk delivering her ultimatums he had ached to protect her; to cherish her and let her see that with him she need never be afraid.

He had wanted women before, but never like this. He admired women who made their own way in life, independent, slightly acid women who could match him intellectually as well as physically, and he had never, apart from Amanda, wanted to protect them. Pepper touched something inside him that was an elemental part of his life; a deep well-spring of emotion. It was almost as though some part of him had always known they would meet again and that she would be part of his life.

He wanted to go to her and plead with her to retract her demands, to make her see the risk she was running; to show her how dangerous Simon Herries really was, but he knew she wouldn't even listen to him, never mind believe him.

The frustration of not being able to talk to her, to show her . . . To show her what? he asked himself wryly. To show her how much he wanted her? He could just imagine her reaction to that!

At the time she had delivered her ultimatums he had acted impulsively, doing the first thing that came into his head to protect her. Would it work? It could do, if he could manage to convince the world at large that the pair of them were lovers.

Which brought him back to the problem of Simon Herries. Simon hadn't liked him taking charge—Simon didn't trust him, he had seen that much in his eyes. Miles was going to be walking a tightrope between the two of them. Herries would check every move he made, he knew that. No, for Pepper's own sake it was better that she continue to believe he had been a party to her rape.

He suspected she didn't realise how very dangerous Simon Herries actually was . . . Miles frowned again as he picked up the sheet of paper relating to Simon Herries. Pepper knew about his violent streak, of course. Against his will his mind replayed back for him in faultless detail the scene in his room at Oxford the night that Simon had raped her. Yes, he could understand how a woman would want to exact retribution for an act such as that.

Richard and Alex he dismissed as being merely pawns caught up in the real game; they posed no true threat to Pepper; not in the way that Simon Herries did.

His researcher had penned a handwritten note at the bottom of Simon Herries' sheet, and he read it thoughtfully. It seemed that Simon Herries had

returned from Cumbria after what was an annual
family holiday without his wife and children and that
moreover the staff at the London house had not seen
Elizabeth Herries or her two children since the day
she left to join Simon in the country. She had left him,
obviously, but why? And why had he not made any
attempt to gain custody of his children? A man like
Simon Herries, ambitious, driven by a powerful need
to succeed, could scarcely be blind to the fact that it
could only improve his public image if he was seen to
be a caring father, especially since Elizabeth seemed
to have been the one to have left him. She had not
gone to her family in Boston, so the researcher had
established.

Miles leaned back in his chair thoughtfully, putting
Elizabeth Herries out of his mind and concentrating
instead on Pepper. He had been a lawyer for long
enough to know that there were men, perfectly respectable, upright and honest men, who genuinely believed
that no good decent woman was ever raped. He had
seen some of his colleagues waste years of their lives
trying to show them otherwise, and he himself had
come face to face with the reality of mindless and
appalling violence in too many of its various forms to
be naïve about it any more. Even so, what he read in
the brief report worried him.

He had always known about Simon's homosexual
tendencies, but he had hitherto dismissed them as
youthful experimentation—Herries hadn't been the
only student to indulge in that particular form of
gratification and then later produce both a wife and a
family—but this statement about young boys being
picked up off the street and then left half beaten to
death. There was no evidence to corroborate it; it was
merely a comment, but Miles was a lawyer and he
knew that the most respectable and reputable of men

could have the most secret lives.

He had seen the shock and hatred in Simon's eyes when Pepper handed them her ultimatum and he had no illusions about how Simon felt about her. He would have killed her on the spot if he could.

As he had once before, he felt again that in Simon Herries' case the thin line dividing sanity and madness was very fragile indeed in places. His hatred of Pepper was almost obsessional—a sure sign of a deranged mind.

If he could prove it, get the man committed even if only temporarily . . . but Miles knew already that that wasn't the answer. He told himself that there was no reason for him to be involved. Even if Pepper did reveal the truth he doubted that it would have much effect on his career. He was not in as vulnerable a position as the others; he could afford to turn his back on her and walk away, but he knew he wasn't going to.

He was attracted to her—he might as well admit it. Attracted to her and challenged by her. And he was also increasingly afraid for her. She was a very brave and courageous woman, and in some ways he admired the stand she had taken, but she didn't know the danger she was putting herself in.

If he hadn't stepped in and taken matters into his own hands by assuming command he suspected that Herries would have gone to almost any lengths to silence her, even murder.

And maybe not for the first time.

All kinds of gossip had gone the rounds at Oxford after Tim Wilding's death; the kind of macabre black-humoured jokes that undergraduates delight in. Then he had dismissed the whole thing as merely another speculative item of gossip. Now . . . Miles frowned again . . . there was no doubt in his mind that

Herries had some sort of hold over the other two. He had watched them carefully and observed the way they allowed him to take control. Alex Barnett he could understand—he had never been a particularly forceful type, but Richard Howell . . .

It made no difference to the outcome of Pepper's attempt to blackmail them, of course, but still it might be interesting to see just how and why Herries held them in his power.

It was his lawyer's mind that hated loose ends, Miles told himself as he checked in his diary and then rang through to his office.

His clerk wasn't used to him cancelling appointments at such short notice, and Miles grinned to himself as he heard the disapproval in the older man's voice. Barristers' clerks were the real power in chambers; they ran and ruled the small élite world, and woe betide anyone who didn't acknowledge it.

Now that he had the week free, he needed to decide what he intended to do with it. He couldn't afford to waste too much time. Herries would soon grow impatient, he suspected, and even if he were of a mind to warn Pepper Minesse of the danger he suspected she was courting he doubted if she would listen to him.

He packed a small case and booked himself into a hotel on the outskirts of Oxford. He had friends in the area whom he could visit, and thus kill two birds with one stone. He had a godson in Oxford whom he hadn't seen since he was christened, and if he was lucky and everything went according to plan he might just have sufficient time to be able to call at the Manor on the way back.

Colonel Whitegate's heir had not been able to maintain the house for very long, and when it eventually came on the market Miles had helped to raise the money to buy it and convert it into a home for mentally handicapped children. Whenever he was in the area, he tried to make time to call in, and to visit the orphanage where he had been brought up. Things had changed since his day, but he still recognised the intense loneliness and apartness of the children there, and he knew it was something that no amount of community care and charity could ever wipe out. It was a burden they would have to carry all their lives. Something they would have to come to terms with as he had done.

Like him, there would be times when they would yearn desperately for a family of their own; when they would question what it was they had done that had put them in such a place, but he also hoped that like him, as time went by, they would be able to develop enough self-confidence to realise that the blame was not theirs. He had had to do so. There were times when he had been tempted to try to trace his parents, but he had seen too often the outcome of such heart-breaking searches to believe that it would really solve the problems that being deserted as a child had fostered.

He was one of the lucky ones, he acknowledged. He had found the strength to put the past behind him and go on into the future. Many others did not.

He knew quite well what had brought on this introspective mood. He looked down at the two sheets of closely typed paper again. This was the dossier his informant had prepared on Pepper. One fact leapt glaringly off the paper again and again. During the time she had been staying with the Simms, Mary Simms had produced a son. Was Miles being unduly suspicious? Was it not, after all, possible that a woman of forty might well conceive after fifteen years of marriage despite the fact that she had previously had a history of miscarriages?

And yet by his reckoning the child had been born just about nine months after the night Simon Herries had raped Pepper. Coincidence, or . . .

Miles could feel the beginning of a migraine building up behind his skull. Too much tension, too many late nights. For the first time in his life, the variety of a constant parade of women through his life was beginning to pall. Marriage had always been something he had scrupulously avoided. He didn't have what it took to make a permanent commitment, he had often told himself. He had tried to put himself in Pepper's mind . . . to imagine what it would have been like to be that seventeen-year-old, alone in the world. The Simms had taken her in. Might she not out of gratitude to them have . . . have given them her child?

He thought of the controlled, triumphant woman behind that imposing desk and grimaced wryly. It seemed too out of character. He was after all simply leaping to conclusions. But what if these conclusions were the right ones? What if Pepper had actually borne Herries a child?

He tried to think of the sort of heritage a child of that conception might carry, and acknowledged, not for the first time, that sometimes it was in a child's interests for it not to know its antecedents.

It was a disturbing, challenging thought and he pushed it to one side. Every instinct he possessed— and he was that rare kind of man who did not take his instincts lightly—told him that Pepper Minesse was in danger. But how to remove her from it, and at the same time not alert Simon's suspicions? Because he was suspicious, Miles had seen it in his eyes. He had not liked having control of the situation taken from him.

Simon Herries was a man poised on the edge of a

chasm which if successfully crossed could lead on to
the peak, the ultimate seat of power, or so he believed.
Pepper was a burden coiled round his ankles, and he
would kick her down into the chasm without a qualm
to free himself if he had to, without even realising that
she could, by clinging to him, drag him down there
with her.

Herries, Miles suspected, had no awareness of the
real harshness of life. He seemed to believe himself
inviolate, and Miles believed he was dangerous enough
to kill if he had to. He wouldn't get away with it, of
course. He would be caught and there would be a
cause célèbre in the papers for a few weeks, but none
of that would breathe life back into Pepper's corpse.

No . . . somehow he had to get Pepper away.

His phone rang and he picked it up. It was his
secretary, reminding him that he was due to meet a
client later in the day. He had been asked to represent
a women's refuge in North London who were having
problems with their landlord. The popular press were
beginning to refer to him as a knight in shining
armour, always ready to champion the underdog. It
wasn't quite true, but Miles's own upbringing left him
with a strong sense of gratitude, a need in some small
way to pay back the kindness and generosity he
himself had received, and so from time to time he
took on these cases virtually free of charge.

He made a note of the appointment and went back
to his mental résumé of his progress with Pepper. His
campaign to establish himself as her would-be lover
was well in hand. He had bombarded her office with
flowers and telephone calls, and had even on one
occasion parked his car virtually on her doorstep.

Pepper had seen him as she emerged from her office
and had determinedly turned her back on him. In
other circumstances Miles would have found the

challenge of breaking through barriers an intoxicating one, but because he knew the reason behind her hatred of him he felt no amusement at her behaviour.

The security guards at both her office and home now recognised him. Pepper had told them both that she wanted nothing to do with him. He had countered by telling them that he and Pepper were lovers who had quarrelled. Two newspaper gossip columns had run items on them, both carefully and deliberately leaked by himself. As far as the world was concerned, it would no longer be surprised to hear their names linked together. All very well as far as it went, but Miles was still a long, long way from keeping her safe from Simon.

He was due to play squash this evening and then he was having dinner at his club. He needed the expertise of a doctor, and he thought he knew where he could get it.

This weekend in Oxford he would find out as much as he could about Herries' activities while he was there, and then next week—Miles checked a list he had on his desk. It covered all Pepper's social engagements for the coming fortnight. His eyebrows lifted slightly as he saw that she was due to attend the polo match at Smith's Lawn on Saturday. Windsor wasn't that far from Oxford. The father of his godson was a polo aficionado who used to play for the Guards.

The gods, it seemed, were smiling on him.

The women's refuge was in a run-down, shabby building, down a narrow side street. It was a Victorian villa with a narrow strip of front garden. As Miles rang the bell he could hear a child crying, a thin wailing, despairing sound.

The woman who opened the door to him looked at

him cautiously. She was in her thirties, blonde and too thin.

Miles introduced himself and saw her expression lighten. Had she thought he was an angry husband come in pursuit of a runaway wife?

It wasn't really so amusing. He knew that it happened.

The woman who ran the refuge was an ex-nurse. She took Miles into the room she used as her office and outlined the problems she was having with the landlord, explaining that he was trying to increase their rent.

"Most of the women who come here have no money; they can't afford to pay their way, and so we're funded in the main by whatever we can raise. Quite frankly, it isn't enough to line the pockets of a greedy landlord."

They talked for a while, while Miles decided how best he could help, then Sarah James offered him a cup of tea. He accepted, and Sarah disappeared for several minutes, returning to announce that tea would not be long. As she opened the door Miles heard the sound of children's voices.

"Just back from school," Sarah explained. "We send two mothers with them to take and collect them just to make sure they aren't snatched by their fathers. It does happen," she assured him. "Violent men don't like losing control of their wives, and they're quite ready to use any means they can to blackmail them into going back; even if that means hurting their own children."

"And do they?" Miles asked her.

She looked at him and frowned.

"We don't handle cases of child abuse here, if that's what you mean. We aren't qualified to; that's a matter for the proper authorities, although getting a woman to tell them exactly what's going on isn't always easy. We've a case in point now . . . a woman with two children. She came to us some time ago. Her husband had been violent to her throughout her marriage, but she's only recently discovered that he's also been sexually abusing their son. She knows she ought to report him, but she's too terrified to do so. She's worried that she won't be believed, and that somehow she'll be forced to go back to her husband. And this is an educated woman, Mr. French—a woman, moreover, who's married to an extremely prominent man!"

Her indignation showed in her voice, her eyes sparkling with the force of her emotion. The door opened, silencing her for a moment, and Miles turned to smile at the woman bringing in their tea.

He recognised her straight away. Elizabeth Herries! Only his legal training allowed him to control his shock. He waited until she had gone and then relied on his instincts, asking quietly,

"I presume that's the woman you've just been telling me about?"

"Remarkably quick of you, Mr. French," Mrs James frowned. "You realise of course that what I've just told you was in the strictest confidence." She was plainly rather put out that he had recognised Elizabeth as the woman she had just described, and Miles could understand why.

He thought fast, not sure yet how he could use the information to his advantage without endangering Elizabeth Herries herself. He would have liked to have talked to her, but he suspected she would simply clam up on him. If he was going to get her to talk to him he was going to have to enlist the help of the woman sitting in front of him.

"I should like to talk to her," he said quietly,

holding up his hand when Sarah James would have interrupted to add, "No, I promise you I mean no harm. Quite the opposite. I know who she is and I know her husband—a very dangerous man."

After a brief pause she told him reluctantly, "She wants to divorce him, but she's terrified he'll try to take the children from her."

"I think I can help her," said Miles, and he meant it.

Mrs James looked at him consideringly and then said abruptly, "I'll go and have a word with her, if you'd like to wait . . ."

He wasn't going to make it for his squash game, Miles acknowledged as he drove away. Elizabeth Herries had been nervous to the point of dread, but eventually she had told him everything. He had assured her that he believed her and he had managed to convince her that she needed to divorce Simon, for her own sake and that of her two children, but he had not disputed the very real danger she was in. She badly needed her family's support, but she was too afraid to approach them, convinced that they would not believe her. She had confided to Miles that her husband was determined to be a future Conservative Prime Minister. It was no secret that the existing PM was planning on retiring, and Simon was one of several men being groomed for eventual leadership.

The PM was known as a man who had very strong moral views. Elizabeth Herries' family could hardly refuse to support her if Elizabeth had the Prime Minister's condemnation of Simon to substantiate her claims.

But Elizabeth was totally against any form of publicity. She was terrified about the effect it might have on her children.

There had to be a way round the problem, and Miles was determined that he would find it.

Pepper frowned as Miranda tapped on her door and walked in carrying a vase full of flowers. They weren't the usual hothouse type of blooms, but soft pastel-coloured cottage garden flowers nestled in a mist of silver-white foliage.

Pepper looked and pretended to be studying her diary, but inwardly she was seething. She knew without taking the card from Miranda who they would be from. What did Miles French think he was trying to do? Did he honestly think that in pretending to be physically attracted to her he could swerve her from her chosen course? The man must have an ego the size of a mountain if he really believed his sexual appeal was such that she would simply give up all she had worked for, because he chose to smile at her!

"Aren't they gorgeous?" Miranda enthused, putting the flowers down on her desk. She looked surreptitiously at the downbent red head. The whole of the office was agog with the very obvious and lavish attentions of their boss's new man. There had been other men before him, of course, droves of them, but never one like this.

"Take them away and put them in the boardroom, please," Pepper commanded her curtly. "They give me hay fever."

It was a lie, and had she had her way she would have picked up the flowers, vase and all, and thrown them into the street, but she couldn't afford to behave so emotionally. It would be totally out of character.

"Mr French rang four times this morning," Miranda told her. "Er . . . I told him you'd said you didn't want to speak to him . . ."

Pepper felt her skin prickle with irritation and

something else she didn't want to name. She refused to look up, but she knew that Miranda was still standing beside her desk.

"He . . . he—er—told me to tell you that he'd be round tonight as usual and that if you really want your key back he'll bring it with him."

Pepper gripped hold of her pen and stared disbelievingly at her secretary. She opened her mouth to deliver a blistering retort, then realised that nothing she could say would do any good. One look at Miranda's face had convinced her that her secretary could never be convinced that she and Miles French were not engaged in a very passionate affair.

Damn him! If he was here now . . .

She let Miranda escape and then paced her office angrily. Miles French thought he was so clever, putting her in this position, making it impossible for her to refute his claims that they were lovers. Pepper stopped pacing and discovered that she was actually grinding her teeth. She stared out of her office window and into the busy street.

She needed to get away. She was tense and on edge. To get away . . . She laughed to herself. She never needed to get away; she loved her work and devoted herself to it wholeheartedly. Nick had given up trying to persuade her to take time off. He had asked her to go away with him often enough, but she always refused. She knew she was safer on her own home ground, and she always knew that Nick was still determined that they were going to be lovers.

Miranda came back in with some letters for signing just as Pepper was massaging her aching neck.

"Tired?" Miranda asked her sympathetically. "You need a holiday."

"Yes . . . Yes, I think I do," Pepper agreed tiredly. She certainly needed something, if only the opportunity to get away from Miles French's constant bombardment of tokens of his totally fictitious affection.

She was due to spend the weekend with Isabelle and Jeremy, but that would hardly be relaxing. She thought of Oxford and Mary and Philip, but visiting them this weekend was out unless she left the office early on Friday.

She nibbled on the edge of her pen. The polo match she was attending with Isabelle and her husband was an important one. Nick Howarth's team would be playing. He was captain of it now and no longer quite the rarity he had once been. Smith's Lawn abounded with millionaire pop stars turned country squirearchy, and wealthy businessmen ready to put their hands into their pockets and sponsor such a socially potentially rewarding sport.

Pepper mentally reviewed her wardrobe, deciding what she would wear. Isabelle was giving a dinner in the evening and it would be a formal affair. She would wear the new creation she had just bought from Parker's. It wasn't in her usual style, being slightly less sexy and rather more softly feminine. She frowned, checking slightly, wondering why she had chosen to deviate from her habitual style.

She had lost two pounds this week—a sign that she was worrying about something. And yet hadn't she every reason not to worry? Hadn't she just reached a goal she had been striving for for ten years? Surely that was just cause for self-congratulation? So why then was she suffering this faint feeling of malaise; this sombreness that shadowed her thoughts and her dreams? Why was she allowing Miles French's pseudo attentions to unsettle her so much? She had far more important things to worry about. She had delivered her ultimatums and there was no way her victims would dare not to meet them. For now she had work to do if she was taking the weekend off. She had heard reports of a new potential tennis star, in Cheshire of all places, and she wanted to go and check out the report for herself. Tennis sponsorship was very big business. So far Pepper only had a small slice of it, but in five years' time it would be much larger. She waited for the thrill that planning the expansion of her business always brought her, but strangely it didn't come. A tiny frisson of anxiety rippled across her skin, but she dismissed it, concentrating instead on the report on her desk.

It was one of her major gifts that she could be single-minded enough to concentrate on the here and now, rather than drift into time-wasting thoughts of the past and the future, but despite her concentration she still remained vaguely unsettled. And she knew deep inside herself that somehow this was due to Miles French.

She looked up and realised that Miranda had forgotten to remove the flowers. They reminded her very much of Philip's garden, or going even further back, of the wild flowers that she had seen growing during the years of her childhood.

Miles's choice of bouquet surprised her. She would have expected expensive hothouse blooms, not these delicate, pastel-hued, velvet-petalled flowers, and it disturbed her that he was capable of doing something she had not associated with him. It made her wonder how accurate her total assessment of him had been—or more worryingly, how *in*accurate.

Julia Barnett stared unseeingly out of her bedroom window. She had started sleeping in here alone on odd nights six months ago, consumed by a guilt she could no longer fight. Alex was at work—at least that was where he told her he had gone. Her once pretty mouth twisted bitterly. She had rung him half an hour ago, and his secretary had sounded surprised that Julia didn't know he wasn't due in.

She picked up the piece of paper she found on the floor of their bedroom, only now Alex sometimes slept alone in it. She had smoothed it out and now it lay on the bed beside her.

Alex's strong handwriting was instantly recognisable, even if she hadn't kept every love letter he had written her. There were only two words on this piece; a name, written over and over again, with a compulsiveness that spoke volumes.

Julia stared at it, and blinked.

Pepper Minesse . . . another woman . . . the other woman . . . Julia knew who she was. She had seen her on television not long ago, in a BBC 2 series featuring successful women.

Alex, her Alex, was having an affair with Pepper Minesse. She felt the tightness inside her chest grow and clamped her teeth together, to prevent the scream of hysterical fear engulfing her. She had known this would happen. She had known all along she would be punished for what she had done to their child. She started to tremble, and the faintness she often experienced these days started to overwhelm her.

She wasn't conscious of passing out, only of coming to, to find herself lying on the bedroom floor. She got up awkwardly, still dizzy, pressing her hand to her flat stomach. She hadn't eaten for two days, but she didn't connect that with her dizziness. It was all part of her punishment—punishment she justly deserved. But Pepper Minesse should be punished too. She was stealing her husband. She would give him the children that she, Julia, could not.

She remembered how remote the adoption people

had been . . . kind but remote. She knew they would
not get their child, but would find out about what she
had done, and then . . . And then Alex would leave
her and she would be completely on her own. But
wasn't that what she deserved? She had killed their
child . . .

She wasn't aware of walking to the station or of
getting on the London train. She arrived at Pepper's
office just after lunch. Pepper had not eaten out, and
she was sitting at her desk, studying a report, when
her secretary came in.

"There's a woman outside asking for you." Miranda
frowned uncomfortably. "I'm afraid . . . she's rather
odd . . ."

"Odd? In what sense?"

"Well, she seems to think you've . . . you've stolen
her husband."

Pepper's eyebrows rose. There had been many times
over the years when her name had been linked with
that of men both married and unmarried, but this was
the first time an angry wife had turned up outside her
door.

"What does she expect me to do?" Pepper asked
coolly. "Unlock a safe and hand him back? Who is
she, by the way?"

"Well, we had some difficulty getting her name.
She's . . . well, she looks very distraught. She said
her name was Julia . . . Julia Barnett."

Julia Barnett. Alex Barnett's wife. Did she really
think that Pepper was having an affair with her
husband? On the point of telling Miranda to get rid
of her, Pepper changed her mind.

"Show her in here. I'll have a word with her."

"Do you think you should?" murmured Miranda.
"She's in a pretty bad state . . ." The girl flushed
under Pepper's querying stare. "Well, maybe not

dangerous exactly, but . . . well, verging on the hysterical, almost certainly." She bit her lip and added uncertainly, "She isn't even dressed properly."

"Show her in," Pepper repeated firmly.

She saw what Miranda meant the moment the door opened. The woman standing on its threshold must have once been very pretty and could still have been very attractive. Instead her blonde hair was unstyled and faded, her face free of make up and drawn into harsh lines of pain. She was wearing clothes that made Pepper's fastidious mouth curl; a pair of what looked like old slippers on her feet and a loose smock-like dress that did nothing to hide her appalling thinness.

"You've stolen my husband and I want him back."

The bald trembling statement broke the silence. Pepper said nothing, just sat watching. The woman stirred a feeling of pity deep inside her that she would much rather not have felt.

"I know why he wants you." The words came out in a rush. "It's because you can give him a child . . . Well, I'm not going to let you!" She moved so quickly that Pepper was caught off guard. One moment the woman was standing by the door, the next she was up against the edge of the desk brandishing what looked like a carving knife.

Pepper didn't have time to be frightened; there was only an overwhelming sensation of unreality; the incongruity of the whole situation struck her as ridiculously funny. Here was this woman accusing her of stealing her husband, threatening to end her life, when in reality . . .

"I'm not trying to take your husband away from you." Pepper spoke calmly and quietly. "I promise you that. Look, why don't you sit down and we'll have a cup of coffee and talk about it?" She saw the woman's face change, soften and then crumple into almost childish lines.

"I lost my baby," she said helplessly.

"I know. I know all about it."

"God keeps punishing me. That's why he let you take Alex from me."

"God doesn't want to punish you, really. He understands what you did."

She saw the uncertainty flicker in the blue eyes as they focused on her for the first time. She saw the tiny gleam of hope lighten them and wondered disbelievingly what on earth she was doing. Counselling distraught women was not her line of work; she couldn't care less about Alex Barnett's wife. So why did she have this appalling sense of compassion for her? Why did she have this need to reach out and help her? She could not understand it.

"Let's sit down and talk," she suggested quietly. "I know all about your baby, Julia. I know all about you."

"You do?"

"Yes . . . and I promise you I'm not going to take Alex away."

"He doesn't know what I did. I lied to him . . . I can't have any more babies, but he can . . . He . . ."

"Alex only wants *you*."

She had the woman's attention now. The hand holding the knife relaxed, but Pepper made no attempt to reach for it. Oddly, she had not felt a second's fear that she was in any real danger, but she waited until Julia had placed the knife on the desk before reaching for it and taking it from her.

She rang for Miranda and when the girl came in she said evenly, "Miranda, two cups of coffee, please, and then I'm going to take the rest of the day off. Mrs Barnett and I will be going out shopping."

"Shopping?" The blue eyes stared at her, the faded lips forming the word as though it was totally unfamiliar.

"Alex likes you to look pretty, doesn't he?" Pepper said firmly.

"Yes. Yes, he does." Frail fingers plucked nervously at the worn dress.

Here was a woman suffering under an immense burden of guilt; a woman in desperate need of proper psychiatric help, Pepper recognised. A woman she would have expected a man like Alex Barnett to have discarded years ago, and yet he still loved her. All the reports had confirmed the fact. Could a man who loved a woman so faithfully and intensely really . . .?

Really what? She hadn't imagined being kidnapped by him and then raped. She owed it to herself to exact her just measure of retribution, and yet here when she was faced with the ultimate weapon when she could have so easily have called the police and had his wife forcibly and publicly removed and held up to ridicule, she hadn't done so. Why?

Perhaps it was because of the woman sitting in front of her. She had photographs in her file of the old Julia and the difference was almost painful, and yet what had this woman done? Nothing that Pepper had not contemplated doing herself. Her guilt, her punishment, was all self-inflicted. It was one thing to read in a report that to destroy Alex Barnett's chances of adopting a child would send his wife over the edge into complete despair. It was another to be confronted with the reality of that woman and her pain.

Even without being ready to admit it to herself, Pepper knew that she just could not do it . . . That she would have to find another way of punishing him.

The decision was made almost without her being

aware of it, and with its making came an odd lightness
of heart.

She got Miranda to track down Alex Barnett, who
was eventually found in Whitehall, trying to discover
the outcome of his tender. Pepper had asked Miranda
to leave a message that he was to call at her office. In
the meantime, as she had promised, she took Julia
shopping. It was almost like being in charge of a
helpless child, and she was in turn angry and appalled
at what could happen to a member of her own sex,
simply through guilt.

When she felt her charge had had enough she
shepherded her back to her office. Once inside she sat
her down and said firmly,

"Julia, you must tell Alex the truth."

She felt the woman tremble beneath her light touch
on her shoulder.

"I can't . . . I can't!"

"You must," Pepper insisted. "You must be strong.
That's what Alex would want. You must share
your . . . your pain with him."

She had no idea why she was doing all this. She
should simply have rung the police, she told herself
angrily. She hated what this woman was doing to her
own emotions. They were see-sawing up and down
like mercury in a thermometer . . . She hated herself
for being so ridiculously emotional.

"God won't let me," Julia protested.

Pepper took a deep breath.

"Yes, yes, he will. That's why he sent you here to
me, Julia, because he wanted me to tell you that he
has forgiven you. He wants you to tell Alex everything . . . because he wants Alex to take care of a
very special child for him."

She could tell that she had Julia's attention.

"God has a child for us?"

The whole thing was like a farce, Pepper thought fiercely, but she had to see it through. She was being pulled apart by her own conflicting feelings, and yet she couldn't sacrifice this woman to the hell of her own depression. She was still governed in so much by her gypsy genes, and they told her that there was a higher purpose; a higher awareness, a higher ordering of much that occurred in life, and that this was a test for her. Almost she could feel her own grandmother at her side, and the skin on her scalp prickled with prehensile awareness. She never thought about that other life now, those other mores . . . but they were still there, and she carried her awareness that there was much in life that is inexplicable and not subject to reason without her being aware of it. This woman had been sent to her for a purpose . . . she could sense it. In her mind's eye she visualised Julia as a desperate creature trapped in a pit of sticky clinging mud, which would eventually drag her down and destroy her. She was reaching out her hands to Pepper, and if she ignored her, if she turned her back on her . . .

She took a deep breath and with only her instinct to go on, said firmly, "Yes. Yes, he does, Julia. Soon Alex will be here. He'll take you home and you'll tell him all about your baby."

"And then . . . then God will send us another child?"

She was trembling visibly, and Pepper fought to control her own inner panic. What was she doing, interfering like this? She wasn't God, she couldn't make such promises, and yet . . . and yet . . . As though the words came from someone else, she heard herself saying an old Romany blessing, a favourite of her grandmother's, and almost instantly the tension in the room disappeared, and it was filled with a warmth like the sun coming out on a cloudy day.

Julia felt it too. Suddenly her trembling ceased and her eyes cleared. Pepper held her breath. Her internal phone rang, cutting through the golden stillness.

"Alex Barnett has just arrived," Miranda told her.

"Right. Give me two minutes and then show him in.

"Alex is here," she told Julia as she replaced the receiver. "When he comes in just tell him that you want to go home. And then when you get home, tell him all about your baby. You must do that, do you understand, Julia?"

"If I do will God forgive me?"

"God wants you to tell Alex," Pepper told her firmly. "And when you have done you're going to feel a lot better. God will forgive you."

She only hoped that the woman would forgive herself, Pepper thought as she let herself out of her office via another door that led into the private meeting room.

The last person Alex had expected to discover in Pepper's office had been his wife. He rushed over to her in concern.

"Julia . . ."

"Take me home, Alex. I want to go home."

He saw the way she was dressed, but the wild and unfocused look in her eyes that went with these increasingly common depressed moods wasn't there.

"I want to go home . . . I have to talk to you . . ." she muttered.

"What are you doing here?" Alex demanded.

"I had to come," Julia told him quietly. "I had to come."

"While they were talking Pepper walked into the foyer.

"I'm leaving now, Miranda. Would you go into my

office and give Mr Barnett a message for me? Please tell him that his wife arrived here in a rather distressed state, and I think that it would be best if he took her home."

Alex received the message in a state of semi-shock. He had no idea what was going on, or what had brought Julia here, and even more important, exactly what Pepper Minesse had been saying to her. And yet Julia seemed calmer and more rational than she had been in a long time.

He smiled rather distantly at Miranda, unaware of the length of her legs, or the lush promise of her smile, but when he looked at his wife his entire expression changed, softening and warming, and as Miranda commented wryly to one of the girls after they had gone,

"There aren't many of that kind around, worse luck!"

Pepper was late leaving the office on Friday afternoon after all. Alex Barnett had rung her several times during the week, but she had refused to take his calls. She couldn't understand what on earth had motivated her to behave in such a stupid and emotional fashion. And as for thinking that her grandmother . . . Well, that was total idiocy. Firmly dismissing both the Barnetts from her mind, Pepper got into her car.

Her clothes were already packed. A quick bath and something light to eat and she could be on her way.

With any luck she could reach Oxford before Oliver went to bed. She checked the thought as it formed. Oliver meant nothing to her. She had no right to want to see him. Oliver was Philip and Mary's child.

If she carried on like this for much longer she was likely to become as mentally unstable as Julia Barnett, she derided herself—first imagining that she could

sense her grandmother's spirit and now mooning over
a child she never wanted in the first place.

And yet . . . and yet when she reached Oxford just
after nine and she was greeted by Oliver's welcoming
smile, she couldn't disguise the curious fluttery,
pleasurable sensation that rose up inside her.

Her visit was only a brief one. She left in the
morning straight after breakfast. Mary kissed her
gently as she drove off.

"She loves him," she said quietly to Philip later
when they were alone. "I knew one day she would."
He squeezed her hand and wondered why it was that
fate so often decreed that those who were most meek
and innocent among human kind should suffer so
dreadfully.

"Does it hurt badly?" he asked her.

She shook her head.

"No, not really." She got up and smiled at him.
"Oliver will be in soon. I'd better make a start on
lunch."

Isabelle had organised a picnic lunch to be eaten at
Smith's Lawn.

Jeremy had already gone on ahead, and watching
as Isabelle manoeuvred the huge picnic basket and
what seemed like half a dozen children and was in
fact only three, into the back of a large Range Rover,
Pepper was both amused and saddened by how much
her scatty friend had changed. Now she was the
complete Sloane Ranger wife and mother; those days
in Oxford might never have been, and Pepper knew
with certainty that the Isabelle of these days would
never have stopped to talk to a stranger in the street,
nor certainly to have so quickly and impetuously
offered her friendship. Without their mutual connection with polo to tie them together Pepper suspected

the friendship would have faded long ago.

"I'm thrilled that you're presenting the Cup. It's quite an honour, you know. Last year the Princess of Wales did it".

"Jeremy thinks Nick's team will win," said Isabelle. "He's quite miffed about it really. He says it isn't fair that they should be able to buy in so much South American talent. We don't know who half of them are, you know . . ."

There was a good deal more in the same vein, and Pepper wished she could drive to the game in her own car. However, Isabelle had made all the arrangements, and Isabelle hated her arrangements being changed.

"In fact Jeremy's not himself at all these days. I expect it's something to do with all this 'big Bang' fuss in the City." She pulled a wry face, and Pepper, who suspected that Jeremy was far more likely to be involved in an extra-marital affair than concerned about an event that could only lead to a huge increase in his income, said nothing. She knew Isabelle of old, and if she wanted to she would eventually find a way to get round to the subject that was really bothering her. Isabelle was no fool; she was also an extremely attractive woman—plumper now after the birth of three children, but Pepper suspected that she wasn't entirely true to her marriage vows herself. Of course, everything was done discreetly, one didn't flaunt one's small peccadilloes, but Pepper hadn't missed the glances Isabelle had been exchanging with the husband of one of her cronies, the last time she had been down.

She settled herself in the front of the Range Rover, while Isabelle cautioned the children to be quiet. Jeremy's black Labrador was in the back, his tail thumping against the grille separating him from the children.

"All ready?"

The match they were attending was one of the most important in the polo sporting year. Sponsored by Cartier, it was of international importance, and when they arrived at the Guards' Polo Club at Smith's Lawn, it was to find the ground sprinkled with an assortment of elegant marquees.

This was the fourth year that Pepper had attended this particular event, but it was the first occasion on which she had been asked to present the winner's trophy. She had no delusions about what Isabelle had told her in an awed whisper was a great honour; if the Princess of Wales and the Duchess of York had not been away on holiday with their respective husbands, she would not have even been considered. However, her company had become so closely involved with the game and her face so well known that as she and Isabelle made their way to Cartier's reception marquee, they drew curious and envious glances from the huge crowd of onlookers.

Luckily the day was fine and the flower-decorated marquee not too crowded. Pepper acknowledged smiles from several members of the Hurlingham Polo Association as she made her way to the top table. Once not so long ago this old-guard governing body of the sport would have looked askance at sponsorship for their game, but now it had become so much the norm as to draw very little attention at all.

Lunch was the noisy, gossipy occasion Pepper had expected it to be; she smiled and talked, and all the time she kept her ears open and managed to pick up two rather interesting bits of gossip which she suspected she would be able to turn to her own advantage later. Isabelle had drifted away to talk to some of her county cronies. Nick was deep in conversation with a fellow player.

Pepper glanced across the crowded marquee—and

suddenly froze. That man with his back to her . . . that dark head . . .

Miles had already seen her—how could he not? She was the cynosure of all eyes, both male and female. She played her part well, he acknowledged, amused and admiring of her skill and dexterity. She was dressed elegantly, in a white spotted cornflower blue silk suit with a matching hat that set off her extraordinary hair. Pearls gleamed lustrously at her throat. She was wearing decorous white gloves. He knew all about her relationship with Nick Howarth. They were supposed to be lovers. He knew a lot about Pepper now, and about how she kept her men at a distance. Inside that beautiful packaging she was a woman who was unable to come to terms with her sexuality. Miles was ready almost to bet his reputation on his belief that none of the men who so assiduously danced attendance on her had ever shared her bed. He didn't know why he was so convinced of this; all the evidence dictated otherwise. She had been very clever with her camouflage. One man would be put off by the intimation that she was in love with another; someone else the promise that one day perhaps . . . and yet another with a further piece of adroit manipulation. Pepper Minesse was one very clever lady, he admitted, still watching her; clever enough not to antagonise the male sex with an outright refusal, clever enough to manufacture for herself a reputation that made it next to impossible for anyone to believe that her sexual experience was limited to one frenzied act of lust.

He looked at Nick Howarth. He was a supremely fit male specimen; physically attractive, wealthy . . . and obviously very attracted to Pepper.

The announcement that the formalities of the day were about to begin intruded into his thoughts. There was a general exodus outside during which he was

careful to ensure that he kept out of sight. Pepper
looked in vain for the dark head as the bands of the
Artillery Company and the Irish Guards played the
national anthems of the two competing countries.

The first chukka started, the game fiercely contested
and played dangerously fast. The week had left Pepper
curiously drained and weak in a way that she found
disconcerting. She must have imagined that brief
sighting of Miles French, she comforted herself. She
was beginning to feel as though the wretched man was
almost haunting her. Dismissing him from her mind,
she tried to concentrate on the game in progress.

Halfway through the afternoon there was a break
for tea. Jeremy and Nick joined them, and the talk at
the table was all of the merits and demerits of the
rival teams. Pepper was not a particular devotee of
polo, but it disconcerted her to realise how much that
intrusion of Miles French into her mind had unsettled
her. She felt restless, almost bored even by Nick's
conversation, relieved, and yet at the same time in
some odd way disappointed that Miles French wasn't
really there. Disappointed? She caught herself up on
the thought, frowning so deeply that Nick broke off
his conversation to ask if she was all right. He touched
her wrist as he did so, and she had to stop herself
from flinching away from him.

Nick had introduced a new pony to his string, and
soon he was deep in discussion with Jeremy about the
animal's potential.

"It's a little on the nervy side as yet, but it's early
days . . ."

Pepper shut her mind to the conversation, glancing
away. Why on earth was Miles French occupying so
much of her attention? It was ridiculous, it was
dangerous.

The men got up, and Pepper and Isabelle followed

them. Pepper and Isabelle resumed their seats; the second half started. Nick's team had been knocked out before the afternoon tea interval, and he came over to talk to them.

"Come and have a look at my latest acquisition," he invited Pepper. She didn't want to go, but guilt and a certain irritation with herself for allowing Miles French to intrude so much into her thoughts made her do so.

Nick placed his arm proprietorially around her shoulders as they walked over to where the ponies were tethered. She wanted to move away, but restrained herself. There had been many women in Nick's life since they had first met, but she knew that he still had hopes of their becoming lovers. It would never be; she knew that, but he did not . . . not yet.

Nick stopped to talk to someone and she broke away from him. She heard someone cry out a sharp warning, and wheeled round. One of the polo ponies had broken loose from its string and was heading straight towards her. Paralysed with shock, she could only stare at it . . . someone was screaming in the distance, a high pitched terror-stricken sound, and then the breath was forced out of her lungs as someone grabbed hold of her and pushed her to the ground. She felt the weight and warmth of an unmistakably masculine body covering her own, pinning her down.

Time spun crazily out of focus and she gave into the surge of blind panic engulfing her. She tried to fight, to push the weight off her. She couldn't breathe, her lungs laboured to take in air, panic and fear obliterating the concerned sounds of the onlookers. Only one reality reached her, and that was that for the second time in her life a man was inflicting himself on her, touching her, terrifying her.

She opened her mouth to scream, but no sound

came out. Blackness engulfed her, dizzily speckled with a thousand bursting coloured stars.

"She's fainted!"

Miles got up, carefully examining Pepper's inert body for broken bones. The crowd of admiring onlookers praised him for his quickwittedness. Isabelle, who was standing at his side with her children, said shakily,

"Oh my God! Pepper could have been killed! She just stood there . . ."

"Shock and fright," Miles told her, giving her his lazy, warm smile.

"She hasn't broken anything. I'll carry her over to my car, out of the way of this crowd . . ."

Flashbulbs exploded, but no one took any notice apart from Miles. If he had arranged the whole thing deliberately, it could not have been better. Tomorrow morning their pictures would be plastered all over the press. He had seen what was happening from yards away, but no one else had made any move to snatch Pepper out of the way. Like her, they had all been stricken by shock.

"Do—do you know her?" Isabelle was obviously puzzled.

"Yes. Yes, I do know her." Miles gave her a smile and a look that said quite explicitly what their relationship was. Instantly Isabelle was all flustered. "Oh. Oh, I see. I thought I hadn't seen you here before . . . That is, one becomes accustomed to a certain set of faces and I . . . Oh dear!"

"You and she were at college together, weren't you?" he added, mentally blessing the handiwork of his informant. Isabelle liked him. There was something about him, something very masculine and yet at the same time very gentle.

"She hasn't said anything about you . . . Oh look,

she's coming round."

Pepper froze as awareness flooded back. She was instantly conscious of being surrounded by man smell, by man strength, by a maleness so intense that her whole being cried out in protest against it.

"Pepper, are you all right?"

"Isabelle." She recognised her friend's voice and clung to it, opening her eyes. She couldn't see Isabelle. All she could see was Miles French. Miles French! She froze, her eyes dilating in panic. What was happening?

"My God, Pepper, what happened?"

Nick . . . She twisted round in Miles French's grasp, her breasts pushing against his chest, as she tried to extricate herself. The contact burned her, scalding her flesh, throwing her into a wild panic.

"She was so lucky, Nick . . . Miles saved her. Miles, why don't you join us for dinner tonight?"

It would put out Isabelle's numbers, but luckily she knew of a girlfriend who would be only too happy to partner Nick Howarth. Why on earth hadn't Pepper told her about this new man in her life? Isabelle wondered, a little chagrined.

"Pepper darling, why doesn't Miles run you home? You can lie down and have a rest and . . ."

"No!" The sharpness of her response drew three pairs of eyes. Only Miles French's held understanding, and she flinched from it, fighting for breath and self-control. Just that moment of awareness in his arms had made her realise how impossible it would ever be for her to take any man as her lover. Her fear of him overwhelmed her reluctant liking for Miles. She felt contaminated by his touch, whirled back to that morning when she had woken up in his bed, when he had leaned down and she had been filled with a panicky vulnerable fear that it was all going to happen again. In some way she hated him more than she hated Simon Herries . . . although she couldn't have said why. Perhaps it was because of her very vulnerability to him, because of the look she had seen in his eyes so briefly that morning—an awareness of her fear and a compassion for it. Pepper shook her head. What on earth was she thinking? He hadn't felt compassion for her . . . he had actively encouraged what happened to her. He must have done, for her to have been taken to his room.

He had released her now and she stood shakily, fighting to appear calm and in control.

"I'm fine, Isabelle. There's no need for Miles to take me anywhere." She gave him a taut smile and extended her hand. "Thank you so much. I . . ."

Isabelle interrupted.

"Darling, I'm afraid it's no good playing dumb. Miles has already spilled the beans." The coquettish look she gave them both said it all. A savage bitter anger filled Pepper as she saw the look on Nick's face. What was Miles French trying to do to her? Was this his petty idea of getting back at her?

"I've invited Miles to join us for dinner . . ."

Isabelle's prattle washed over her. She felt trapped . . . trapped and afraid. She wanted to scream out that she didn't want Miles French invading her life; that she was frightened of him. She wanted to run to Nick and beg him to protect her, and yet her pride, that fierce gypsy pride, and her intrinsic deep-rooted fear of the male sex, stopped her. How did she know that she would fare any better with Nick than with Miles? At heart weren't all men predators in the end? Didn't they all enjoy inflicting pain, damaging, destroying? Wasn't it all part and parcel of the whole male persona?

Fate was indeed favouring him, Miles reflected as

he made his excuses and went back to his friends.

Pepper reminded him of a frantic wild animal, desperate for escape, unaware of her own danger or the fact that he was trying to save her from it. He had felt the furious beat of her heart when she came out of her faint; had caught her gasp of shock and fear. What would it take to tame her? To win her confidence?

He frowned, irritated with himself for even thinking the question. Pepper Minesse was simply a problem in his life that had to be overcome, nothing more, nothing less. She did not fit into the mould of his women. She would never be the calm complacent type of lover he preferred. She would . . . He caught himself up and sealed off the thought before it could be properly formed. Emotionalism was a deterrent to achievement. He would do well to remember that simple cynical but very accurate fact.

CHAPTER SIXTEEN

THE SOUND of her office door slamming as Pepper walked into it caused Miranda and the receptionist to exchange raised eyebrowed looks.

"What's got into her?" Helena asked. "I've never seen her react like that before . . . wonder what's caused it?"

"The same thing that causes all women's problems," Miranda retorted acidly. "A man." She had had a bad weekend with her fiancé. He wanted her to give up her job when they got married and play at being Mrs Cabbage, and she wasn't going to.

In her office Pepper ran irate fingers through her hair. Her head ached with tension, her shoulders were stiff with it, and she was aware of a deep and intense inner rage that nothing could dissipate.

She knew who to blame for it, of course.

Miles French.

God, when she thought of how he had ruined her weekend . . . *Ruined* it! He had assassinated it.

On Saturday evening, when he turned up at Isabelle's for dinner, it had been bad enough, but the way he had appropriated Pepper, had begun to give a star performance as her doting lover . . . She ground her teeth. No amount of persuasion had been able to convince Isabelle that Pepper loathed the sight of him. The stupid idiot was an incurable romantic. Isabelle had giggled away Pepper's insistence that the man meant nothing to her; nothing at all.

What on earth was he playing at? She knew that he

was trying to throw her off balance, but was there a deeper purpose to his behaviour? He hadn't struck her as the sort of man who would give up nearly an entire weekend, simply for the purpose of being annoying.

The problem was that she couldn't really confide in Isabelle and tell her the truth, and Miles knew that, damn him. He seemed to have developed a sixth sense about her . . . Pepper's skin grew hot, her eyes flashing bitterly as she remembered how he had whispered to her over dinner, flirting with her, drawing everyone's attention to them, including Nick's.

It was hardly surprising that Nick had gone off in a huff. And then as though that wasn't enough, just as she was starting to bring Nick round on Sunday, who should turn up at the quiet pub where they were having lunch but Miles, claiming that she had agreed to meet him there the previous evening.

Isabelle must have told him where they were going. There couldn't have been any other way he could have found out.

Of course Nick had been furious.

Pepper sighed, leaning back in her chair, trying to massage the tension out of her forehead. It was pointless getting all wrought up about the man; he was perfectly capable of causing enough havoc without her aiding him.

She opened her diary and settled down to work. Normally she didn't have the slightest difficulty in putting aside the private side of her life, but today, irrationally, it kept on intruding. Every time her attention wandered she found herself thinking about the weekend, remembering how well Miles had fitted in to Isabelle's circle, how cleverly he had manipulated them all, and yet, like her, part of him remained outside it, and like her he had to fight to get where he was. Like her . . .

Exasperated with herself, she flung down her pen. This was getting her nowhere. She looked out of her office window. The sun was out and it was a clear bright day. She had a sudden longing to feel the breeze, see the countryside; a vague, disturbing yearning that she knew belonged to that side of her nature she had ruthlessly suppressed for so long.

She rang through for Miranda and when the girl came in said coolly, "I'm taking the rest of the day off, Miranda. If anyone wants me, I shall be here tomorrow."

She ignored the way her secretary gaped at her. Pepper never took time off, never left the office without giving a number where she could be reached.

"What's going on?" the receptionist hissed, as she watched Pepper walk out of the building. "She's never done anything like this before!"

"Like I said, it's got to be a man," Miranda told her positively.

Ten minutes later the receptionist came into her office bursting with excitement, waving a newspaper at her.

"It looks like you're right—take a look at this!"

The photograph had caught them just at the psychological moment when Miles had reached out to snatch Pepper away from the runaway polo pony. They looked like two lovers caught in a passionate clinch, and the slightly purple prose captioning the photograph hinted at more than a casual relationship.

"Miles French . . .phew! He looks gorgeous, doesn't he? I wouldn't mind a man like that myself. No wonder she's taking the day off!"

Pepper's staff weren't the only ones to see and speculate on the photograph. Richard Howell saw it and mentally congratulated his co-conspirator on his success. After the way Pepper had treated them in her office he hadn't believed for a moment that French had the slightest chance of putting up a convincing display that they were lovers. He had forgotten the appetite of the public for sentiment, he thought cynically. And then he frowned. Time was running out. All right, so French had managed to convince the world at large that he and Pepper were heavily involved, but he still had to carry out the second and more dangerous half of his plan. And Simon was getting impatient. He didn't like or trust French. Only yesterday he had insisted on having lunch with Richard.

He had been very much on edge, very tense, and if Richard hadn't known him better he might almost have suspected he was sitting across the table from a man suffering from some very deep mental problems, rather than the prominent and very astute MP he knew him to be. Simon had talked wildly about them taking matters into their own hands and ignoring Miles's plans. Richard hadn't taken up the hints he was dropping. It had been one thing to allow Simon to force him into kidnapping the girl when he was just another Oxford undergraduate. If he got embroiled in a similar sort of thing now . . . in his position . . . and somehow this time he didn't think it was merely rape that Simon had in mind. It seemed impossible to believe that a man in Herries' position could actually be contemplating what was in actual fact murder, but Herries' hatred of the woman had been so apparent, so all consuming that it had left Richard himself feeling acutely uncomfortable.

He needed to talk to Miles, he decided, reaching for the phone, and then replacing it. There was no point in taking unnecessary risks, he would ring him from the car; that way he wouldn't be overheard.

Miles was working in his study when the telephone rang, ostensibly on the case he was taking to defend the women's refuge, but in reality his mind was on Pepper and the problem of how to remove her to a place of safety. He thought he had the answer, but what he was contemplating was very risky and full of potential hazards.

He had talked to his doctor friend and had managed to extract from him a cocktail of drugs, guaranteed to give an immediate loss of consciousness with no after-effects. Miles had told him that he was sleeping badly and suffering from stress. He had claimed that he didn't want to approach his own doctor because he had a bias against tranquillisers and sleeping tablets of any kind. It had been a very thin excuse, but luckily it had been accepted.

He had several other arrangements yet to make, including finding somewhere where he could keep Pepper until he had convinced her of her danger.

He picked up the receiver, not particularly surprised to hear Richard Howell on the end of the line. They had been keeping in contact, although Miles suspected that like Simon, Richard was not altogether sure that he trusted him.

Alex Barnett, unlike the other two, had seemed frankly relieved to leave everything in his hands, and Miles suspected that if he never heard another word about Pepper or her ultimatums he would be a very happy man.

"Nice work," Richard announced. "I've seen the piece in the papers. As far as the rest of the world is concerned at least, you and Ms Minesse are now something of an item!"

"Is that why you're telephoning me—To congratulate me?" Miles asked him drily.

There was a moment's silence and then Richard admitted,

"No. Look, Simon's putting pressure on me to . . . well, to be quite frank, I don't think he's too happy with the way you're handling things. Time's running out."

Miles had been expecting something like this from the moment Pepper delivered her ultimatums. Unless he acted fast he suspected that Simon Herries would take matters into his own hands, and that was the last thing he wanted. He had had another meeting with Elizabeth Herries and had managed to persuade her to agree to see the Prime Minister. A meeting had been arranged, very discreetly, in his name, and he had only been able to achieve that much by ruthlessly using all his contacts. He had said nothing about the purpose of his appointment save that it concerned the behaviour of a prominent MP. Right now he needed time. Time to get Pepper away to a place of safety, and time to persuade Elizabeth Herries to go through with her divorce.

"Look, why don't we have a meeting?" he suggested.

"Yes, I think that's advisable and we'd better contact Alex, too. But you should know that Simon's out for Pepper Minesse's blood," Richard told Miles frankly. "We met for lunch the other day, and to be honest, he worried me. He's talking about getting rid of her— permanently." He paused and then said grimly, "If he tries anything like that we'll all be dragged even further into the whole mess."

"You could always go to the police and tell them everything," Miles suggested, knowing even as he spoke that it was a very forlorn hope.

"You know I can't do that," Richard told him curtly, confirming his thoughts. "None of us can. No, the sooner you can get her to retract, the better.

Simon doesn't trust you," he added flatly, "and unless you do something soon he's going to take matters into his own hands."

Tell me something I don't know, Miles thought grimly as he replaced the receiver. There must be some way of getting Pepper to safety, somewhere he could take her. His glance fell on a brief he had put on one side to be filed away. It had involved a very intricate copyright case for a billionaire industrialist. He had been very grateful to Miles for winning him his case— so grateful in fact that he had offered him the use of one of his many overseas properties for just as long as he wished. Miles had told him at the time that barristers couldn't afford to take indefinite holidays. A thought struck him and he picked up his telephone.

"Get me Ralph Ryde, will you, please?" he asked his secretary.

Three minutes later his phone rang.

"Ralph, do you still have that property in Goa?" he asked without preamble. He had visited it once, and the house and its setting had caught his imagination.

"Yes . . . yes, I do. Don't go there much though now . . . it's too remote. But if you want the use of it—"

Offering his thanks, Miles ended the call and sat in thought. The more he looked into Simon's past, the more concerned he became about Pepper's future. He suspected she didn't know how dangerous the man was, and Miles had been relieved to discover from a fellow member of one of his clubs that despite Simon's own convictions, the Conservative Party had no intention of proposing him for a Cabinet post.

"Too unstable, don't you know, old chap," his contact had confided. "Not quite the sort we're looking for." His fellow club member had cleared his throat and added gruffly, "Heard one or two unsavoury items about the chappie from time to time . . ."

The club was one which Colonel Whitegate had sponsored him for when he was first at the bar, and Miles kept up the membership out of a certain sentimental gratitude to the older man. Its members were all very much in the same gruff Army mould, good sterling British stock.

Phoning Richard back Miles confirmed the need for a meeting. "Could you make it this evening at my place?"

It had occurred to Miles that it might be a good idea to get Alex and Richard on their own without Simon around. He might discover then exactly what hold the other man had had on them.

Alex Barnett sounded rather preoccupied when Miles rang him, but confirmed that he would be there.

There was only one small task left to complete now. He picked up the phone and dialled. A pleasantly spoken girl answered him.

"I'd like to book a flight to Goa for two, please. Yes, Goa."

Ten minutes later he replaced the receiver and smiled rather grimly to himself. What he was contemplating doing broke just about every rule in the book. He only hoped he could get away with it, because if he couldn't . . . He picked up the phone again.

Miranda was rather surprised to find Miles French on the phone asking for Pepper. She had assumed that when Pepper took the day off it was because she intended to spend it with him.

He even managed to sound sexy on the phone, she thought, relishing the smooth maleness of his voice. She explained to him that Pepper had taken the day off.

"Ah, good!" There was a suggestion of laughter in

his voice, a hint of shared intimacy which she liked. "I wonder if I could persuade you to enter a small conspiracy with me, then. I want to take Pepper away on holiday, but I'm sure you know how your boss feels about leaving her office."

Miranda made a wry sound of agreement.

"Well, I think I've found the answer. I'm going to abduct her . . . I've made all the arrangements, but it's just struck me I'm going to need her passport. Do you have access to it?"

Miranda did. It was kept locked in the small office safe which also housed important documents and day-to-day petty cash.

As she said later to her boyfriend, it was one of the most romantic things she had ever heard of. Just think . . . to be whisked off to the airport and flown away to some secluded spot!

"You wouldn't think it was romantic," said the boyfriend. "You'd be complaining about not having the right clothes."

"Not if it was Miles French I was with I wouldn't!" Miranda countered recklessly. Even so, her boyfriend had a point. She had made a note to remind Miles when he came in for Pepper's passport that he would need to organise some clothes for her. It never even crossed her mind that Pepper wouldn't want to go. What woman in her right senses would turn down a man like Miles French?

Miles could see the moment Alex Barnett arrived that evening that he had something on his mind. Hitherto he found him rather quiet and shy. His previous impression of him had been that Alex was a man who had been dragged unwillingly into a situation which had now completely overtaken him. Miles had seen enough of the seamier side of human nature over the years to consider himself a reasonable judge of character, and Alex was the very last person he would have anticipated finding involved in something like this.

He explained to them both how far along his plans were, watching them carefully. Richard Howell expressed nothing other than relief, but Alex Barnett looked uncomfortable and for a moment Miles thought he was going to interrupt.

The moment passed and Miles asked smoothly,

"I only realised the other day that the three of you were all members of Tim Wilding's would-be Hell Fire Club, weren't you?"

The effect was electric. Richard Howell's eyes narrowed and before anyone else could speak he said harshly,

"Look, if you've got any idea of taking over from Herries and trying a spot of blackmail on your own account you can forget it!"

He broke off and flushed darkly. Miles told him calmly, "I can assure you I have no intention of doing any such thing. How long has he been blackmailing you?"

"Virtually ever since I took over the bank."

"He got in touch with *me* once my company started hitting the headlines," Alex supplied miserably, "and I suspect we're not the only ones."

"Damn right we're not!" Richard interrupted with some force. "I've done a little discreet checking up of my own, and every one of our fellow members of that thrice damned club who's made anything of his life is facing the same problem. He's got files . . . photographs . . . copies of membership papers . . . God, even then he must have been planning to use them . . . and we thought *he* was the crazy one!"

"Crazy?" Miles asked sharply.

"Well, you remember what he was like . . . Tim Wilding at least really thought they could raise the Devil, I'm sure of it, and then when Tim died . . . well, Simon simply went to pieces."

"It was just after Tim's death that he raped Pepper, wasn't it?"

"Yes . . . he called it 'just punishment'. He blamed her for Tim's death, said she'd put a curse on him or some such nonsense. We *had* to do it . . . we didn't have any choice. It was either go along with him or risk being exposed as members of the Club and sent down. Of course, neither of us knew exactly what he had in mind."

Miles's eyebrows rose. "A man asks you to kidnap a girl and dump her in his rooms and you don't know what he has in mind?"

Richard flushed again. "Come on . . . you roomed with him. You know damn well what I mean. His tastes ran in other directions . . . He and Wilding . . ."

"So what did you think he *did* want to do to her?"

"I don't know. We were too damn scared to think beyond what would happen to *us* if we didn't go along with him."

There was a small silence as though each man was reliving those days, and then Alex Barnett said uncomfortably, "There's something I should tell you. My wife—my wife went to see Pepper the other day. She'd got this idea into her head that Pepper and I were having an affair. She's not well . . ." He flushed. "An—an accident a long time ago left her sterile, and she longs desperately for a child. She went to see Pepper to beg her to give me up—I don't understand the woman. Pepper took my wife out shopping and then sent her home and told her to talk to me. She could have pushed Julia to the edge of insanity, but instead she went out of her way to reassure her. She even . . ." Alex's thin face flushed, but he went on doggedly, "She even somehow managed to give Julia some hope, something to hold on to. We've been trying to adopt, but there just aren't enough children to go round . . . now Julia's talking about there being a special child somewhere waiting for us."

It was patently obvious that it was painful for him to disclose his private grief to them. Miles could see the mistrust and disbelief in Richard Howell's eyes.

"It's all a trick . . . she's trying to gain your wife's confidence so that she can do even more damage later. She . . ."

"Julia needs something to do to take her mind off the fact that we can't have our own children. I've suggested every manner of work, voluntary and otherwise, but until now she's ignored everything I've said. Now she's talking about working with handi-capped children. There's a new place opened up near us . . . Ranger's Hall."

Miles frowned. Ranger's Hall was Colonel White-gate's old home. He had had no idea that the Barnetts lived so close to it. He made a mental note to have a word with the couple who ran it. Provided they were satisfied that she was physically and mentally capable of working there, there was no reason why a part-time voluntary job couldn't be found for Julia Barnett.

All the time new and different facets of Pepper's personality were being revealed to him. He listened without interrupting while Alex talked about Julia's abortion; his own shock and sense of failure that he had not been able to help her; that he had not known, sensing that the other man needed the catharsis of pouring the whole thing out.

"I'm confused," Alex admitted when he had finished. "This woman is my enemy, and yet she's helped my wife. What will you do to her once you've abducted her?''

Miles gave him an icy look and said coldly, *"I'm* not Simon Herries. I only intend to keep her out of the country long enough for her to become worried about the future of her company and to hand over those files, that's all.''

It wasn't all, though. There was his own deep inner conviction that Simon Herries was dangerous. That if he got the opportunity he would offer Pepper physical harm. A man who had killed once always found it easier a second time.

Miles veiled his eyes. He hadn't told the other two what he had discovered in his investigations, and he was pretty sure he was right. It had been hard to discover the truth surrounding the suicide of Tim Wilding's sister . . . hard, but not impossible.

Deborah Wilding's mother had told him that once long ago there had been a curse laid on the family. She had laughed when she said it, but with two children dead it must be very hard not to believe there was some substance in the old tale. Why was it that so many powerful, wealthy families were burdened with more than their fair share of tragedy? Was it because their very power incited too much jealously, too much passion in others? Or was it more simply that great power could so often go hand in hand with great evil?

Absolute power corrupts absolutely, unless one was very strong . . . Impossibly strong, perhaps.

"I'd better go. I don't like leaving Julia on her own for too long." Alex stood up awkwardly.

Richard got to his feet as well. His wife would be at the TV studio—he frowned. She had been talking rather a lot of late about a certain producer they had just taken on. It came to him that he was almost halfway through his allotted span and yet he had not found the contentment and security he had once craved. Owning the bank had not brought him the sense of achievement he had anticipated. In point of fact he had enjoyed himself more in his old entrepreneurial days. He grinned to himself, remembering some of the more spectacular deals he had pulled off. These days he sat back and watched while others made the deals.

He was still frowning as he got into his car. What on earth was the matter with him? He had everything he had ever wanted in life; everything he had ever promised himself. It was a wise man who knew when he had achieved enough. What more was there for him? Expanding the bank? But he didn't want that . . . He shifted uncomfortably in his seat, disliking this odd mood of introspection. He wasn't given to delving too deeply into his inner self. It must have been the letter from Morris that had brought it on.

It had been a long time since Richard had had any contact with his cousin. As far as he knew he was with Rothschild's now and doing quite well in a plodding sort of fashion. It occurred to him that Morris would have been ideal for his job. He would have loved the steady humdrum daily round that so bored and irritated him.

He stopped the car, ignoring the furious and noisy protests of other drivers. Bored, irritated . . . what on earth was he thinking? He had worked all his life for what he had now, how could he be bored with it?

Angrily he took his foot off the brake and slid the car forward. He was getting maudlin, that was what it was. What he needed was a good strong Martini and then an enthusiastic blonde . . . that would soon put the life back in him. He didn't want to go home,

there was no point . . . Linda wouldn't be there, and
so instead he found himself heading for the bank. The
sight of it no longer brought the old thrill. He remembered the excitement that had coursed through him
when he realised he had the wealth and the power to
take it over.

Jessica's money had helped there . . . Richard had
more than doubled the money he had taken from her
as the price of his silence and her freedom. He could
easily afford to repay her.

Repay her. He stopped the car and stared into the
darkness. What the hell was getting into him? Perhaps
Herries had been right and Pepper Minesse *was* a
witch . . . Well, if so, he would like to see her get the
better of Miles French. Now there was a man he
wouldn't like to get the wrong side of! *He* wasn't like
Herries. He didn't need to be . . . One look from
those cold astute eyes and you felt as though every
small meanness, every greediness and vice you had
ever possessed was being stripped bare and revealed
to him.

Tiredly he restarted the car . . . perhaps Linda
would be home by now. If so, he hoped to God she
would have the good sense to keep her eulogies on
her new producer to herself. An open marriage was
all well and good, but there were times when there
was a lot to be said for the old traditions. A man
knew where he was with the woman in his life
then . . . she stayed at home and produced children.
She cooked his meals and washed his socks . . .

Richard laughed to himself. God, he must be more
Jewish than he had ever realised! Kids . . . who
wanted them? Look at the mess Alex Barnett had got
himself into over them. And yet . . .

In their darkened studio Linda stood watching the

man with her.

"Have you told him yet?" he asked.

She shook her head.

"No, I can't . . ."

"Well, it isn't going to go away, is it? What are you so frightened of?"

She touched her stomach protectively.

"You think he'll want you to get rid of it."

She winced at Gary's words. They had trained together at a hick TV station, now long buried under a pile of debts so high that no one could ever remember it. He had been a shoulder to lean on when Linda discovered she was pregnant. An ear to listen to her woes . . . He was gay and happy with it, he could also make her laugh.

She had been trying to work up the courage for weeks to tell Richard, but the time never seemed to be right . . . and never would be right. They had agreed when they got married that it would be an open, "no holds" affair. Children had never been intended to come into it . . . and yet here she was pregnant, all because of one miserable bout of sickness.

It should have been the easiest decision in the world. She had never wanted children, didn't know the first thing about them and always had abhorred the messiness of uncontrolled emotionalism, and yet here she was torn in half by conflicting yearnings. Wanting Richard and yet wanting their child too . . . Well, she would have to make up her mind soon. Unless of course—darkly, temptingly, the thought slid into her mind—she could simply wait until it was too late . . .

Linda resisted the temptation, pushing it away. No, she wasn't going to sink to that. If she decided to keep the child then she would do so honestly and openly. She would tell Richard and if he didn't want them both then . . . She stopped, appalled by the way the truth had sneaked up on her. She had no intention of even contemplating terminating her pregnancy and never had had. She wanted this child, and intended to keep it.

She hugged the knowledge to herself, swept by a fierce joy, an uprush of relief and release so intense that it overcame her dread of losing the man she loved.

She would have to tell him soon. She would tell him and let him make his decision. She had made hers and she intended to abide by it.

Miles collected Elizabeth Herries himself from the women's refuge. She was trembling with nerves as she got into his car.

They arrived on time for the appointment, but had to wait for almost half an hour as the previous one had overrun.

Miles half suspected that Elizabeth would get up and run out; as it was, every time the door to the waiting room opened she tensed, and Miles knew she was dreading seeing her husband walk in.

The Prime Minister received them kindly, giving them a brisk smile that warned them time was precious and short. Miles told him calmly and unemotionally what Elizabeth had discovered, and immediately he knew that he had judged the PM's reaction correctly. He could see that the man was extremely concerned. He was also relieved that he didn't for one moment appear to doubt Elizabeth's story.

"I'm afraid what you say only confirms my own doubts about your husband. Unfortunately there are those among my Cabinet colleagues who don't agree with me. I think the best thing we can do is to initiate a full investigation into your husband's life-style. I shall let it be known that certain information has come to me without revealing who from."

"It would help if Mrs Herries could have a copy of the report once it's received," Miles interrupted. "She needs to convince her family that her accusations are just before she can ask them to support her in her divorce petition. Obviously she doesn't want the truth to come out in court because of her children, especially her son. We want to make sure that Herries will give up all rights to his children before we petition for divorce.

"He's a very dangerous man," he told the Prime Minister. "A very mentally disturbed man, in my view."

"Yes, I think you're right," he agreed. "Really it's amazing how few men do have to retire from public life because of the stress it involves when one thinks about it, but it does happen."

He was telling them what would happen to Simon, Miles suspected. Obviously the Government would not be able to come out into the open and announce exactly why one of the country's most lauded MPs was giving up his seat. If indeed he could be compelled to give it up.

"Don't worry, Mrs Herries," the Prime Minister smiled reassuringly at Elizabeth. "I promise you that your husband will have no inkling that you and I have met."

"From now until the time the divorce goes through I'd like you and the children to stay at my house in the country. I'm employing a bodyguard who'll stay there with you. It's for the best, Elizabeth," Miles told her when she would have demurred. "You'll all be perfectly safe there."

He was dropping her outside the refuge when Pepper saw them. She was considering buying a property in the area, which was at present run down, but which she had heard on the grapevine was gradually being invaded by the lower end of the up-and-coming "yuppie" market.

She recognised Elizabeth immediately from photographs on her file, but what was *she* doing with Miles French? She dismissed the thought that they were involved in a sexual relationship almost before it was born. There was nothing sexual in the way Miles was both holding and talking to the other woman. But there was concern, and compassion. Concern—compassion, from a man like Miles French.

Pepper left without either of them seeing her, her interest in the potential property boom subdued beneath her curiosity about Miles and Elizabeth Herries.

It was one of his allies in the Cabinet who told Simon Herries what was going on.

"An investigation?" he echoed. Panic hit him, clawing at him, sending him wild with fear and rage.

It was that Minesse woman's doing—he knew it. He should have got rid of her. He shouldn't have let French take control . . .

Somehow Simon mastered his reaction and smiled tightly at his colleague, thanking him for the information.

An investigation . . . They couldn't discover anything, he reassured himself. They couldn't . . . And then remembered Elizabeth. Where was she? He had to find her and make her come back to him, and then he had to destroy Pepper Minesse.

He bumped into a fellow MP as he left the building and swore vitriolically at him without even seeing him properly. Yes, Pepper Minesse was to blame. Well, he would punish her for it, but first he would make sure she was sorry for what she had done. Oh yes, she would be sorry—very, very sorry!

Simon could feel the rage rising inside him, engorging his body, obliterating everything else. He thought of Tim and how Pepper had taken him from him. Tim had wanted to sacrifice her, believing that through her death he could raise the Devil. Simon had laughed at him, but perhaps Tim had been right. He could feel the madness starting to engulf him and he pushed it back, knowing he needed to be calm, to plan . . .

First he must find Elizabeth. She had no money and few friends, so it shouldn't be very difficult to track her down.

CHAPTER SEVENTEEN

As SHE came out of the hairdressers, Pepper didn't notice the car parked at the side of the road. Why should she? It was ordinary enough, and besides, she had too many other things on her mind.

Her hairdressers was only a short distance from her office and unless the weather was really bad she always walked. She would have to ring Jeff Stowell when she got back about that new tennis player she wanted to see. She frowned as she remembered that Miranda had forgotten to give her this message. She didn't know what was wrong with her secretary at the moment; she seemed unusually forgetful. There had been an air of expectant excitement not unmingled with envy about her this morning. Pepper shrugged the thought aside. The girl was probably having problems with her love life.

Miles sat in the car and watched her, admiring the feminine movement of her hips. Only seconds after Pepper had left her office Miranda had phoned him and given him their pre-arranged signal.

He supposed he would have found a way to put his plans into action without the secretary's help, but it wouldn't have been easy. He had planned everything in the most minute detail. He had gone through Pepper's schedule with Miranda a dozen or more times. Today was the day, and had he not been able to pick her up now, he would have followed Pepper to lunch and tried again then.

He got out of the car smoothly as she drew level

with him. He registered the surprise in her eyes, and
then the shock as he reached for her. He was blocking
her way, stopping her from moving.

Pepper opened her mouth to scream—and instantly
found herself gasping for air as Miles's mouth came
down on hers. The shock of being kissed so unexpectedly and so publicly deprived her of the ability to
think. She tried weakly to struggle, but Miles's grip
on her was too strong. He was slowly dragging her
towards the car, she realised in panic. He was going
to kidnap her! His mouth lifted as he pulled her into
the car with him. She felt something cold and hard
pressed against her ribs and her heart bounded in
fright.

"All right!" Miles called out to the driver, and then
before Pepper could speak, he murmured menacingly
against her ear, "One word . . . just one word, Pepper,
and I promise you it will be your last!"

All her normal composure and alertness deserted
her. She was completely panic-stricken. Too many
memories came crowding back for her to think ration-
ally. Miles was still holding her in that macabre
parody of a lovers' embrace with his gun into the
softness of her body. Her mouth still tingled from his
kiss. She was enveloped in the scent and heat of him.
It smothered her, choking off her breath, depriving
her of enough oxygen to make her brain cells work.
She made a tiny moaning protest of fear under her
breath, and instantly his grip tightened.

Dazed, she stared out of the window. Where was
he taking her? She remembered Oxford and that bare,
old-fashioned panelled room and her stomach churned
sickly, her skin turning cold with fear. She wanted to
cry out . . . She ought to cry out, and yet somehow
she couldn't. The man driving the car wouldn't help

her anyway, she admitted bitterly. They were both in it together.

The sunshine was suddenly blanked out and they were in darkness. Panic hit her again, and then she realised they had entered an underground garage. Almost as though he wanted to soothe her fear, Miles leaned towards her and said softly,

"It's all right, I'm not going to hurt you."

Not going to hurt her, when he was threatening her with a gun? The car stopped. The driver got out and opened the door. Miles got out first, then hauled Pepper out alongside him, still holding on to her. The driver averted his eyes . . . almost as though in fact they were lovers, Pepper thought bemusedly.

Miles said something to him, in a murmur too low for her to catch, but she thought she heard him mention a time, and then Miles was half dragging, half carrying her towards a lift.

She shivered with tension. What would she find when she reached her eventual destination? Would Alex Barnett be there, and Richard Howell . . . and Simon Herries?

They were inside the lift. It was dark and hot, but Pepper still felt intensely cold. Almost as though he was aware of it, Miles started to rub the frozen flesh of her arms. In another man the gesture might almost have been comforting. It made her feel protected, cherished . . . like a little girl . . . She banished the thought, frightened suddenly by the extent of her vulnerability. This was what kidnappers did to their victims, wasn't it? Lured them into a position of false dependence, teaching them to accept and then need those whom they should most fear. Well, that wasn't going to happen to her. Wasn't it a technique the Nazis had perfected on their prisoners during the war? Round and round her thoughts circled, like vultures waiting for blood.

The lift stopped. Pepper clung to the door, refusing to move. Miles looked at her, his eyes hard and dark. She tensed as he picked her up. The ignominy of being so easily defeated frightened her. Her face was pushed into his shoulder and her body prickled with fear and dislike at being so close to him. He stopped and she heard him unlocking the door. She struggled in his arms, frantic for escape, but there was none.

She door slammed behind them and she saw the narrow walls of a small hallway. It opened out into a huge room with a panoramic view of the city.

"A flat I've borrowed from a friend," Miles told her as he dropped her on one of the cream suede settees.

It was a woman's home, Pepper recognised instinctively, a sensual, physical woman who enjoyed the stroke of suede against her skin, and the richness of thick cream rugs on the floor. Had this woman and Miles been lovers? Were they lovers now?

"Now," Miles told her calmly, "we can do this the easy way, or we can take the hard path. It all depends on you."

"Where are the others?" Her throat was dry and cracked, her voice a painful whisper. "Aren't you going to let them in on my humiliation?"

"Which one of them did you want in particular?" Miles asked her drily, giving her an assessing look. "Simon Herries?"

Pepper went white, and he had a moment's compunction. Under that closed, shuttered little face, she must be terrified, but she wasn't showing it. He didn't make the mistake of believing that she had no emotions as so many others had. He knew too much about her for that. She had them all right, and right now they would be tormenting the hell out of her.

"You and I are doing this alone, Pepper. After all, it only takes one man to . . ."

"Don't!" The tormented, agonised cry cut right across what he was saying. Pepper pressed her hands to her ears. He was going to rape her . . . to attack her as she had been attacked before. He was . . .

"As I was saying, it only takes one of us to make you realise that you're in as vulnerable a position as the rest of us, and I elected to be that one."

He had her attention now. She was staring at him, caught somewhere between fear and a small glimmering hope that perhaps after all he did not mean to hurt her.

"Why do you think I've been at such pain to establish us as lovers, Pepper?"

She frowned. "We aren't lovers!"

"No, but the rest of the world thinks we are, doesn't it?"

She couldn't deny it.

"How do you think Minesse Management will fare without you to take charge?"

Pepper stared at him in disbelief.

"You can't get away with this," she told him huskily as enlightenment dawned. Why, oh, why hadn't she thought of this?

"Give me your files and your written promise that nothing in them will be publicly revealed and we won't have to," Miles told her reasonably.

He waited, praying that she would refuse. Things had gone too far now. She knew too much. He doubted that anything other than her complete destruction would satisfy Simon Herries, but he didn't want her to know that yet. Later, when he had taught her to trust him . . . If he could teach her to trust him, he thought wryly, remembering the fear and revulsion betrayed by every part of her body whenever he so much as touched her.

"You'll never be able to do it . . . They'll be looking for me . . . for us . . . When they find out you've kidnapped me . . ."

"Kidnapped?" His eyebrows rose. "Oh, they won't think that, surely? A woman goes away with her latest lover . . . especially a woman like Pepper Minesse, no one is going to think she's going unwillingly."

Pepper stared at him. Too late now she saw his purpose. And damn him, he was quite right . . . no one would question her disappearance with him.

"And if I refuse to hand over the papers?"

"A statement in our leading papers discreetly announcing that Miss Pepper Minesse is taking—er—an indefinite rest owing to overwork and nervous strain."

Pepper stared at him, appalled. If he carried through that threat her business empire would disappear overnight. No one would want to touch her . . . she would be ruined . . .

"You can't do that!" she gasped.

"Oh, I think you'll find that I can, but it needn't be necessary—just hand over those files."

"Never!" The word exploded between them, and Pepper was too angry to see the gleam of relief in Miles's eyes.

"Very well then," he said silkily, "let's see if a short time—say two weeks away from Minesse Management, won't make you change your mind. An uncaptained ship can sail into some dangerous waters, as I'm sure you know."

She wasn't going to give in, Pepper decided. There must be a way she could escape from him.

"Two weeks?" she said derisively. "You intend to keep me cooped up here fourteen days?"

"Not here." Miles smiled at her, and there was

something in that smile that awakened every one of her primitive instincts. This man wanted more from her than simple retribution . . . more even than her agreement to his plans. He wanted . . . She looked at him, her mind unable to cope with the enormity of what her emotions were relaying to her. She had been desired by men before, countless numbers of them, but never a man like this, she admitted to herself. And his desire was different from theirs, less overt, less sexual and more cerebral . . . and much, much more dangerous.

She dismissed the thought, knowing that to contemplate it was to weaken herself.

"I'm going to have a cup of coffee. Do you want one?"

Pride tempted her to refuse, but she had missed her coffee at the hairdressers because they had been very busy, and her mouth watered at the thought.

Miles got up and said casually, "By the way, just to avoid any embarrassment for you, I might as well tell you that the phone has been disconnected, and that the only door to this place is well and truly locked."

Pepper looked at him with acute dislike. He must have guessed that she had intended to try to escape the moment he turned his back, and of course, he would have thought of that contingency and made plans against it. Miles French, it seemed, was a master planner . . . but then being a lawyer no doubt he would be . . . every 'i' dotted, every 't' crossed. He would probably be just as meticulous when he made love, she thought bitterly—meticulous and wholly unspontaneous, she added nastily to herself.

She looked up and discovered that he was grinning at her. For one appalled moment she thought he had read her mind and was about to verbally discount her theories, and then she realised he was probably amused by the thought that he had stopped her escaping from him.

"No coffee for me," she told him abruptly, and then seconds later wished she had not been so obstinate, when she caught the delicious scent of newly ground beans wafting from the kitchen. Her stomach protested at its unwanted immolation on the altar of her pride, her taste buds rioting in furious disorder at what they were being denied.

When Miles came in with a jug of coffee and two mugs on the tray he said casually,

"Just in case you wanted to change your mind."

There was also a small jug of hot milk . . . Pepper wavered, and then he poured his own coffee. He drank it black, and the smell was just too much for her.

"Perhaps I will have some after all," she said grudgingly, not daring to look at him. If he gloated . . . if he laughed . . . but instead all he did was pour the fresh-made fragrant dark liquid into the other mug. She stopped him when it was three quarters full.

"I like mine white."

"Help yourself." He indicated the jug of hot milk. "I heated some up just in case."

She poured it into her coffee and picked up the mug, warming her chilled fingers. There was something comforting both about the warmth and the smell. She took a sip and then another. Five minutes later it was gone and she looked longingly at the coffee remaining in the pot. She was just reaching for it when Miles whipped it away from her.

What *was* this? she wondered irately. Some new form of torture? "I wanted another cup . . ."

"This has gone cold. I'll make some more."

Pepper opened her mouth to protest and found to

her surprise that she was yawning. That was odd, she felt quite sleepy all of a sudden . . . very sleepy, in fact, and almost relaxed. She leaned back in her seat, and felt her eyelids close. Panic was slow to hit her, but when it did and she realised what was happening, she opened her eyes, fighting against the relentless tide of sleepiness overwhelming her, her voice blurred and soft as she cried out accusingly, "You've drugged me!"

And then, impossibly, she was fast asleep.

Looking down at her, Miles grimaced. God, but that had been a near thing! As it was he had hated giving her the stuff, but his doctor friend had assured him it would do no harm. What he hadn't expected was that she would want a second drink of coffee. That had really panicked him. Lucky the stuff worked so fast. He had been at his wits' end as to how to get it into her, disliking the idea of force, until Miranda had happened to mention her boss's love of freshly made milky coffee . . . He grimaced as he looked down at his own barely touched mug. He loathed the stuff black, but hadn't wanted to alert Pepper's suspicions by bringing in two readymade mugs.

Now all that remained was for him to put the final part of his plan into operation.

Their flight was already booked. His chauffeur would drive them to the airport. The chauffeur was the son of Colonel Whitegate's ex-batman, and had been quite happy to accept Miles's story of a romantic involvement with a lady who was pretending to be slightly unwilling.

Slightly unwilling. Miles grimaced at the memory of Pepper's taut, bitterly rejecting body. He could almost kill Herries for that alone . . .

He dragged his thoughts away from the past. What was done was done, and there was no going back . . .

only going forward. At the airport when he took his comatose 'girlfriend' on board the jet, Miles would explain to the staff that she was terrified of flying. A tranquilliser too many, plus a good stiff drink . . . it wasn't the first time it had happened, and it wouldn't be the last.

He looked down at Pepper's sleeping figure. She was slumped against the cushions at an awkward angle, and with great tenderness Miles moved them, frowning over the task as he made every endeavour not to actually touch her. It was odd, this need he felt in himself not to infringe upon her privacy more than was absolutely necessary . . . Almost as though he was thinking that at some later date she might acknowledge and be grateful for his care of her. He grimaced at the thought. Grateful! He was more likely to have a spitting, clawing cat on his hands when she finally came round.

He doubted that even revealing to her the danger he suspected she was in would soften her mood of antagonism. She probably wouldn't believe him no matter what he told her, he thought moodily.

It was crazy, this habit he had fallen into of trying to anticipate her thoughts, of almost knowing how she would think and react. He had felt it before, on some of his more demanding criminal cases, but never to this extent . . . never with this degree of intimacy. One of his tutors had once told him that he was an instinctive creature, and that no amount of logic would ever make him totally forget that deep-running vein within him. Miles knew that he had been right. It was still there, and there were many occasions when he had allowed himself to be guided by it.

It was in force now, telling him that once he was on that plane he would have set his foot on the first step of his journey from which there would be no going back. He looked down at Pepper. There were a dozen or more other places he could take her . . . and yet . . . He thought of the villa in Goa, of its tropical gardens and appealing air of decay . . . of its lushness, the warm sensuality of the air . . . His watch buzzed and he flicked back his cuff, staring at it.

Time to go.

Their cases were already in the car. Miles grinned a little to himself. Miranda had been right to warn him that no woman wants to be abducted without her favourite clothes, but he wondered what Pepper would make of the ones he had chosen for her. He hoped he had gauged the sizes correctly.

He picked her up. She was a dead weight in his arms, and yet so small that his conscience pricked at him. But what alternative did he really have? Simon Herries was a dangerous, half-crazed man, who would not even think twice about harming her, if he felt the need.

Something would have to be done about him . . . he had taken the first step, and he hoped the words of warning he had dropped gently into a prominent M.P.'s ear had had the right effect.

Everything went as planned. The girls on the check-in desk were all sympathetic understanding and mild envy for Pepper as Miles explained her delicate state. Once on the plane he tucked her into the inside seat and fastened her seat belt. She hadn't even stirred . . . he looked at his watch. She shouldn't come round until they were well on their way, and he hoped to God his medical friend had not been over-enthusiastic with his cocktail of drugs.

The droning in her ears was familiar and persistent. Pepper struggled through layers of unconsciousness to reach out and recognise it. A plane, she thought sleepily . . . she was on a plane. Why did she find the thought so comforting? Such a relief . . . something unpleasant and unwanted tugged at her memory. Behind her closed eyelids a variety of images danced . . . a car, an unfamiliar room, Miles French's face . . . fear. Muzzy unclear impressions like those recalled from a nightmare.

A nightmare . . . yes, that was it! Relief warmed her. She was on a plane and she must have fallen asleep and had a bad dream. But where was she going? Her brain felt thick and woolly . . . She struggled to open her eyes.

"Pepper."

The familiar voice, so close at hand, froze her. It wasn't a dream. It was real. Somehow Miles French was here with her on the plane . . .

Weakly she closed her eyes and feigned sleep. She didn't feel able to cope with the reality of him right now. She would wait until her brain had cleared a little bit more.

At her side, Miles, who knew quite well that she was awake, grimaced to himself but said nothing. Soon their flight would be over. Transport to their destination had been arranged for them, but once they were there they would be as effectively cut off from the outside world as though they were on an uninhabited island.

The staff at the villa spoke only Portuguese; they were a small enclosed community, descendants of the servants brought out to India by the first Portuguese settlers. There was no telephone, no transport other than mule and cart, and the owner had been at great pains to preserve the villa's remoteness.

Although she had closed her eyes, Pepper was far from unaware of Miles's presence at her side. She thought of his threat and how it held the potential to destroy all that she worked so hard for. It was sheer blackmail, and stubbornly she decided that she wasn't going to give in to it.

It struck her as the thought formed that he could well be feeling exactly the same way about her threats against him, but she dismissed such anarchist mental meanderings, reminding herself virtuously that she, unlike Miles had moral right on her side.

She felt the plane start to lose height. She had never liked flying, and instinctively her fingers clutched at the armrest of her seat. The shock of having her cold hand taken within the comfortingly warm grasp of someone else's forced her eyes wide open. She glared at Miles and tried to tug her hand away.

"Don't let go," he murmured, smiling at her. "I'm scared!"

Pepper opened her mouth to deliver a blistering put-down, and at that moment the plane hit an air pocket and lurched drunkenly, dropping several hundred feet. She managed to stop herself from screaming, but there was no way she could stop herself from flinging herself almost bodily into Miles's arms, her face buried in the curve of his shoulder. Instantly his arms came round her, holding her, his voice a soothing murmur of inanities in her ear that helped her body to stop its wild trembling and her fear to subside.

The plane levelled out; the pilot announced that they would soon be landing. Pepper, her face red with embarrassment and rage, extricated herself from Miles's body, her face deliberately averted from him. One word . . . just let him say one word, make one mocking comment, and she would kill him!

But he said nothing, and eventually she was forced to conquer her own emotions and turn to look at him.

He was calmly reading his newspaper, and as he felt her attention focus on him he put it down and looked enquiringly at her.

He really was the most complicated and unfathomable man! Where she had expected him to crow over her cowardice he was acting as though it had simply never happened. No other man she knew would have been able to resist drawing a comparison between her tough businesslike behaviour and her complete and to their minds feminine panic at the first hint of any danger.

"You won't get away with this!" she told him fiercely. "The moment this plane lands I'm going to tell the authorities that you've abducted me!"

Miles surveyed her with interest.

"Really? Well, if you're thinking of appealing to the cabin crew, I should forget it . . . . I've told them that we've had a fight and that you'll probably pretend I'm abducting you, just to get back at me."

Pepper glared at him, knowing he had spiked her guns.

The plane landed; the airport was hot and busy, the night air full of unfamiliar scents and voices. Pepper stood stock still, bemused by the alienness of her surroundings. India . . . she recognised that they were somewhere in India. She heard Miles call her name, but when she turned round she couldn't see him. She was surrounded by a seething throng of unfamiliar faces speaking an unknown language.

The shock of being abducted, the strangeness of her unknown surroundings sent her into an uncharacteristic panic. She started to tremble, the blood racing fearfully round her veins. She looked desperately for Miles, searching among the turbanned figures for his bare dark head. She couldn't see him, and for one fearful moment she thought he might actually leave her here among these unknown people whose language she couldn't speak, without money or papers. The effect was instantaneous; a throw back from her days with the Lee tribe; a feeling of panicky alienation swept over her, a fear of the people around her and their reaction to her "difference". She wanted to run and hide herself to escape from their curious glances.

Someone touched her and she swung round. Miles was standing behind her, frowning slightly. He saw the way she was trembling and drew her closer to his side. Almost instantly Pepper felt comforted and reassured by the proximity of him. Although she didn't want to admit it, even in the privacy of her own thoughts, she was glad of his presence.

All through the Customs and Immigration the shock of her discovery kept her silent. She wasn't used to having to depend on any other human being, never mind one like Miles French who was actually her enemy.

Her docility puzzled Miles. Concern for her coloured his relief at having carried out his plan successfully. Rage, tantrums, even personal violence, he had all been prepared for, but not this too pacific, dull acceptance. Had the drug he had given her been too strong? Had the fact that he had abducted her had some deep pyschological effect on her connected with her previous abduction by Alex and Richard?

Now for the first time he began to doubt the wisdom of his plans, but what other alternative had he had? Pepper was so much safer away from Simon Herries, and yet if he tried to tell her that she would not believe his warning to be altruistic. In her mind he was firmly linked with Herries and the others, and he doubted that anything he could do would convince her otherwise.

The feeling that touched him as he acknowledged

this shocked him. He had liked, admired, and even loved many women in his life, but for none had he felt this protective, fierce anger. For none had he felt this sharp desire spiked with the grim realisation that it was a desire that would probably never be satisfied.

From the moment he had realised that there had been no lovers in Pepper's life he had been aware of the damage Simon Herries had wreaked. To love a woman carrying such a burden was the last thing any sensible man would do.

Love? Miles caught himself up, frowning. What on earth was he thinking? He barely knew her . . . had talked to her on a handful of occasions, no more.

But you do know her, an inner, stronger voice taunted. You know everything there is to know about her.

And it was true. He did. From the reports he had gathered; from his own knowledge, from everything he had assimilated about Pepper, he knew her as intimately and thoroughly as though they had spent their whole lives in the knowledge of one another. It was a disturbing thought . . . a disturbing acknowledgement. How often during his life had Miles been aware somewhere deep within him of an inner, relentless searching for a oneness with another human being that would fill the empty space in his life?

But that woman could not be Pepper Minesse, surely? He had grown to adulthood knowing of this inner need within him; his intelligence told him it sprang from his own childhood . . . from not having any parents, from being alone. And while his intelligence had derided it, his instinct had allowed it to flourish; had been wise enough to know that it was an essential and important part of him, and that if he tried to destroy it, he would be destroying a very vital element of himself. Without that inner vulnerability he would not be the successful barrister that he was; he was sure of it. Others might deride instinct, and call it superstition, but it was so much a part of himself he rarely even questioned it any more.

Until now . . . Until it had told him that he had found what he had always wanted in the person of the woman standing at his side. He looked at her. Even after the long flight she looked beautiful. The wildness was subdued; the gloss gone, but the essential woman remained. Miles wanted to reach out and touch her skin, push the heaviness of her hair off her face, to cushion her protectively against his side.

He grimaced to himself, imagining Pepper's reaction if she were able to read his thoughts. Most of his women friends were of the new breed of dynamic career women, and he had long ago acknowledged that womankind had no need of the male sex for her protection or existence.

"Where are we going?"

The rusty sound of Pepper's voice checked him. He looked down at her, wishing there could have been an easier way of doing this.

"Wait and see." He touched her arm, directing her towards the helicopter terminal where his friend housed his private transport. The pilot was waiting for them. A porter brought their luggage. Pepper gaped at the machine, and sensing her reluctance to board it, Miles picked her up. The pilot grinned at him, and Pepper, furious and frightened, glared at them both. It was too dark for her to see where they were going, and besides, she was frightened of doing so, in case she started to feel even sicker than she did already.

Miles took one look at her white face and clenched hands and reached out to touch her comfortingly. Pepper opened her eyes and glared at him. She reminded him of an angry, frightened kitten, all ready

to spit and claw. He smiled to himself at the blatant
sexism of his comparison, and acknowledged wryly
that, equality or not, there were still some things so
deeply ingrained in the male psyche that they were
not easily rooted out.

The helicopter ride seemed to last an eternity, but
at least they were putting down. Pepper opened her
eyes and then closed them again, blinded by the
battery of light illuminating the landing area. The
helicopter bumped on to the concrete and then settled.
Miles opened his door and got out, turning to lift her
down. She wanted to refuse his help, but the drop to
the ground was too high for her to make alone. The
pilot removed their luggage, and what seemed like a
dozen pairs of eager brown hands took it away. The
pilot got back in his seat, and as Miles drew her away
into the dark shadows beyond the lights, it took off
again.

She watched it go, shivering with a mixture of
apprehension and excitement. Excitement? She shivered
harder and risked a glance at the man standing beside
her. Excitement wasn't an emotion she was used to
experiencing in any context, and certainly not in
connection with a man; unless it was caused by an
opportunity of putting one down. She looked away,
unsettled by her thoughts, acknowledging that there
was precious little chance of her putting Miles French
down. The combination of lazy good humour and
iron determination that he used to such good effect
defeated her. And that was frightening.

"This way." He touched her arm, directing her past
terracotta pots full of tumbling plants, their colours
muted by the diffused light. The night sky was full of
stars, the moon waning. Pepper had a jumbled impression of towers and trellises, of archways, and the rich
scent of heavily perfumed flowers, as Miles led her

down a flight of steps and through a doorway into the almost icy coolness of a dimly lit square room.

Her heels rang noisily on the chequered tiled floor. Heavy, carved furniture hugged the walls in formal array; rich hangings blanketing the windows.

The room was almost Moorish in conception, and that confused her. A woman came in, gliding so smoothly it was impossible to imagine how such fluid movements were perfected. She was plump and saried, a caste-mark on her forehead. She smiled at them both and greeted Miles in a language Pepper couldn't begin to understand.

He listened and then translated.

"Maja says that food is prepared for us if we want it, but that also your room is ready if you prefer to rest."

Pepper was totally disorientated. She had no idea what time of night it was. She was totally exhausted, and suddenly the thought of the privacy and silence of her bedroom was so blissfully tempting that she didn't have to think of making a choice.

Maja smiled and bowed, indicating that she was to follow her. Pepper went with her down what seemed to be a maze of corridors until finally they stopped outside a heavily carved door. Maja opened it and indicated that Pepper was to go in.

Like the other room this too was furnished with ornate, heavily carved furniture, expensive silk draped the huge bed, beneath the protective mosquito nets. The floor was bare and polished, its dark expanse broken up here and there with softly silky rugs.

Maja smiled as she waited for Pepper to absorb the magnificence of her surroundings—and magnificent was the only way to describe them, Pepper acknowledged, reverently touching one of the silk-covered ottomans.

When she had judged that Pepper had had sufficient time to adjust to her surroundings, Maja crossed the room and opened another door. Pepper followed her through it. She was in a long corridor-like room lined with mirrors and cupboards, obviously a dressing room. Another door off it led into her private bathroom. The size of the round marble bath astounded her. The fitments were gold inlaid with jade and the floor a rich polished malachite. Pepper had never seen anything like it in her life. Visions of Cecil B deMille extravaganzas danced before her eyes, but they had nothing on the reality and sumptuousness of this room. It was a suite designed for a pampered woman whose only role was to please the man who provided her with such luxuries, and Pepper wondered wildly if Miles French had deliberately chosen this suite for her. He knew so much about her . . . too much. If he knew that her much vaunted sexual experience was a total sham . . . She shivered, despite the moist heat in the air.

Maja, seeing the fear darkening her eyes, touched her arm in concern. Pepper smiled at her. If only she had some way of communicating with this woman, of asking her all the questions that tormented her mind. Where on earth was she? Somewhere or other in the Indian subcontinent, but where?

Maja indicated the bath and turned on the taps, miming that Pepper should undress, and Pepper realised that the woman intended to stay with her while she did so. But in what capacity? As a maid or a guard?

Pepper was too exhausted to dwell on the question; too exhausted to marvel at the incongruity of the fact that she, who had always been so determinedly independent, should be so unquestioningly accepting Maja's ministrations, almost as docilely as though she

herself were indeed just another possession among
many owned by a man wealthy enough to own such
a house and so many riches.

CHAPTER EIGHTEEN

SHE SLEPT deeply and well, opening her eyes to the morning sunlight, stretching languorously in what surely must be the most comfortable bed she had ever occupied. The mosquito netting diffused the light, giving it a faint haziness. Pepper had slept nude, too exhausted to wait until Maja had unpacked her luggage, but now she saw that a robe had been folded carefully over the ottoman at the bottom of the bed.

She picked it up, frowning over its tobacco satin extravagance. It was cut in a severe, almost masculine style, and yet as she slid the fabric over her sleep-warm body she had a shivery, tormenting mental image of Miles French.

The heat must be getting to her already, she thought grimly. Last night she might have been stupid enough to let Miles think he could get away with abducting her, but today he was going to discover that she was far from being a passive pawn in his game.

She bathed and dressed in the clothes she found hanging in the cupboard—cool, comfortable cottons, all in exactly the right size. She frowned over the labels, recognising them; even knowing the Knightsbridge shops they must have come from. Had Miles himself bought them for her? The thought made her feel restless and uncomfortable. She disliked the idea of him handling the brief items of cotton underwear she was wearing. It was almost as though he had in some intimate way reached out and touched her.

She dismissed the thought as fanciful, and combed

her hair. Now that she was up she felt restless and
trapped. She didn't even know how to find her way
back to last night's salon, from her room.

Almost as though her thoughts had conjured her
up, there was a tap on her door and Maja appeared.
She beamed when she saw Pepper up and dressed and
by mime indicated that she was to follow her. They
went down another maze of corridors, emerging into
the sunlight of a shadowy courtyard. A central fountain
tinkled musically, the whole scene one of tranquillity,
and Pepper stiffened instinctively when she saw Miles
seated in one of the chairs pulled up at a table laden
with fresh fruit, a pot of coffee and what smelled like
freshly baked cinnamon rolls.

She looked round, trying to get her bearings, as
Maja glided silently away. Pale pink-washed walls,
furniture that looked Spanish, or was it Portuguese,
in conception—and yet Maja was obviously Indian;
the airport, the rich smell of spices in the air there . . .
these did not belong to Europe. So where exactly were
they?

Pepper looked again at the tropical climbers smothering the walls and felt the moist heat of the air
around her. Miles pulled out a chair for her, and like
a sleepwalker, with no will of her own, she subsided
into it.

"Where are we?" she asked.

She had meant to demand, instead she sounded
more as though she were pleading.

"Goa," Miles told her promptly. "The Portuguese
colonised it in the fourteenth century, I think it was.
This villa belonged to a member of the Portuguese
nobility, a *conde*, in fact, but the rich spice trade that
made his family wealthy has gone, and so he sold this
estate to a client of mine. It's virtually inaccessible
other than by helicopter."

Pepper looked at him, and sensed that he was telling her the truth.

"What were once cultivated fields have long ago given way to jungle. The nearest village is twenty miles away and the nearest railway closer to fifty. This is a forgotten part of the world, although unfortunately not for much longer. The coast is unbelievable—soft pink beaches, the deepest blue ocean I've ever seen, the kind of solitude I'd forgotten existed, but we're too far away from it for you to enjoy it."

In point of fact they were only a matter of a dozen miles from the coast and one of the villa's outhouses housed the ancient Land Rover that was capable of taking them there, but Miles wasn't going to tell Pepper that.

Without her make-up and her hair loose, she looked like a young girl. Her vulnerability caught him off guard. He wanted to go up to her and comfort her, to take away that brief flash of panic he had seen seize hold of her when she saw him. He wanted to reassure her that she had nothing to fear, and yet conversely he knew that he could not.

He had arranged that the helicopter would come for them in two weeks' time. By then he hoped to have persuaded Pepper to drop her vendetta. He hoped to have convinced her how dangerous Simon Herries really was.

"Come and sit down and have some breakfast," he invited.

Pepper wanted to refuse, but what was the point in starving herself? Shrugging slightly, she sat down, resolving that no matter what he said to her she would simply pretend that Miles French did not exist. Yes, that was what she would do. For as long as he kept her captive here she would pretend she was here alone. She would ignore him completely and totally.

Only things didn't work out quite like that.

After their mutually silent breakfast Miles excused himself and said he was sure Pepper would prefer to be alone.

"I've brought some work with me that I want to do. Why don't you walk through the gardens? They're truly magnificent. Maja will accompany you."

So Maja *was* her guard! Pepper stifled a feeling of resentment as the Indian woman appeared and she and Miles started talking away together, both of them laughing at some joke that Miles had obviously made.

It was ridiculous to feel excluded, and yet she did. She turned her head away, determined to ignore his suggestion, and yet after ten minutes or so she was so wrought up with tension and tired of her own company that she was only too glad to go with Maja when the other woman indicated with gestures and smiles that she was ready to accompany Pepper on a tour.

Over the next few days Pepper become more familiar with the grounds and the villa itself. It was one of the most beautiful places she had ever seen; and yet the very air here seemed to be imbued with an atmosphere of heady sensuality; of lazy concupiscence so totally at odds with her own personality that it made her on edge.

She knew now that a small army of people worked and lived within the walls of the villa, keeping it in a state of instant readiness for its owner. She learned also that Miles had told her the truth when describing their remoteness. There was no phone, no means of communication with the outside world at all.

While she fussed and fumed about being so out of touch with the rest of the world, Miles was calmly involved in the work he had brought with him.

Her self-imposed silence hadn't lasted very long.

Pepper was discovering that it was pleasanter to have
someone to vent her wrath upon than to maintain an
icy silence, and no matter how much she argued or
demanded, Miles maintained that same façade of easy
companionability. But Pepper wasn't deceived. Here
indeed was the iron fist within the velvet glove. Here
indeed was a man who meant what he said.

"Doesn't it worry you?" she fretted one evening
when they had finished their meal. "People might be
wanting to get in touch with you. You could be losing
important cases . . ."

"No . . . cases are like buses, there's always another
one coming along," he mocked. "And besides, I don't
believe in a man allowing his work to dominate his
life. Work is simply one facet of a whole." He smiled
at her and mocked, "All things in moderation . . .
that's my creed for living."

It was a creed that Pepper found hard to comprehend, and yet it held familiar overtones. She
remembered Naomi telling her much the same thing.
She relaxed into her chair, smiling softly at the memory
of her grandmother.

"Who are you thinking of?" Miles asked her softly.

"My grandmother." The answer slipped out past
unguarded lips.

"Of course. Naomi, the queen of the Lee tribe."

Pepper sat up tensely. "How did you know that?"

Miles shrugged. "I'm a barrister, used to ferreting
out facts. I know all there is to know about you,
Rachel," he told her softly, deliberately using her old
name.

He hadn't moved, and yet instantly she felt threatened. She tensed and her tongue clove to the roof of
her mouth. Was he going to deride her, to taunt her
with her childhood? But no, he couldn't—she remembered his had been even more bereft of love than had

her own. She ached to put some physical distance between them, but she was too proud to move.

Was this it—was this the moment she had dreaded deep down inside herself ever since he had abducted her? Was this where he proved to her that he was just like any other man she had ever known, that beneath his urbanity and good humour, beneath the compassion she had glimpsed within him occasionally, he too was driven by a lust to possess her?

He desired her, she knew that. She had seen it in his eyes when he watched her. Would he try to inflict that desire on her? Would he . . .

Her eyes grew enormous in her pale face, her tension filling the room, making the atmosphere almost crackle with it.

Miles felt it, and instantly knew the reason for it. He had been waiting for this moment, knowing that they must both some time confront it. He had been scrupulous about not touching Pepper, not invading her personal space or intruding on her privacy, but time was running out and now he needed desperately to talk to her. He had deliberately banked down his own sensuality, forcing back his response to her. He wanted to make love to her, but before that could happen he had to win her trust, to convince her that he meant her no harm. To show her that there did exist a man who could understand and break through her web of fear.

"I know everything," he repeated slowly, standing up.

Pepper froze, waiting for him to come towards her, instead he walked over to the window and stood staring out into the night.

She sensed that he was weighing up something, coming to an important decision, and her muscles clenched protestingly.

"I want to talk to you about why I brought you here, Pepper."

It was such an anticlimax after the physical assault she had been dreading that it took her several seconds to respond. At first all she could do was to simply stare at him in confusion, and then she pulled herself together and said bitterly,

"I already *know* why. You *told* me, remember?"

"I lied to you . . . at least in part. Is that really what you think of me, Pepper—that I want to hurt you, to frighten you?"

It was almost as though he was pleading with her to deny it, but why should he plead with her for anything? Miles saw her face close up and sighed. It was not going to be easy, but then he had never believed it would be.

"Look, Pepper—I had nothing whatsoever to do with your rape. *Nothing at all.* I'm a man who prides himself on his honesty, both with myself and with others. I had no part in what happened that night. Do you honestly realise what you're dealing with— what kind of man Herries is?" he demanded before Pepper could refute his first statement.

"A man who raped me!" she challenged him flatly.

"And a man who beats and abuses his wife and son . . . a man who takes young boys off the street and . . ." He saw her flinch and pushed his hand through his already untidy hair in a gesture of self-disgust. "How can I get through to you, Pepper? Simon Herries is dangerous, almost insanely so. I suspect that you're in very grave danger—in danger of losing your life, if you don't abandon this crazy vendetta."

"First Simon's crazy and now I'm crazy!" Pepper taunted him. "You'll have to do better than that, Miles. I haven't forgotten that it was your bed I woke up in. You were bending over me . . ."

"Yes. But shall I tell you why you were in my bed, Pepper? You were there because Herries hates me almost as much as he hates you. He put you there because it amused him to do so . . . because he knew you'd think I was party to what had happened, and because he knew how I would feel about what he'd done.

"At first when I walked into my room that night and saw you in my bed I thought Herries had persuaded you to wait for me there—he and Tim. It was the sort of thing he and Tim would have done, and then when I tried to wake you . . ."

He broke off, and Pepper saw the unmistakable compassion and pain in his eyes. She wanted to run from it, to cry out that it wasn't real and that he was deceiving her, but she couldn't move. For the first time since it had happened, she was sharing the horror of her rape with someone else; and moreover, sharing it with a person who had been there with her, who had known exactly what Simon Herries had done to her body and her soul. An unfamiliar sense of release rose up inside her, a sensation of a very heavy burden being shared with a fellow human being. She didn't like it, and she fought against it, but Miles was still talking.

"I'll never forget how you looked," he told her quietly. "I'm not a violent man, but if Herries had been there . . ." He turned away from her for a moment, but not before Pepper had seen the quick glimmer of tears in his eyes.

Tears . . . for her?

"I cleaned you up as best I could, put you in clean sheets and left you to sleep. I was going to talk to you, to ask you what had happened—to warn you to keep away from Herries in the future, but when you woke up you were so petrified, you so obviously believed that I was involved, that I daredn't come after you in case I terrified you even more.

"I've brought you here to try and make you see sense—not for my sake. I couldn't care less what you reveal about my past. Yes, technically I broke the law, but I did it to help an old friend who was desperate. What would you have done in my shoes, Pepper? Would you have let that idiotic teenager destroy their lives—her father's career, and her stepmother's peace of mind? Perhaps I should have done, but I couldn't. I'm not God, Pepper . . ."

What was he saying . . . that she was usurping a role that no human being should ever aspire to? The Greeks called it hubris, she remembered vaguely. He looked and sounded tired, and she wavered, caught between suspicion and a very odd desire to walk up to him and tell him she believed him.

"Simon Herries is a very dangerous man—a man poised on the edge of madness, in my opinion. Don't be deceived about him. He won't give in easily. He isn't like the rest of us, Pepper. Howell and Barnett were dragged in by blackmail. I had no knowledge of what was intended, but Herries plotted and planned to rape you. I think he would have liked to have killed you then, but he didn't dare. He had too much hanging over him already. Wilding's death, for one thing—that fall may or may not have been an accident, I don't know, but the suicide of Wilding's sister . . . that was no accident." He saw Pepper go white and start to shake. "You didn't know about that? Well, it was well covered up. But you haven't been his only victim, you know."

"He hates woman," Pepper told him flatly.

"Yes, I think you're right, and I'm certain his wife would agree with you."

Pepper shot a look at him. Why was he mentioning Elizabeth Herries?

"I saw you with her," she told him emotionlessly. "Herries' wife . . ."

"You saw us? Where?" Miles seemed more perturbed than she would have thought her comment merited.

"In London. She was just getting out of your car." She mentioned the area, and saw him frown.

"Elizabeth Herries has left her husband," Miles told her, quickly making up his mind that she might as well know the full truth. "She wants to sue for divorce, but she's terrified that somehow or other Simon will force her to go back to him. She found he was abusing their son," he added flatly.

Pepper stared at him in shock.

"I've managed to persuade Elizabeth to see the Prime Minister, who's instituting an enquiry into Herries. Backed up with what comes out at that, I only hope Elizabeth's family will support her in the divorce. Elizabeth won't bring an action against him involving her son, for the child's sake."

"But . . . but that will ruin his career!"

"Far more effectively than you could have done," Miles pointed out drily. "But until that investigation takes place you're safer here. Once the news of that breaks Herries will have far more to worry about than your attempts at moral blackmail."

Pepper sat down.

"How do I know that any of this is true? Why should you want to . . . to protect me?"

"Is it so unbelievable?" Miles queried, his mouth twisting slightly as he looked at her and saw the struggle going on inside her. He ached to take her in his arms and tell her how much he wanted her . . . how much he loved her. He frowned, wondering abruptly how long he had hidden his feelings from himself; how long he had pretended to himself that what he felt was compassion and concern, not unmixed with a very natural desire, when in reality . . . when in reality he loved her.

"You want me to believe you actually want to protect me from Simon Herries?"

"Yes . . . Yes, I do," he told her huskily. "Even if I had been a party to your rape I would hardly want you dead—think of the effect it would have on my career if it ever got out!" he added self-mockingly.

Pepper wasn't listening, he realised. At the very sound of the word rape she had gone rigid, almost trancelike in her stillness.

"Pepper." Miles went up to her. "Pepper!" He reached out to touch her, and as he did so her eyes focused on him. The horror and terror in them chilled him to the heart. She opened her mouth to scream, but no sound emerged. Instead she slid into a dead faint.

He caught her as she fell, picking her up as though she weighed no more than a child. So much for his hope that he was gradually winning her trust, he reflected bitterly. He was a fool for trying to rush her, but time was running out.

They had only ten days left here . . . ten days before the helicopter would be coming to take them back. Somehow, even if he couldn't convince her in that time that she could trust him, he must find a way of convincing her to drop her vendetta. If she didn't . . . If she didn't Simon Herries would surely find a way of destroying her. He would try to kill her. Miles was convinced of it. He knew criminals; he knew insanity. Simon Herries had no conception of the restraints other men place on their behaviour. He acknowledged no laws, no rules . . . and he was all the more dangerous because of it.

Miles carried Pepper to her room and placed her carefully on her bed. When she came round Maja was sitting with her. She could almost have believed she had dreamed the whole thing, but the concern on Maja's face told her otherwise.

The Indian woman helped her to undress, and then bathe. She was becoming almost sybaritic in her enjoyment of the warm scented water and the luxury of scarcely having to lift a hand for herself, Pepper acknowledged. She had even begun to forget about her business for whole minutes at a time. What was happening to her? Was it the slower pace of life that was putting its spell on her, or was it Miles French who was infecting her with his dangerously revolutionary ideas?

Miles . . . Pepper sat up, quivering with an unfamiliar sensation. Some instinct deeply buried and long ignored told her that here was a man who would break through all her barriers, who could be more dangerous to her than half a dozen Simon Herries.

Had he been telling the truth? She no longer knew what to believe. He had been so convincing . . . But if he *was* telling the truth then she was guilty of pursuing a vendetta against a wholly innocent man.

She remembered waking up in his bed, her body clean and sweet-smelling, where she had expected it to be putrid with the atrocities Simon had inflicted upon her. How had it got like that? The thought of Miles touching her, cleansing her, made her heart lurch and then beat at twice its normal rate.

Maja got up and picked up a tall glass of sherbet. Pepper took it thirstily, drinking almost all of it in one go. Almost immediately she started to feel sleepy, and recognised that Maja had put some sort of sleeping potion in it. The gardens around the villa abounded with herbs, many of which had originally come from

Europe. Living in such a remote spot, no doubt the chatelaines of this enormous complex must once have had to make up their own remedies for sickness. The villa was a village complete in itself in many ways. Pepper closed her eyes and let sleep wash over her. She was changing, she acknowledged drowsily. Where once she would have fought wildly against the drug, now she accepted its potency. Was it the same with Miles French? When the time came would she accept him instead of fighting him?

She fell asleep on the thought.

The dream came later. Pepper had such a vivid impression of Naomi's presence that the dream seemed totally real, and yet she knew herself to be an adult, and the Naomi who stood at her side was not the old woman of her memories, but a younger, healthier Naomi, who nevertheless she knew instantly to be her grandmother.

She was saying something to her, using the ancient Romany tongue which by some miracle Pepper herself could understand. Naomi was warning her against something . . . like a mirage Pepper saw herself in Miles's bed, and then saw Miles himself leaning over her, his face grave.

In her ear Naomi's voice said clearly,

"He is a good man . . . Your man, my chavvy."

And then the vision faded, to be replaced by another. This time it was Simon Herries whom she saw. His face was drawn into a virulent mask of hatred, and like sulphur, she could smell the scent of corruption and hatred in the air. She could smell fear too, and knew dimly that it was not her own. She saw a child, white-faced and close to the point of death. Through the mists of her dream she heard Naomi saying a name, but it was too dim for her to hear, and then incredibly she saw Oliver, her own child, and heard Naomi saying quite clearly,

"You and your son are both in danger, my chavvy. Beware . . . you must beware . . ." And then the vision faded, and no matter how much she cried out Naomi's name her grandmother would not come back.

It was Pepper's scream that woke Miles. Disorientated and half asleep, at first he thought that somehow or other Simon Herries had actually broken in and attacked her, and then the mists of sleep dispersed and he was on his feet heading for her room.

He found her sitting up, her eyes wide open but unfocused as she called out a name. He recognised it instantly.

"Naomi!" Her grandmother. He went up to her, pushing back the mosquito netting as he caught hold of her.

"Pepper—wake up! It's only a dream . . ."

He shouldn't have let Maja give her that sleeping potion. It had obviously caused her to have nightmares. Pepper turned her head and focused on him, coming slowly out of her trancelike state. She started to tremble and her arms felt so cold Miles started to chafe them instinctively.

"It's all right . . . it's all right . . . it was only a bad dream . . ." He talked to her as he would have done to a frightened child, soothing her with the sound of his voice and the action of his hands. Gradually the trembling died down. He sat down on the bed beside her and took her into his arms, half alarmed by the passivity with which she accepted him.

Pepper had no energy to object. She was still caught up in that half dream-world where her grandmother had been so real. The heritage of her ancestors rose strongly within her, both gypsy and Celtic, and she

was convinced that what she had seen had in fact been
the spirit of her grandmother, warning her, as Miles
had warned her, about Simon Herries.

Her man, Naomi had called him. She turned her
head and looked at him, and to her own astonishment
heard herself saying slowly,

"Make love to me, Miles . . . make love to me
now."

Miles stared at her. Did she know what she was
saying, or was she still affected by the drug? What on
earth was it anyway? Maja had no right to doctor her
with her own weird potions . . . heaven knows what
damage she might have done. And yet Pepper seemed
perfectly aware of what she was saying, of what she
was asking.

He reached out and pushed the soft fall of her hair
off her face, and miraculously she didn't flinch away.

Through the fine satin of her nightgown he could
see the outline of her breasts. A need so sharp and
intense that it couldn't be denied rose up inside him.
He eased her back against the pillows, careful to keep
his weight off her, holding her as though he thought
she was so fragile that she might break.

His heart was thumping like a sledgehammer . . .
what if she should suddenly change her mind? What
if . . .? He bent his head and found her mouth,
feathering it experimentally with his own. Her lips felt
moist and full, they parted slightly and he captured
the faint sigh of her breath.

A feeling of joy filled him. He didn't know how it
happened, but somehow a miracle had occurred, and
Pepper wanted him. Who was he to question such a
gift from the gods? He looked down at her peaceful,
beautiful face, and noted its abstracted air, and was
jealous of it. What thoughts did those veiled eyes hide
from him? What had wrought this transformation?

And then almost as though there was someone in the room with them he heard a voice, thick and unfamiliar, saying gently.

"Take her, she is yours and you have earned her. The first plunge of the knife must always cause pain and takes courage, but once done it is over and the wound can heal."

Pepper gave no sign of having heard anything at all, but when he looked at her her eyes were not focusing on him but looking instead at the darkness in the corner of the room. His skin chilled into a rash of goosebumps as he heard her breathe softly.

"Naomi . . ."

Miles didn't believe in ghosts, spirits, call them what you will, and yet . . . Impossible, he told himself, and yet the words lingered and he even thought he knew what they meant.

"Pepper." He said her name and she looked up at him and froze, tension invading every muscle of her body.

"You wanted me to make love to you," he reminded her, correctly reading her rejection.

"No. No . . . I don't want you!" she cried instinctively, and yet she lay quietly supine, knowing that something had changed. She had changed.

She remained still as Miles removed first her clothes and then his own. Her body was completely supine, neither accepting nor rejecting. It was her mind that rejected him, her mind that knew fear and horror. She waited, anticipating the slow caress of his mouth and hands, knowing that she would react to him as she had done to all the others. He was a very physically desirable man, but she did not desire him, she could not desire him.

He straddled her body, his movements so determined and purposeful that they seemed to mock her frozen stillness. A smile curled his mouth, some hidden amusement seeming to darken his eyes. It annoyed her that he should find her amusing. She waited for him to touch her, to start trying to coax her to respond, and then realised with shock that he had no intention of coaxing her to do anything.

"No," she heard him whisper. "Before there can be anything else there must first be this." And then he was entering her, not painfully, but determinedly, his body slowly, oh, so slowly enforcing itself on herself, until her flesh was forced to accommodate the hardness of his.

There was no frenzy of passion in his eyes, no tension in his body, just its slow, sure movement within her own, as though they were both engaged in some primaeval ritual that had to be accomplished. Only when he was fully immersed in her did his movements cease.

"Now," he said softly, "now you can't block me out of your mind or retreat from me, because I'm already a part of you. There isn't going to be any lovemaking that will end in rape, because I'm already inside you." He smiled at her then, darkly and brilliantly. "Your body already accepts me. Now I'm going to teach *you* to accept me, and to want me."

Impossible, her mind screamed, but something told her that this man possessed the sorcerer's magic of making the impossible possible. She stared up at him, mesmerised by him, wanting to tell him that he was wrong; that he had simply managed to possess her by a trick, that he had been able to enter her simply because she had not guessed what he was going to do. How could he have known of those other men who had tried and been defeated, who had lost both their manhood and their desire in the face of her body's rigid refusal to accept them? She had braced herself against a long, languorous assault on her senses, and what she had got had been a basic physical possession which had nothing to do with the rape she had endured, nor anything in common with the frantic caresses of the men who over the years had tried so unsuccessfully to persuade her to share their desire.

Every time Miles moved, every time he touched her, caressed her, kissed her, his body moved with hers, and it was like being lapped in warmth, like being heated and melted; and a thousand other sensations Pepper couldn't even begin to analyse. He was a part of her, accepted by her flesh to the point where it clung moistly to the heat of him. His tongue-tip stroked along her skin, finding the pulse thudding at the base of her throat. The pulse jumped and quivered as his hand closed over her breast. An aching, unfamiliar sensation spread through her, a wanton urgent need to arch her body against his hand. She just managed to suppress the moan building in her throat, but almost as though he had heard it Miles bit delicately into her flesh. It pulsed and quivered, her nipples hard and thrusting into his palms. She moved, her body pulsing to a fierce new rhythm. He stroked, teased and cajoled, using every ounce of expertise and control he possessed to give her the ultimate in pleasure. He couldn't afford to lose control now. Not when he was so close to gaining the prize he had yearned for all his life.

Thoughts flashed in and out of his mind, weaving themselves into a complex tapestry. This was his woman, his other half. He had known it the moment he saw Pepper again. Within hers his body throbbed and pulsed, her breasts filled his hands, the heated musky scent of her filling his senses. She was everything he had ever wanted, and somehow he would teach her to want him with the same intensity. He was never going to let her go. Never.

She cried out, a thin sharp sound that he knew wasn't caused by pain, and he bit lovingly into the rigid swell of her breast, recognising and answering her need.

Pepper was beyond thought, beyond logic, beyond anything other than the fierce urgent tide carrying her along on its crest. She reacted instinctively to the call of her blood and senses, revelling in the ultimate ecstasy of her climax, hedonistically and voluptuously revelling in it, while Miles watched her with loving awareness that for her this was the first time she had known this experience.

Later they made love again. This time he showed her how to give him pleasure as well as to take it for herself. She fell asleep with her head pillowed on his chest.

He had been right to fear her, he thought tiredly, watching her sleep. His life would never be the same again. He loved her and he wanted her with him for the rest of eternity.

The shock of waking up and finding Miles lying beside her was lessened slightly by Pepper's vivid memories of their lovemaking. She seemed to have slipped so easily from the role she had cast for herself back into the more primitive role of her mother's people, that it almost frightened her. Even in the clarity of the morning sunlight she could not dismiss her conviction that Naomi had come to her. She didn't tell Miles about it, though. He was her lover, and she was prepared to admit now that she loved him, but she didn't entirely trust him. How could she? These were days out of time, unreal, an escape, but reality existed and one day she would have to return to it. For the present she was content to bask in the hot sun, and absorb its sensuality into her flesh, so that she might give it out again to Miles in the coolness of their shadowy room. From loathing and abhorring the mere thought of making love Pepper had gone to an imperious sensuality that made Miles at once both bitterly regretful for all she had missed and yet malely triumphant that he had been the one to release the passionate woman imprisoned within her fear.

Neither of them spoke of love, Pepper because she was still wary of his motives, Miles because he didn't want to crowd her. Sometimes he feared that he was in danger of forgetting why he had brought her here in the first place. He repeatedly tried to warn her against Simon, but whenever he mentioned him Pepper clammed up.

Neither of them had broached the subject of Oliver. On their last night together Miles knew that he had to do so.

After they had made love he placed his hand possessively over Pepper's belly and looked at her.

"If you conceive my child, I don't want you to keep it secret from me the way you did Herries."

Pepper went still. He *knew* about Oliver! Her mouth was dry and bitter. She turned her head and looked at him. The wide light eyes betrayed nothing other than compassion and tenderness. She looked in vain for contempt or disdain.

"I wanted to abort it." She hardly knew why she was telling him this. "I wanted to destroy his child before it was born."

She could feel the pain welling up inside her, a pain remembered from long ago and ruthlessly suppressed. Without her knowing it she had started to cry, tears welling up and running down her face. Miles cradled her in his arms, appalled by her despair, wishing he had never brought up the subject.

Both of them knew what it was to lack parents, and he knew Pepper was thinking of this when she added huskily,

"Philip and Mary wanted him so desperately; they had so much love to give him. I was eighteen . . . I couldn't have kept him. I couldn't face having one day to tell him how he was conceived, who his father was."

"You did the right thing."

He knew it was true, and somehow in saying the words, he laid for ever his own ghosts of the past. How often as a child had he yearned to know his parents? How often had he cursed his mother for deserting him, and yet hadn't Colonel Whitegate been more of a father to him than many sons ever know? Hadn't he set him an example he would be proud to follow with his own children? Against his breast Pepper wept—for her child, for herself, for the whole of mankind and all that it has to suffer.

"We must go back," Miles told her gently when she had stopped. "Tomorrow we're going home. Before we leave I want your word, Pepper, that you'll drop this revenge business."

Her mouth set in stubborn lines.

"I can't give it. It's meant too much to me for too long, Miles," she protested, when he remained silent. "I can't give it up just like that! He deserves to be punished . . ."

"But not by you," Miles told her quietly. "You can't set yourself above the law, Pepper, either God's or man's—you must see that."

Stubbornly she remained silent. Miles sighed. He had known she wouldn't be easy to convince, and the fact that they were now lovers didn't make it any easier. He knew that she still mistrusted him, just as he knew that she loved him, but for him, one had to go hand in hand with the other, otherwise it wasn't worth having.

"It's late," he told her tiredly. "We both need to get some sleep."

Pepper turned away from him, leaving a cool space between their bodies, but at some point in the night she turned back again, and when Miles woke in the early hours she was entwined with his body, her hair wrapped round his arm like a silken bond. He made love to her with passionate intensity, making her cry out sharply in the fierce throes of delight, as he drove them both from one peak to another, until they were too exhausted to do anything other than lie sated in one another's arms.

Pepper knew that she had not conceived his child. It was an instinctive knowledge, something she didn't even have to think about. Later she would question *how* she knew, and why the knowledge should hurt her, for now she had to concentrate on keeping herself from falling apart at the thought of returning to her normal everyday life.

Minesse Management had faded into almost total insignificance, and she hated herself for allowing Miles to take such an important role in her life.

It would be different when she got home, she told herself. She would feel differently away from this place, with its ancient magic. She would feel more in control, more herself . . . less a part of Miles.

She heard the helicopter while she was showering. It was over. The idyll had come to an end.

CHAPTER NINETEEN

IT WAS a small, rather nondescript room, tucked away behind the formal elegance of Number Ten's lavishly decorated reception rooms. Heavy, old-fashioned dun-coloured velvet curtains hung at the windows, obscuring almost all the natural daylight. The table around which they sat was scarred and the chairs with their shiny leather seats far from comfortable, but none of the ten occupants of the room was really aware of their surroundings. They had more important business on hand.

All of them looked grave, one or two of them, those who had actively supported and championed Simon Herries in his bid to get a Cabinet post, looked uneasy as well.

The Prime Minister opened the meeting.

"You all know why we're here," he began crisply. "Certain information has come to my attention regarding Simon Herries. As was arranged at the time, a full investigation has now been carried out."

He handed each of them a photo-copy of the report. Dutifully the other members of the committee studied the report, leaving the Prime Minister free to study them. Those who had favoured Simon Herries' bid for Cabinet rank looked most uncomfortable—and who could blame them? The kindest thing one could find to say about him was that the man was the victim of his own brutal childhood and that this had resulted in a dangerous form of insanity.

It amazed the Prime Minister that he had managed

to keep that side of his life a secret for so long. It was fortunate that it had come to light now when pressure could be put on him to resign quietly and disappear from public life.

"Do you want to speak to him, Prime Minister, or . . ."

"I think it would be better coming from you, George," he responded drily to the Deputy Chairman of the Party. "Don't you?"

George MacBride sighed heavily. He was new to the post and only knew Simon Herries slightly. However, he was not looking forward to the task of telling him that he must resign. They were both members of the same Club, which didn't make it any easier. George MacBride arranged to have dinner there with Simon.

Simon knew even before he kept the appointment; someone had alerted him to what the report contained. But he needed to know more. He needed to know who had alerted the PM in the first place.

George MacBride, not having been fully briefed, saw no reason to withhold the information.

"Well, I think it was your wife who originally told the PM, old chum. She went to see him some time ago. Took a legal chappie with her . . . French, I think his name was."

Across the table from him he noticed uncomfortably how Simon's eyes glittered, and wished he had been a little more discreet. Too late now to regret those relaxing gins he had downed before dinner . . . "Miles French," Simon said softly. "I should have guessed." He got up, excusing himself. "My resignation will be in tomorrow's post."

Feeling rather relieved, George MacBride shook hands with him and congratulated himself that the whole thing had passed off rather well. Herries had done the decent thing, without any unpleasantness. Just as one might expect from a fellow old Etonian.

Feeling as though a weight had fallen from his shoulders, George poured himself another glass of port.

Rage burned in Simon with the cold pure heat of arctic ice. The urge to physically destroy those who had worked against him raged in him like a fever, but like a dam holding back the fierce tide of his mania, cold, calculating common sense warned him not to act too hastily. French would be expecting some form of retaliation. He would have to act carefully.

The first thing he did was to summon Alex and Richard to a meeting. He needed to know how much they knew of what was going on. The answer was very little, but his instincts, always sensitive where his own well-being was concerned, warned him that they were slowly slipping out of his control.

"Have either of you heard anything from French recently?" he asked nonchalantly when he judged the moment was right.

Alex and Richard exchanged puzzled looks.

"Not since he left the country with Pepper Minesse," Richard told him, and then seeing the start of shock he was too slow to control, he added frowningly, "Surely he told you what he intended to do?"

"You mean that crazy plan of his to abduct the woman and blackmail her into giving up those files?"

"Not so crazy, as it turns out," Richard intervened. "He's managed to pull it off."

"Where's he taken her?" Simon had no intention of wasting time listening to Richard's fatuous praise of Miles French.

"That I don't know. He said it was better that we

didn't, for our own safety, just in case anything went wrong."

Alex, listening to the exchange, felt the rage emanating from Simon. How had he managed to remain blind to how dangerous the man was? Before leaving the country, Miles had alerted them both to what was likely to happen, and he had warned them to say as little to Simon as they could. Richard hadn't lied when he claimed that Miles hadn't told them where he was taking Pepper; it was the truth.

In exposing Simon, Miles had additionally freed them from the threat of blackmail. Simon sensed the change in their attitude towards him, like a wary animal scenting danger. These two would not help him now. No, now he was on his own, and it was all Pepper Minesse's fault. He would make her pay . . . somehow he would make her pay. She might think she was safe with Miles French . . . the pair of them might think they had won, but they would soon discover that he wasn't so easily bested.

Hatred filled him, a black, tearing rage so intense that he could almost taste it in his mouth. He would punish Pepper Minesse, and this time . . . this time he would do it properly. But first he had to find her. It didn't matter where French had taken her, he would track them down, and when he did he would exact a vengeance so complete that she would never, ever be able to torment him again. The madness grew inside him, blossoming and swelling, destroying his hazardous grasp on reality.

When Simon left them Alex shivered slightly and reflected that he was glad he wasn't in either Miles's or Pepper's shoes.

Richard, less imaginative, simply shrugged off the meeting and dismissed it. He had more important things to think about. The bank was beginning to

bore him. He had known that for some time; now he
was admitting it. He thought about Morris and
wondered how he would feel about taking over the
chairmanship of the bank, so that he himself could
head a new offshoot devoted entirely to the more
entrepreneurial end of the market. It was just the sort
of challenge he loved. He would have to discuss it
with Linda, of course. He frowned again. She was
very elusive these days, withdrawn from him, almost.
She seemed to be spending a lot more time at the
studios. His old insecurity, the one he thought he had
banished after Jessica left him, surfaced to torment
him. Jessica's refusal to share his bed had affected him
on a far deeper level than he ever allowed anyone to
know. And now these last few weeks Linda had
exhibited a growing reluctance to make love, pushing
him away sometimes when he attempted to touch her.
Had she found someone else?

Perhaps if he took her away for a few days . . .

He stopped outside a travel agents on his way back
to his office and on impulse booked a short luxury
cruise in the Mediterranean. It was only for five days,
he could manage to take that much time off, and it
should appease her.

He didn't want to let himself think that it might be
more than annoyance at being neglected in favour of
the bank that was responsible for his wife's changed
attitude towards him.

He lingered deliberately at the office, not wanting
to return to the house ahead of her. It felt curiously
empty when he did, and he was beginning to dread
walking into its unwelcoming coldness.

Linda had in fact returned from work early. She had
been feeling sick all afternoon—and not just because
of the baby. She was dreading telling Richard, but

soon he would *have* to be told. She was still determined on keeping her baby, no matter what Richard
had to say.

At first when he unlocked the door he thought she
was still out, and then he saw her sitting on the cream
leather sofa, staring into space. He recognised the look
and anxiety clutched at his muscles. Ignoring it, he
walked up to her and bent to kiss her.

"Guess what—I've organised a little surprise for
you!" Almost he winced to hear the false heartiness in
his voice. "I've booked us both on to a Mediterranean
cruise. I . . ."

"I can't go."

Her brusque refusal was the last thing Richard had
expected, and for a moment all he could do was to
stare at her, while pain exploded inside him. So that
was it. Until this moment he hadn't admitted to
himself how much Linda meant to him.

She turned to face him, and he saw how white and
tense she looked.

"I can't go on the cruise, Richard." Her hands
twisted together and he saw that her wedding ring was
loose. It seemed an ominous sign.

"I . . . I'm pregnant."

Pregnant? He stared at her as though the meaning
of the word was completely unknown to him.

His blank reception so neatly dovetailed with her
secret and terrified belief that he would not want the
baby, and she rushed immediately into her prepared
speech.

"Don't ask me to get rid of it—I'm not going to.
This is *our* child, Richard . . . but if you don't want
it, I'm quite prepared to bring it up on my own. All
right, I know we didn't plan on having a family, but
now that I *am* pregnant . . ." She lifted her head and
looked at him. "Now that I am pregnant I intend to

keep our child, even if that means that I lose you."

"A baby . . . you're having a baby?" Richard shook his head like a man coming up through deep water. "But I thought . . ." He shook his head again, his mind suddenly clearing as he recognised what she had said. She wasn't having an affair with anyone else. She wasn't tired of him. She was having a child . . . their child!

"You're having our child." He said it softly and went up to her, pulling her to her feet and into his arms. OK, so he might not have planned to become a father, but he was traditional enough to feel an entirely male thrill of pride in knowing that he had impregnated her.

Later, after they had eaten their supper and drunk the champagne, while Linda slept with her head on his shoulder, Richard reflected on the events of the day and for the first time in his life suffered an urge to appease the gods just in case they chose to punish his son for his own misdeeds. It came to him that the easiest way to jettison any burden of retribution his child might be called upon to bear would be to repay to Jessica the money he had blackmailed from her. He could afford to, after all; that original two million had been increased several times over through his astute business dealings. The more he thought about it, the more the idea appealed to him. He would do it for his son's sake, he told himself chauvinistically. Yes . . . Yes, he liked the idea of that very much . . . very much indeed.

After the meeting with Richard, Alex returned home in a very worried frame of mind. Miles had warned him what Simon was, but until this evening he had not really seen it. It seemed incredible that such a man was free to walk the streets, a respected member of society. He reflected on what Miles had told him privately about Simon's life and shivered to himself.

Miles had taken him into his confidence just before he and Pepper left the country, but he had not even told him where he was taking her. When they came back both of them would be in danger. When they came back.

Julia was waiting for him when he got home. The introduction Miles had given them to the children's home had opened a new door in their lives. Julia spent as much time there as she could. She seemed to have a gift for communicating with these very special children, and already they were talking tentatively about the possibilities of adopting.

Additionally, Alex had been approached by a large conglomerate who wanted to take over his main line of business, despite the fact that they had not won the Government contract. The money he received from them would relieve him of all his financial worries, and he would be free to do what he enjoyed the most—developing and researching more and more advanced uses for the micro-chip. They would be able to keep the house, but Julia had even said she would have been quite happy to move to something smaller. They were communicating in a way Alex had almost forgotten existed. Julia was a different woman. No, not a different woman; Julia was once again the woman he had fallen in love with.

It seemed naïve to believe that a shadow had been removed from his life, but that was how he felt, and he could almost believe that that shadow had come with his involvement in Pepper's rape, and that all that happened in his life since, both good and bad, had been part and parcel of some form of atonement.

These weren't feelings he could discuss with anyone else, not even Julia; they seemed too fanciful—*too* fairytale almost for a man of science and logic such as Alex prided himself on being, but the thought remained nestled in a far corner of his mind, and while he listened to Julia and shared in her joy at their new way of life, he also wondered about Miles and Pepper and how he could warn them that Simon's dismissal from candidacy for the Cabinet seemed to have finally tipped him over into madness.

He would have been even more concerned if he could have seen into Simon's mind.

Pepper herself had no such fears. When Miles warned her that he thought she was in danger she laughed at him. Her whole life had taken on a new meaning, the past had faded to nothing, and Simon Herries with it. Throughout the flight back to Heathrow, Miles tried to persuade her to allow him to hire a bodyguard for her.

"Then at least move into my place," he urged.

Pepper shook her head.

"No—not yet."

"You still don't fully trust me, do you?"

Pepper smiled at him and placed her fingers against his lips, a delicious sensation quivering through her as she felt the warmth of his breath. She had never known there could be such physical pleasure as that that Miles had shown her. She felt almost drunk on it, giddy with the release of discovering her own sexuality. When they made love she wanted to purr like a cat. Miles only had to look at her and she could feel her bones melting. Even now while they argued as he reached out to touch her she wanted to arch against him. She wanted . . .

"For God's sake don't look at me like that!" she heard him muttering fiercely. "Not here!"

She smiled at him—a long slow, seductive smile that made him feel he was completely losing his sanity.

There was nothing he wanted more than to take her in his arms and feel her mouth and her body beneath his own. These last days had been such a special, wonderful time. He had known before that he loved her, but he had never dreamed the woman she would be once she was freed from the trauma of her rape. He had never guessed she could be so sensual, so responsive to his every touch. He wanted to make love to her and go on making love to her until there was no way she would ever let him go, and yet at the same time he wanted to shake her for her refusal to accept the danger she was in.

She seemed to think that Simon Herries had somehow ceased to exist. In Goa Miles had been able to keep her safe, but once they were home . . . He shuddered to think of Simon's reaction to his dismissal from the Party.

Miles had picked up a newspaper before their flight left. It was several days old and had carried a leader about the golden boy of politics' sudden decision to resign. There had been a good deal of speculation about the reasons, most of them coupled with the fact that Simon was no longer living with his wife, but as far as Miles could judge the media had not got hold of the real reason for Simon's resignation.

If only he could make Pepper see sense! That suggestion that she should move in with him had been a last-ditch attempt to get her to see her danger. He had never expected that she would agree. It was something they had already discussed at great length.

This was the first time he had ever wanted any woman living with him on a permanent basis . . . the kind of permanent basis that involved exchanging vows and making promises that lasted for a lifetime, he recognised wryly.

But not yet. First he had to make Pepper see how

vulnerable she was. She had refused to have a
bodyguard, but Miles was determined to hire one for
her, someone who would shadow her discreetly and
make sure that she was in no danger.

He wasn't sure why he should be so convinced that
Simon would try to harm her; after all, it was his wife
who was responsible for his dismissal from the Party,
but Simon wasn't a sane man; he was a man who had
already tried to destroy Pepper once, and Miles had
seen for himself just how violently, almost demonia-
cally he hated her.

Simon meanwhile watched and waited. If the staff at
Pepper's office knew where she was they weren't telling
anyone. He dared not question them in person, just in
case one of them recognised him. He had developed
the sixth sense that sometimes goes hand in hand with
a maniacal personality—and what if his obsession to
destroy Pepper meant that he had to spend hour upon
hour every day watching her office and her home? He
had nothing else to do with his time now.

Once the truth about the reason behind his resignation percolated through to his one-time colleagues
they dropped him like a hot brick. He suspected that
he could blame the Prime Minister for that. Officially
no one was supposed to know why he had resigned,
but when more than half a dozen of his ex-colleagues
had made excuses when he suggested meeting for a
drink or dinner he guessed the truth.

He returned from watching outside Pepper's office
one afternoon to discover that he had a visitor.

He hadn't had much time to think about how his
father-in-law was likely to react to Elizabeth's accusations; he had been too busy thinking about Pepper, so
the sight of Henry Calvert sitting waiting for him in
his own study brought him to an abrupt halt.

"How did you get in here?" he demanded, crossing over to the Sheraton bureau and pouring himself a drink. Some of the whisky splashed down on to the polished mahogany that Elizabeth had taken such a pride in keeping beautifully waxed, and part of his attention watched the liquid form into a large globule on the satin surface.

Henry Calvert hated flying. He also hated being proved wrong, but there was no way he could refuse to support his daughter in her divorce petition. A cynical man all his life, Henry was not going to pretend that he was shocked by what she had had to tell him. Mentally he cursed his son-in-law for being stupid enough to attempt to vent his lust on his own son. Already he had been dropping hints in Washington that his son-in-law looked like being a future Conservative Prime Minister; now unless he could think of a good excuse to cover Simon's resignation he was going to look a complete fool, and that was one thing he abhorred more than anything else.

The Governor had been talking about inviting Simon over for Thanksgiving; the President would have been attending the dinner; useful contacts could have been made. Henry Calvert had been looking forward to the added influence he would be able to wield once Simon was in the Cabinet—and now this. There was only one way he and his family could emerge from the stigma caused by Simon's resignation with their honour intact, and that was to throw Elizabeth to the wolves and to publicly admit what Simon had done. He had it all planned already. His righteously indignant speech; his explanation that his daughter had been so desperately in love with her Englishman that he, her father, had allowed himself to be persuaded against his better judgement, but that upon discovering how his grandson was being abused he had insisted on Elizabeth returning to the good old US of A where such sickness did not exist . . . at least not among good Boston families.

"I used my daughter's key," he said now in response to Simon's harsh question. "After all, this is *her* house."

"*Our* house," Simon contradicted him. "In this country the marital home belongs equally to both partners. Where is my wife, by the way?"

"Back home in Boston."

Henry hadn't wanted to do it, but as his sons had pointed out, once the scandal broke it would look decidedly odd if Elizabeth wasn't seen to be at home, recovering from her ordeal in the bosom of her family.

Luckily she had already announced that she didn't intend to stay with them. The boy, who had spent far too much time tied to his mother's apron strings as far as Henry Calvert was concerned, would be sent to a good school and Elizabeth would be persuaded to live somewhere quietly out of the public eye.

"What do you want?" Simon demanded broodingly.

"Your signed statement admitting your sexual abuse of your son and an uncontested divorce."

He hadn't told Elizabeth about that first bit. She was determined that her children would remain in ignorance of the real reasons for the divorce. The last thing she wanted was for the whole thing to be splashed all over the papers. She didn't realise how damaging it might be to the whole family if they did not come up with a concrete reason for the divorce. Already Henry had entered into several deals purely on the strength of being a future Cabinet Minister's father-in-law. But those deals weren't going to stand up once the news got out . . . not unless he had a cast-iron excuse for it. No Calvert ever liked to lose

money, even money that he had not actually earned
yet.

"And if I don't?" sneered Simon.

"I'll be forced to give the whole story to the British
press," Henry told Simon uncompromisingly, adding
bitterly, "You fool . . . why the hell did you have to
involve your own son?"

His scorn cut through the wall of fantasy Simon
had erected between himself and the real world as
easily as a laser through concrete. Simon wasn't used
to enduring the contempt of his peers, and just for a
moment he ached to give in to the searing need to
take his father-in-law's neck between his hands and
squeeze his throat until he had stopped breathing.

He had the strength to do it. He could do it . . .
and then he remembered Pepper. His father-in-law
could wait. Pepper must come first . . . Pepper's
punishment was far far more important than any
momentary satisfaction he might get out of silencing
Henry.

The statements were already prepared. Simon signed
them recklessly, and as Henry Calvert put them in his
briefcase and got ready to leave he didn't know that
in reality what Simon had just signed was Pepper
Minesse's death warrant.

Miles and Pepper's flight arrived at Heathrow late in
the evening. She ought to have been suffering from
jet-leg, Pepper recognised, but instead she was on such
a high that she doubted she would sleep for weeks.

When they got into the taxi she felt a fleeting regret
that she had not agreed to Miles's plea that she move
in with him straight away. This would be the first
night they had slept apart in almost two weeks, but
sensibly she knew she needed some time apart from
him, back in the real world, to assess the true depth

of her feelings for him. She had no doubts that she loved him, nor that she could trust him with her life. It was just that the idea of any kind of permanent relationship in her life was so new that she needed time to come to terms with it.

She knew instinctively that Miles was not the man to be happy with half measures. He would want all of her, and for ever, and she wasn't sure if she had it in her to give that sort of commitment. More, she loved Miles enough not to want to cheat him by pretending a permanency she did not feel.

No, some time apart was what they both needed. In Goa it had seemed natural and right that they should spend every waking and sleeping moment together. Neither of them had ever been bored, even when they sat in silence there was a communion between them, an awareness of one another. But they couldn't live like that for ever. Miles had his career and she had hers . . .

Miles, sensing all that she was feeling and more, squeezed her hand. "You're right. We both need time apart to come to terms with what's happened to us. I just wish you'd change your mind about that bodyguard, Pepper. Simon is very dangerous . . ."

"He'll surely be too busy worrying about his divorce now to be bothered with me."

It should have been true, but somehow Miles doubted that it was. He had a niggling sense of approaching danger, a sharply acute awareness of an anxiety that wouldn't go away.

"I take it I'm still allowed to take you out to dinner tomorrow night?" he said humorously instead of trying to persuade her. She would have a bodyguard whether she agreed to it or not.

It would seem strange going out to dinner with Miles and then going home to her own bed, Pepper thought. Would he try to persuade her to go back to his home? Would she need any persuasion? she asked herself honestly, remembering how she had responded to his lovemaking. Somehow she doubted it.

They didn't kiss in the taxi. Miles simply touched her hand and then walked with her to her apartment door. Neither of them said anything, but Pepper knew that he genuinely believed she was in danger. For herself she felt that Simon Herries would have far more important things on his mind than her. And anyway, she had decided to drop her vendetta. Retribution no longer seemed important to her, and she marvelled at the ease with which she had stepped from the old to the new way of life. Miles had become the centre of her universe, but she would never be a dependent clinging woman—that was not her way.

They kissed briefly in the shadow of her doorway, and as he walked away she ached to call him back; to tell him that she couldn't spend the night without him.

Once inside she felt a little better. She started to unpack—and then stopped as she lifted out a dress she had worn that Miles had particularly admired. Her skin quivered as she remembered with what care he had stripped it from her; with what love he had caressed her body; with what tender desire he had possessed her. She went to bed and lay there without sleep, wondering if *he* was thinking about her, and then chided herself for behaving like a teenager, reminding herself that she had to get up early in the morning.

Miles was thinking about her, but not because he missed her sexually. He hadn't gone straight home, but had got the taxi to drop him off at a small private library he belonged to which opened almost twenty-four hours a day. They had copies of all the newspapers and it didn't take him long to check through the indexes and take photo-copies of every article relating to Simon Herries. He read them at his desk, drinking black coffee to keep himself awake, trying to put himself in the other man's shoes. Simon Herries wasn't the first mentally ill person Miles had had to deal with. His legal training should have made it easier for him to try to get inside the man's mind, to try to establish what motivated and moved him, but all he could think about was Pepper. In the end he gave in to his anxiety, and despite the fact that it was gone one in the morning he dialled Alex Barnett's telephone number. Alex answered the phone himself, coming abruptly awake as he recognised Miles's voice.

"I've been checking through the newspaper reports on Herries. Have you seen anything of him while I've been away?"

"Not much. He got in touch with us once. He seemed to think you'd betrayed him," Alex told him.

"And Pepper?" Miles asked. "Did he say anything about Pepper?"

"Nothing that he hasn't said before. He hates her, Miles, and I think you're right when you say she's in danger. To be honest, I don't think he trusts me either—in fact I doubt if he trusts anyone."

Which didn't take him much further forward, Miles admitted as he replaced the receiver. First thing in the morning he intended to hire a discreet bodyguard for Pepper.

He found exactly what he wanted through a contact in the legal world, an ex-policewoman who ran her own small agency and who he was assured would provide just the kind of discreet surveillance that was needed. He briefed her as best he could and warned her that Pepper was not to know that she was being guarded.

If his colleagues in chambers found him rather

distracted and withdrawn they were too tactful to mention it. Pepper's staff were equally discreet—at least to her face.

"I thought you said she was going somewhere hot," the receptionist whispered to Miranda once Pepper was safely installed in her office. "I didn't see much of a tan." She giggled when Miranda tried to frown reprovingly, and added, "Oh, come on . . . would you have spent any time sunbathing if you'd been whisked off to a tropical paradise by a hunk like Miles French."

"I should be so lucky!" was Miranda's tart response.

Lucy, the receptionist, made a face behind her back and muttered under her breath, "Someone's having boyfriend troubles. I'll bet!"

Lucy was inclined to be a bit of a daydreamer who spent half her life indulging in romantic flights of fantasy that enlivened the boredom of her routine tasks. She was fairly new at Minesse, having been taken on to help out during the summer holiday season. Simon, who had been watching the office for days and now knew enough about the staff to recognise that she wasn't one of its regular members, bumped into her in the street as she was carrying the morning's letters to the post on her way to lunch.

She smiled at him, her eyes widening fractionally as she studied him. She liked fair men, and this one looked as though he knew his way around the world. Rich, by the looks of him . . . and good-looking too, she added mentally, giving him another appreciative smile.

"I'm so sorry," Simon apologised. "Careless of me . . . Have we got them all?"

He helped her to pick up the scattered letters and then invited her to join him for lunch. The wine bar he mentioned was only just down the road and familiar to her. There seemed no harm in accepting his invitation.

Over lunch he encouraged her to chatter, subtly nudging her in the direction he wanted her to go. Very soon he had learned that the head of Minesse Management was just back from holiday and moreover that she was heavily involved in a new affair. The girl could be useful to him, although she wasn't his type; too full-breasted and feminine for him.

Lucy had no idea what Simon was thinking as he escorted her halfway back to the office, explaining that his office lay in the opposite direction. She only just managed to stop herself from asking if she would see him again. He was the most exciting thing that had happened to her in weeks, and she mentally cursed the fact that she was on the reception desk on her own and so wouldn't be able to spend the afternoon enthusing about him.

Pepper didn't go out for lunch. She had too many things to catch up on. Miranda had actually seen her flush slightly when she asked if she had had a good holiday. Nothing had been said about her own part in its arrangement, but there was no doubt that the Pepper Minesse sitting opposite her now was a very different woman from the one who had left this office just over two weeks before. She had that glow that women in love are supposed to have, Miranda noted enviously, and more . . . she had the sleek supple look of a woman whose sex life is abundantly joyful.

"I want to leave early tonight," Pepper told her briskly. "About four."

She wasn't meeting Miles until eight, but there were things she had to do. She must ring Mary and . . . She bit her lip as she looked down at the list of telephone calls there had been while she was away. She had to speak to Nick some time. She owed him

some kind of explanation. They were not committed
to one another in any emotional or physical way, but
unspoken between them had always been her own
feeling that if she could admit any man to her bed
that man would be Nick. He had rung several times
while she was away. She would ring him tonight when
she got home.

Pepper had her own very strict code of honesty,
and her relationship with Miles was not something
she could explain to Nick over the telephone. He
sounded guarded when they spoke and Pepper
suspected that he already knew what she was going to
say, but she felt she owed it to him and to herself to
make her explanation in person. They arranged to
meet the following evening at a small restaurant that
had been one of their regular haunts.

Pepper decided to say nothing to Miles about her
dinner date with Nick. She suspected it would only
give him a further opportunity to urge her to accept
the protection of a bodyguard—something which her
fiercely independent spirit railed against.

After she had spoken with Nick she walked into
her bedroom to look for something to wear. Was it
customary for women in love to feel that everything
already in their wardrobe was completely unsatisfac-
tory? she wondered a little wryly. She had a sudden
urge to wear softly sensuous silks in drifting styles
and cool misty colours. The sharp lines of her strikingly coloured existing clothes didn't feel right any
more. She wanted something softer, something more
in tune with her present mood.

In the end she settled for a dress she had bought on
impulse only weeks ago. Not strictly in her usual style,
the white jersey clung seductively to her body, the
discreet smattering of emerald green sparkle scattered
across the skirt adding a more formal touch to what

was basically a very demure dress. Oddly enough it suited her, she recognised, and she marvelled again about the ability of the human personality to grow and change.

Miles arrived early. Pepper was just completing the finishing touches to her make-up when he knocked on her door. The security guard had already announced him, and putting down her lipstick she hurried to let him in.

Her hallway was only quite small, and with Miles inside it, it seemed even smaller. He reached for her as he closed the door, kissing her lingeringly. There was just enough passion in the hard grip of his fingers to bring a frisson of sexual arousal to her skin. He felt it and thought she shivered. Immediately he apologised, releasing his grip slightly.

"Sorry. It's just that it seems a hell of a long time since yesterday. I forget sometimes how fragile you are."

"You didn't hurt me," Pepper assured him.

The look in her eyes told him what she wasn't saying. Pepper heard him groan as he took her back in his arms, his voice thick and slightly raw as he whispered in her ear,

"Do you really want to go out to dinner?"

Immediately she knew she didn't. She had known that some time during the evening this moment would come, but she had not expected that when it did come she would be as hungrily eager for the touch of his body as he was for hers.

They might have been apart for months instead of just hours. She let him strip off the dress and drop it to her bedroom floor without the slightest qualm. The sensation of his hands sliding over her skin made her shiver with pleasure. She looked down and watched him as he caressed her and felt her body quicken with need.

They made love quickly, eagerly, like teenagers, Pepper's body matching Miles's fierce thrusts.

"I love you, do you know that?" he demanded later, cupping her face and kissing her lingeringly. "Marry me, Pepper."

She had known that it would come, and Miles cursed himself as he acknowledged that he had moved too fast. He was rushing her, and that was the last thing he had intended. She loved him, he was sure of it, but love . . . passion; these were new emotions to her and she needed time to come to terms with them.

"It's all right," he told when she didn't answer. "You need time. I know that."

He left her just after midnight. Pepper felt bereft when he had gone. She turned over in bed, automatically reaching for him, her body chilling with emptiness when she realised he wasn't there. She didn't know why she had hesitated like that. She knew she loved him. She even knew she would probably marry him. But he was right. It was still too soon. She had an odd feeling hanging over her, an awareness of something unfinished and somehow threatening.

Perhaps she would feel better once she had spoken to Nick. Whatever it was that had brought on this odd mood of disquiet, until it was gone she felt that she wouldn't be free to share Miles's life with him.

Lucy was over the moon when Simon rang her mid-morning. He hadn't given her his real name, calling himself Greg Lucas. He asked her out for lunch, suggesting that she meet him at another wine bar, this time a little further away from the office.

She didn't mind at all that she was the one who did most of the talking—normally it was the men who talked while she had to listen. Greg was different; he seemed so interested in everything she did, even her quite boring job. Blithely unaware of his real purpose in asking her out, Lucy chattered on about Minesse Management and her new boss.

He wasn't learning anything from her that he didn't already know, but there was time yet. Time was a commodity Simon had in vast quantities now . . . thanks to Pepper.

He had a score to settle with Miles French as well, but the more he listened to Lucy the more he believed that in destroying Pepper he would be punishing Miles. Miles French in love . . . He sneered slightly at the thought, remembering Tim's unsuccessful attempts to get him into bed, and Lucy, seeing that look, paused uncertainly.

Immediately Simon checked his thoughts. This stupid little girl must be the world's biggest bore, but right now he needed her. He stretched out and covered her hand with his, playing with her fingers.

"I've got to get back to my office, but why don't we have lunch again tomorrow?"

"Here?" Lucy suggested, breathless with delight.

"No, not here." He didn't want to run the risk of being recognised and remembered, although it was unlikely so far away from his normal haunts.

CHAPTER TWENTY

"WHAT do you mean, you can't have dinner with me tonight?"

"Exactly what I said, Miles. I have a . . . a previous commitment."

Pepper felt the tension humming along the telephone line and she automatically gripped the receiver harder. She ought to have anticipated this and she hated lying, but Miles wasn't in a receptive enough mood for her to be able to explain about Nick.

"I see . . . Somehow I thought the relationship we had pre-empted all other commitments," he announced silkily.

Panic struck her. She felt like a wild animal with the nets closing in around her, and she struck out accordingly.

"I'm not your private property, Miles! I . . ."

At the other end of the line Miles forced himself not to react. What the hell was the matter with him? This was crazy! Of course she had other commitments. So had he. He knew quite well what was wrong—he was going crazy with worry about Simon Herries. All his discreet enquiries about Herries had met with no response. He seemed to have disappeared. The London house was closed up and for sale, and no one knew where Simon had gone. That worried Miles. He would have felt happier knowing where he was and what he was doing. It also worried him that he couldn't seem to get Pepper to see how dangerous the man was. She seemed to think just because she was no longer concerned about the past that Herries was going to forget it as well. Miles knew that he wasn't. He couldn't have told anyone how he knew . . . he just did.

"I'm sorry," he apologised now. "I don't know what got into me . . . Frustration perhaps," he added wryly. "I miss not sleeping with you and I wake up in the morning aching like hell."

"Me too," Pepper told him softly.

"Why don't we spend the weekend together?" he suggested, then cursed. "Damn it, I can't. There's a meeting of the trustees of the children's home and I've got to be there. We could have dinner together on Friday night, though."

"I'd like that," Pepper agreed.

By then she should be feeling more relaxed. The interview with Nick would be behind her. She was sure it was that that was making her feel so jumpy and on edge. They talked for a few more moments, both of them silently acknowledging their reluctance to end the phone call and both of them still surprised by the intensity of their emotion. It was still so new for both of them; this need to give and take commitment; this sharing of feelings that extended far beyond the level of mere desire.

At last Pepper hung up. As always when she had been speaking to Miles on the phone she felt the loss of his physical presence. There were whole hours at a time when she sat at home when she should be working on the reports she had brought back from the office, simply staring into space and re-living their time in Goa . . . She loved him, and slowly, oh, so slowly she was beginning to trust him, and to admit him into her future.

A plan was slowly taking shape in Simon's mind. He

knew exactly how he was going to punish Pepper now.

He was living in a small anonymous flat he had rented in a false name. The landlord had been too glad to take his cash deposit to question him deeply. The flat was tucked away in a rabbit warren of similar dwellings in a large Victorian house, run down and shabby now and housing in the main victims of the eighties mania for divorce. No one concerned themselves with his comings and goings, and, as Miles was beginning to discover, to all intents and purposes Simon Herries had disappeared.

He had brought with him very little from his old life—his clothes, his filing cabinets with the secret records that he and Tim had built up.

Tim . . . His old friend seemed so close to him these days, so close that sometimes he felt as though he actually was there with him. If Tim had lived his life would have been different, but Tim had died, and she had killed him. For that alone she should be punished. But he had already punished her for that . . . Round and round swirled his thoughts, dark and tainted with the madness growing within him. At night he dreamed that he and Tim were together again at Marchington.

He stroked the gun he had brought with him. It had been his father's Service pistol; never handed in after the end of the war. For years it had lain in a desk drawer in the house in Cumbria until Elizabeth had found it and demanded that it be locked away, complaining that it was too dangerous to simply leave lying around. Simon had kept it in his desk ever since.

He liked handling it. The cool smooth sensation of the metal beneath his fingertips was oddly pleasing to him . . . soothing almost. He had the ammunition for it as well. He had found it tucked away in the same drawer that had housed the gun.

On Thursday he didn't lunch with Lucy. He had a poste restante box from which he collected the mail and there had been a letter from his solicitors in with the others, asking him to call and see them. It would be about the divorce. When he had punished Pepper Minesse he would have to punish Elizabeth as well. She had taken his children away from him; she had betrayed him to his enemies.

Simon had enemies all around him now. Tim came to him in his sleep and warned him about them. When he went out he moved furtively, with the cunning of the dangerously deranged, choosing different routes to reach his chosen destinations, watching always to make sure that he wasn't followed. Tim had warned him that Pepper Minesse was a very clever woman and that he would have to be cautious.

This time he would do the job properly. He had been too lenient with her before.

The madness came down over him as it always did when he thought about Pepper. It was like a black cloud filling his brain, obliterating everything else. It made him feel sick; his heart pounding rapidly, as though a fever ran through his blood, and yet elated at the same time, every perception heightened so that he felt something approaching a state of euphoria. He paced his small flat mouthing her name possessed by a blood lust so strong that it overwhelmed everything else.

Afterwards when the feeling had receded it left him feeling beatifically calm and trancelike, as though he was in some state of grace, and it was while he was on this almost ecstatically elevated mental plane that Tim came to him most clearly.

Pepper was slightly late leaving the office on Thursday evening and she wondered wryly if her tardiness was perhaps due to a psychological dread of seeing Nick.

She had to rush to be ready on time for him to pick her up. The bodyguard Miles had hired watched them leave and dutifully followed in her anonymous hire car. She saw them go into an exclusive London restaurant and discreetly prepared to wait.

Inside the restaurant Pepper tensed when Nick helped her off with her coat, refusing a pre-dinner drink. She was so on edge that all she wanted to do was to tell him about Miles and then go home. She could tell Nick was aware of her tension from the way he looked at her.

The maitre d'hôtel led them to their table and flourished an ornate menu. Pepper had never felt less like eating. Around them most of the other tables were occupied. This was one of London's most fashionable restaurants. Here the aristocracy of the stage and media world mingled with the genuine article. This was no flash, here today, gone tomorrow eaterie but a restaurant that had built up its reputation over several decades.

After an unsuccessful attempt to study the menu Pepper put it down.

"Nick, there's something I have to tell you . . ."

Nick Howarth had known Pepper for several years. From the moment she first walked into his office he had wanted her. He had stalked her carefully, knowing instinctively that the slightest wrong move would panic her. He knew all about her reputation with men, but he had his own opinions on that. A hard-headed businessman who had made his own way through life, he was not inclined to put much store on human emotions. His own parents had divorced when he was seven; a vulnerable age. He had stayed with his mother until she remarried. Her new husband hadn't wanted him either. When Nick looked back on his childhood he felt a mild irritation for the child he had been; for allowing himself to be hurt. It was different now. He was armoured against that kind of pain. He liked women; he enjoyed their company; he liked making love to them, but he believed that a man was a fool if he ever allowed any other human being to become too important to him. That was the way he had run his life. Until he met Pepper.

He looked across the table at her and knew immediately what had happened. Before he had thought they were two of a kind. He didn't know why she held him at bay, but he had known instinctively that to break through her reserve he must win her trust; and he wanted her enough to take the time to do that. Almost seven long years, dammit . . . seven long years of playing it cool and hoping that one day he would pique her interest enough to get her to come to him, and now she was going to tell him that there was someone else.

And he even knew who that someone was. The popular press hadn't been slow to reveal the romance blooming between the eminent barrister and London's top businesswoman.

Everything that had made Nick Howarth what he was rose up in him now, urging him to deny that Pepper had ever meant any more to him than any other woman. Only one tiny corner of his mind refused to accept what it was being told; and that one tiny corner mourned what he knew now would never be.

Oh, he would marry, he would have a family. His wife would be beautiful and accomplished, but he would always withhold the greater part of himself from her, and she in turn would learn to give her love to her children and the odd discreet lover.

"You're in love with Miles French," he told her,

not allowing her to go on. "So what's new, Pepper?"

She swallowed hard. What had she expected? That he would be angry? That he would demand to know why she had not told him before? He had every right; their relationship . . .

She looked at Nick as he picked up his menu and started to study it, knowing that the subject of their relationship was closed.

The old Pepper would have been quite satisfied with this, would not even have wanted to prolong the conversation; would certainly not have wanted to enter into a potentially emotionally dangerous dialogue, but the new Pepper ached to explain to Nick, to show him what she had found; to tell him that it could be the same for him.

"Nick." She reached tentatively across the table and touched his arm. Immediately a muscle jumped under his skin.

"I think I'll start with oysters."

She withdrew her hand, knowing that he would rebuff all her attempts to talk to him. The only thing she could do was to take her cue from him. Over dinner he told her about the latest business deal he had pulled off in the States. Never once did he ask Pepper about her future plans; and it gave her the eerie sensation that somehow the two of them were playing out false roles.

When they had finished eating Nick helped her on with her coat. Outside the restaurant she turned impulsively to him and said quietly, "Nick, perhaps it might be better if I got a taxi . . ."

She half expected him to demur, but his face was in the shadows and she couldn't quite read his expression. Coming outside into the cool night air made her shiver, and immediately he took hold of her.

His touch wasn't Miles's and her flesh shrank

beneath it. He bent his head and even though she
knew he was going to kiss her she didn't move. She
owed him this final courtesy at least.

His kiss was cool, emotionless . . . the kind of kiss
exchanged by old friends. The bodyguard, witnessing
it, saw Nick's hand tighten briefly on Pepper's
shoulders before he released her. Enviously she noted
that he was a very good-looking man.

"I'm due back in the States at the end of the week.
I could be gone for some time. I'll be in touch when I
get back," Nick told Pepper. He smiled at her and
added quietly, "I think it might be as well if you did
get that taxi. I'm only human, Pepper, and I've
dreamed about having you in my bed for too long, I
suspect."

It made her want to cry; she who never cried. She
wanted to reach out and embrace him as a mother
embraces a hurt child, and yet she knew she could
not. She wanted to tell him that a part of her did love
him, but she knew it was not the kind of love he
wanted.

He summoned a taxi for her and saw her safely into
it. Her bodyguard followed her home, and then waited
for her relief to come and take over for the night-
shift. Twenty-four-hour protection; that was what
Miles had requested, and the agency specialised in
providing just that.

Her weekly report would be on Miles French's desk
first thing in the morning. One of the girls she was
training would deliver it for her.

Miles read the report while drinking a cup of coffee.
He had arranged that they would be delivered to his
home rather than his chambers, and he frowned as he
came to the last bit. Pepper had said nothing to him
about having dinner with Nick Howarth.

Jealousy, an unfamiliar and therefore unrecognisable emotion, curled through him. Why had Pepper not told him about her date with Nick Howarth? Common sense told him that the explanation must be innocent, but what man desperately in love ever listens to common sense? Nick Howarth was a singularly attractive man; and one, moreover, who desired Pepper and had done so for many years. And now Pepper was having dinner with him secretly.

Miles managed to resist the temptation to ring her straight away, but by lunchtime he couldn't contain his feelings any longer.

Pepper was surprised to get the phone call asking her to meet him for lunch. He sounded oddly terse and her stomach muscles contracted. She had told him that she was not concerned about Simon Herries, but suddenly she felt apprehensive.

Lucy put the call through to her and sighed enviously. She was not seeing Greg, as Simon called himself to her, until the evening, and then only for a quick drink after work. It had crossed her mind that he might be married and that she might be involving herself in a clandestine affair with a man who had no intention of ever allowing her to be anything other than a pleasant diversion in his life, but she dismissed it, not wanting to listen to that small warning voice.

They were meeting at Pepper's restaurant. Miles was there first and had to wait in growing anger as she responded to several greetings from people who knew her. He realised that he was behaving unreasonably; almost childishly, but for once was powerless to control himself. He was jealous—intensely, aggravatingly jealous, and the last thing he wanted was to admit it.

"What's wrong?" Pepper asked him quietly as she sat down. She could see how tense he was, his forehead creased in an unfamiliar frown.

"Why did you have dinner with Howarth last night?"

The harsh question took her off guard. She blinked uncertainly and stared at him.

"How . . . how do you know that?"

It was the worst possible thing she could have said, as she admitted ruefully to herself later. Miles immediately took her response as an admission of guilt and demanded to know bitterly exactly what her relationship with Nick was.

Pepper's anger rose to meet Miles's. She was not used to having to account for her movements to anyone, and it hurt that Miles so obviously didn't trust her. She didn't stop to think that his jealousy was as unfamiliar to him as it was to her; both of them were as unused to the darker side of being deeply in love as they were to the lighter.

Instead she was challenging him angrily, demanding to know how he knew she had seen Nick.

"What have you been doing? Following me around to see where I am when we're not together!"

She never imagined for one moment that he had, and so it came as a shock when he told her quietly,

"I hired a bodyguard to keep watch over you. It was in their report."

Pepper was stunned—stunned and furious. How dared he set someone to . . . to spy on her without telling her! How dared he assume that he had the right to . . . to take charge of her life, to interfere in what she did . . .

Anger, righteous and forceful, welled up inside her. They were both oblivious to the interest of the other diners as they exchanged speculative and amused looks.

Pepper couldn't remember the last time she had really lost her temper. Perhaps as a child when she was tormented by those Northern village children, but not since then. But she lost it now, standing up, her eyes glittering wildly, her hair almost seeming to give off sparks.

"How dare you have me followed and watched!" she demanded furiously. "How dare you think you have the right to interfere in my life!" And to Miles's consternation she turned on her heel and walked out of the restaurant.

Nothing like it had ever happened to him before. He liked women; he rarely quarrelled with them, and certainly never as publicly or as violently as this.

And over what? Before she stormed out on him Pepper had told him bitterly,

"I had dinner with Nick to tell him about us. As it happened he already knew, but I felt I owed it to him to tell him myself. I didn't tell you about it, Miles, because I felt uncomfortable with the fact that Nick knew nothing about our relationship—or so I thought."

She had every right to be annoyed with him, Miles admitted later when he had cooled down. He had been idiotically jealous, and in her shoes wouldn't he have wanted to do the same thing? He admitted that he would. He also admitted that at the root of his jealousy lay his fear that Pepper wouldn't commit herself to him, and he wanted that commitment. He wanted the life he knew the two of them could have together . . . But before there could be any of that he had to be sure that she was safe from Simon Herries, and now, through his own almost criminal stupidity, he had effectively destroyed his chances of persuading her to accept the necessity of having a bodyguard. He winced as he remembered the bitter comments she had thrown at him . . . how she had accused him of wanting to spy on her. Nothing was further from the truth, but what chance did he have of persuading her to believe that now?

Pepper couldn't calm down quite as quickly. This was her first experience of the intensity of love. She knew quite well that had their positions been reversed she would have felt exactly the same way, but it jarred that Miles had gone behind her back; that he had hired a bodyguard for her, without telling her about it.

She knew that he was genuinely concerned about Simon Herries; she knew that spying on her had been the very last thing in his mind, but there was still that raw sore place caused by the knowledge that he didn't fully trust her. How could he, after what he had said?

There was a sour taste in her mouth, a heaviness in her heart. On impulse she picked up the phone and rang Mary. She wanted someone to talk to . . . she needed someone to confide in, and it was only now with the new-found awareness that love had brought her that she recognised how instinctively she turned to the older woman. She had chosen Mary to be Oliver's mother because she had recognised in Mary a quality that she had ached and yearned to have for herself, she had known how much Mary would love and protect her child.

She arranged to spend the weekend with them. She needed the break, she told herself, trying to placate the conscience that had told her that it was childish to simply disappear without telling Miles where she was going.

She shrugged, angry with herself for not being able to maintain her feeling of ill-usage. He would be away for the weekend himself; he did not own her . . . she had no need to tell him what she intended doing with her time, and yet the tiny feeling of guilt persisted and grew as she tried to clear the work on her desk ready for an early departure. Miles would hardly expect her to have dinner with him after this lunchtime's débâcle.

And yet . . . On her way out of the building, she hesitated beside Lucy's desk, some impulse causing her to say to the girl,

"If Mr French rings will you tell him that I've left early and that I shall be spending the weekend with friends in Oxford."

Miles held out for as long as he could, but Pepper's angry face kept coming between him and the brief he was studying. He reached for the phone, just as his secretary came in to tell him that a client was waiting to see him. He would ring Pepper after the meeting, he decided.

It was four o'clock and the meeting didn't finish until almost five. He caught Lucy just as she was on the point of leaving, and she duly delivered Pepper's message.

Miles swore under his breath as he tried Pepper's home number. He supposed it was no more than he deserved, and as he had half expected, no one answered the phone in Pepper's apartment.

Obviously she had already left for Oxford. She would be going to see Mary and Philip Simms. She mentioned them a lot—them and Oliver—but never once had she suggested that he might like to meet them. That hurt, he recognised. They were an important part of her life—and a part of her life that in some way she seemed to want to keep separate from him. Another sign that she didn't fully trust him.

He had known that her trust would be difficult to win, but until today he had not recognised how difficult.

If it wasn't for this damn meeting tomorrow he would be tempted to throw a few clothes into a case and follow her to Oxford, but he couldn't let the other members of the committee down. They wanted to talk about installing an indoor swimming pool at the home, and how best to raise the finance for such a venture. Miles had intended suggesting one or two businessmen who he felt might respond generously to a request for a donation towards the ultimate cost.

By the time Simon met Lucy at the wine bar, Pepper was already well on her way to Oxford.

Almost he had not gone, but he had nothing else to do, and now as he listened to Lucy's irritating chatter he froze, his body tensing with excitement.

"Say that again!" he demanded abruptly.

Lucy frowned, puzzled by the glitter in his eyes and the painful way he was gripping his wrist. Suddenly she felt almost uncomfortable with him . . . frightened in some way, although she could not understand why.

"Er . . . Pepper left the office early. She met Miles French for lunch and when she came back Miranda said she was in a real temper. They were supposed to be having dinner tonight, but she's gone off to Oxford on her own. She's got friends down there . . ."

Oxford . . . Simon relaxed his grip on Lucy's wrist, unaware of the bruises he had caused. His eyes closed and a feeling of pleasure swept through him. Oxford . . . how fitting that would be, how right and proper. Almost he could see some influence that was not human at work here . . . he shivered and thought of Tim. Tim had already told him how he should punish Pepper. He had read up on what he would need to do and had been careful to buy the books from different shops . . . And yet how similar they had all been. Small secretive places where no one looked at you . . . where the very silence seemed to be imbued with a thick dangerous potency.

Once long ago Tim had sworn that he would raise the Devil and Simon secretly laughed at him for it. Now . . . His mind clouded, old images supplanting reality. Voices seemed to call him . . . Images danced before his eyes. He got up, ignoring Lucy's cry of protest, almost knocking over their glasses of wine. He didn't hear Lucy call out to him as he left. He had things to do.

He thought about the fate Tim had planned for Pepper, and how he had mocked his beliefs in the ancient ritual. Now he acknowledged that he had been wrong. Pepper Minesse was dangerous. She possessed strange powers, he was sure of it . . . otherwise how could a gypsy brat have achieved what she had? She must be destroyed. Simon went first to his flat and lovingly took the gun from the cloth in which it was wrapped. A smile lit his face as he stroked it. Soon . . . soon now . . . And he said the words out loud as though there were someone in the room with him to hear them.

CHAPTER TWENTY-ONE

LONG BEFORE she reached Oxford Pepper's mood had changed. A dull kind of emptiness took the place of her earlier anger. She ached to turn round and drive back; she ached for the comfort of Miles's arms around her, and she used the back of her hand inelegantly to wipe away the tears that had come from nowhere to cloud her vision.

Only now when the heat of her own rage was gone did she actually feel the full shock of their quarrel. It hurt almost physically, making her stomach cramp and her muscles ache. The cause of their fight was unimportant—forgotten almost. All she wanted to do was have Miles here with her.

Only the fact that she knew Mary would be expecting her stopped her from going back—that and a growing, curious sensation that for some reason she had to go to Oxford. She blinked, surprised by the momentary vision that flashed in front of her eyes.

Oliver! Suddenly she shivered, remembering the dream she had had in her bedroom at Goa; remembering Naomi and the warning she had given her that she and Oliver were in danger.

She shivered again, goosebumps lacing her skin; she was imagining things . . . it was her heightened emotional state that was responsible for this sensation she had of Naomi somehow being close at hand. And yet . . . and yet . . . She was not so sophisticated, so out of touch with her roots that she could totally deny them. She remembered things Naomi herself had

told her, and her own strange awareness of her grandmother's imminent death, and she shivered for a third
time.

In Oxford Mary waited. It was half term and Oliver
was playing in the garden. As he grew older, his
heritage from Pepper became more plain. He was a
physically attractive boy, with thick dark hair and
smooth, faintly olive skin. His eyes were light-coloured
and very serious, but when he smiled his whole face
lit up. Everyone who met him loved him—he was that
kind of child, quick and intelligent and yet compassionate as well, so essentially sweet-natured that one
could not help but be aware of it. Mary adored him,
although she and Philip both tried desperately not to
spoil him; not to let him know how precious and
special they thought him.

She had had him for ten joyous years, but soon . . .
The pain within her body bit deeply and she tensed
against it.

Her death would be slow and lingering; she had
read that in her doctor's eyes and had shrunk from it.
She had always feared pain, and her fear was no less
now that she was intimately acquainted with it.

There was no question of an operation, her cancer
was too deep-rooted for that. Later she could, if she
chose, opt to go into a hospice run to care for people
like herself who were close to death.

She still hadn't told Oliver. Now she was going to
do so. She sensed that it was right for her to do so
now, when Pepper was here. They would need one
another then, those two. Philip had a weak heart; she
had always been the physically strong one. Oliver
could so easily be left an orphan. That weighed heavily
on Mary. That wasn't what she wanted for him. She
looked at her watch. Soon Pepper would be here. If

only she had more time . . . If only she could be sure that Pepper . . . The pain struck again and everything was suborned to it, every other thought banished.

When it finally receded Mary went to the door and called Oliver. He came at once, and she knew without having to say anything to him that he was aware, as sensitive children are, that there was something wrong.

She sat him down in her own small sitting room, where he had crawled on the floor as a baby and then later learned to pull himself to his feet and walk. So many memories; so much happiness . . .

Slowly and carefully she explained to him that she was ill and that she was not going to get better. He listened gravely, his eyes filming with tears that he didn't shed.

"I'm telling you this, Oliver, because when I'm gone, if anything happens to Daddy, I want you to go and live with Pepper."

She prayed as she said it that she was doing the right thing . . . If need be she was not afraid of resorting to emotional blackmail, she knew Pepper would not refuse to take him, but would she make him happy? Would she realise the wonderful gift she had in her child, would she . . .? Mary clamped down on the thought, making herself concentrate on Oliver and what she had to say to him. She had so little time . . . so little strength; she must not waste any of it.

She saw the surprise cross his face and said quickly,

"Pepper is your godmother. She will take care of you and love you . . ."

Her voice thickened and she suppressed her own tears. She had to be strong now, for Oliver's sake. He had been their gift; but always she had had the sense of only having him on loan. She could not tell him the truth. Pepper had bound them to their word, and besides . . . she looked at him and knew that Pepper had acted wisely. No, she could not tell him the truth, but she could prepare him for what was to come.

"I'm going to talk to Pepper when she arrives,"she went on. "She will understand."

"And will I have to go and live in London with her?"

"Yes," Mary told him firmly. "And Oliver, you must promise not to forget what I'm telling you, not to say anything to Pepper until I've spoken to her."

Some inner wisdom she had only recently come by told her that Pepper would accept her death far less easily than would Oliver . . . that Pepper would be the one to rail and protest against her fate. Pepper loved her, Mary acknowledged sadly.

Simon drove straight down to Oxford and booked into a small hotel. Tomorrow would be soon enough to look for Pepper. He would find her—he knew it. For now he had other things to do.

He drove down to Marchington. The house had been closed up for some time and the once immaculate gates were slightly rusty. He didn't use the main drive, but instead drove round the back, down a narrow bumpy track that went straight to the stables and outbuildings.

Tim's father had died two years ago, the only remaining heir, a cousin, had died too, and since there was now no direct male heir, squabbles had broken out in the family over who really had the right to Marchington. The result was that until the squabbles were legally settled no one was living there.

Simon already knew this. From the first moment the idea had come to him he had been working deliberately to this end. Marchington . . . Tim's home, the place Tim himself had chosen for Pepper's death.

It was only fitting that he should destroy her there.

He broke in through the french windows of the library. It had been one of the late Earl's foibles that he had flatly refused to install any formal type of burglar alarm. Instead they had had guard dogs which patrolled the grounds, but these were now gone and there was no one to see Simon walk through the gathering darkness of the empty rooms.

What had happened to the paintings and furniture? Stored away somewhere, no doubt, pending the result of the court case. The house looked ill at ease and shabby in the half light. He daren't take the risk of switching on the lights, always assuming the electricity was still working, but he didn't need lights to find his way down to the chapel.

He was carrying a large parcel under his arm, and when he walked into the chapel he placed it on the simple altar. It was here that Deborah had died, the blood pouring from her body in a red tide.

Simon unwrapped his parcel and set the tall candles in the holders he had brought with him. He wasn't going to light them yet, but his body trembled with excitement as he touched them. It had been surprisingly easy to find them, and the proprietor of the small shop where he had bought them had evinced no interest at all in them or in his other purchases, but then given the type of merchandise he was selling it was perhaps not surprising.

Black magic, Satanism . . . these were joke words to many, but Simon had been surprised to discover how very strong some people's belief in the power of the rituals of evil actually was. Perhaps Tim was right and he was wrong. He shivered slightly. He wasn't here to raise the Devil, he was here to pass sentence on Pepper Minesse, and this time there would be no clemency.

He used the torch he had brought with him to check that everything was in order. He had been through this ritual so many times in his mind, lying in the narrow single bed in his bleak flat, that it was now automatic, soothing almost, calming the febrile excitement beating up inside him.

As he worked he talked quietly, addressing the one companion who followed him through his increasingly insane thoughts. Tim had become as real to him as though he was in fact alive. Talking to him like this elevated him to a mental plane where he felt a power so strong that it was almost like taking a drug.

It was not just himself he was avenging but Tim as well, Tim who would not be dead if it wasn't for that bitch. So his thoughts ran, increasingly out of touch with reality, and when at last he drove away from Marchington Simon Herries, urbane Member of Parliament and hopeful future Prime Minister, was gone for ever, and in his place was a man who looked perfectly normal and sane, but who was in fact dangerously unbalanced.

Mary sent Oliver to bed before Pepper arrived. She wanted to see her on her own, although Philip had protested. In the end he had given way. It frightened him to see his strong, dependable wife slowly weakening beneath the onslaught of her illness. Every day she seemed to lose a little more ground as though slowly she was slipping away from him.

They had talked about Oliver and Philip had concurred with all she had said, but how would Pepper feel? Mary was convinced that she would take the child. But would she?

Pepper knew the moment she walked in that something was wrong; not because Oliver was missing, but because she felt it, smelled it, tasted it almost, with every instinct she had inherited from her ancestors. Naomi's presence was so real to her that she almost turned her head to look at her.

She had come to Mary like a hurt child running to its mother, but now she realised that Mary was the one who was hurt.

Mary told her about her cancer quietly and calmly. For a moment Pepper couldn't respond, her shock and grief lay within her like a heavy stone.

"Surely there must be some form of treatment . . . an operation?"

Mary shook her head.

"No—it's too advanced. I'm going to die, Pepper, and probably quite soon. If you hadn't come down this weekend, I was going to telephone you anyway."

Pepper wanted to scream her pain and denial, but somehow her emotion could not be released. Like a dark shadow, grief stalked her, and not even her awareness of Naomi's presence could ease her anguish. She had lost so much already . . . she didn't want to lose Mary . . . Mary who had never hurt a soul in her life, Mary who . . .

"If anything happens to Philip I want you to promise to take Oliver, Pepper."

The quiet words cut right across her thoughts. They were sitting in Mary's room, and now Pepper realised how carefully Mary had planned this whole interview, because she reached across the small table in front of her and picked up a worn Bible.

"This Bible belonged to my grandmother. The date she was given it, the date of her marriage and the births of her children are all recorded in here, as are their deaths—theirs and hers. My mother wrote in it too, and so have I. I want you to swear to me on this Bible that I hold sacred that you will do as I ask."

How could Pepper refuse? Did she even want to

refuse? Oliver was her son and in her pain she found she could now acknowledge how much she loved him . . . How much she had always loved him.

She took the Bible and made the promise Mary wanted.

They talked for a long time . . . or at least Mary talked and Pepper listened . . . Mary told Pepper about her childhood, about how happy she had been then and during her marriage to Philip.

"It's old-fashioned of me, I know, but I pray that you will have a Philip in your life one day, Pepper."

"I think I already have."

The words were out before Pepper could silence them, and once spoken demanded elucidation. Even talking about Miles made her ache to have him with her. Why had she been such a fool? Why had she lost her temper with him like that? Was it really because she had been frightened by the strength of her own emotion? She knew that it was. Her need to give Miles the commitment he wanted from her terrified her, and so she had fought against it in the only way she knew.

"You look sad," Mary told her. "Have you quarrelled with him?"

What could Pepper say? How could she explain Miles's fears for her? They would only frighten Mary, and she had enough to bear as it was.

"Yes."

"Go and ring him," Mary urged her.

"He might not be in," Pepper protested, but she was already reaching for the telephone.

Miles answered it on the second ring, and from the rough urgency in his voice she knew he regretted their fight as much as she did herself.

"I'm at Mary's," she told him huskily.

"I hoped you'd ring. God, Pepper, I'm sorry . . . but I was so damn jealous. I miss you like hell. I wish

I could be there with you."

"So do I!"

His quick ear caught the undertone of despair in her voice; a despair that came from much more than their quarrel, and he had an urgent desire to put down the phone and go to her, and to hell with the committee meeting.

He took a deep breath and said quietly,

"We need to talk. When do you plan to come back?"

"Sunday," Pepper told him. She owed it to Mary to at least stay the full weekend, much as she ached to be with Miles.

"I'll take the train down on Sunday, then, and we could drive back together."

She could introduce him to Philip and Mary . . . and Oliver. Suddenly she found she was gripping the receiver too tightly.

"I . . ." she began.

"Why don't you invite him for Sunday lunch?" Mary suggested quietly at her side, but not so quietly that Miles didn't hear her.

"It's a long time since I enjoyed a traditional Sunday lunch," he said. "I'd love to be there."

Pepper gave him directions and thought of all the things she ached to say that she couldn't over the telephone.

"How long have you known him?" Mary asked her when she replaced the receiver.

The words "for ever" trembled on her lips and Pepper only just caught them back, realising with a small shock of surprise how apt they were. That was how she felt about Miles, as though in fact she had known him not just all her life, but throughout eternity itself.

"I met him briefly years ago in Oxford," she said

instead. "I think you'll like him. He's a barrister."

The only paper Philip read was *The Times*, so they were hardly likely to have seen the gossip about them. Sensing Mary's interest, Pepper told her a little more, leaving out the true reason Miles had taken her to Goa and substituting instead the small white lie that they had gone there on holiday.

"He knows . . . about Oliver," Pepper added quietly. "He knew what happened to me and he . . . he guessed that I conceived a child. He's like me, an orphan. He was brought up in a children's home."

Did she realise how much she betrayed with those few words, Mary wondered, or was it simply now that she herself was so near death that she had been granted the insight to see so much more? She knew, for instance, how much Pepper loved Oliver, something she had never been totally sure of before. She knew as though Pepper had told her so herself that she had given him to them out of love for them and out of love for Oliver himself, knowing with a painful wisdom that no girl of her age should have had that he would be better off with them than her.

Philip and Mary liked to go to bed fairly early. Pepper went up at the same time, to the same room she had had when they had brought her home from hospital. Some of her clothes still hung in the wardrobe, her small personal belongings were scattered around in its cupboards. It was her room, and oddly, for all its simplicity she felt at home here.

She showered in the old-fashioned rather spartan bathroom, wrapping herself in the thick white towel that had been part of Mary's bottom drawer, then went to bed. She lay back in bed and stared up at the ceiling. Mary dying . . . Mary being eaten alive by pain and her own flesh. She shuddered and her throat closed up with pain.

Then suddenly she was aware of a presence in the room with her, and she said the name that came instinctively to her lips, sitting up and staring at the door.

Only it wasn't Naomi who stood there but Oliver.

He came over to the bed and stood there looking at her. He was so physically like her, this child of her flesh. Pepper wanted to reach out and embrace him, but could not. She looked at him, and in the depths of his serious gaze she saw his own pain and understanding, and for the first time something within him that was purely Naomi . . . a kind of acceptance she herself with her restless spirit had never had and bitterly regretted not having.

While her eyes burned with tears of grief and gratitude she realised that she had been given the gift of a child old in the understanding of mankind with all its weaknesses . . . one of those elevated spirits who chose to return to an earthbound plane for the benefit of others. As though Naomi stood at her shoulder and told her so, Pepper saw the strength and gentleness that would one day make her child a man revered and respected by all who knew him. And many would. He had nothing of Simon Herries in him, nothing at all, and none of her own weaknesses and failings either. As instinctively as though she had held him every day since the moment of his birth she opened her arms, and he walked into them. Without words they formed a bond, a communion that went deeper than the mere bond of blood.

How long they remained like that, mourning silently for the woman they both loved, Pepper didn't know, but eventually Oliver disengaged himself and went back to his own room as silently as he had arrived. How had he known how much she needed that contact with him? Again her grandmother's face seemed to form itself in her mind.

She slept and dreamed joyously of a beautiful garden where she walked with those whom she loved. Miles held one of Oliver's hands and she held the other, and Mary was on her other side with Philip, and then suddenly the golden warmth of the garden was stolen away and she was filled with a sense of fear. Something menaced that beautiful paradise, and suddenly she and Oliver were alone in a frighteningly dangerous place. She saw Naomi again, warning her . . . urging her to do something—but what?

Pepper woke up shivering and frightened and told herself that her dream was only her fear of Mary's death.

But what if it was more? What if Miles was right to fear Simon Herries? What if Naomi herself was warning he against him? No—she wasn't going to think like that . . .

She woke up early as she always did at Philip and Mary's. The soft fruit was beginning to ripen and after breakfast she joined Mary picking raspberries. Would Mary be alive to eat this year's jam?

The thought wouldn't go away, and as though she had read her mind Mary touched her arm and said quietly,

"It won't be long, Pepper."

"You're being so brave."

Why were they both whispering? There was no one here to listen to them—unless it was the shadow of death.

"No . . . I'm terrified of the pain. It's bad enough now." Mary shivered, her eyes clouding.

"They'll give you drugs," said Pepper, trying to comfort her.

"But will they be enough?"

Both of them fell silent.

"Oliver needs new clothes—he's growing so fast," said Mary. "Come with me this afternoon to Oxford and help me buy them. We'll all go and have lunch out."

It was a beautiful cloudless day with the sun shining from a perfectly blue sky. Oxford shimmered under the warm summer heat haze, and the quality of the light seemed so pure that the ancient buildings appeared to float above the ground.

It had been on a day as perfect as this that Pepper had seen Marchington.

Marchington. Why was she thinking of that now? Pepper wondered tensely as she parked her car. Philip hadn't come with them, preferring to stay at home with his books. He wasn't a man who enjoyed shopping.

Oliver stayed close to Mary's side. Not for his own sake, but for hers, Pepper recognised, overwhelmed by her love for this child she had so desperately wanted to hate. By what miracle had fate ordained that from that bestial coupling should come this boy? She wanted to reach out and touch him . . . to give thanks for the special gift she had received. How had she managed to live so long without realising that there was this very deep emotional side to her nature; this need to be at one with her own universe; this joy in the beauty that was all around her that she had never known before?

"Because you would not allow yourself to know it."

So real was the sound of Naomi's voice that Pepper stopped in the street and looked over her shoulder. From being disconcerting this awareness of her grandmother's watchful presence had become reassuring. She saw that Oliver was looking at her, and thinking she had alarmed him she summoned a reassuring

smile—then she realised he was looking beyond her.
Was he too aware of Naomi's presence? Her heart
skipped a beat. How her grandmother would have
loved him! How she would have cherished and taught
him.

Without realising it she had parked close to Miles's
old college, Christ Church. They had to walk past the
entrance to Tom Quad and she paused for a moment
outside it, remembering.

Simon had been up early as well. He ignored the hotel
dining room—food was of no interest to him. He had
other things to do. He drove out to Marchington
while the dew was still on the grass. No one was there.
He went down to the chapel. Nothing had been
disturbed. It was as he had thought, but it was as well
to check.

As he walked through the empty rooms it was as
though Tim walked with him.

"It won't be long now," he promised him.

The madness had finally taken over, the psychosis
inherited with his genes and begun as an escape from
his father's sexual debasement of him; a fantasy land
with a gate which he could open and close at will now
imprisoned him, the gate back to reality now closed
for ever.

Only Simon didn't see it that way. He felt buoyant,
his body surging with energy and delight. He felt alive
with the power of his own thoughts; elevated above
all other men; with the strength to destroy a hundred
Pepper Minesses.

He had gone beyond hatred of her now, his madness
deepening beyond that point. He saw himself as an
executioner sent by a greater force to destroy an
enemy of that force. He was a disciple following the
orders of his master. Euphoria possessed him. He had

forgotten how he had once privately mocked Tim for his obsession with Satanism and remembered only the pleasure Tim promised he would experience through the sacrifice of Pepper.

Now it was time for that sacrifice to take place, and he had been charged with the task of doing it.

He left Marchington in an intense state of euphoria and drove back to Oxford. He didn't want to eat; he was too restless, too keyed up. Now he had to find the woman.

He saw her quite by accident, just as he was crossing the road outside the entrance to Tom Quad. She was standing there staring at it. There was a boy with her and an older woman, but he didn't pay much attention to them. He had found her! It had been so easy. A further sign that what he was doing had some higher approval. Keeping Pepper well in sight, he followed her, an anonymous figure in his Savile Row suit and white shirt.

Simon hadn't been following her for very long when he realised something. Someone else was following her as well. Slipping into the shadows of a narrow alleyway, he watched as Pepper and her companions paused outside a shoeshop, and sure enough when they moved, so did the woman in jeans and a sweatshirt who seemed to have been marking their every move. Everywhere the small party went their two shadows followed them. Simon had no idea who the woman was, but she was interfering with his plans. She was in his way, and he would have to find some means of getting rid of her.

Pepper, Mary and Oliver lunched at a new seafood restaurant, but none of them really did justice to the meal.

Oliver's new clothes were soon bought, winter things for the coming school term. Pepper's eyes misted over as she watched Mary choose them, both of them knowing that she might not be alive to see him put them on. A tight strained look came over Mary's face as they left the shop and without her saying anything Pepper knew she was in pain, and seeing Oliver slipping his hand into the older woman's she suspected that he knew it as well.

It was a strain pretending to a cheerfulness she could not feel. Naomi had taught her that death was more friend than foe; death might be, but this mortal agony, this suffering . . . surely there was no virtue or reward in that?

She longed for Miles's calm rational presence. Sunday lunchtime could not come soon enough.

They left Oxford after lunch. Two cars followed them back.

As Laura Bates had already discovered, there was nowhere to discreetly conceal her car down the narrow lane that led only to the Simms' house. Last night her relief had parked hers on the main road, secure in the knowledge that no one could leave or enter the lane without her seeing them.

Country manners were not London manners, she had reported to Laura when they switched over. She had apparently lost count of the number of would-be knights of the road who had stopped to ask her if she was in difficulty.

Simon, already aware that Pepper was being shadowed, took good care to keep out of sight of the small blue Fiesta following the Aston Martin. He saw it drive past the opening to the lane Pepper drove down, and park up several yards away. He drove past it without turning his head, and then several miles on he turned round and drove back to Oxford.

It wasn't difficult to find a bookshop selling maps

of the area, and from the one he bought he was able
to see that there was only one house down the lane.
Was Pepper staying there or was she just a visitor?

He waited until late afternoon and drove out of
Oxford again, slowing down well before turning into
the lane, and skilfully mimicking the uncertain driving
of a person looking for an unfamiliar landmark.

Less than half a mile down the lane he saw the
house, with Pepper's car parked outside and, better
still, Pepper herself playing cricket with the dark-
haired boy who had been with her earlier, on a piece
of uncultivated lawn to the side of the house. His
instincts told Simon that she was staying at the house,
but for how long? He couldn't afford to delay. This
was the golden opportunity.

He drove back up the lane and wondered if the
person driving the blue Fiesta was marking down his
number plate. Just to be on the safe side, when he got
back to Oxford he handed in the car, which was only
rented, and hired out another from a different
company.

Soon it would be dusk. A good time to act. Simon
went back to his room and lay on the bed preparing
himself for his self-appointed task.

Miles's meeting was over, but the other members of
the committee were pressing him to stay and join them
for dinner. There was no reason why he shouldn't;
Pepper wasn't expecting him until tomorrow and he
could hardly inflict himself on her friends half way
through the evening. And yet . . . and yet he had this
nagging feeling that he should go to her. Almost it
was as though someone was telling him that he must
go to her.

It was silly really. He could pick up the phone and
speak to her. Almost without consciously making up

his mind, he refused the proffered invitation, and somehow or other found he was in his car and heading for Oxford.

Foolish, illogical . . . both those things, perhaps, and yet the moment he got into his car Miles felt an intense sense of relief in the air all around him, coupled with a strong impulse to drive to Oxford just as fast as he could.

Not unusual behaviour in a man in love, perhaps, but Miles acknowledged to himself that it went deeper than that. That there was more to his feelings than mere emotional need to be with the woman he loved.

Laura Bates yawned and glanced at her watch. Another four hours before she was relieved. It was boring sitting here like this. So far one car and two cyclists had turned down the lane and then come back again, that was all. She was beginning to think that Miles French was wasting his money.

She saw the yellow car approach and slow down as it stopped alongside her own without any feeling of alarm. A man got out, tall, fair and vaguely familiar. He came towards her and opened the door of her car, and as she looked into his eyes she recognised him— and shock jolted through her.

She tried to cry out, but his hands were already around her throat, squeezing it with manic strength. Laura Bates was trained to defend herself, but not against strength like this. Bubbles of air gurgled in the vacuum that was her lungs. She tried to breathe, to tear at the hands clutching at her throat, but it was no use.

Darkness came down over her, and her last thought was that Miles French had been right after all, but she would have no way of telling him, because Simon Herries would have killed her.

Simon let her body sag and then pushed her into the passenger seat, fastening the seat belt. She looked as though she was asleep. He moved his own car, then pulled on the gloves he had brought with him and got into hers.

A small spinney spread out to one side of the lane and it was an easy task to conceal the small blue car in its depths. The failing light helped him. It would be discovered in the morning, no doubt, but by then it would all be over anyway.

Back in his own car he stripped off the gloves and started the engine.

The garden was empty, lights streaming from the house. Simon parked behind Pepper's car, blocking her exit. A sense of elation filled him as he walked up to the front door.

Oliver answered his knock. Simon took hold of him quite gently, pulling him against his body with his left hand while in the right he held the gun.

Neither of them spoke—there was no need. Simon had the boy and soon he would have the others. He knew from the way the old woman had fussed over the child.

He was right.

Mary came first, calling out, "Who is it, Oliver?" And then she screamed, a high petrified sound that brought the others running.

"It's me he wants," Pepper said quietly. She hadn't taken her eyes off Simon since the moment she saw him. "He'll let the rest of you go."

She stepped past Mary, willing herself not to betray her fear. She had no option but to go with him. He had Oliver.

"No!" Philip objected rawly, stepping up to Simon and trying to wrench Oliver away.

It was the wrong thing to do. Mary cried out as

Simon raised the gun and clubbed Philip to the ground. Pepper wanted to say something . . . anything, but her throat was tight with shock and fear.

"Get in the car, the rest of you," Simon demanded savagely. He had enjoyed hitting the man, even though it hadn't been part of his plan. The fool should have known better than to approach him.

Didn't he have the gun?

"Simon . . ." He turned his head as Pepper touched his arm. His eyes glittered maniacally, his mouth curled into a rictus smile of triumph. "Let Mary and Oliver go," she begged him. "They have nothing to do with this. It's just between you and me."

Please . . . please let him agree, she prayed, but even as she did so, she remembered Naomi's warning and knew he would refuse.

"Do you think I'm a fool? If I let them go they'll be on the phone to the police. You," he gestured to Mary, "you and the boy . . . in the back."

"Philip . . . my husband . . . he has a weak heart. You can't leave him lying here! He could die!" Mary protested, and Pepper felt ashamed because her fear had nearly all been for Oliver. She bent down to touch Philip and felt the stickiness of the blood on the side of his head where Simon had clubbed him. She suspected that Philip was already dead, but she daredn't say so.

"Crazy fool! He shouldn't have interfered," Simon snarled, then he laughed, a maniacal sound that chilled Pepper's blood.

Now she knew why Naomi had been trying to warn her, and of what. Why, oh, why hadn't she realised just how dangerous Simon Herries was? Dangerous and mad.

She heard Mary scream and turned in shock to see that Simon had levelled the gun at Philip's prone body. Oliver struggled in his arms and the gun went off. Pepper heard the shot, smelled the stench of burning flesh and cordite. Behind her she could hear Mary being sick. Oliver was staring at them both, his eyes huge and agonised.

She couldn't bear to look at Philip's poor body. She knew if he hadn't already been dead that that shot must have killed him.

"Get in the car," Simon repeated. "Otherwise the boy goes next."

He was loving this, high on the power of the control he had over them. He had enjoyed killing the man. It was surprising how satisfying it had been, though not as satisfying as killing Pepper would be. He looked at her and frowned. She should be more afraid—cowering, begging him for mercy.

"I think we'd better do as he says," Pepper told Mary. Privately she was wondering if there was any point in prolonging their agony. Simon would kill them all in the end, she had seen it in his eyes. She was tempted to plead for Mary's and Oliver's lives, but she suspected that if he thought they were important to her he would take even greater pleasure in killing them.

How he had found her she had no idea. She could hardly think straight at all as she got into the back of the small car. Oliver was at her side. Simon made Mary get into the driver's seat and then he climbed into the passenger seat beside her, the gun pressed hard against her side.

Mary started the engine. She was trembling so much it took her several minutes to get the car started, and all the time the tension within it grew.

"Where . . . where do you want me to go?" Mary asked Simon drily. Odd how her pain had subsided now that she actually was faced with death. She contemplated driving to the nearest police station, but she knew that Oliver and Pepper would be dead before anyone could help them. She knew who Simon was . . . she had recognised him instantly . . . and his madness.

Pray God Oliver would never learn that this madman was his father! She shuddered at the thought.

Originally Simon hadn't planned on taking anyone other than Pepper, but he had seen the fiercely protective way she had stood close to the child. He would enjoy what he had to do.

He would sacrifice the boy first, he decided calmly. He would enjoy watching Pepper's face as he made the ritual incisions. It would give her an idea of what lay ahead of her. She would die in the same kind of mortal agony she had inflicted on him. He would punish her as she truly deserved to be punished, the way Tim would have wanted her to be punished.

Pepper had only been to Marchington once, but she had recognised the route instantly, even in the dark. Generations of ancestors accustomed to living close to nature and its powers had given her instinct a deep inner knowledge out of step with modern living.

She knew instantly what Simon intended to do. He might just as well have screamed the words at her. She saw the chapel, felt its evil coldness. She saw the black candles, the words of the satanic Black Mass. She closed her eyes and prayed . . . Not to God of whom she knew nothing, but to older, stronger powers, to Naomi who she knew to be watching over her.

Oliver, sensing her tension, reached out and touched her. She withdrew slightly from him, frightened that he might sense through touch and understand what lay in her mind, and silently, over and over again, she repeated the words that her race had used almost since the dawn of time itself when committing the bodies of their young children to burial.

Miles found the turning into the lane without too much difficulty, even in the dark. He could see the light blazing from the house and in his anxiety to be with Pepper thought nothing of the fact that there was no sign of Laura Bates or one of her employees.

It was only when his headlights picked out Philip Simms' prone body that he began to feel real fear.

He stopped his car and got out. Philip was dead. As Miles knelt in front of him he was possessed by such a savage surge of urgency that he was half way back to his car before he realised what he was doing. It was an effort of will to make himself go back into the house and telephone the police. Within ten minutes they were with him.

At first they were efficient and polite, and no more, but Miles was not a leading barrister for nothing, and his story sounded too improbable not to be the truth.

"So you think this . . . Simon Herries has kidnapped your fiancée and perhaps two other people as well because of some private vendetta?"

He explained as simply as he could, and all the time the urgency inside him grew until he felt he could explode with the force of it.

"I don't suppose you've any idea where he might have taken them, have you, sir?"

The Inspector's attention was distracted when a uniformed constable came up to him, looking sick and shaken. He was only young, nineteen, maybe, no more.

"We've found a car in the spinney at the top of the lane, sir. There's a body in it . . . a woman."

Not Pepper! Dear God, no! Every instinct Miles possessed was screaming that she was still alive.

"Tall, heavily built . . . dark hair."

No, not Pepper, it sounded more like . . .

"Laura—Laura Bates, a private investigator," he said numbly. "I was worried about Pepper. She wouldn't listen to me, so I hired Laura as her bodyguard."

Now he had the inspector's full attention.

"And you've no idea where this Simon Herries could have taken them?"

"Marchington . . . he's taken them to Marchington."

Miles felt as amazed as the Inspector looked. How had he known that? Where had the words come from? Not from him, although he had been the one to speak them.

"Marchington?" the Inspector repeated.

"It's the family seat of the Earls of Marchington. Simon had a very close relationship with the Earl's grandson Tim Wilding at Oxford. They were planning to revive the old Hell Fire Club when Tim was killed. That was how it all started." Miles told them what Pepper herself had told him, willing himself not to show his impatience while with every breath he took, his sense of urgency grew.

Whoever started the rumour that the British police have no imagination was wrong, Miles acknowledged an hour later when a casually dressed, laconic detective, with an unshaven jaw and a quantity of dark, untidy hair, said, "I think we'd better check it out." He looked up at the sky and said something that Miles himself hadn't noticed. "There's a full moon tonight. If your theory's right . . . Johnson, Austin, get the cars," he called over his shoulder, and added to Miles, "You realise if he does have them there we're probably going to have to talk him into surrendering. It could be a long wait . . . I'll send one of the squad cars."

He didn't want him with them, Miles recognised, but there was no way he wasn't going, and he said so. Pepper needed him. He shook off his exhaustion, and wondered what on earth the detective would say if he told him that he was almost haunted by a thin old woman with a gnarled walnut face and distinctive Romany features who told him constantly that Pepper needed him. Probably have him locked up! he decided wryly.

"What we need now is some idea of the layout of the building. They'll try to get that for us back at the station. I can't promise you we're going to get them out alive," the Inspector told Miles frankly. "It all depends on Herries. You say he's insane? If that's true . . ."

It was what he didn't say rather than what he did that lay so heavily on his heart, Miles acknowledged, and there was much he had not told the police. Like the fact that Oliver was Simon's son . . .

As they drove past the end of the lane Miles noticed two policemen removing a shrouded body from the blue car. Laura Bates . . . he shuddered deeply. Indirectly he was responsible for her death.

No one in the chapel at Marchington heard the police arrive. Mary, beyond shock and pain, was sitting with Oliver, holding on to him. For the past three hours they had had to sit and listen while Simon talked.

Little of what he said made sense to anyone other than Pepper. She saw that he blamed her for Tim's death, even though she knew that he was responsible. His hatred of her, of her whole sex, spewed up inside him like lava from a volcano. He talked of Deborah and her suicide, and Pepper's heightened awareness made it almost possible for her to see the other girl as she lay on the coldness of the chapel floor. She had to fight to suppress her sickness as Simon told them what he had done to her. For a girl brought up as Deborah had been, innocent, naïve, a girl whose sexuality had never been awakened, the torment she had experienced must have been unendurable.

And lastly he talked of Pepper herself, of her rape . . . of his pleasure in it, but listening to his ranting Pepper found that she might almost have been listening to him talking about someone else. His words no longer had the power to hurt her. She was free . . . Miles had freed her.

All the time Simon talked, he never took his eyes off them nor relaxed his grip on the gun. He would shoot them the moment they tried to move—Pepper knew that.

She also knew why he was delaying so long. He would not start the Black Mass ritual that would lead to their deaths until midnight.

She prayed as she had never done in her life before that neither Oliver nor Mary understood what was in store for them. She would kill her child herself before she would allow Simon Herries to touch him, and she fully intended to do so.

Miles had been right to warn her. Miles . . . this was the first time she had allowed herself to think of him. She hadn't dared before, knowing that to do so was to weaken herself. She wanted him; she loved him, and now too late she knew that all her dreams of revenge and retribution had been nothing more than a throwing away of so many years of her life. But they had brought her Miles. Good out of bad, love out of hate—like Oliver, the child of her enforced union with a man who was now going to kill them both. How could she have guessed when she had been so desperate to destroy her unborn foetus just what her child would be . . . would have been, she corrected herself bitterly.

They found the car straight away. The house was in darkness. The police fanned out silently around it.

"Door forced here, sir," one of the men told the Inspector.

They went inside. The Inspector had suggested that Miles remain by the security of the police cars, but he had refused. His awareness of Naomi's presence was so strong now he was surprised that no one else was aware of her.

"They're down here somewhere," he told the Inspector, heading for the passage that led to the chapel.

The Inspector and the man at his side exchanged glances. Both of them were too experienced . . . had seen too much to question how he knew.

"Carefully now, sir," was all the Inspector said.

The chapel was illuminated with candles for the Black Mass. The wax hissed and dripped, giving off a drugging odour. The ingredients that went into their making were secret; special incantations said over them. Once, long ago, the drug content in them, made from wild poppies, had been put there to soothe the fears of a coven's victims. Then the rite of sacrifice had been an accepted part of rural village life.

Like animals, human beings have instincts that pass from generation to generation, although civilisation has glossed over them. As the men approached the entrance to the chapel all of them felt an atavistic and instinctive urge to withdraw.

Pepper saw them first, her heart leaping into her throat. She sensed them there, even while they were still cloaked in the shadows, and she measured the distance to safety with fierce eyes . . . not for herself, for Oliver, for her child. He had won the school sprint race, Mary had told her with pride. A child, no matter how fast on his feet, could not run faster than a bullet . . . unless someone stood in its way. Pepper inched forward carefully—and froze as Simon saw her.

He stopped in full spate, suspicion narrowing his eyes. Like an animal he could smell fear around him . . . fear and danger. The candles guttered slightly as though somewhere someone had opened a door.

Watching the scene, Miles felt his stomach roll over. No one spoke. The police were armed, but how could they risk rushing Simon? If they tried he would kill all three of them before they could reach him.

Simon grimaced and advanced on Pepper. It was five to twelve. Soon it would begin. He could feel the pleasure building up inside him. There was a pressure inside his skull that was almost a pain, an excitement that went beyond anything he had ever known—and then abruptly it started to fade. He stopped moving, bewildered by the sudden loss of exhilaration, his eyes unfocused and wild as he stared into the dark corners of the chapel. Where was Tim? He had promised Simon he would be here to share this with him . . . he had told him so. Confusion clouded Simon's mind. He wanted the sharpness of his earlier exhilaration back. He wanted to feel again that keenness, that euphoria, that ecstasy that would be his when he saw Pepper's body spread out on the altar . . . He told Pepper as much, relishing the words, while his unseen listeners froze.

"You were right—he is mad," the detective told Miles grimly. "We need to distract him."

"Can't risk it," one of his men said tersely. "We wouldn't have enough time. We might be able to save one of them . . ."

Simon frowned. It was almost time. Where was the

exhilaration he needed to feel . . . he had to feel? Where was Tim? He had promised he would be here . . .

Pepper watched him, her heart in her throat, sensing the dull clouding of his senses. Now . . . it had to be now. There wouldn't be a better time. The gun was still pointing at them.

Outside in the darkened corridor the Inspector turned to Miles. "We've got a marksman here. We'll get him up and into position, but at the moment there's not a damn thing he can do. The others are in the way."

Pepper gripped hold of Oliver's shoulder, and he looked up at her. She looked towards the corridor and immediately he understood. This communion between them was still so new to him and yet at the same time so very old; something that had come into this life with him and that would go out of it with him as well. Pepper wanted him to run. He knew that one of them was going to die, although he didn't know which one, but Pepper wanted him to run, and run he would.

Her fingers still gripped him. She watched Simon struggling against the darkness dulling his brain. He turned his head.

The moment was upon them. She released Oliver's shoulder and he ran. Simon called out, levelling the gun. Pepper rushed in front of him to protect her child, but Mary beat her to it, pushing her to the floor with surprising strength, flinging herself at Simon's chest, arms outstretched.

The impact of the bullet killed her instantly. Her inert body was still draped against Simon's when the police marksman's bullet entered his brain.

As death embraced her, Mary saw a woman waiting for her, her hand outstretched, and a feeling of intense

happiness overwhelmed her. In the shadows behind
the gypsy woman stood Philip. And as she floated
towards him the gypsy woman turned her so that she
could look down on the scene she had just left, and
she thought she heard her saying,

"It is over. The child is safe."

In a daze Pepper saw the men emerge from the
passageway, policemen, and another—another whose
face she felt she should know. He was carrying a little
boy. He said her name—at least she thought it was
her name. He said it again, his forehead creased in
anxiety, and then she knew. She got up and ran to
him, and his free arm opened, gathering her close to
him.

"It's over, Pepper—it's over. You're both safe."

They were safe, yes, but Mary and Philip were dead.

"It is as it was ordained to be." Pepper heard the
words and yet knew that no one had spoken them.
She smiled shakily, her lips forming a name.

"Naomi . . ."

She would not see her grandmother again—not in
this life. She knew it instinctively. From that other
world, her grandmother's task was done.

She felt Oliver's hand on her arm and looked at
him.

"Mary's at peace now, Oliver," she told him.

He looked back at her, his eyes grave and knowing.

"Yes . . . I saw her," he told her quietly.

Miles watched them both, knowing they were
sharing something from which he was excluded and
yet not resenting it.

"I should have listened to you," Pepper admitted later
when the formalities were done with and she and
Oliver were safely installed in Miles's flat.

"And I should have been more understanding."

"That poor girl!"

They were both silent for a moment. Oliver was upstairs in bed, and Pepper turned to Miles and said quietly,

"Oliver is my responsibility. I promised Mary I would take care of him, and even if I hadn't done so, I would want to . . ."

"He's our responsibility," Miles amended quietly. "He's a very special child, Pepper."

"Yes." Her head was bent, her hair falling against her cheek. In the firelight she could have almost been a young girl. It was four o'clock in the morning, but neither of them felt like sleep.

"I was frightened of committing myself to you . . ." she told Miles.

"And I was frightened of losing you." He took hold of her hand. "We can't alter what happened, Pepper."

"No . . . it was already ordained," she agreed quietly.

"We could always live in London, sell both our flats and buy something bigger," Miles suggested.

Pepper shook her head.

"No, Oliver is used to the country, and that's what I want for our children."

"You'll find it tiring commuting between London and the country every day," Miles warned her. "It's different for me—I can work from home."

Besides, he had been approached with a hint that he was being considered as a circuit judge. He would be one of the youngest in the country, his work load would be heavy, but he wouldn't need to be based in London.

"No," Pepper told him. They were sitting in her drawing room discussing their plans. They had been married quietly at the weekend, with Oliver and only a handful of friends to witness the ceremony.

"I'm giving up the business." She avoided looking at Miles. "It's served its purpose now."

He understood immediately.

"Minesse—Nemesis. Was it worth it, Pepper?"

She shook her head.

"No . . . nothing is worth the loss of people like Philip and Mary, and I could have lost Oliver as well."

Sensing the guilt underlying her words, Miles took hold of her hand.

"And yet look at the good that has come out of it as well," he reminded her. "Look at Alex and Julia."

"Do you think they'll get permission to adopt Randolph?" Pepper asked him, referring to the half English, half West Indian physically handicapped baby the Barnetts were hoping to make their own.

"I don't see why not. You're a very special lady," Miles added softly, "but you aren't superhuman. None of us can change what life holds in store for us, we can't alter the circumstances, only mitigate them."

"But if I hadn't tried to blackmail all of you— Simon Herries . . ."

"Would still have destroyed himself and possibly others as well, but in a different way. It's over, Pepper, and we've all got to go on with our lives. Will you ever tell Oliver?" he asked her.

"I don't know. I don't think so. I want him to grow up free of any burdens." She paused and added quietly, "If we have a daughter I'd like to call her Naomi."

"I think she'd like that," he agreed, and both of them knew that he wasn't referring to their unborn child.

She would sell Minesse Management, Pepper

decided; she had several potential buyers for the business. She and Miles would buy an old rambling house somewhere in the country and she would direct her formidable energies to bringing up their children. They would give them all that they had not had themselves; and with any luck all that they had had.

She touched her still flat stomach, smiling secretively at her own inner knowledge. She had conceived Miles's child, she was sure of it, and its conception was a sign of her own rebirth; a sign that the past was dead and its burden of bitterness with it. Pepper had tried to bargain with fate, forgetting that others might be called upon to meet the price for her. Now she knew better.

"Come on," Miles demanded prosaically. "I'm hungry! Let's go and get something to eat, and then we'd better go and relieve Alex and Julia of the burden of our son."

The other couple had offered to look after Oliver for them for a few days so that they could have some time alone. Already Pepper missed him.

She looked down at her wrist. The key was gone and in its place she wore a small charm that was the Romany symbol for peace and hope. She touched it gently and smiled before slipping her arm through that of her husband. Sunlight touched their faces, warm through the glass. Pepper lifted hers up instinctively and Miles, looking down at her, thought she had never looked more beautiful, more desirable, more womanly. Sorrow had touched her and left its mark. He had her now and he would never let her go. Never.

He saw her smile and asked softly, "What are you thinking?"

"An old saying, one that goes. 'Living well is the best revenge.' And that's exactly what I intend to do from now on."

All things have a purpose, a meaning that it is not always given to us to understand. Out of rage Pepper had found love; out of grief she had been given hope; out of danger had come peace, and she intended to be worthy of those gifts.

HARLEQUIN

American Romance®

**Beginning next month
Share in the**

Join American Romance in celebrating the magical charm of the Colorado Rockies at a very special place— The Stanley Hotel. Meet three women friends whose lives are touched with magic and who will never be the same, who find love in a very special way, the way of enchantment.

Read and love
#329 BEST WISHES by Julie Kistler, February 1990
#333 SIGHT UNSEEN by Kathy Clark, March 1990 and
#337 RETURN TO SUMMER by Emma Merritt, April 1990

ROCKY MOUNTAIN MAGIC—All it takes is an open heart.
Only from Harlequin American Romance

All the Rocky Mountain Magic Romances take place at
the beautiful Stanley Hotel.

RMM-1

February brings you . . .

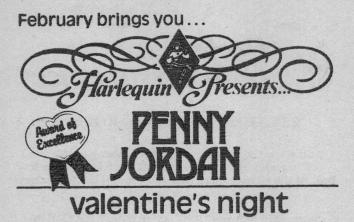

valentine's night

Sorrel didn't particularly want to meet her long-lost cousin Val from Australia. However, since the girl had come all this way just to make contact, it seemed a little churlish not to welcome her.

As there was no room at home, it was agreed that Sorrel and Val would share the Welsh farmhouse that was being renovated for Sorrel's brother and his wife. Conditions were a bit primitive, but that didn't matter.

At least, not until Sorrel found herself snowed in with the long-lost cousin, who turned out to be a handsome, six-foot male!

Also, look for the next Harlequin Presents Award of Excellence title in April:

Elusive as the Unicorn
by Carole Mortimer

HP1243-1

Harlequin Superromance®

LET THE GOOD TIMES ROLL...

Add some Cajun spice to liven up your New Year's celebrations and join Superromance for a romantic tour of the rich Acadian marshlands and the legendary Louisiana bayous.

Starting in January 1990, we're launching CAJUN MELODIES, a three-book tribute to the fun-loving people who've enriched America by introducing us to crawfish étouffé and gumbo, zydeco music and the Saturday night party, the *fais-dodo*. And learn about loving, Cajun-style, as you meet the tall, dark, handsome men who win their ladies' hearts with a beautiful, haunting melody....

Book One: *Julianne's Song*, January 1990
Book Two: *Catherine's Song*, February 1990
Book Three: *Jessica's Song*, March 1990